Maggie knew it was wrong, but it felt right

Why now, after all this time, did she finally feel connected to someone? There were so many reasons why Nate was wrong for her. He was a man who lived for his work, and thought nothing of putting himself in danger. He had his life ahead of him. They didn't even live in the same country.

And in a very short time, he'd be gone. And she was shocked to find, in the circle of his arms, that she would miss him when he left.

But she had right now, and she burrowed deeper into his chest, letting the clean scent of him surround her. Letting his body form a cocoon as the slightest bit of healing trickled into her.

Dear Reader,

Why is it that sometimes the thing we want the least is exactly what we need the most?

When I was writing *Hired by the Cowboy* and *Marriage at Circle M,* I got to wondering about Mike's cousin, Maggie. Maggie became Mike's foster parent when she wasn't that much older than he was, and I wanted to know what had happened to her. I got to know her, and realized that the strength she displayed in her childhood had been tested in her adult years—so much so that she had resolved never to love again.

I realized she needed a hero who could restore her faith… in herself, in life, in love. And that hero was Nate Griffith, a U.S. marshal sent to Canada on a case. The kind of man she shied away from—young, vibrant, principled and in a profession that carried far more danger than she was comfortable with. The kind of man who could show her that there was more to life than complacency and fear. That living without risk isn't living at all…it's just existing.

Nate comes to realize that his job isn't always about punishing the guilty. It's also about protecting the innocent, and when Maggie sees this—sees this code of honor and duty—she finds she's unable to resist Nate for long.

I enjoyed writing this book very much. I enjoyed creating Mountain Haven Bed and Breakfast and loved how Maggie somehow started cooking some of my favorite recipes for Nate! I hope you enjoy it, too.

You can visit me at my Web site, www.donnaalward.com, or write to me care of Harlequin. I'd love to hear from you.

Love,

Donna

DONNA ALWARD

Falling for Mr. Dark
& Dangerous

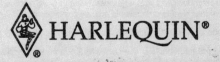

TORONTO • NEW YORK • LONDON
AMSTERDAM • PARIS • SYDNEY • HAMBURG
STOCKHOLM • ATHENS • TOKYO • MILAN • MADRID
PRAGUE • WARSAW • BUDAPEST • AUCKLAND

ISBN-13: 978-0-373-17534-5
ISBN-10:   0-373-17534-5

FALLING FOR MR. DARK & DANGEROUS

First North American Publication 2008.

Printed in U.S.A.

Just like having a heart to heart
with your best friend, these stories will take you
from laughter to tears and back again!

Curl up and have a

Heart *to* Heart

with
Harlequin Romance®

So heartwarming and emotional
you'll want to have some tissues handy!

Her Millionaire, His Miracle
by Myrna Mackenzie
in November 2008

The Italian's Family Miracle
by Lucy Gordon
in December 2008

Acknowledgments

When I decided I wanted to write a book with a cop hero,
I turned to Mark Graham, U.S. Marshal, who not only
provided me with all the law-enforcement information I
needed, but also gave me a glimpse into what it's actually
like to do the job that he does. Thank you, Mark,
for the info and the laughs. You rock.

Dedication

My paternal Grandmother was an avid reader.
Even bringing up several children during the Depression
and beyond, her attachment to Harlequin romances is
legendary in our family. So much so that at one point
or another, we've all been called "Myrtle," after her—
my mother, my sisters, even me. Now my own children have
taken on that tradition; this summer found my girls on a
bunk with a book more often than not. And at one point
or another they were dubbed "Myrtle."

My Gram passed away when I was seventeen,
but I think of her often these days as I'm now writing
the stories that she loved so much.

I dedicate this book to my Gram, for passing on her love
for books to all of us, and hope that in some small way
I have done her proud.

This is for you, Grammie.

CHAPTER ONE

THE crunch of tires on snow let Maggie Taylor know he was here. The U.S. marshal. The man who'd thrown a monkey wrench into things before he'd ever even arrived.

She parted the curtains and looked out over the white-capped yard. A late March storm had dropped several centimeters of snow earlier in the week and then the temperature had plunged. Now it looked more like Christmas than impending spring.

Maggie sighed as the black SUV pulled up beside her truck. She'd almost booked a trip to get away from the late surge of winter. She'd always found an excuse not to travel, but now that Jen was away from home, she'd decided to treat herself for once and go somewhere hot, where she'd be catered to instead of doing the catering. In fact, she'd been taking extra time browsing around the travel agent's on a trip to Red Deer when *he* had called, requesting a room for a prolonged stay.

Of course, since she'd been out at the time, Jennifer had taken the call and booked him in without even asking. Not only had it spoiled her plans, but it had caused a huge argument between her and Jennifer. She pressed her thumbs against her index fingers, snapping the knuckles. If it hadn't been about that, it would have been something else. They were always arguing, it seemed. They never saw eye to eye on anything anymore.

As if preordained, Jennifer chose that moment to gallop down the stairs. Maggie stared at the pink plaid flannel that covered her daughter's bottom half, topped by a battered gray sweatshirt that had seen far better days. Maggie felt guilty at the relief she knew she'd feel when Jennifer went back to school after her spring break. These days they got along much better when there were several miles between them.

She dropped the curtain back into place, obscuring her view of the man getting out of the vehicle.

"Honestly, Jen. You're still in your pyjamas and our guest is here." She ran her hands down her navy slacks and straightened the hem of the thick gray sweater she'd put on to ward off the chill.

"I haven't done my laundry yet." Jennifer skirted past her and headed straight for the kitchen.

Maggie sighed. Even though Jen complained that there was *nothing* to do around here, she somehow always left laundry and chores up to Maggie. And Maggie did them rather than frustrate herself with yet another argument. Their relationship was fragile enough.

When Jen had informed her of this particular booking, Maggie had lost her cool instead of thanking her daughter for actually taking some initiative with the business. Instead she'd harped about her ruined vacation plans.

She should just let the resentment go. Mexico wasn't going anywhere. She'd go another time, that was all. And the money from this off-season booking would come in handy come summer, when repairs to the house would need to be undertaken.

The marshal was a guest here and it was her job to make him feel welcome. Even if she had her doubts. A cop, of all people. He was probably rigid and scheduled and had no sense of humor.

Letting out a breath and pasting on her smile, she went to the door and opened it before he had a chance to ring the bell.

"Welcome to Mountain Haven Bed and Breakfast," she got out, but the rest of the words of her rehearsed greeting flew out of her head as she stared a long way up into blue-green eyes.

"Thank you." His lips moved above a gray and black parka that was zipped precisely to the top. "I know it's off-season, and I appreciate your willingness to open for me. I hope it hasn't inconvenienced you."

It was a struggle to keep her mouth from dropping open, to keep the welcome smile curving her lips. His introductory speech had locked her gaze on his face and she was staggered. She'd be spending the next three weeks with *this* man? In an otherwise empty bed and breakfast? Jennifer would only be here another few days, and then it was back to school. It would be just the two of them.

What had started out as an annoying business necessity was now curled with intimacy. He was, very possibly, the most gorgeous man she'd ever seen. Even bundled in winter gear she sensed his lean, strong build, the way he carried his body. With purpose and intent. His voice was smooth with just a hint of gravel, giving it a rumbling texture; the well-shaped lips unsmiling despite his polite speech. And he had killer eyes…eyes that gleamed brilliantly in contrast to his dark clothing.

"I *am* in the right place, aren't I?" He turned his head and looked at the truck, then back at her, frowning a bit as she remained stupidly silent.

Pull yourself together, she told herself. She stepped back, opening the door wider to welcome him in. "If you're Nathaniel Griffith, you're in the right place."

He smiled finally, a quick upturn of the lips, and exhaled, a cloud forming in the frigid air. "That's a relief. I was afraid

I'd gotten lost. And please—" he pulled off his glove and held out his hand "—call me Nate. I only get called Nathaniel when I'm in trouble with my boss or my mother."

She smiled back, genuinely this time, as she shook his hand. It was warm and firm and enveloped her smaller fingers completely. She couldn't imagine him in trouble for *anything*. He looked like Mr. All-American.

"I'm Maggie Taylor, the owner. Please, come in. I'll show you your room and get you familiar with the place."

"I'll just get my bags," he said, stepping back outside the door.

He jogged to the truck, reaching into the back seat for a large black duffel. He leaned across the seat for something else and the back of his jacket slid up, revealing a delicious rear-view clad in faded denim. A dark thrill shot through her at the sight.

"Wow. That's *yum*," came Jen's voice just behind her shoulder.

Maggie stepped back into the shadows behind the door, feeling the heat rise in her cheeks. "Jennifer! For God's sake, keep your voice down. This is our guest."

Jen took a bite of the toast she'd prepared, looking remarkably unconcerned by either her words or her appearance. "The cop, right? The one I booked? Mom, if the front's anything like the back, it totally beats Mexico."

Nate turned around, bags in hand and Maggie pressed a hand to her belly. This was silly. It was a visceral, physical reaction, nothing more. He was good-looking. So what? She was his hostess. It wasn't her style to have an attraction to a guest.

It wasn't her style to feel that sort of pull to anyone for that matter, not these days. It was just Jen pointing out his attributes. Maggie wasn't blind, after all.

His booted steps echoed on the veranda and he stomped the snow from his boots before coming in and putting down the bags.

Maggie shut the door behind him. Enough draft had been let in by the exchange and already the foyer was chilly.

"I'm Jen." Jennifer plopped her piece of peanut butter toast back to her plate and held out her hand.

"Nate," he answered, taking her hand and shaking it.

When he pulled back, a smudge of peanut butter stuck to his knuckle.

"My daughter," Maggie said weakly.

"I gathered," he answered, then with an unexpected grin, licked the smudge from his thumb.

Jen beamed up at him, unfazed, while Maggie blushed.

"You took my reservation," he offered, smiling at Jennifer.

Jen nodded. "I'm on spring break."

Maggie held out her hand. "Let me take your coat," she offered politely. "The closet's just here."

He shrugged out of the jacket and Maggie realized how very tall he was. Easily over six feet, he towered over her modest height. He handed her the coat, along with thick gloves. She smiled as she turned to the closet, the weight of the parka heavy in her hands. For a man from the sunny south, he sure knew how to dress for an Alberta winter.

The phone rang, and Jen raced to answer it. Nate's eyes followed her from the room, then fell on Maggie.

"Teenagers and phones." She raised her shoulders as if to say, "What can you do?"

"I remember." He looked around. "She gave great directions. I found you pretty easily."

"You drove, then?" Maggie hadn't had a chance to get a glimpse of his plates. Maybe the SUV was a rental. He could easily have flown into Calgary or Edmonton and picked up a vehicle there.

"The truck's on loan from a friend. He met me at Coutts, and I dropped him off before driving the rest of the way."

Maggie shut the closet door and turned back, getting more

comfortable as they settled into polite, if cool, chitchat. This was what she did for a living, after all. There was no need to feel awkward with a guest, despite Jen's innuendoes.

"Where does your friend live?" Maggie asked. Nate gripped the duffel by the short handles. Maggie paused her question. "Would you like some help with your bags?"

"I've got it." He moved purposefully, sliding the pack over his shoulder and gripping the duffel.

Maggie stood nonplussed. His words had been short and clipped, but she'd only been offering a simple courtesy.

Her lack of response stretched out awkwardly while Jennifer's muffled voice sounded from the kitchen. Inconvenience at his arrival was now becoming discomfort. Perhaps she'd been right after all when she'd thought about having a cop underfoot. Terse and aloof. She prided herself on a friendly, comfortable atmosphere, but it took two to accomplish it. By the hard set of his jaw, her work was clearly cut out for her.

Nate spoke, finally breaking the tension.

"I'm sorry. I didn't mean to be rude. I'm just used to looking after myself." He smiled disarmingly. "My mother would flay me alive if I let a woman carry my things."

Maggie wondered what his mother would say if she knew Maggie looked after running the business *and* all the repairs on the large house single-handedly. She was used to being on her own and doing everything from starting a business to repairing a roof to raising a daughter.

"Chivalry isn't dead, I see." Her words came out cooler than she wanted as she moved past him to the stairs.

"No, ma'am." His steps echoed behind her as she started up the staircase.

When they reached the top, she paused. Perhaps because of his job he was naturally suspicious, but she was trying hard not to feel snubbed after his curt words in the foyer. It should have been implicitly understood that whatever was in his bags was his business. She'd never go through a guest's belongings!

"The Mountain Haven Bed and Breakfast is exactly that. A haven." She led him to a sturdy white door, opened it. "A place to get away from worries and stress. I hope you'll enjoy your stay here."

He looked down into her eyes, but she couldn't read his expression. It was like he was deliberately keeping it blank. She'd hoped her words would thaw his cool manner just a bit, but he only replied, "I appreciate your discretion."

He went inside, putting his duffel on the floor and the backpack on the wing chair in the corner.

"Local calls are free, long distance go on your bill, unless of course you use a prepaid card." Maggie dismissed the futility of trying to draw him out and gave him the basic rundown instead. "There's no television in your room, but there is a den downstairs that you're welcome to use."

Maggie paused. Nate was waiting patiently for her to finish her spiel. It was very odd, with him being her only guest. Knowing he'd be the *only* guest for the next few weeks. It didn't seem right, telling him mealtimes and rules.

She softened her expression. "Look, normally there's a whole schedule thing with meals and everything, but you're my only guest. I think we can be a little more flexible. I usually serve breakfast between eight and nine, so if that suits you, great. I can work around your plans. Dinner is served at six-thirty. For lunch, things are fluid. I can provide it or not, for a minimum charge on your overall bill. I'm happy to tell you about local areas of interest, and you have dial-up Internet access in your room."

Nate tucked his hands into his jeans pockets. "I'm your only guest?"

"That's right. It's not my busiest time right now."

"Then…" His eyes met hers sheepishly. "Look, I'm going to feel awkward eating alone. I don't suppose…we could all eat together."

Nate watched her closely and she felt color creep into her cheeks yet again. Silly Jennifer and her suggestive comments. The front side *was* as attractive as the back and Maggie couldn't help but notice as they stood together in the quiet room. It wasn't how things were usually done. Normally guests ate in the dining room and she ate at the nook or she and Jen at the kitchen table. Yet it would seem odd, serving him all alone in the dining room. It was antisocial, somehow.

She struggled to keep her voice low and even. "Basically your stay should be enjoyable. If you prefer to eat with us, that would be fine. And if there's anything I can do to make your stay more comfortable, let me know."

"Everything here looks great, Ms. Taylor."

"Then I'll leave you to unpack. The bathroom is two doors down, and as my only guest it's yours alone. Jennifer and I each have our own so you won't have to share. I'll be downstairs. Let me know if there's anything you need. Otherwise, I'll see you for dinner."

She courteously shut the door, then leaned against it, closing her eyes. Nate Griffith wasn't an ordinary guest, that much she knew already. She couldn't shake the irrational feeling that he was hiding something. He hadn't said or done anything to really make her think so, beyond being proprietary with his backpack. But something niggled at the back of her mind, something that made her uncomfortable. Given his profession, she should be reassured. Who could be safer than someone in law enforcement? Why would he have any sort of ulterior motive?

His good looks were something she'd simply have to ignore. She'd have to get over her silly awkwardness in a hurry, since they were going to be essentially roommates for the next few weeks. Jen wouldn't be here to run interference much longer, and Maggie would rely on her normal professional, warm persona. Piece of cake.

He was just a man, after all. A man on vacation from a stressful job. A man with an expense account that would make up for her lost plans by helping pay for her next trip.

Nate heaved out a sigh as the door shut with a firm click. Thank goodness she was gone.

He looked around the room. Very nice. Grant had assured him that the rural location didn't mean substandard lodging, and so far he was right. What he'd seen of the house was clean, warm and welcoming. His room was no different.

The furniture was all of sturdy golden pine; the spread on the bed was thick and looked homemade with its country design in navy, burgundy, deep green and cream. An extra blanket in rich red lay over the foot of the bed. He ran his hand over the footboard. He would have preferred no footboard, so he could stretch out. But it didn't matter. What mattered was that he was here and he had all the amenities he needed. To anyone in the area, he'd be a vacationing guest. To his superiors, he'd be consistently connected through the Internet and in liaison with local authorities. Creature comforts were secondary, but not unwelcome. Lord knew he'd stayed in a lot worse places while on assignment.

He unpacked his duffel, laying clothing neatly in the empty dresser drawers. His hand paused on a black sweater. When Grant had mentioned a bed and breakfast, Nate had instantly thought of some middle-aged couple. When he'd learned Maggie ran Mountain Haven alone, he'd pictured a woman in her mid-to-late forties who crocheted afghans for the furniture and exchanged recipes for chicken pot pie with her guests. Maggie Taylor didn't fit his profile at all. Neither did Jen. He'd known she was here, but she seemed precocious and typically teenage. Certainly not the kind to get in trouble with the police.

He rested his hips on the curved footboard and frowned. It was hard to discern Maggie's age. Initially he'd thought her maybe a year or two older than himself. But the appearance of her nearly grown daughter had changed that impression. He couldn't tell for sure, but she had to be at least late thirties to have a daughter that age. Yet…her skin was still creamy and unlined, her eyes blue and full-lashed. Her hand had been much smaller than his, and soft.

But it was Maggie's eyes that stuck in his mind. Eyes that smiled warmly with welcome but that held a hint of cool caution in their depths. Eyes that told him whatever her path had been, it probably hadn't been an easy one.

He stood up abruptly and reached for the jeans in his duffel, going to hang them in the closet. He wasn't here to make calf-eyes at the proprietress. That was the last thing he should be thinking about. He had a job to do. That was all. He had information to gather and who better to ask than someone in the know, someone who would take his questions for tourist curiosity? Inviting himself to dinner had put her on the spot, but with the desired results.

The afternoon light was already starting to wane when he dug out his laptop and set it up on the small desk to the left of the bed. Within seconds it was booted up, connected and ready to go. He logged in with his password, checked his e-mail…and waited for everything to download. Once he'd taken care of everything that needed his immediate attention, he quickly composed a few short notes, hitting the send button and waiting what seemed an age for them to leave the Outbox.

"I miss high speed Internet," he muttered, tapping his fingers on the desk, waiting for the dial-up connection to send his messages. Waiting was not something he did well.

But perhaps learning to wait was a life lesson he needed.

He'd been one to act first and think later too many times. Dealing with the aftermath of mistakes had caused him to be put on leave in the first place. He hadn't even been two weeks into his leave when it had been cut short and he'd been given this assignment, and he was glad of it. He wasn't keen on sitting around twiddling his thumbs.

Grant had asked for him personally. As a favor. And this wasn't a job to be rushed. It was a time for watching and waiting.

He frowned at the monitor as the messages finally went through. He didn't want to run up a long distance bill while he was here, but staying in communication was important. For now, his laptop *was* his connection to the outside world. It was a tiny community. The less conspicuous he was, the better.

He realized that his room had grown quite dark, and checked his watch. It was after six already, and Maggie had said dinner was at six-thirty. He didn't want to get things off to a bad start on his first day, so he shut down the computer and put his backpack beneath the empty duffel in the closet.

Maggie heard his footsteps moving around upstairs for a long time, listening to the muffled thump as she mixed dough and browned ground beef for the soup.

Nate Griffith. U.S. Marshal. The name had conjured an image of a flat faced cop when Jennifer had told her about the reservation. Despite the flashes of coolness, he was anything but. He couldn't be more than thirty, thirty-one. And it hadn't taken but a moment to realize he was all legs and broad shoulders, and polite manners.

"Whatcha making?"

Jennifer's voice interrupted and for once Maggie was glad of it. She'd already spent too long thinking about her latest lodger.

"Pasta e fagioli and foccacia bread."

"Excellent." Jen grabbed a cookie from a beige pottery jar and leaned against the counter, munching.

Maggie watched her. There were some days she really missed the preteen years. Parenting had been so much simpler then. Yet hard as it was, she hated to see Jen leave again.

"Day after tomorrow, huh. Did you book your bus ticket?"

"I booked it return when I came, remember?" She reached in the jar for another cookie.

"You'll spoil your supper," Maggie warned.

Jen simply raised an eyebrow as if to say, *I'm not twelve, Mother.*

"You should be glad I'm leaving. That leaves you alone with Detective Hottie."

Maggie glared.

"Oh, come on, Mom. He's a little old for me, even if he is a fine specimen. But he's just about right for you."

Maggie put the spoon down with more force than she intended. "First of all, keep your voice down. He is a paying guest in this house." She ignored the flutter that skittered through her at Jen's attempt at matchmaking. "He wouldn't be here at all if you'd asked first and booked later."

Jennifer stopped munching. "You're still mad about that, huh."

Maggie sighed, forgetting all about his footsteps. It wasn't all Jen's fault. She did her own share of picking fights. She should be trying to keep Jen close, not pushing her away.

"I just wish…I wish you'd give some thought to things first, instead of racing headlong and then having to backtrack. You took the reservation without even consulting me."

"I was trying to help. I told you I was sorry about it. And they did come through with the cash, so what's the big deal?"

How could Maggie explain that the big deal was that she worried over Jen day and night? She hadn't been blind the last few years. Jen had skated through without getting badly hurt. Yet.

But she'd had her share of trouble and Maggie was terrified that one day she'd get a phone call that something truly awful had happened. She wished Jen took it as seriously as she did.

"Let's not argue about it anymore, okay?" Arguing over the reservation was irrelevant now. Maggie had been irritated with Jennifer at the time for not taking a credit card number, but it had ceased to matter. The United States Marshals Service was picking up the tab. All of it. A day after Nate had reserved the room, someone from his office had called and made arrangements for payment, not even blinking when she'd told them the rate, or the cost of extras. And she'd charged them high season rates, just because she'd been so put out at having to put her travel plans on hold.

She pressed dough into two round pans, dimpling the tops with her fingers before putting them under a tea towel to rise. No matter how much she wished she were lying on a beach in Cancún right now, she still derived pleasure from doing what she did best. Cooking for one was a dull, lonely procedure and her spirits lightened as she added ingredients to the large stockpot on the stove. Jen had been home for the last week, but it wasn't the same now that she was nearly adult and spreading her wings. Having guests meant having someone else to do for. It was why she'd chosen a bed and breakfast in the first place.

The footsteps halted above her, the house falling completely silent as their argument faltered.

"I didn't mean to pick a fight with you."

"Me, either." Jen shuffled to the kitchen doorway and Maggie longed to mend fences, although she didn't know how.

"Supper in an hour," she called gently, but it went ignored.

Maggie reached across the counter to turn on the radio. She hummed quietly with a recent country hit as she turned her attention to pastry. Her foot tapped along with the beat until she slid everything into the oven, added tiny tubes of pasta to the pot, and cleaned up the cooking mess, the process of cooking and cleaning therapeutic.

At precisely six-twenty, he appeared at the kitchen door.

She turned with the bread pans in her hands, surprised to see him there. Again, she felt a warning thump at his presence. Why in the world was she reacting this way to a complete stranger? It was more than a simple admiration of his good looks. A sliver of danger snuck down her spine. She knew nothing about him. He looked like a normal, nice guy. But how would she know? She didn't even know the reason why he was on a leave of absence. What could have happened to make him need to take extended time off? Suddenly all her misgivings, ones she rarely gave credence to, came bubbling up to the surface. Most of the time she was confident in her abilities to look after herself. Something about Nate Griffith challenged that. And very soon, it would just be the two of them in the house.

"Is something wrong?"

She shook her head, giving a start and putting the pans down on top of the stove. "No, not at all. You just surprised me."

Maggie took a deep breath, keeping her back to him. "Dinner's not quite ready. It won't be long."

"Is there anything I can do to help?"

He took a few steps into the kitchen. It was her job to make him at ease and feel at home, so why on earth was she finding it so difficult? She forced a smile as she flipped the round loaves out of the pans and on to a cooling rack. "Jen should be down soon. Besides, it's my job to look after you, remember?"

"Well, sure." He leaned easily against the side of the refrigerator. "But I thought we were going to play it a little less formal."

He had her there. She thought for a moment as she got the dishes out of the cupboard. He was only here for a few weeks. What harm could come of being friendly, after all? Her voices of doubt were just being silly; she was making something out of nothing. He'd be gone back to his job and the palm trees before she knew it.

"All right." She held out bread plates and bowls. "Informal it is. We can use the kitchen or the dining room, whichever you prefer. If you could set the table with these, I'll finish up here."

He pushed himself upright with an elbow. "Absolutely." He moved to take the dishes and their fingers brushed. Without thinking, her gaze darted up to his with alarm. For a second she held her breath. But then he turned away to the table as if nothing had connected.

Only she knew it had. And that was bad, bad news.

CHAPTER TWO

HE'D set the three places at one end of the table; one at the head and the other two flanking it. There was little chance of her getting away with sitting across from him. He'd be close. Too close. With his long legs, their knees might bump under the table. Her pulse fluttered at the thought and she frowned. It wasn't like her to be so twitchy.

As she watched, he lit the thick candles at the center of the table with the butane lighter.

Maggie paused at the intimacy of the setting and shook it off again, putting the soup tureen on the table. It shouldn't make her feel so threatened, but it did. Even with Jennifer here, a simple dinner had somehow transformed into something more. Maggie simply didn't *do* relationships of any kind. Not even casual ones. It always ended badly with her being left to try to pick up the pieces. After the last time, with Tom, there hadn't been many pieces left to pick up. She had to hold on to every single one. All that she had left was put into raising Jennifer and running her business. She didn't know why he'd go to the bother of setting the atmosphere, and it unsettled her.

"Ms. Taylor?"

Maggie realized she'd been staring at the table. She laughed lightly. "I'm sorry. You were saying?"

"I asked if you ran the Haven alone. I'm afraid I didn't get many details when I booked."

"I do, yes." She brought the basket of bread to the table and invited him to sit with a hand. She was surprised when he waited until she was seated before seating himself. "Jennifer attends school in Edmonton, so she's not around much anymore."

"Which makes you sad."

Maggie smiled, pleasantly surprised by his small, but accurate insight. The house did seem unbearably lonely when Jen was gone. "Despite teenage angst and troubles, yes, it does. I miss having her close by. Speaking of, she should be here by now."

She pushed her chair back and stood, fluttering a hand when he made a similar move out of courtesy. "It's okay. Jen knows to be on time. I'll call her."

Maggie made her way to the bottom of the stairs. What she'd said was true. She did miss having Jen closer, even though at times she was glad Jen was away from here and making new friends. Not all her acquaintances at home were ones Maggie would have chosen. And the last thing Maggie needed was for the marshal to know about Jen's brush with the law.

"Jennifer. Dinner," she called up the stairs.

There was a muffled thump from Jen's room, then she came down, earbuds still stuck in her ears and her MP3 player stuffed in her pocket.

They went to the kitchen together, but when Jen sat and reached for the bread, Maggie shook her head.

"Not at the table, please."

Jen seemed unconcerned as she plucked the buds from her ears. "Hey, Nate," she greeted, snagging the piece of bread as though it were the most natural thing in the world.

Maggie saw Nate try to hide a smile. Honestly, she wondered sometimes if the manners she'd tried to instill had gone in one ear and out the other.

"Hey, Jennifer." Nate politely answered the greeting and broke the awkwardness by starting a conversation. "So… spring break is just about over. You looking forward to getting back to school?"

Maggie relaxed and ladled soup into bowls. Nate apparently had paid good attention to *his* upbringing. Manners and a natural sense of small talk. And for once, Jen didn't seem to mind answering.

"I guess. It's been kind of boring around here. Nothing to do."

"Oh, I don't know. With all this snow…there must be winter sports. Skiing, skating, tobogganing…or are those things uncool these days?"

Maggie grinned behind her water glass. She'd suggested a day of cross-country skiing earlier in the week, only to have the idea vetoed by Jen. The same Jen who a few years ago would have jumped at the chance.

"I dunno," Jen replied.

Nate nodded. "I'm looking forward to spending lots of time outdoors," he said. "No snow where I live. This is a real treat for me."

Maggie pictured him bundled up, his boots strapped into a pair of snowshoes, with his eyes gleaming like sapphire bullets beneath his toque. Her heart thumped heavily. His lean, strong build made the outdoors a natural choice.

"I suppose you're all athletic and stuff." Jennifer paused and tilted her head as if examining him.

"It's part of my job. I have to stay in good shape. Just because I'm not…working, doesn't mean I can ignore the routine." He paused to take a spoonful of soup. "Besides, if I eat your mother's cooking for the next two weeks, I'm really going to have to watch myself." His smile sparkled at Maggie. "This is delicious."

"Thanks," Maggie responded. She was used to receiving polite compliments on her cooking. It made no sense that his praise caused her heart to pitter-patter like a schoolgirl's.

She considered steering the conversation so that Jen didn't monopolize it, but she realized two things. Jen was more animated than she'd been the whole break, and Maggie was learning a whole lot more about Nate by sitting back and listening to their exchange.

"So, Nate…when you're not vacationing, what's your job like? Are you like a regular cop or what?" She popped a spoonful of soup into her mouth while waiting for his answer.

Nate concentrated on adding grated parmesan to the top of his soup. "No, not like a regular cop. I get to do special stuff. A lot of what I do is finding fugitives, people who have committed crimes and are on the run."

"You mean like *America's Most Wanted*?" Jen leaned forward now, her dinner forgotten.

Nate nodded. "Exactly like that. And sometimes I'm sent out on high profile security details, too."

"Isn't that dangerous?" Maggie's voice intruded. A cop was bad enough, but even she knew that a police officer dealt with a lot of the mundane. This seemed like a whole other level. "Don't you worry about getting killed?"

His eyes were steady on hers. "Yes, but not as much as I worry about getting the job done."

Maggie's chin flattened. Tall, strong and handsome was one thing, but having a target painted on his chest was quite another. She couldn't imagine anyone choosing such a lifestyle.

"Have you ever killed anyone?"

"Jennifer!" Maggie put down her spoon and glared at her daughter for her crassness in asking such a thing. Nate's eyes made the transition to look at Jennifer, the smile disappearing completely.

"Jen, that was beyond inappropriate." Maggie spoke sharply. "Please apologize."

But Nate shook his head. "There's no need. It's a valid question. I get it a lot." He took a drink of water. "I work as part of a team. And our goal is to bring fugitives to justice, or to protect those we are assigned to protect. Of course we prefer to bring them in unharmed. But if we're fired upon, we have to fire back."

Silence fell over the table.

Maggie tried to fill the uncomfortable gap the way a hostess should, yet all she could see was Nate, holding a smoking gun. The thought chilled her considerably.

"That must be very stressful."

Nate nodded. "It can be, yes."

Jen's voice interrupted again. "Is that why you're here?"

Maggie kicked her beneath the table. Jen bit down on her lip but watched him, undeterred.

Nate swallowed. "Part of it, yes. I was directed to take some time off after a…particularly challenging case. A little rest and relaxation is just what the doctor ordered."

He smiled, but it wasn't as warm as before. "In keeping with that, I'd appreciate if you'd keep my presence here low-key. I realize it's a small community, but right now I want to enjoy the outdoors and not worry about speculation."

Maggie aimed a stern look at Jennifer before turning to Nate and answering.

"Of course. You are a guest here, and of course we'll respect your wishes. That's what the Haven is all about." At least she didn't have to worry right now. He was on vacation. What he did for a living had no bearing on anything.

"Thank you," he murmured. He picked up his spoon again and resumed eating, and Jennifer wisely let the subject drop for the rest of the meal.

"Dessert, Mr. Griffith?"

Nate looked up at Maggie as she removed his plate and bowl. The meal had had its uncomfortable moments, but he was actually glad the questions had been asked and answered.

He got the feeling that Maggie would have been too polite to ask point-blank what her daughter had. Not only that, but the questions had provided a natural way to introduce his cover. Even if he did feel a bit guilty about the half-lie. He'd deliberately prodded her about some things, like asking if she ran the bed and breakfast alone when he knew darn well she did. Still…it was all necessary.

Maggie was waiting, her lips curved pleasantly in what he now realized was her hostess smile. "I shouldn't…but maybe you could tell me what it is first."

Her lips twitched…a good sign, he thought. She'd looked far too serious throughout the rest of the meal. If he could get her to relax a bit, it would go a lot easier toward getting what he needed to know without her feeling like she was being questioned.

"Peach and blueberry tart with ice cream," she answered.

Jennifer clattered around the kitchen, already scooping out servings. "Can't really resist that, now can I," he acquiesced. "So…yes, please. And stop calling me Mr. Griffith. Mr. Griffith is my father or my uncle."

Maggie put on coffee while Jennifer finished doling out servings of the tart, taking hers and escaping to the den and the television. When Maggie placed the dessert before him, the smell alone was enough to remind him of home. Sweets weren't something he indulged in much anymore, but his mother was a fantastic baker and plied him with goodies whenever he visited. Right now the scent of fruit and cinnamon took him back to when things were much simpler. Made him wish this were that simple, instead of him having to work his way through hidden motives. But this was the closest lodging to where he needed to be and the most private. There hadn't been much of a choice, so he had to work with what he'd been given.

"What made you decide to take on a business such as this?"

He decided to draw her out by talking about herself. "It has to be a huge job for one person."

Maggie avoided answering by pouring coffee into thick pottery mugs.

"I had this house and a whole lot of empty rooms," she explained. Her pulse quickened as she was drawn back nearly twenty years. "I had a house and a baby and a foster child and needed to support us all."

Nate's fork paused midair. "Children? As in plural?"

Maggie smiled thinly. "Yes, for a while I looked after my cousin, until he grew up and did his own thing. He's thirty-one now."

His fork dipped into a slice of peach but Maggie noticed a pair of creases between his brows. She tried to lighten the mood by cracking a joke. "Now you're doing the math. How old must I be to have an eighteen-year-old daughter and a foster child of thirty-one?"

He swallowed and reached for his water as a snort of mirth bubbled out at her directness, easing the tension. "I guess I am."

"I'll save you the trouble. I'm forty-two. I was twenty-four when Jennifer was born. Mike was thirteen. He came to me when he was eleven—when I was twenty-two."

She passed him the cream and sugar, then resumed her seat. "And now you want to ask the question and don't know how to do it politely."

Her heart fluttered. Talking about it was hard, and no matter how many times she answered, it never seemed to get any easier. But by now she knew that it was best to get it over with, quick and clean.

Nate had given up all pretense of eating and was watching her closely, so she tried her safest smile. "When I was twenty-five, my husband, Jennifer's dad, was killed in a work accident."

"I'm so sorry."

"It was a long time ago."

Conversation halted. Probing the topic further would be presumptuous, which was part of the reason why Maggie tended to get it over with as soon as possible. Once it was out there, most dropped the subject, uncomfortable with the idea of asking how it had happened, or worse, why she hadn't married again. She knew her reasons. That was enough.

Nate put a bite of pastry and ice cream in his mouth. Her answers had been plain at best, and he knew she was skimming the surface, evading deeper responses. It would be rude to press further. And how much did he *really* want to know? He was here for a short time. It would be best if he stayed out of her way as much as possible, kept her questions to a minimum. Get the answers he needed and no more.

Besides, there were some questions about his life he wouldn't want to answer. If she wanted to keep her life private, that was fine by him. What he needed from her had nothing to do with her private life beyond Jennifer's—and her—involvement.

The candle at the center of the table flickered and he watched the flame dance.

Maggie sipped her coffee and changed the subject. "So what brings you to back roads Alberta? Most would choose a more touristy area. Like Banff, or somewhere south of the border. Montana or Colorado. There's nothing around here besides snow and prairie and a bunch of ranches mixed in with the gas industry."

"If this is your tourism pitch, I can see why your beds are empty," he joked.

"This isn't our big season," she answered. "Like I said, most would head to the mountains for the skiing and richer comforts. We get most of our traffic in the summer."

"I'm surprised you don't vacation in the winter, then," Nate suggested.

When she didn't answer right away, he peered closer at her face and it struck him. "You *do* usually travel, don't you? Is my being here…" He paused, knew he was right by the uncomfortable way her gaze evaded his. "You canceled plans because I was coming." He hadn't thought of that. Hadn't thought of anything beyond doing this assignment, and then dealing with the details.

She shook her head. "It's no bother. I hadn't even booked anything yet."

"But you were going to," he confirmed.

Maggie looked up at him and he was struck again by how young she looked. If he didn't know better, he'd have thought they were close to the same age.

"Mexico isn't going anywhere." She smiled shyly, and their gazes caught.

She tried to cover the moment with her own question. "How long have you been a marshal?"

"Five years. Before that I was in the marines."

"Oh."

He grinned at her. "And now *you're* trying to do the math. I'll save you the trouble. I'm thirty-three."

"And you like it?"

"I couldn't do it otherwise."

Somehow their voices had softened in the candlelight, taking on an intimacy that surprised him, pleasantly. He watched as Maggie bit the inside of her lower lip and released it. She had a beautiful mouth. A mouth made for kissing.

When he lifted his gaze she was watching him, and her expression was fascination mixed with shock that he'd been staring at her lips.

Attraction, he realized. It had been a long time since he'd felt it. But there was definitely a familiar surge in his blood as his eyes locked with Maggie's, blocking out the muted sound of the television coming from the den. Maggie Taylor raised his temperature and he couldn't for the life of him understand why.

It was a complication he didn't need. All he really wanted to do was what he'd been sent here to do. He'd put on a good face; pretended this was just a vacation for some relaxation, but he wouldn't have chosen this for a holiday. His idea of fun wasn't in the middle of some godforsaken Canadian Prairie at a bed and breakfast. He certainly hadn't expected to feel whatever it was he was feeling for the proprietress. He wasn't sure if the desire to flirt with her was a detriment or a bonus.

The light from the candles sputtered, throwing shadows on her face. She was as different from his regular type as sun was from rain. Subdued, polite, grounded, yet anything but boring. It took a woman of character and stamina to lose a husband so young and still bring up a family and run a business. How had she done it all alone?

Jen coughed in the den and Maggie looked away as the moment ended. Nate caught his breath as the color bloomed in her cheeks. He hadn't imagined it, then.

"Excuse me, I should clean this up." Her voice was over-bright as she scrambled up from the table, knocking over her empty mug.

It crashed to the floor, breaking into three distinct pieces.

"Oh, how clumsy of me!" Without looking at him, she knelt to the floor to pick up the pieces. Nate watched, amused. It had been a long time since he'd met a woman who intrigued him, and even longer since he'd had the power to fluster one the way Maggie seemed to be right now.

"Let me help you," he suggested, pushing out of his chair and squatting down beside her.

"Ow!"

Maggie sat back, one of the pieces of pottery in her left hand and a small shard sticking out of a finger on the opposite hand. A drop of blood formed around the tip.

"Maggie, take a breath." Nate took her hand gently in his. "Are you sure coffee was a good idea?" He chuckled as he concentrated on her finger, pinching the fragment between his thumb and forefinger. "Perhaps decaf next time, hmmm?"

He pulled out the shard, but it had gone deeper than he expected and the drop of blood turned into a substantial streak.

"Do you have a first-aid kit?"

Her voice was subdued. "Of course I do. Under the sink in the bathroom."

He rose and headed for the stairs.

"The one over there. In my living quarters."

He stopped and looked at the closed door leading off the kitchen. She had wrapped a napkin around the finger and stood up, taking the larger pieces of the mug and placing them gently on the table.

"I'll get it," she said.

"No, you sit tight. I will."

Nate changed direction and went through the door, feeling somehow like he was trespassing. This was crazy. Less than six hours here and he was flirting with the owner and wandering around her private living space. He went into the bathroom, surprised by the scent of cinnamon and apples coming from a scented oil dispenser plugged into the wall. Switching on a light, he was bathed in an intimate glow—no blaring bulbs here. Soothing blue and deep red splashes of color accented the ivory decor. Nate felt very much like he was intruding.

He searched the small vanity cupboard until he found a white box with a red cross on the top. He shut off the light and went back to the kitchen, where he found Maggie at the sink, the napkin off her finger as she ran it beneath cold water. She lifted it out of the stream and looked at it closely in the soft light from above the sink.

"I think all of it came out," she explained. "What a klutz I am."

"Not at all." Nate sat the kit down on the counter and flipped open the lid. "It's not deep, so you just need a small bandage."

"I can get it, truly."

"You're right handed, aren't you? Putting it on lefty would be awkward. I've got two capable hands."

Maggie looked down at his fingers holding the bandage. Capable indeed. His hands were wide, with long tapering fingers. She swallowed, but held out her finger anyway.

The sound of the paper wrapper tearing off the bandage echoed through the kitchen. Nate stepped closer, anchoring one sticky end and then holding her hand before wrapping the rest around and sticking it to itself. Her heart pounded painfully; she was sure he could hear it as he applied the small wrap.

"All better," he said softly.

"Thank you," she whispered.

He started to pull his hand away, but for a long moment his fingertips stayed on hers. She lifted her eyes to his and found him watching her steadily. Oxygen seemed scarce as she fell entranced by his intense eyes, the shape of his lips. Lips that leaned in ever so slightly.

"You're welcome." And he lifted her finger to his lips and kissed the tip.

CHAPTER THREE

NATE flipped through the channels aimlessly. There really wasn't going to be much to do here in the evenings, especially when the days were still fairly short. At the end of March, this far north, it was full dark early in the evening. Whatever work he did, it would be during the day. It was becoming very clear that after dinner he'd either spend his time here, in the den, or upstairs in his room reading or working online.

He'd rather be upstairs, putting his thoughts together, but on the off-chance that Maggie might come in, he stayed.

He had questions, ones whose answers could get him started in the right direction. Not to mention the fact that he'd enjoyed their little interplay in the kitchen earlier. It had been a long time since he'd indulged in a little harmless flirtation.

Maggie entered with a coffee carafe and mugs on a tray. She put them down on the coffee table. "I thought you might like some coffee," she offered. "I made a fresh pot and promise not to break any more mugs." She smiled tentatively.

The brew smelled wonderful and Nate brushed aside the thought that he'd be up all night if he drank too much of it. He wasn't about to refuse the gesture. If nothing else, it would give him more time with her, and that wasn't a hardship. "That would be wonderful." When she poured the first cup, he nodded to the second. "Are you joining me?"

She smiled. "If you like."

Nate looked up into her eyes. They were warm and friendly with something more. Perhaps a shy invitation, definitely a quiet curiosity. "I would like." He returned her smile. "It's quiet. The company would be nice."

Maggie took her own cup and sat, not on the sofa next to him, but in a nearby chair. Nate was taking up the couch and she was far too aware of him to sit next to him. In the winter months, this room became the family room, and she often snuggled up on the couch with a blanket and a DVD. In season, it was where the guests went to relax.

Normally she didn't socialize with her guests, either. But normally her guests didn't travel alone at the end of winter. She was accustomed to guests traveling in pairs. A romantic getaway, or a stop on the way to somewhere else. Very rarely did she have singles, and when she did, it was nearly always in prime season when they were out exploring the area or the nearby Rockies, or when other guests were present to facilitate conversation.

But Nate was definitely here alone. She'd noticed the absence of a wedding ring at dinner.

"This gives me a chance to pick your brain," he was saying, and she stopped staring at his hands and paid attention. The tingling sensation that he was more than he seemed prickled once more.

"Pick my brain?"

"About things to do while I'm here."

She exhaled slowly. Just tourist information, then. She'd had the uncomfortable feeling after their interchange in the kitchen that he was about to get personal. "Well, there are always day trips into the mountains. I have pamphlets, but there are lots of winter activities there." She crossed her legs, adopting the tour-guide voice she used with guests. "Or a few hours either northeast or south will take you to major cities for shopping, the arts, whatever you want."

"I meant more locally. What I can do with *Mountain Haven* as my base." Nate put down his cup and leaned forward slightly. He wasn't going to let her off the hook, it seemed.

Maggie swallowed. His voice was deep and a little rough; it rumbled with soft seduction through the room. The remembrance of her finger against his lips rippled through her.

"We're…we're usually closed this time of year. I'm afraid I haven't given it much thought."

"I see." He looked down into his cup, frowning, then took a drink.

"But…I have some personal gear I could loan you." His disappointment in her answer was clear and she instantly regretted being so cool. She punctuated the offer with a soft smile.

"Personal gear?"

Maggie hesitated. She knew that out in the shed she'd find Tom's things—cross-country skis, snowshoes, even his old hockey skates. They'd been out there over fifteen years, and she'd never had the heart to throw them away.

But holding on to them didn't make much sense anymore. For the last several years, she'd nearly forgotten they were even there. If Nate could get some use out of them, why shouldn't he?

"My husband's things. Snowshoes, skis, that sort of thing." She took a sip of hot coffee to cover the tiny waver she heard in her own voice.

The television still chattered in the background, but Nate went very still. She heard nothing beyond the quiet resonance of his voice.

"That's not necessary. I can outfit myself, if you can tell me where to shop."

Maggie nodded slightly. "I understand if you're uncomfortable with using Tom's things." What man would truly want the leftovers of a dead man, after all?

"I don't mind at all. I thought maybe *you* were uncomfortable with it, which I completely understand."

Maggie looked up. Nate was watching her calmly, one ankle crossed over his knee. His lips were unsmiling, but not cold. No, never cold, she realized. She was starting to understand that what she'd mistaken for coolness earlier was just him waiting, accepting. Like he understood far more than he should for someone so young.

And he was young. When she thought about the numbers, she realized there was much *behind* her and much *ahead* for him. She'd been married, raised a child, knew what to expect from life and had accepted it. But he had so much yet to discover. She was good at reading people, doing what she did, and unless she missed her guess, Nate had all those things ahead of him.

But when she looked into his eyes like she was now, the numbers faded away into nothingness. Somehow, without knowing each other hardly at all, she got the feeling they were strangely coming from a similar place. Like she recognized something in him though they'd never met before. Something that superseded the difference in their ages.

"It's not doing anyone any good in storage. You are most welcome to it."

"In that case, thanks. I appreciate it, Maggie."

He used her given name again and it felt very personal. Like they'd crossed a threshold moving them from simple guest/proprietor relationship to something more. Which was ridiculous, wasn't it?

Maggie leaned ahead and poured herself more coffee. It was good Nate was going to use the things. Letting go of Tom had taken a long time. But the sense of loss never left her completely. Or the sense of regret. She had a box of small trinkets she kept all the time, mementos of those she'd loved, tucked away in a box in her closet. She had memories and other reminders of Tom; the skis and snowshoes wouldn't be missed. It was a long time ago and in most respects, she'd moved on.

And in the others...that was none of his business.

Jennifer popped in the door, grinning first at Nate and then over at Maggie. "I thought I smelled coffee."

Maggie was glad of the interruption. "You'll have to grab a mug from the kitchen."

With a flashy smile, Jen saluted and disappeared. Maggie couldn't repress the smirk that twisted her lips. Nate looked over at her with raised eyebrows, and Maggie let out a soft laugh. For all of her troubles, Jen was the breath of fresh air that brightened the house when she was home.

"She's got lots of energy," Nate commented dryly, his hand cradled around his mug as he lifted an eyebrow at Maggie.

"That comes from being eighteen."

"You make it sound like you're in your dotage."

She laughed. "Well, I'm a lot closer than I care to admit."

Nate put down his empty cup and rested his elbows on his knees, linking his hands together. "Believe me, Maggie. You're anything but *too old*."

Maggie's pulse leaped as his gaze locked with hers. Too old for what? For him? She couldn't deny the undercurrents that kept running through their conversation, or the way he'd kissed the tip of her finger. The way she'd caught him staring at her lips. Perhaps flirtation came naturally to him. But she was very out of practice.

"I'm old enough to have a grown daughter to worry about."

Jen popped back in the door and headed straight for the coffeepot, oblivious to the tension in the room. As she poured, she gave her mother the update. "Three loads down, one more to go and my term paper is printing as we speak."

"Atta girl." It was a relief for Maggie to turn her attention to Jen and away from Nate's probing glances.

"Hmph." Jen grumbled as she stirred milk and two heaping teaspoons of sugar into her mug. "Break would have been more fun if I could have gone out instead of being cooped up here writing about the War of 1812."

"What exactly do you do for fun around here?" Nate took a sip of coffee.

Maggie looked at Jen. Maggie's idea of going out for fun wasn't quite the same as Jen's. Maggie preferred for Jen to hang out with girls her own age. Maybe go into Sundre to a movie or something. It was one thing about living in a very small community. Maggie remembered it well. Someone would make a liquor run and everyone would converge on an agreed spot. Most of the time it was harmless, but not always. As they both well knew.

"I, uh…" Jen actually faltered, looking at her mother.

Good, thought Maggie. Perhaps Jen was realizing now that what she'd done was serious. And that it definitely wouldn't seem funny to a cop.

"Um, you know, hang out with other kids and stuff. There's not much to do around here. No place to go other than the store."

"The store?"

Maggie answered the question. "The General Store. Unless you go into Sundre or Olds, it's the only place around to pick up what you need." Maggie looked at Jen, who was staring into her coffee cup. "I'm afraid kids tend to be at loose ends a lot of the time. It's good that Jen's going to school in Edmonton. There's more there for her to see and do."

Jen's head lifted in surprise and Maggie offered a warm smile. Sure, in her heart she also knew there was potential for Jen to get into much more trouble, and that worried her. But by the same token, there was more to catch Jen's interest and keep her busy. It was just hard not being there to make sure she was making good choices.

Maggie went to pour more coffee and realized the cream was empty.

"If you'll excuse me, I'll be right back."

Nate watched her leave, then casually leaned back on the couch, crossing an ankle over his knee again.

"I get the feeling you and your mom just had a whole conversation."

Jen looked up, her cheeks pink. "Well…yeah. Maybe. How'd you know?"

Nate chuckled softly, settling back into the cushions. "Ah. I, too, have a mother. One that saw far more than I ever thought she did."

"My mom sees everything."

Nate purposefully kept his pose relaxed, inviting. It might be his only opportunity. "See now? It sounds like there's a bigger story in there somewhere. You get in some trouble, Jen?"

Her lips thinned and he recognized the stubborn rebellion in her eyes.

"You're a cop. If I did, it would be dumb to tell you, wouldn't it."

Nate nodded. When she got that obstinate jut to her chin, she looked remarkably like her mother. He couldn't help but smile at the thought. "I can see how you'd think that. But you know, I'm not here to bust you for anything. And sometimes an impartial ear comes in handy."

"Why don't you ask my mom?"

"Because I'm asking you. Because maybe I also became a cop to help people."

Again, Jen stared into her cup, avoiding looking him in the eye. "I got into some trouble with the RCMP last year."

"Doing?"

"I got caught with drugs." Her fingers turned her coffee cup around, avoiding him.

"Were you using?" Nate was careful to voice the question gently, without censure.

"No. I mean, I'd tried a joint or two, I guess. Like everyone else. I thought it was gross. I was just…I didn't sell it or anything."

"You weren't using and you weren't selling. Delivery?"

"Yeah, I guess you could say that." Her eyes slid up to his and he knew he'd been right to take it plain and simple. Her fingers stopped fiddling with the mug.

"You were a go-between. And you got caught with it."

She nodded. "Yes. I mean…I know it was wrong, but it was only pot. My mom was so mad. I was…scared to say much of anything, but in the end she made it okay. She made it so I could come home. And then she sent me away to school. A change of scenery, she said."

But Nate knew that tone of voice. He could tell Jen resented being sent away. But his job wasn't to mend fences between Maggie and Jennifer. He held his breath, listening for any evidence that Maggie was coming back. If only she would stay away another five minutes, he might have what he needed. An ID.

"Jen, who were you doing it for? A boyfriend? Did someone threaten you?"

She shook her head so hard he knew whatever came next would only be a partial truth, if that.

"No. No. Pete was never my boyfriend. He's…he's just the go-to guy, you know? On a Saturday when you can't make it into Sundre to the liquor store, or whatever, you go see Pete, and he sets you up."

Nate gritted his teeth. Small potatoes crime, the kind everyone hated but mostly turned a blind eye to as if it would never affect them. "Booze and recreational drugs?" He forced his voice to remain calm and inviting. Damn. Pete seemed to have changed professions, just like Grant had said. There was no doubt in his mind that the local residents probably considered him the community miscreant, but had no idea of his real past.

If he was indeed the man he'd been sent here to find. More than ever now he had to be sure.

"It started out as something fun, something *exciting,* you know? But then it all changed and I wasn't sure how to get out. And I was scared to talk to Mom. I knew she'd blow her top about it. In one way…" She blushed. "I guess in a way I'm glad I got caught. Because then it was over and done with. I just hate that I disappointed her."

Suddenly Jen's face changed, no longer embarrassed but fearful. "You're not going to say anything, are you? I mean… gosh, I probably said too much…we just sort of got to a place where we're okay, you know? Not fighting about it all the time."

Nate felt guilt spiral through him. He'd actually inspired her trust and now he was indeed going to use what she'd told him. The only thing that made it okay was knowing that in the big picture he was doing the right thing. He had no desire to hurt Jen, or Maggie. On the contrary.

"It's okay, Jen. I wouldn't use what you told me against you."

"You're sure?"

"I'm sure. Like I said, my job is also to help people." *Helping people by getting rid of scum,* he reminded himself. *Helping people by getting the information right.*

"Yeah, and besides, you're from the States. So there's no jurisdiction, right?"

He swallowed. It didn't matter how long he did this, some things simply didn't sit right even when they were necessary. He reminded himself of the bigger purpose and lied. "Yeah, that's right."

"My mom…she was mad, but I think she was more upset that maybe I was in big trouble. I…I don't want to hurt my mom again."

Nate smiled. Jen was a good kid, no matter how much trouble she'd gotten into. He hoped Maggie knew it. It spoke well of her that she was worried about her mom's feelings. But his concern was Pete.

"How old is this Pete? I mean, does he usually use young girls to move his stuff?"

"I dunno. Old. Like in his forties, I guess. He just moved here a few years ago. He, you know. Tries to keep it on the low. He's not really hurting anybody. It's just parties and stuff."

Nate hid another smile at Jen's perspective of "old." At eighteen, he supposed it seemed that way. Yet Maggie fell into that bracket and he wouldn't consider her old at all. He remembered the sound of her breath catching in her throat when he'd kissed the tip of her finger. No, there was nothing old about Maggie.

He heard a door shut down the hall and he realized whatever information he'd received was all he'd get. But it was enough.

"Hey, Jen, you want some friendly advice?"

"I guess."

"Make sure you always learn from your mistakes. I can tell that the experience isn't something you'd care to repeat. Take your lessons learned with you."

Take your own advice, buddy, a voice inside him said.

"You're not going to tell my mom? That I told you?"

"Not unless she asks. And you know, she might be really glad to know what you just said. About not wanting to hurt her. Might be a good way to mend some fences."

"I'll think about it."

When Maggie came back in, she put down the cream and ruffled Jen's hair. "I put your last load in the dryer for you. And hung up your sweater."

"Thanks."

Nate tasted cold coffee and suddenly knew what had been plaguing him for the last few weeks. He was homesick. He was missing someone being there for him when he got in trouble, the way Maggie was there for Jennifer. Someone who cared enough to do the little things, for no reason at all. And despite how complicated the trip was rapidly becoming, he was glad he'd somehow ended up at Mountain Haven.

* * *

Maggie breathed on her fingers, fumbled with the key and finally got it shoved in the lock.

It turned hard, stiff from the cold and lack of use, but finally the padlock sprung apart and she opened the shed door with a flourish.

"Enter, if you dare."

She aimed a bright smile up at Nate. He'd been quiet last night after she'd come back in the room, and had excused himself soon after. But this morning he was back to what she assumed was his friendly self. Now he was with her, ready to dig out Tom's things and see if they were fit for use.

He smiled back, his even teeth flashing white in the frosty air. "I think I mentioned that I was also a marine. I'm not afraid of an itty-bitty shed."

"Not even of spiders?"

He laughed. "It's minus a million out here. If they can get through this parka, they deserve a meal."

He ducked into the shed while Maggie waited just outside the door. His sense of humor was a surprise, but it wasn't unwelcome.

"You find anything?" Her breath came out in puffy clouds as she called in after him.

"Yeah. Hang on." A few things rattled and banged as he rearranged articles, pulling things free. Maggie caught a glimpse of his backside as he bent to pick something up from the floor. She stepped away from the door. He was becoming far too alluring and she had to keep her head.

"Incoming!"

She sidestepped quickly as a pair of snowshoes came flying out. When he emerged, cobwebs clung to his coat and hat. She resisted the temptation to reach up and brush them away. Touching him would be a big no-no. She was at least self-aware enough to understand that much.

He proudly held a pair of cross-country skis in one hand and the poles in the other.

"Did you find the boots?"

"Hang on." He pitched the skis in the snow and went back inside, returning with a dusty pair of black boots with square toes. "Size eleven and a half. Should fit all right, even if I double my socks."

"You're crazy to want to go out in this cold." He wouldn't know where he was going and she knew she'd worry in this weather. "With the windchill it's nearly minus thirty."

"Bracing, wouldn't you say?"

"More like frostbite."

"Yes, but then I'll be out of your hair."

Maggie's lips twitched. "Guests at Mountain Haven Bed and Breakfast are *never* in the proprietress's hair."

"You say that now, but I'm god-awful when I'm bored. Disposition of a gator."

Maggie laughed and folded her mittened hands as he tried sliding his feet into the snowshoe harnesses. Despite her words, it would be easier for her if he weren't around 24/7. No matter what *should* be, the two of them alone in the house held a certain degree of intimacy. Intimacy she didn't want or understand. It had never happened with a guest before, but she could feel it stirring between them already. Amicability. The feeling that perhaps they were similar sorts of people. And yes, a level of physical attraction that couldn't be ignored.

"I can't seem to get this on right."

Maggie watched him struggle for a minute, then went to him and knelt in the snow, showing him how to fit his boots into the harness and buckle up the ends.

As she knelt, he bent to see what she was doing and Maggie felt the heat from his body blocking the wind. He was too close. She fumbled with the straps, so took off her mittens to buckle them with her bare hands. Touching him in any way was a mistake. Each time they were together the ridiculous urges grew. He was big and strong and she'd already seen glimpses of compassion and humor. How was she supposed to stay immune to that?

"Try that." She went to get up, and immediately felt the pressure of his hand at her elbow, helping her.

She stepped away.

He took a few steps, gained confidence, picked up the pace, and promptly fell.

Maggie giggled into the wool of her mittens, she couldn't help it. One side of his body, from jeans to the side of his toque, was covered in snow.

"You need some help, tough guy?"

"Not from a scrawny thing like you." He planted his hands and hopped up. "Go ahead and laugh. I bet you couldn't do it."

Maggie's snickers died away as he tried again, the gait awkward but steady. He didn't look back so couldn't see the look on her face, see how his casually tossed out words hurt her.

But the truth was she could do it. She used to snowshoe a lot. First she'd taught Mike when he'd lived with her in Sundre. Then she'd met Tom and she'd gotten pregnant, and they'd married and moved here. That first winter they'd gone on long jaunts with Mike and Jen in a baby backpack.

She turned away, closing the shed door and putting the lock back on it. She hadn't realized what she'd had, and had squandered so much time asking what if. By the time the truth hit her, Tom was gone and she was left alone again. Only this time with the responsibility of a teenage foster child and a baby.

Nate jogged back to her, leaving gigantic bird-shaped tracks behind him in the snow. "Thanks for this. It's going to be fun wandering around."

"You're welcome. You can leave the skis and stuff on the porch, and bring the boots inside."

"Maggie?"

She looked up at him. His green-blue eyes pierced her. "Are you sure you're okay with me using these? You're quiet all of a sudden. I don't want to intrude, really."

"It's not that. They're not doing anyone any good locked up in there. Don't worry about it." She tried to muster a cheerful smile. "I'm going to make a light lunch before I have to take Jen to the bus station."

"You're going to miss her." His voice was quiet in the winter stillness.

"Yeah. I am. Even though we fight like cats and dogs. Still…I think she's better off where she is."

She knew Jen was. The last thing she needed was being back home all the time. She'd get bored and want to go out with friends, and get mixed up with the wrong people again. Maggie had been able to bail her out last time. That wouldn't work again. As lonely as it was without her, she knew she'd made the right decision, getting her into a school there.

"Anyway, she's got to go back so I'm going to do the proper mother thing and ply her with food and a care package." She tried a smile but it fell completely flat.

Nate bent to take off the snowshoes. "You might not think she appreciates it now, but she does. And once she's grown up she might even tell you about it."

Maggie had her doubts. "Are you close with your parents?"

She grabbed the skis and poles while Nate carried the snowshoes and boots and they walked slowly to the house.

"Yes, I am. I have a brother and a sister who chose nice, safe professions, and me, who picked the military and then law enforcement. I know my mom worries. But you know, even when I was overseas, she still sent care packages. The one thing about living in Florida and having them up north is not seeing them as often as I'd like."

"It sounds as though you had a perfect childhood."

"I suppose, although I'd probably just call it normal."

Maggie swallowed. Nate would never understand *her* life. He'd had brothers and sisters and two parents and he still had them. This whole family system in place, even if they were miles apart. The only family she had now was Mike and Jen.

"What about you, Maggie? Where are your parents?"

Maggie climbed the steps to the veranda and leaned the skis against the wall. She put her hand on the doorknob but paused, knowing he was behind her waiting for an answer.

"In a plot next to my husband," she replied tonelessly, before turning the knob and going inside.

CHAPTER FOUR

THE restaurant was nearly empty, and when Maggie walked in she was surprised to see Nate sitting at a table with Grant Simms. She caught her breath and held it for a moment. Grant wasn't a bad sort, he just *knew* things. Things she would rather Nate not find out.

She wondered briefly why they were together, but then realized it was natural that enforcement types would gravitate to each other. Nate had probably seen Grant come in and looked for some company. Lord knew she wasn't the best conversationalist today.

Nate turned toward the door as she came in and his eyes lit, the intimate look warming her. She smiled back despite her misgivings. There was a magnetism—a pull—that she would never admit aloud but couldn't deny to herself. A feeling so unexpected, unfamiliar in its long absence. She couldn't bring herself to feel sorry about the attraction rising up now. It provided a welcome distraction. The alternative was going home to an empty, quiet house. A reminder of how lonely she was when Jen was gone. A taste of how it would be when Jen moved on with her own life and Maggie would be left alone.

She pulled off her gloves and approached the table.

"Jen get off okay?"

"Yes, the bus is gone." His words brought her firmly out

of the moment and back to the very real present. She nearly choked on her reply, swallowed against the sudden tightening in her throat as she said the word "gone." Saying goodbye had been emotional to put it lightly. She hated watching Jen go away, hated the helpless feeling that flooded her every time she left. Hated the fear that somehow this could be the last time. In her head she knew it was irrational, but her heart didn't quite get it. Knowing Jen was out of her sight frightened her more than she'd ever admit.

But she said nothing, because Nate didn't need to know, and besides, he wasn't alone. Her eyes skittered to his companion.

His gaze followed hers and he performed introductions. "Maggie, this is Grant Simms."

"Constable Simms." She held out her hand, surprised when the man rose politely and took it.

"Nice to see you, Maggie. Nate tells me you're treating him well."

"Well, as the only guest, I don't have to play favorites, it's true."

"You know each other." Nate looked from one to the other.

"It's a small town, Nate." Grant laughed lightly, but it sounded false to Maggie.

Maggie forced the smile to remain on her lips. In another time she might have liked Grant. He was in his mid-forties, handsome in a crisp, efficient sort of way. But last summer when they'd met it had been in less pleasant circumstances that she'd rather forget. She commented out of politeness only.

"And now you two have met."

"Grant and I attended a conference in Toronto together a few years ago," Nate explained. "We've been catching up."

The two men exchanged a look. Maggie narrowed her eyes. They knew each other before today, then. It was just a crazy coincidence that they'd met up here. How much had Grant told him about her, about Jen? What would Nate think?

Grant Simms was part of the reason why Maggie had been so persistent in Jen going away to school. She knew she should feel gratitude. Things could have been so much worse. But today of all days, it was a bitter reminder of how much she missed the girl she'd known; how far apart she and Jen had grown that it had come to this. Regrets.

A waitress appeared, bearing a coffeepot. "Sit down, Maggie," Nate invited. "Have a coffee."

She didn't see a way to properly refuse, besides, she was suddenly feeling quite raw. She took the chair Nate held out, sat gratefully.

"Cream?"

He held out the saucer containing tiny plastic cups of creamer. She took two, biting her lip as her fingers began to tremble.

The waitress filled her mug while she struggled with the tab on the creamer. It finally peeled back, but by this time her hands were shaking so badly she jostled the cup as she went to pour, sloshing coffee over the edge and on to the table, staining the cloth.

"Oh, how clumsy of me!" She blinked furiously, out of humiliation and sheer emotionalism. Why couldn't this get any easier? It should get better each time. Instead it was always the same. She functioned through goodbye and then fell spectacularly apart later. Why couldn't she have made it another hour so she could do it in private, instead of in front of the two men she'd least want to witness it?

"It's okay, Maggie. I've got it." Nate dabbed at the spilled coffee, making her feel even more foolish.

She tried to catch her breath. It would be fine. Jen's bus would drive into Edmonton and she'd go back to campus and her dorm room and in two months she'd be home for summer break. They'd get back to how things were. They could do it, she knew it in her heart. She'd seen glimpses of it today. Her fears were groundless.

Only they weren't. Silly, perhaps, but not groundless. Life could change on a dime.

"Are you okay?"

Nate's voice murmured into her ear, low enough that no one could hear. His warm breath tickled the hair behind her earlobe and she focused on inhaling and exhaling. When she opened her eyes, Grant had gone to see the waitress about a towel and fresh coffee.

Maggie looked at Simms's retreating back and then up into Nate's concerned eyes. She wished he didn't see so much, it made her feel naked. "I'm fine. I just want to go home, if that's all right with you."

Nate dug in his wallet and dropped a bill on the table as Grant came back with a tea towel in his hand. "Grant, I think we're going to be off. It was nice to see you again." He held out his hand and the other officer shook it.

"Give me a call while you're around, Nate. We should shoot some pool or something."

"Will do. See you later."

"Nice to see you, Maggie."

He was friendly looking and polite but there was something in the other man's eyes she didn't quite trust. He knew. Had he shared that information with Nate after all?

Her response came out frosty. "You, too." She could feel Nate's hand, warm and reassuring against her back. She tipped her lips up in a perfunctory smile.

"Let's go then."

They were almost to the truck when Nate's rough voice stopped her progress. "Hey, Maggie? Why don't you let me drive back?"

She stopped and turned. He'd pulled his collar up in an attempt to keep some warmth close to his ears, but they turned pink in the frigid air. She wished again that she didn't find him so attractive, especially now when she knew she was raw and vulnerable. His clipped hair, straight bearing and sheer size didn't intimidate her, not at all. She was drawn to it. It was the oddest thing. She'd never gone for the clean-cut, military type before. There was something about them she didn't trust. Whether it was because of past history or simply knowing how dangerous their lives were, Maggie had never gravitated toward that type of man.

But with Nate, even after a few short hours, there was a constant curiosity that took her by surprise. Knowing there was much more to him than met the eye and wondering what it could be; wanting to dig below the surface to find out what mattered to Nate Griffith.

"You want to drive my old beater? Why?"

He laughed, the masculine sound turning her knees to jelly. He had a strong, rich laugh, one that rippled. "I'd hardly call it a beater. But…sorry, it's a guy thing. I feel kind of weird having you chauffeur me around."

"It's okay. Consider it part of the vacation treatment." It was tempting to let him drive. Her hands were still shaking and she was thankful he'd gotten her out of the restaurant so quickly. But over the years she'd handled everything thrown her way on her own. Knew she could. It was the one thing she was sure of. The last thing she needed was to let him see how fragile she was. "I can drive."

He stopped her at the driver's side door. "Please, Maggie. You were trembling in there." His hands turned her gently so she was facing him, blocked from the wind by his massive body. "Saying goodbye to Jennifer didn't go well, did it?"

He was hard to resist when he looked down at her with obvious concern. When was the last time anyone had been concerned about her? The relief of it was almost enough to make her want to sag against his body and let him carry a little of the burden. But that was ridiculous. He was a virtual stranger.

"It never does. It's just a parent's worry."

"Worry to the point of shaking, and turning white as a sheet?"

She swallowed. She hadn't realized it was that obvious. Somehow saying goodbye set off a reaction every time, but she hadn't realized it showed so very much. She got the feeling he'd keep up the inquisition, and she tried a plain answer, hoping it would stop him from prying more.

"I've lost a lot of people in my life, Nate. Sometimes it hits even though it's been a long time. Saying goodbye…" She took a big breath. Met his eyes and said it all at once. "Saying goodbye triggers a lot of those old feelings of panic. It'll pass. It always does."

"Then you worry about decompressing and I'll worry about the road. This once." He held out his hand, unsmiling, simply waiting.

She took the keys from her pocket and placed them into his hand. He was steady, she already got that. His warm fingers closed over hers.

"Maggie, she'll be fine. She's a good kid."

Grant must have kept quiet then. Nate wouldn't have said such a thing if he knew about her arrest last year. A tiny sliver of relief threaded through her.

They got in the truck and he started the ignition. Maggie reached over and cranked up the heater, trying to halt the chills that wouldn't seem to stop shaking her body.

"You want to talk about it, Maggie?" He pulled out of the parking lot, watching her from the corner of his eye.

Her smile wavered a little. Did she? Perhaps. Maybe it would be nice to talk to someone who didn't know everything, who didn't look at her like *that widow that never remarried.* Too many people here knew her past. But she'd kept it all inside for so long she wasn't comfortable delving too deeply.

"I'm fine. It's just…" Her eyes held his as he waited before putting the truck in gear. "I can't protect her when she's away. But she's eighteen. It's right for her to be where she is."

"All moms worry. It's part of the job description." Nate smiled again and she felt it spread over her. He turned on to the highway, leaning back in the seat and resting a hand comfortably on the steering wheel. "But I get the feeling there's more to it than that."

Maggie stared out the window. Her relationship with Jen was so complicated. It had been easier when Jennifer had been small, and life had been simple. But Jen had grown up, wanted her independence. Didn't understand Maggie's need to keep her sheltered and fought her every step of the way. Without Nate understanding that, she didn't think he could understand how much a simple hug of farewell and "I love you" meant. She didn't have anyone to talk to about it and appreciated the impartial ear.

"Jen and I don't often see eye to eye. But today…today was different."

"How so?"

"I didn't get the level of hostility I normally do. We talked about summer vacation. It was…nice. But it felt…"

The sense of panic settled in her gut again and she pursed her lips.

"It felt?"

She was glad his eyes were on the road so he didn't see the tears flickering on her lashes. "It felt like goodbye. Like making peace. And it scared the hell out of me."

She sighed when he didn't answer. "I know. It's a fatalistic approach and it sucks."

He laughed. "Well, you're very self-aware."

Tension drained out of her at the sound of his chuckle. Telling him had been good. She'd stopped confiding in her friends long ago. The last thing she wanted to do was bore them to tears about the fears that never quite went away. She'd picked up her life and made something of it. She had a successful business, was a mother. It didn't make sense to most of them that she still had issues. Besides, she wanted people to forget about Jen's troubles, and talking about it wouldn't help at all. But Nate was safe. In the overall scheme of things, it would be forgotten soon enough, when he was gone.

"I'm hungry. Let's stop at the store."

"The store?"

"Up here." She pointed to the turnoff. "I'll pick up something special for dinner."

"You got it." He followed her directions, pulling into a parking space and killing the engine.

Nate hopped out of the cab and trotted over to her side before she could blink. He opened her door and she slid out, self-conscious at his solicitude.

They stood there for long seconds. Nate's heart thudded erratically at the continued closeness, the same feeling he'd had this morning when she'd kneeled to strap on the snowshoes. She'd trusted him today, and lately trust had been in short supply. The more he talked with her the more he realized it couldn't have been easy. Not for a self-sufficient woman like her. As the pieces started to come together, he could understand how putting her kid on a bus today was a big event.

"Nate, I..." She paused, looking up at him. Her eyes were blue, the color of the Atlantic on a clear day and her lips were parted as she paused, seeming to search for words. For a fleeting second he thought about putting his lips against hers just to see what would happen. If the need he felt stirring for her was real or imagined. If the warmth of her mouth would take away some of his own misgivings, as well as appease some of her own.

But that would hardly be fair, so he waited for her to finish what she was saying.

The silence drew out, until he prompted her with "You..."

She blinked slowly. He wasn't imagining it, then. There *was* some sort of a connection between them. It hadn't just been the candlelight at dinner last night.

She cleared her throat. "I was just going to ask if you'd like to rent a movie after. There's a video store in Sundre. It's not far."

If he were home he'd work out or read, or flip through TV channels much as he had last night. It was different now. They would need something to fill the time. To keep him from thinking about how pretty she looked or how she kept him from feeling lonely. They would be alone together. It would be getting dark, there would be dinner with just the two of them and a long evening stretching before them. They'd only be fooling themselves now, insisting it was a hostess-guest relationship. Something more had been forged between them today. A movie would be just the thing to quell the silly urge to spend the evening with her in his arms.

"That might be nice."

She let out a breath, the air forming a cloud above her head. She had to move soon or he'd reconsider kissing her. Which would be a huge mistake, especially in front of the only store in the community with everyone watching. Even he understood about gossip in small towns. More than she realized. He'd pretended to be surprised she knew Grant, but he wasn't, not at all. He knew all about their past association. How could he, in all conscience, kiss a woman he'd lied to less than an hour before?

"Maggie?"

"Yes?" She shoved her hands into her pockets.

"What's for dinner?"

She smiled at him then and he suddenly realized he'd been waiting for it. Maggie smiling sucked all the bitterness out of the cold air and replaced it with something else. He felt better than he had in a long time, and rather than analyze it to death, shoulds or shouldn'ts, he simply enjoyed it.

"Come inside and we'll find out," she suggested impishly, darting for the door, her dark hair streaming out behind her in the wind.

Movie be damned. Nate was starting to realize it would take more than a DVD to keep him from thinking about Maggie Taylor.

Nate followed her into the store, more intrigued than he remembered being in a long time. He'd sensed a lot of things about Maggie since arriving, but a sense of fun wasn't one of them. Especially this afternoon when she'd nearly come undone in front of Grant. Yet watching her eyes twinkle at him as she flicked her hair out of her face, he realized there was more to Maggie than met the eye. Much more. He was beginning to regret not kissing her when he'd had the chance.

"Hey, Nate, you helping here or what?"

He straightened, pinning a smile on his face. "Helping with what?"

"Dinner. You pick it, I cook it."

She was standing at the meat counter. He went up beside her and noticed she was quite serious about choosing choice cuts. "Steak?"

"Yeah." The corners of her lips flickered in teasing. "You caveman. Like red meat, yah?"

He couldn't stop the snort, surprising both of them. "Yah, red meat good."

"T-bones or rib eyes?"

The very thought had his mouth watering. He was used to cooking for himself, pointless as it seemed. It had been a long time since any woman had taken care making him a meal. To be given the choice…

"Rib eyes. And mushrooms."

She ordered the steaks, adding in a good-size portion of stewing beef for another meal.

"Any other requests?"

She turned with the paper packages in her hands and he swallowed. She was making an effort, he realized. To dispel the gloom from the start of the afternoon and replace it with something bright and shiny.

"I trust your culinary judgment completely. Surprise me."

She started down another aisle, but turned her head at the last moment. "I just might, Nate. I just might."

He had no doubt about it.

CHAPTER FIVE

IT SEEMED changed somehow.

The house actually felt different with Jen gone. Her presence had been a barrier between Maggie and Nate in one way, and brought them together in another. Now, with just the two of them at Mountain Haven, the opposite was true. Her absence was forcing them together physically, but propriety reared its head again and Maggie tried to keep things how they were supposed to be. She'd said enough this afternoon, when Nate had invited her confidence. It really wouldn't be wise to smudge the lines any further. No matter how empty the house felt with Jen gone. No matter how tempting Nate's company could be.

She opened the oven and pulled out the cookie sheet, placing it on the stove and turning the roasted potatoes so they'd brown evenly. She was a hostess cooking dinner for a paying guest. That was all.

Then why, oh why, did it feel like a date, for heaven's sake?

She paused, the spatula frozen midturn. *Because after only two days she'd allowed him in.* She'd broken her own personal rule about becoming friends with guests and had told him personal things that had been incredibly painful to verbalize. It had felt good to talk, and she'd needed it, but Maggie knew it couldn't happen again. She couldn't let herself become vulnerable to him. To anyone.

She slid the pan back in the oven and turned her attention to the Caesar salad. Cooking soothed her, warmed her soul. It was more than nourishment, always had been. She'd learned to cook at her mother's elbow at a young age, and when she'd been orphaned, it had been the one task that gave her any sense of comfort, of connection. It still did.

Nate came to the door and she wondered, in a moment of sheer fantasy, what it would be like if he came up behind her and slid his arms around her waist. To feel the comfort tangibly from his touch, more than the pressure of his hand on hers as he took her keys, like this afternoon. He looked like he'd perhaps taken advantage of the time to have a nap. His cotton shirt was wrinkled and his hair was slightly mussed. There was definitely something to be said for the rumpled look, she thought as her mouth went dry.

"Smells good."

She reached into a jug, pulling out her favorite salad utensils, using dinner preparations as a refuge. Talking out of turn while she was raw and upset was one thing, but she'd had time to pull herself together. It was up to her to set the tone where it ought to be.

"Thanks. I thought we'd eat in the dining room tonight." She held out the salad bowl. "The steaks are almost done, but if you could take this in, I'll be there in a minute."

When she entered the dining room, she was struck yet again by the sense of intimacy. It was the custom for her guests to eat here, but she'd never experienced a feeling of "specialness" to the room before. Now, with Nate present, it looked—felt—changed somehow. Richer, darker, smaller.

It would have been an out-and-out lie to think that the extra effort she put into the meal was completely platonic. She'd wanted to impress him, to do something special. Perhaps because of how nice he'd been to Jen, or because he'd put up with her episode this afternoon and had listened to her troubles.

Perhaps because she was tired of being lonely, of going through the motions, and he was a willing ear.

She put down the tray and unloaded the serving bowls. Nate stood at the corner of the table, pouring the merlot she'd uncorked.

"Thank you." She took the glass from his hand when he held it out.

"No, thank you," he murmured. A candle hissed and sputtered before finding its flame once more. "You've outdone yourself, I can tell."

"Nonsense."

He waited until she was seated before taking his own, and she glowed inwardly at the presence of manners.

"This looks wonderful, Maggie." She handed him the platter, steaks surrounded by herbed and browned potatoes and he helped himself.

"All in the line of duty." She brushed it off with a glib comment.

His hand paused, then put down the platter. He seemed to think for a moment, his lips pursing in a thin line. "I get the feeling you've been doing things in the line of duty for a really long time. Especially after what you told me this afternoon."

She looked away. Was she that transparent? She'd told him little about her life in the greater scheme of things. Just the basic facts. But what he said was true. She'd shut away so much of life, had focused on what she did and bringing up Jen. It was easier than letting her heart get involved again.

"I enjoy what I do." She put him off. Talking about the bed and breakfast was a nice, safe topic.

"When was the last time you did something purely selfish? Just for yourself?"

She couldn't remember, and she was disconcerted that he'd been able to read between the lines so easily.

She made her hands busy by filling his salad bowl. "I love my job, you know. I couldn't do it otherwise. It makes me happy."

"I don't mean your job."

He put his hand over hers, stopping her from fiddling with the salad. "Maggie."

She stalled, caught by the simple touch.

"Whether or not it's your job…thank you. For making me feel at home here."

Maggie looked up. His eyes were completely earnest, caught somewhere between that blue and hazely-green color.

"You're welcome."

His gaze held her captive in the flickering candlelight as he held her hand. "And for trusting me this afternoon. I'd like to think—maybe—that we're becoming friends."

She pulled back. "I don't usually befriend my guests, Nate."

He thought for a moment, then a smile brightened his face, as if he knew that was exactly what she was supposed to say. "Yes, well, I'm special."

She couldn't help the quiver of her lips at his teasing. How was she to answer that? She got the feeling that he was, indeed, special. Different. But to say so wasn't wise.

"Don't let it go to your head. And thank you. For being so kind today. I'm sorry I was all over the map. I don't usually fall apart in front of my patrons."

"You're welcome." He pulled back, buttered his bread and broke it into crusty pieces as they enjoyed the meal she'd prepared.

"So, anything else I should know about Maggie Taylor?"

She'd hoped that thanking him would put an end to the personal talk, but that wish fluttered away. She wondered if it was the cop in him, the need to ask so many questions. She focused on spearing a lettuce leaf. "I told you anything that's interesting. I'm really very boring."

He laughed, cutting into his steak. "Yeah, right, Maggie. The last word I'd use to describe you is dull."

She picked up her wine and drank to hide her face. Was he serious? Dull is exactly how she'd put it. She'd had the same life for the last decade and a half. Running this business and raising a daughter. Watching middle age creep up on her. Nothing exciting in that.

"What do you want to know, then? How much starch I put in my pillowcases? Do I grow my own herbs?" She tried to make a joke of it.

"Sure, if that's what's important to you."

A smile teased her lips before she straightened once more, the picture of propriety. "I sprinkle, not starch and I grow some of my own herbs, but not all."

"Did that hurt?"

"No, I guess it didn't."

They ate in silence for a few more minutes and then Nate spoke again. "I'm more interested in how you became the person you are now. How you grew up and what made you choose this as your livelihood."

The crisp romaine leaves wilted in her mouth. She swallowed. Damn him. "The life story of Maggie Taylor? Only if you're having trouble sleeping."

"Why do you do that?" Nate pushed away his plate and cradled his goblet. "Why do you diminish who you are, what you do? I wouldn't have asked, Maggie, if I didn't think it was worth knowing."

She flushed. She had no wish to unearth the pain and disappointment she tried to keep buried every day. Or go into the sad and lonely reasons why she'd chosen to open a bed and breakfast. What she'd revealed earlier was all he was getting today. It was time to put a stop to this line of questioning right now, because she was beginning to feel like this was an interrogation, not a heart-to-heart. Like he wanted her to tell him things she shouldn't. She stood, piling his plate on top of hers. "Do you want dessert? There's pumpkin cake with caramel sauce."

His eyes assessed her; she could feel them burning into her as she cleared the dishes.

"I'm sorry, I'm prying. It's unfair of me."

"Yes, it is. I appreciate your listening to me this afternoon when I was upset. But the details of my life are personal. And I know you will respect that."

"I like you, Maggie. I was simply curious."

She couldn't seem to come up with a response. He stood and gathered what was left of the dirty dishes and followed her into the kitchen, putting them on the empty counter.

"Maggie?"

"What." She put down the dishes and turned to face him. She couldn't do this. Being stuck with someone every hour of the day was for some reason, very difficult. Most who came to Mountain Haven were interested in the area, in *their* lives—not hers. Trouble was, she wanted to tell him. To unload all the pain she'd held inside for so many years. She didn't understand it. Couldn't fathom *why* he was different. She'd never felt such a compulsion before.

He didn't say anything. He stood not five feet in front of her, but nothing came out of his mouth. She saw the muscles bunch beneath his shirt and she wondered what it would be like to run her fingers over the skin of his arms, of his broad shoulders.

"What," she whispered again, shocked when she heard her voice come out warm and husky, like the caramel sauce she'd made for the cake.

Without warning, he took two steps forward, curled his hand around her head and kissed her.

His lips were warm and tasted faintly of the acidic richness of the merlot. Taken by surprise, and on the heels of her own thoughts, she didn't push away. Her lashes fluttered down as his arm came around her, tucking her close to his hard body as his lips opened wider, taking the kiss deeper.

And oh, he felt marvelous. Strong and patient and thorough. Her heart pounded, sending the blood rushing through her veins, awakening her. He was vibrant and young and mysterious and so very, very real. Her hands slid over his shoulder blades, down, down, until they encountered the back pockets of his jeans.

He broke the kiss off in stages: gentle, fluttering tiny kisses on the corners of her mouth, making her weak in the knees and wanting more, not less. She chased him with her lips, and he caught her bottom one in his teeth before letting go and putting a few inches between them.

She looked up, frightened by the intensity of his gaze, more frightened that perhaps her own mirrored it so blatantly. It was a shock to realize that she wanted him. Wanted a man she hardly knew. Wanted him in the most basic way a woman could want a man.

Right now she'd crawl into his skin if he'd let her.

She pushed away blindly, stopping only when her backside hit the counter. Her breaths were shallow, ripe with arousal. All from a single kiss, a few fleeting moments where their bodies touched.

"I've wanted to do that all day."

And the words, huskily spoken in the muted light, sent a rush of desire flooding through her.

Shame reddened her cheeks. This was wrong. He was patiently waiting for her reaction and all she could do was feel embarrassed that he'd affected her so strongly. She'd pushed away her sexual being for so long she'd all but forgotten it existed. Had settled for a dim appreciation of a man's looks on occasion. But she'd never, not since Tom, behaved in such a wanton way.

"I…you…pumpkin cake." She stammered and wanted to

slide through the floor into oblivion. Any pretense of dignity was gone.

"Not right now."

"C...c...coffee?"

"Maggie. Should I apologize?" His words were soft, with that hint of gravel rumbling through and her pulse leaped at the intimacy of it. "I don't want to."

I don't want you too, either. She raised her chin as best she could. She had to put some distance between them somehow. "It would be appropriate."

Who was she kidding? It wasn't like she hadn't participated willingly. He might have initiated it but she'd been right there, keeping up.

"I'm sorry." His voice was husky-soft in the dim light filtering in from the dining room. "I'm sorry you're so damn pretty I had to kiss you."

Holy hell.

She couldn't do this. Couldn't. "Yes, well, I've known you two days. You're a guest in my house. A paying guest. Perhaps you should remember that."

It might have worked if her voice hadn't trembled at the end. She gathered what little bit of pride she had left around her and swept from the room.

He wasn't the only one that needed reminding.

Sunlight filtered through the window of the bedroom as Nate stirred. He squinted against the bright light, checking his watch. Eight-fifteen. He never slept this late.

He usually didn't lie awake until the wee hours thinking, either. But he had last night.

He rose, pulling on the clothes he'd laid out. Thermals beneath heavy gray-toned camouflaged pants. Thick socks and a long-sleeved undershirt under a crew necked cotton pullover. He'd layer today and adjust. Took the backpack out of the bottom of the closet, left in it what he'd need and stowed the rest in the bottom of his duffel.

A day out of the house was definitely in order.

He'd been foolish to kiss Maggie last night. Problem was, he'd been thinking of it all afternoon and through dinner. He enjoyed seeing her flustered, enjoyed the moments of banter between them. But then, seeing her vulnerable, knowing how difficult she found it watching her daughter leave, brought out his protective side. It was something he'd inherited. He couldn't do what he did without it.

He put the pack on the bed, seeing her sad eyes in his mind. It wasn't all about justice. Most people thought so, and for some it was true. But not for him.

Sometimes it wasn't about punishing the guilty, but protecting the innocent.

He padded down the stairs in his stocking feet and wandered into the kitchen. It was quiet; not a dish or crumb in sight. The appliances gleamed and floor shone. He smiled to himself. He was beginning to recognize her penchant for order, especially when she was preoccupied. Had his kiss done that? Or had it simply been because of Jen?

He frowned as his early morning thoughts trickled back. Had she put all that extra effort into the meal, had she kissed him back, simply as a substitute? To keep herself from thinking about her daughter's absence? Had he been a distraction?

And wouldn't that be a good thing? A harmless flirtation was far more desirable than something complicated. Yet…the thought of him being a stand-in chafed, good idea or not.

Nate wondered if Maggie had had the same trouble sleeping and was making up for it now. Quietly he filled the coffeemaker and started the brew filtering. There was no sense dwelling on it. A more important question was whether or not she had a thermos on hand for him to take with him today.

The side door opened and Maggie appeared, completely dressed, pulling her hair back into a sensible ponytail.

When she looked up at him, his heart gave a solid thump. Where had that come from? It was difficult enough being here under the present circumstances. Attraction, kissing…they weren't on the agenda. He couldn't afford to be distracted. And she certainly wouldn't understand if she found out the truth. He offered his best, polite-only smile.

"Good morning."

"Good morning," he answered back. Silence fell, awkward. So the kiss wasn't forgotten, nor forgiven. The smile faded from his face. "I started the coffee. I hope that's all right."

"I'm sorry I wasn't up to see to it."

Great. Now they were speaking—and standing—like wooden statues.

"Maggie, I *am* sorry about last night. I was out of line. Your business is yours. I had no right to pry."

He sensed her relief as the clouds cleared from her eyes. "Thank you, I appreciate that." She offered a small smile and he watched her go to the cupboard and dig out ingredients. Perhaps his greatest transgression hadn't been the kiss then, but the intimate questions.

"I like you, Nate. You're a nice guy." He winced. A nice guy? Hardly. Her words were hollow as she spoke from within the cabinet. "It's understandable that things…progressed, I suppose. But I'm not comfortable with it. It can't happen again."

"I know that."

She turned around, flour bin in hand, her smile a little easier. "I'm glad. And I hope you like pancakes."

She couldn't know. Couldn't possibly know how much he wanted to tell her everything. To tell her why he was really there, how it would help her, and Jen. But he couldn't. It was what it was. It was pancakes and pleasantries and half-truths.

"Pancakes are good." He thought of the day ahead. "With a couple of eggs would be even better."

"Eggs I can do. How do you like them?"

"However you fix them will be fine." He offered her the first truly genuine smile of the day. "I'm used to eating them in all forms, believe me."

She beat the batter in the bowl as the griddle heated. "I suppose you have, with your past history. What's your favorite?"

He grinned at her back. "Over easy."

"Then that's what you'll have. What are your plans for the rest of the day?"

The tension had dispelled with apologies and talks of breakfast. "The temperature's gone up a bit, so I thought I'd give those snowshoes a workout." He went to the counter and took the plates and cutlery she was laying out as the first pancakes sizzled on the pan. "I've been two days without physical activity. Add that with home cooking…"

He put the plates at the kitchen table, turning back as she put the pancakes on the warming tray and cracked eggs into a fry pan.

"There's syrup and juice in the fridge," she called out, pouring two more perfectly round circles on the greased griddle.

It was something he missed, more than he'd realized. Everyday chatter over meal preparations, having someone to sit with at the table. Now it only happened when he was home in Philadelphia for holidays, with his brother and sisters around. Mom cooked for everyone, and ribbing and teasing were the order of the day. He was surprised to find it so far away from his ordinary life.

When the eggs were done, she filled his plate. "Sit down, Nate, I'll bring you some coffee."

The pancakes were light and fluffy and he poured syrup— real maple syrup, not the table version—over the top. Two eggs, done to fragile perfection, sat alongside. He'd heard before that the way to a man's heart was through his stomach. As his own rumbled, he thought that just might be true.

"Hey, Maggie?"

"Hmmm?"

"You wouldn't happen to have a thermos, would you? I'd love to take some coffee along this morning."

"I've got one around here somewhere."

She took her place across from him. "How long are you planning on being out?"

"Most of the day, I think."

"Then you'll need a lunch."

"You don't have to…"

"Don't worry about it. It's all part of the 'extras' I quoted your boss."

The pancakes went dry in his mouth. Of course. The tentative friendship they'd forged was punctuated with reminders that he was a client. It was as she'd said all along. This was her job. She was being paid to see to his needs. Food and comfortable shelter.

"Thank you, then."

He sliced through his pancake. He'd asked for the coffee, but had planned on a few protein bars keeping him going throughout the day. If the USMS was footing the bill, there was no reason for him not to take the lunch. Maggie had reverted to her pleasant, professional self. It was like the emotions of yesterday hadn't happened. It was for the best.

He pushed out his chair. "Thanks for breakfast. I'll go upstairs and get my pack."

In his room he reconsidered his clothing and stripped off his cotton shirt, putting his bulletproof vest beneath it. He wasn't anticipating any trouble, but there was no harm in being cautious. Taking care, an ounce of prevention and all that. He checked his pack one last time and went back downstairs.

"Your lunch."

Maggie appeared in the foyer with an insulated pack and a silver thermos. "Sandwiches and fruit. And a slice of the cake you missed last night. I hope that's okay."

"It's perfect." He took them from her and tucked them carefully into his bag, withdrawing his GPS at the same time and tucking it in his parka.

"Are you sure you know where you're going?"

He nodded. "I have a map of the roads right here." He held up the unit. "As long as I stay within the grid, there's no way I'll get lost."

"I'll see you at dinner then."

He pulled his toque over his ears. "Yes, ma'am."

Outside, he squinted in the sunlight and put on his sunglasses. He strapped on the snowshoes bare-handed and pulled on his gloves. It was cold, but not the frigid bitterness of yesterday.

He started off over the lawn, his gait gaining rhythm as he caught his stride. According to his information, a little over two miles southwest from here he could set up, dig in and enjoy more of her coffee as he watched. And waited.

she'd been crazy not to date all that time, because it took the pressure off, knowing that what Jen was talking about—that spark she felt last night—couldn't lead anywhere. Or maybe it was crazy, when her youth, though it didn't seem so now, was just passing her by.

The thrilling sensation... and she'd imagined more than just the physical pleasure from being with Nate, the way he'd made her feel wanted... she'd forgotten what it was like to be wanted with a mere glance. Oh, Nate had made her feel that way when Jen was there, but with Jen gone that didn't seem to change. And now...

CHAPTER SIX

MAGGIE watched him go, heaving a sigh of relief when he crossed through the grove of trees at the edge of her property. She closed her eyes, breathing deeply, willing her body to relax.

This morning had been nothing more than an acting job, and one she wasn't sure she could keep up.

His apology had gone a long way, but as soon as she'd seen him standing there, looking large and dangerous and undeniably sexy, she'd wanted nothing more than to kiss him again and see if it had really been as good as she remembered.

Something had changed. At first it had been a simple appreciation for a good-looking man, full stop. The last person she'd ever be interested in was someone in law enforcement. Maybe the problem was that he wasn't here in any official capacity. He didn't wear a uniform, or a badge, or carry a weapon. It made it easy to forget. Until something intruded to remind her. Like seeing him with Grant Simms. Or the way he questioned her last night.

And then she forgot all over again when he kissed her and turned her knees to jelly.

She went back to the kitchen and began to tidy the mess. Jen had put the idea in her head, but it hadn't taken much to keep it there. And now Jen was gone and Nate wasn't and it wasn't right that she should have such feelings. Maybe she'd been wrong not to date all this time, because it felt suspiciously like slaking a thirst. Nate was younger and energetic and she found that irresistible. And it was foolish to think she could relive her youth through a man who was just passing through.

This morning was a new day and she'd awakened knowing that keeping distance from Nate was the best thing for everyone. The emotional pitch from yesterday had dissipated and she was left with a clearer head. Nate was leaving within a few weeks and she couldn't get attached to him. Anything that happened between them was temporary. They both knew it, and also knew further episodes like last night's would be pointless. After that kiss…even flirting was a dimension best left unexplored. These weeks at Mountain Haven weren't real. What was real was his life back in the States, the one where he was a marshal who spent his days apprehending criminals.

She spent the morning cleaning, discovering with great interest that Nate was a neat lodger. He'd already made up his bed, and his laptop was closed, the mouse pad and cordless mouse sitting on top of the cover. There were no clothes laying about. In fact, except for the laptop on the desk, she could hardly tell anyone was even staying in the room.

For some odd reason, she didn't find that knowledge very comforting.

She curled up with a book in the afternoon. The sun sliding through the south facing window of her personal "parlor" warmed her, making her drowsy. She hadn't slept until nearly 2:00 a.m., and after the emotional roller coaster of yesterday, the six-plus hours she did get hadn't seemed to have alleviated all her exhaustion.

When she woke, it was after four, dinner wasn't started and Nate wasn't back, despite the darkening shadows of fading daylight. She'd been dreaming, odd dreams with Nate and Jen and Grant. Nothing that made sense. Jen, in handcuffs, with

Nate holding her wrists. Grant coming forward and pinning some sort of medal on Nate's chest.

She stood up, rolling her shoulders and dismissing it. It was silly, that was all. She could puzzle it out easy enough. It was worrying that Nate would find out about Jen, and after seeing Grant and saying goodbye yesterday, it was probably natural.

A niggle of concern skittered down her arms as she realized another hour and he'd be out of daylight. Where could he have gone that would have taken him all day? He had to be exhausted. Had he gotten lost despite his assurances to the contrary?

He'd definitely cooled off when she'd mentioned his boss, too. Knowing she was behind schedule, she put chicken breasts in the microwave to thaw, the sound of the appliance filling the empty house. He hadn't appreciated the work reminder. As soon as she'd brought up the fact that his bill was paid, he'd gone cold and distant. She wondered why that was. Wondered why he'd chosen to come here, of all places. What had forced him to take a leave of absence?

As she kept her hands busy, her mind kept pace. She could understand the leave being paid, but it still didn't quite sit right that his vacation was being paid by the Marshal Service. Not if it were a personal trip.

The sound of his boots on the porch coincided with a sudden thought. She couldn't believe she hadn't thought of it before.

The bill, the location, his contact with Constable Simms.

He was here on a job. It was the only thing that made sense, and an icy spear shot through her body as the door opened.

He stomped inside, cheeks flushed and boots in hand, putting them on the mat so that no snow fell on her floor.

"Sorry I'm late."

Maggie didn't know what to say. She was still reeling from the possibility that had zoomed through her head. What if he had been lying to her all along? What had he really been doing today? How was he connected to the very same constable responsible for Jen's arrest?

And how in the world did she go about getting the truth? Did she even want to know? Really? She took a step backward.

"Maggie, are you okay?" He was across the foyer and in the hall in a flash. "Is it Jen?"

Oh Lord. She was horrible at poker faces. She'd really have to do better, because if her suspicions were correct, he was a heck of a player.

"No, Jen's fine. I fell asleep this afternoon and I think I'm still waking up." She gave a light laugh, then frowned when it came out with a false ring.

"I'm going to go change. Fell down a few times and got wet." He started for the stairs.

"Nate?"

He paused with his hand on the banister.

The words she wanted didn't come. She wasn't sure she was wily enough to trick him into answering, and was afraid of asking point-blank. What if he were here on a job? Would it change anything? Certainly not between them. There *was* no them.

"Nate, I…"

His fingers gripped the railing tighter and she closed her eyes briefly, taking a fortifying breath.

"I had a lot of time to think today and I was wondering what happened that made you need a leave of absence."

She blurted it out in one rapid sentence before she could think of taking it back.

"Well. That's blunt."

His eyes cooled as he pressed his lips together. He didn't want to talk about it. Either that or he was hiding something. Whatever the reason, she found she suddenly wanted to hear the answer very much.

"Perhaps my reasons are private." He turned to go back up the stairs but she persisted.

"But the Service is paying all your expenses, and the first time you go into town I find you talking to local authorities."

Nate stared at her. She was way too close to hitting on the truth. Yesterday he'd thought maybe she'd ask questions after seeing him with Grant, but he realized now she'd merely been wrapped up with Jen. Now that she'd had time to think, not everything added up nice and neat. The way she was looking at him now, it was as though she knew. But on the off-chance she didn't, he kept his expression carefully neutral.

He took his hand off of the banister and stepped off the landing, putting less distance between them. He remembered how she'd felt against him last night. Had thought about it a lot today when the job got boring. There was a chance, a slim one, that he could divert her now.

"You want to know why I had to take time off, is that it?" He made sure he worded it carefully—the reason for his leave, not the reason for being at Mountain Haven. He didn't want to have to out-and-out lie again. He'd rather angle the truth.

Even he knew it was a flimsy distinction.

"I...I do." She folded her hands in front of her. "I know I'm prying. And I told myself I wasn't going to ask. But I'm asking anyway."

"Funny. I asked you about *your* life last night and you closed up tighter than a clam." He'd been tempted to tell her the truth earlier this morning, seeing her warm from her bed, remembering how she'd felt in his arms last night. Thankfully he'd been smart enough not to. Because he was beginning to get the picture that she didn't like cops. First the way she acted around Grant yesterday and the cold way she was looking at him now. He let his gaze drop to her lips. "At least at first."

She blushed at the innuendo but persisted. "I know. But you're a guest in *my* house."

"And when I arrived, you assured me that privacy for your guests was of the utmost importance."

Perhaps if he pushed the topic off track enough she'd take the bait and move on.

"Perhaps concern for my own safety trumps that."

Dear God, what *had* run through her mind today? He wondered briefly if she'd gone through his things, but to ask would only confirm her suspicions and somehow he knew she wouldn't have done that. No, she'd be honest and ask like she was doing right now. And he had no idea what to give her for an answer.

"Where *did* you go today, Nate?"

She wasn't going to let it go. And he knew the only way to appease her was to give her the one story he was allowed to give. Even if he absolutely hated retelling it.

"All right. Let me get changed into dry clothes and I promise I'll tell you."

He jogged up the stairs, avoiding her probing gaze. He had to get out of his gear first. The last thing he needed was for Maggie to discover there was more than skin beneath his street clothes.

When he came back down, she was emptying dishes out of the dishwasher.

"Your things," he said quietly, holding out the thermos and bag.

"Thank you."

She put them down and simply waited, her eyes pinning him to the spot.

"Is this about yesterday, Maggie? Because if it is, we can keep this business only. I admitted I crossed a line. We can stop this right here."

Her cheeks flushed slightly. "It's that bad, then. Bad

enough you'd try changing the subject a hundred times before talking about it." She turned back to her dirty dishes.

She had him to rights there. There was no pleasure rehashing the past. He'd failed, and it ate at him. Almost as much as being forced to go on leave. He didn't need vacation. He needed to focus.

If he didn't feel the strong need to protect her so much, he'd come out with the truth and be done with it. He hated lies.

"It was a month ago." The words sounded strangled to his ears so he cleared his throat and started again. "It was a month ago and a case of bad intel. We were on assignment. My team. To bring in a sex offender. We knew he had firearms on the premises…that much was correct. So we were…armed accordingly."

He paused and swallowed. How much should he tell her? Enough to appease her, he supposed. And not so much as to give away his reason for being there. Maggie closed the dishwasher door and gave him her full attention. He didn't know what to do with his hands, so he hooked his thumbs in the belt loops of his jeans.

"The plan was to go in after him. When we gather information, it's pretty complete, so we can make the best tactical plan possible. It was all organized, everyone had their job. Only somehow he must have known we were coming. I don't know whether he was tipped or saw us or what, but he met us at the door."

He looked at her briefly. She couldn't know how hard this was for him, to admit his worst moment. As he faced her, the images came back. The ones that had forced his break from work to begin with. Sounds of gunfire, everything moving in slow motion when in reality it all went down in a matter of seconds. The prolonged moment when he saw the results, the picture branded on his memory.

"He fired. We fired back. You have to understand. All our

intel said that he was home alone, we had no reason not to trust it. But he wasn't. There was a woman. His daughter. She took a round and was killed."

It all came out like an official report. He looked away. "So now you know."

"Did you shoot her?"

He licked his lips. "Me personally? No."

"Then why do you carry the burden?"

Wasn't it enough that she had the truth? Why did she have to keep asking questions? It didn't matter who had pulled the trigger. It had been a fatal error.

"It was my team, Maggie. I was in charge."

"It was a mistake, a tragic mistake."

His hands pulled away from the loops and his fingers tightened. "You don't get it. I can't make mistakes. Would you say the same thing if it had been Jen in her shoes? If it had been your daughter who'd been killed?"

Nate turned and escaped out the door on to the veranda, into the blessed coolness of winter air. Telling Maggie had only made him angry again. He should have foreseen. There simply wasn't room for that kind of error in his job. Worrying about killing someone, the wrong person, or losing a member of the team far outweighed the feeling of personal danger.

His boss had made the leave nonnegotiable, even though all Nate wanted to do was get back in the field. He needed work, not time off to think of all the things he'd done wrong.

Then, the leave had become part of his cover and he resented it. It was over and done with. He'd learned from his mistake. Now he wanted to move on. He sure as hell didn't like—or want—the look of sympathy he'd seen on Maggie's face.

Maggie came out behind him, pulling a shawl over her shoulders. She put a hand on his arm and he pulled away.

"Nate, I'm sorry. I shouldn't have pried."

"Now you know and can stop asking."

She took a step backward at his harsh tone and he hated himself more for hurting her, too. This was exactly why he wished he could just tell her why he was here and forget all the secrecy.

He didn't like lying to Maggie. He could argue with himself and say he hadn't lied, that he'd stretched the truth, but it was the same thing. And the last thing he needed was her pity. But he couldn't tell her his assignment and protect her, too. He knew which was more important.

"Thank you for telling me." Her voice was quietly apologetic. At least his answers seemed to have satisfied her. As she turned and went back inside, he shook off the guilt at smudging the lines of truth. She'd accepted his story completely, and he'd done his job. As much as he hated it, the truth of his "leave" had satisfied her.

He swallowed, not knowing how to patch things up, knowing they should or else the next several days were going to be torture. He followed her as far as the doorway.

"You've got to understand something, Maggie. This is what I do. I'm a marshal and I do my job and if there are consequences to that, I deal with them."

She turned and faced him for a moment, and the warmth from before vanished. "That's very clear," she murmured. And she walked away from him.

His hand smacked the pillar of the porch in frustration. He hated dishonesty. With a passion. Yet this wasn't about being honest. It was about protection. Protection for her, for himself, for the whole community if it came to that. It was a big picture thing. Shifting the truth shouldn't be a big deal. Maggie was temporary in his life. There wasn't room for feelings.

But as he remembered how her lips had clung to his last night, he felt guilt crawl through him anyway.

Guilt because she was, in a sense, part of the job and all he wanted to do was pull her into his arms again.

Right now the best thing to do was keep his distance.

Maggie hefted the grocery bags in her arms, balancing them carefully so she could still use her keys to get in the house. It was midafternoon; she'd still have time to make the steak and Guinness pie she had planned for dinner. Mealtimes were the only times she saw Nate now. He ate in the morning, took a bagged lunch and spent the whole day outside. The weather was warming, hovering just below zero, and soon the snow would melt enough that he wouldn't be able to use snowshoes or cross-country skis anymore. He came back tired, ate his dinner and spent evenings in his room. The few times she'd spoken to him after 7:00 p.m., he'd either been reading or sitting at his laptop.

She'd been wrong to push. She knew it now, had known it as soon as she'd touched his arm and he'd pulled away.

It was good that he was keeping his distance. Because the more she saw him, the more confused she became.

How could the one thing she disliked about him also be the one thing that seemed to attract her? She shook her head even though no one was there to see her. The last thing she wanted was to be involved with someone in law enforcement. Then why did she find it so unbearably sexy? It was just as well their flirting had stopped.

Her key turned easily in the lock; the door was open. She frowned. She was sure she'd locked the dead bolt when she left.

She put the bags down on the porch and eased inside. The first thing she noticed were Nate's big boots on the mat by the door. She exhaled, relieved. It was only Nate, then.

He appeared around the corner and she tried a smile, hoping eventually he'd thaw out and treat her to one of his own and they could reach some level of comfort. "You're back early," she said easily. "So…how did you get in? I suppose doing what you do, you know all the tricks, right? What was it? Credit card? File and pick?"

He held up a hand. "Spare key. You really shouldn't leave it in so obvious a place."

There was something off. She sensed it. He didn't smile, but there wasn't a tone of chastisement in his voice, either. It wasn't about where she'd put her key. It was something else.

She shut the door, forgetting the groceries sitting outside. "What is it?"

He came forward and her heart started beating faster, a thread of apprehension skimming over her limbs. Whatever it was didn't look good; his face was tight and drawn.

"Jen called."

It seemed as though her heart tripped over itself as her breath caught and held, strangling her.

"There was a stabbing on campus."

The life went out of Maggie's limbs. She felt the floor coming up to meet her when Nate's arms caught her full weight.

"God, Maggie!"

Her head spun, dizzy. Jen. Jen. Jen.

"Maggie. Snap out of it."

His voice came from far away, swimming in the back of her brain.

"Maggie!"

He gave her a shake and she met his gaze, not quite seeing. "Maggie! She's fine. She's fine."

Maggie nodded dumbly.

"Look at me."

He was on his knees, holding her on his thighs, bracing her with an arm. His free hand cupped her chin, forcing her to look upward. His eyes, darkened with worry, anchored her. She clung to them as she tried hard to make sense of his words.

"Maggie. Clear your mind," he ordered. Her gaze dropped

to his lips. "Think. If she weren't okay, she couldn't have called."

It got through. She nodded, letting out her breath and willing some of the panic to release its grip.

Jen was okay.

"I'm sorry. It was a stupid reaction," she stammered.

"I understand. I didn't mean to scare you." He held her with firm hands, taking her weight.

She became aware of the hardness of his legs beneath her, the tight grip of his hands on her arms. She should pull away but she still felt so shaky she didn't trust herself to get up. It felt too right, letting him carry the weight for a while. So long since she'd allowed herself to lean on anyone.

He pulled her close, tucking her head beneath his chin and stroking her back soothingly. "I never thought of how you'd react. I should have, knowing your history. I should have said she was fine first. God, Maggie, you dropped like a rock."

"I feel stupid." His hand was warm and she let herself absorb it, drawing strength from it.

"Don't."

And then she felt it. A smile that she could picture creasing his face, moving against her hair. She closed her eyes, relief sluicing through her, ridiculously happy that he wasn't angry with her anymore. "I thought you were mad at me." He'd hardly spoken to her since the night she'd pried into his past.

"Not at you. Maybe just…angry in general." He kissed her hair lightly and her eyes sprung open. He pushed her away slightly. "Are you all right now?"

She nodded. "I think so."

"I'd meant to tell you that she called because she didn't want you to see it on the news and worry. But you didn't give me a chance."

She pushed out of his arms and stood up, feeling at once

the loss of the security found in his arms. "I don't know why I did that."

He hopped up from his crouched position. The last thing she expected from him was gentleness, not after the way things had been strained for several days. His fingers touched her cheek, stroking softly.

"I think you know exactly why it happened. You said yourself, you've suffered a lot of loss. Do you want to talk about it?"

She looked up into his eyes. He'd passed an olive branch and it was up to her whether or not to accept it. But she didn't talk about her past. No one wanted to hear about it. "Let's face it, Nate. My story's a bit of a downer. It's no big deal."

Another smile tugged at the corner of his lips. "You know, that sounds vaguely familiar."

"Touché."

He let her go, but she felt more connected to him than she ever had before, even more than being held in his arms or kissed. "I'll think about it. For right now, I'm going to bring the bags inside and call Jennifer."

"She's a good kid, Maggie. She knows how much you care and worry. If she didn't, she wouldn't have thought to call you."

Tears stung her eyes. How he seemed to know what she needed to hear was uncanny. "Thanks, Nate. That means a lot."

"Anytime."

She turned her back to him so he couldn't see the naked yearning on her face. Jennifer's welfare was such a hot button for her. The best thing she could do now was leave before she bawled all over him, so she started toward the stairs. He had no idea how tempted she was to take him up on his offer.

CHAPTER SEVEN

"MAGGIE. Wait."

"Just leave me alone, Nate. Please. I'm fine." She stopped at the bottom of the stairs, blinking back tears. She wasn't. She was embarrassed, vulnerable, feeling like a fool. Nate kept seeing her falling apart and he kept picking up the pieces. It was becoming a disturbing trend, and one she needed to put to an end. He was, by trade, a protector. He wasn't *her* protector.

She hadn't realized he'd come up behind her until his hand, wide and warm, fell on her shoulder, kneading gently. "I'm the one that saw your face. The one that caught you as you collapsed. You're not okay. You might as well tell me and get it out."

She tried to exhale but the air came out in shaky jolts, the very sound tearing her apart a little more with each breath. She was so tired. Tired of being afraid, tired of pretending. All it did was exhaust her. He put his other hand on her right shoulder, both hands now massaging gently.

The caring touch ripped away any shred of control she had left, and she dropped her head, two tears splashing over her lashes and down her cheeks. She tried to sniff them away, but failed miserably.

"Please don't be kind. I can't bear it."

"Why?"

The question was what she needed, something to shift the

focus from his hands on her shoulders. She turned to face him, straightening her shoulders. "You want reasons? Let's start with the fact that you're here for a few weeks and then gone again. You're just passing through, Nate, and we both know it. And then…well there's the whole cop thing. You're a marshal first and foremost, as you so eloquently pointed out the other day. Not to mention you're…" She paused, her cheeks flushed as she blurted out, "You're nearly a decade younger than I am!"

The words echoed in the hall. She lowered her voice. "And that's the last thing I need. Or want."

"Did I imply that this was something more?"

She huffed. "Imply? Constantly! Starting with the first night when you kissed my finger!"

She gaped when a smile curled his lips and he leaned against the banister.

"Ah, yes. When you grew so flustered you dropped your cup. And you should know I couldn't care less about your age. It's just a damned number." He slid a few inches closer and she instinctively backed up.

"Don't flirt with me, Nate. We're both past that."

His smile faded. "I only wanted to help you and you're making this my fault. Perhaps you can explain that."

How on earth could she explain that being with him made her feel more vulnerable than she could ever remember being? His profession threatened her. And her attraction for him was equally as frightening. Because she was undeniably attracted to all those things that scared the daylights out of her.

And those fears blended with the hurts of the past and the result was a woman who was incapable of making sense of it all and threatened to be overwhelmed. Above all, the urge to let him help was so strong.

"I can't do this. I can't cry all over a guest. And that's

what you are, though I seem to keep forgetting it. Please… just let me be."

But he ignored her plea. He captured her hand and pulled. "I think we both know that I'm not just a guest. Not anymore." He tugged again, pulling her into the strong circle of his arms.

Oh, the warmth of him, the smell…her own laundry soap blended with his aftershave and that little bit of something that was just him. She couldn't fight him any longer. Emotions that had been building ever since Jennifer's arrest last year snapped and let go. Defeated, Maggie turned her head against his chest and let the tears come. Nate's shoulders relaxed and he tucked her against him, holding her while she finally let everything spill out.

Maggie knew it was wrong, but it felt right. Why now, after all this time, did she finally feel connected to someone? There were so many reasons why he was wrong for her. He was a man who lived for his work, and thought nothing of putting himself in danger. He had his life ahead of him. They didn't even live in the same country.

And in a very short time, he'd be gone. She was shocked to find, in the circle of his arms, that she would miss him when he was gone.

But she had right now, and she burrowed deeper into his chest, letting the clean scent of him surround her. Letting his body form a cocoon as the slightest bit of healing trickled into her body.

The tears abated and she became aware of his hand running up and down her back, slowly, firm and sure. She needed him on so many levels. Desire filled the raw, aching hole and she was tempted to channel everything into a physical manifestation. But that would be wrong.

His lips touched her ear and she turned toward them. He spoke instead.

"Trust me, Maggie," he whispered, and she shivered. "You need to talk to someone. And I'm here."

She wanted to trust him. It was part of the problem.

Maggie made herself pull away and look up into his face. *He's beautiful,* she thought, stunned. Not just his body, not just the color of his eyes, the strong line of his lips or the cleft in his chin. But beautiful on the inside. Strong, yes, and stubborn. But principled and caring and compassionate. She wanted to share everything with him. Needed to. She'd pushed it down, pretended that the past didn't exist to everyone but herself. She couldn't do it anymore.

"What do you want to know?"

His lips curved ever so slightly. "Whatever you want to tell me. I want to know how Maggie Taylor ended up here. I want…"

He stopped and swallowed. Maggie's heart held a moment, waiting for what he'd say next. When he answered, it was as if he were touching her even though they were separated by inches.

"I want to know everything about you."

Maggie chafed her arms, already missing the warmth of his body. She was so tired. Tired of being governed by fear. She needed this.

"Then I'll tell you. Let's get a drink and start a fire. You might want to settle in for the duration."

He smiled. "One fire coming up."

Maggie got glasses and a bottle of rye whiskey from the cupboard. When she went into the living room, flames were licking warmly in the gas fireplace and Nate was sitting on the sofa, his elbows braced on his knees, staring into the orange blaze.

"Here. Hold these."

He held the glasses while she poured a small amount in the bottom of each one, then put the bottle down on the coffee table. She took a seat next to him, sipping the liquor. It warmed a path to her stomach and she closed her eyes and sighed.

"Why don't you start at the beginning, Maggie. I know you lost your parents and your husband, but that really only scratches the surface." Nate's voice touched her and she opened her eyes. He held her gaze so she couldn't back away. "There's clearly more. Like why it still hurts so much. How it's shaped you into who you are, how you got to be owner of a bed and breakfast in the middle of nowhere, looking after everyone else instead of yourself."

Maggie tucked her left foot under her leg, leaning back against the cushions. She had told herself that telling him, no matter how close they seemed to get, would be crossing a line. But they'd already crossed several lines with the kiss and with her sobbing all over him. Perhaps if he knew…really knew… who she was, it would actually have the opposite effect. Part of her wished it would be so. That perhaps the details would be sufficient to keep him at arm's length. What man wanted a woman still grieving for her loss and paralyzed by fear? It would be easier for her to resist him if he resisted her first.

And the other part of her yearned for him to listen, to understand, to accept.

"The beginning? Things were pretty normal for me growing up, until my parents died when I was a teenager and I had to look after myself." She took another fortifying sip of the rye. It sounded cut-and-dried now, but her whole world had been ripped apart, changing everything. She was no longer someone's daughter. She'd become Maggie, the orphan, trying to find her way.

"How did they die?"

"In a car accident."

His free hand dropped to her knee, stayed there. "I'm sorry. That must have been horrible for you."

"Thank you."

"Didn't you have anywhere to go?"

She smiled sadly. "Not really. And seeing I was the age of

majority, I looked after myself. Got a job. Tried to make some sense of things."

"And then?"

She looked down at the sight of his hand on her leg, wished fleetingly it didn't feel quite so good. She didn't feel like she was burdening him with prolonged grief. Nate didn't know her family, her friends. Knowing she could speak freely without the guilt she often felt when talking to others was a relief, and the words came easier with every breath.

She lifted her head and their eyes met. There was no pity on his face. She wouldn't have been able to take that. But there was compassion and patience and she was grateful for it. The tension abated in her neck.

"Then I met Mike. He is my second cousin, the son of a cousin who had a baby far too young and made really bad choices, which resulted in Mike being put in foster care." She looked away from his hand and up into his eyes. "When I met him, I was twenty-two and he was eleven, still being bounced from home to home. And I suppose I thought, here is someone who is my flesh and blood, someone who knows what lonely means. It was the only hint of family I had and I needed to cling to it. Hadn't realized it until he was standing there in front of me."

"You needed him as much as he needed you."

Maggie nodded. She had. Mike had given her purpose. She doubted he knew to this day how much.

"I was working steadily, had an apartment in Sundre. I petitioned the court for guardianship and I got it. I don't know who was more surprised, me or Mike."

"You became each other's family."

"Yes, I suppose we did. Mike was a good kid, he was just scared. Didn't trust people much and I couldn't blame him. I did the best I could, but heck, I was young, too, and still raw from all I'd been through. I met Tom. Mike was a teenager when we got married and had Jen. I suppose he felt in the way after that, although he never said anything about it. Mike never talked about things like that much." She smiled at Nate. "Sounds like someone else I know. Anyway, by the time he graduated, he was rodeoing in season and working odd jobs in the off-times."

Her smile turned wistful. "I didn't think he'd ever find anyone to trust his heart to, but he did."

"Like you did with Tom?"

Maggie suddenly realized that she'd been talking, really talking, more than she'd planned. Maybe it was the fire, or the liquor, or the fact that Nate was safe and comfortable. Regardless, this afternoon they had turned a corner. Somewhere in the mess of confusion she'd made the decision to stop fighting and it shocked her to realize how quickly she'd dropped her guard.

But now Nate had turned the subject to Tom and it was different than talking about Mike. She wasn't sure she could go on. Certainly not as easily as she'd talked about her cousin. Tom had done for her what Grace had done for Mike. Given her a place to put her heart for safekeeping. Or so she'd thought.

Losing him had been the most devastating thing she'd ever been through, and it had taken every ounce of her strength to put her life back together. Even now, pieces were missing and it was incredibly painful. A memory flashed through her mind, not of Tom, but of Nate kissing her in the kitchen. The sheer beauty of it had scared her to death. It couldn't happen again. She couldn't feel like that again. The last time she'd had that depth of feeling, she'd ended up being crushed beneath it. It was an odd position to be in, trusting Nate yet needing to push him away.

Surely talking about one's dead husband would make any man put on the brakes.

"Yes. I did trust my heart to Tom."

"And then he died and you were left with Jen."

Her throat closed up a bit and she nodded.

"Come here."

Nate took her glass away and deposited it on the table with his own. Shifting, he leaned back against the arm of the sofa, running one leg along the inside edge. She knew she should keep her distance, but he felt too good. Unresisting, she let him pull her back until she was cradled in the lee of his legs, his arms around her loosely, his fingers lightly circling her wrists.

"Oh, Nate." She sighed, staring into the dancing flames. Why did he have to be so perfect? Why was it that after all this time, Nate Griffith could make her feel things she hadn't felt in years? Including the need to spill about her past?

She paused for so long he squeezed her wrist. "You're thinking too much. Forget the reasons why and just let it out, Maggie. It's been in there a long time, hasn't it."

She nodded.

He stroked her wrist bone with his thumb. "Can you tell me about him?"

Her throat thickened and she swallowed. "I don't know," she whispered, her voice thin in the rich air.

"I'd like to hear about it, if you want to tell me." He touched his forehead to her hair.

"You have to understand that I really don't talk about Tom. To anyone. Talking about him now…doesn't come easily."

Nate waited.

Maggie closed her eyes and absorbed the warmth and strength of his body into her soul. Why not tell him and be free of it? He'd be going back to his job in a few weeks and they'd never meet again. He'd forget all about her and her dead husband, after all. What would be the benefit of a quick fling? Because after the way he'd kissed her, she knew that was a distinct possibility. He'd leave her behind and she'd be left hurt, all over again. Because she didn't do casual, or temporary. And she didn't do serious relationships, either.

He was alive, breathing, real. And if she weren't careful, she'd set herself up for hurt. It would be foolish to do that when it could easily be avoided. Maybe telling them would bring them closer in one way, but it should certainly cool the jets on any attraction between them.

"I was waitressing and Tom was working the patch." At Nate's pause, she amended, "The oil patch. He was doing security at a refinery north of town and used to come in for breakfast and pie in the mornings. The first time we met, I teased him about eating pie at 6:00 a.m."

An image flirted with her, Tom, young and energetic, blond and teasing dimples. She realized she'd been sitting for a few moments with a smile of remembrance on her lips. "Sorry."

"Don't be. Go on."

"I was trying to raise Mike, and working a couple of jobs to make ends meet. Tom was a breath of fresh air. For our first date, he packed a picnic and waited on me, since, he said, I was always waiting on him. I was twenty-three."

Color crept into her cheeks. "I hadn't planned on life changing so quickly, but I fell hard and fast. I was starved for love and he was everything I could have imagined wanting. We got married three months later. Seven months after that Jen was born."

"And you moved here?"

She nodded. She remembered quite clearly the day he'd brought her here, late in the fall with Jen in a blanket in her arms. She'd been so angry with him when she'd found out he'd already bought it without consulting her. It was stupid, she realized later. Fighting over something so silly, when the truth was she'd adored the place as soon as she'd crossed the threshold. Drafty corners and all.

"Yes, we came here. He was making good money in the patch, and we could have the house and I could stay home and be with Jen. Maybe even have a few more."

Nate lifted his right hand from her arm, stroking her hair. "You wanted more children."

"I did then. He…" She stopped, unsure of how to go on. She did that a lot. She was unused to saying personal things aloud, but it seemed like it was *all* she'd been doing since Nate arrived. "He fixed something in me that had been broken when I lost my family."

"Only then he died, too."

"Yeah. And I think that day I realized that it didn't matter what I did, the people I loved were going to leave me. I only had Jen left."

"And that's why you worry about her so much. You're waiting for something to happen to her, too."

He understood.

Maggie felt all the panic and tension drain out of her body in one long, flowing river. The fact that it made sense to someone other than herself was liberating. "Yes."

Nate closed his eyes and cupped her head in his hand. All the resistance he'd felt vibrating through her body had melted away and she lay against his chest. Trusting, empty.

She'd been hurt so much. He really hadn't had any idea of how deep her hurt had gone. Maybe he should have, after today. The truth was he had wanted to know, to feel close to her. He cared about her, and he was shocked to realize it had only taken a few short days for his feelings to be involved.

But she'd given in easily, told him more than he'd ever expected and he wasn't sure what to do with it.

The one thing he knew for sure, now more than ever, was that he couldn't be responsible for hurting her again. Maggie Taylor was too precious to be trifled with. He'd never met a woman with more pain, yet so strong. He couldn't imagine anyone picking up the pieces of their life in the way she had, with a baby and a foster child and a need to make a living. He knew for damned sure he couldn't be the one to turn that upside down.

Which made it insanely difficult, because he wanted her more than ever.

She'd trusted him today and he'd thought it was what he wanted. Now he knew that was a mistake. If she were to find out why he was really here, all that trust would be broken. No, it would have to be done clean. And when he left, it would be with a smile and warm memories of what they'd shared. How they'd helped each other. He felt the sting of irony that the truth would only tarnish the fleeting relationship they'd built.

It was how it had to be.

Long moments passed and he simply held her in his arms, felt her breathing, felt their connection growing and expanding. Never before had he felt so comfortable with a woman.

He looked around the room over the top of her head. Comfortable, welcoming, cozy. Like her. Yet…a blazing fire, a sparkling glass bottle of dark liquid, splashes of color…vibrant. Also like her. A woman who made her living caring for others but one who knew how to stand on her own two feet. A survivor.

A woman he wanted. Completely.

But he couldn't have her. Not after all that had happened today. It would be completely unfair to her, in every way. He felt guilty enough about misleading her about his work. He knew for damn sure he wouldn't take advantage of her when she was stripped bare. Because he knew she hadn't told him every detail. He wondered how Tom had died. She hadn't told him about the troubles she'd had since, or Jen's brush with the law last year. And he wondered if she'd ever trust him enough to let him in completely.

So he held her in his arms as the afternoon wore on, wondering how the hell he was going to get through the next week.

CHAPTER EIGHT

COOKING. He watched her from the doorway, his arms folded over his chest as he leaned against the woodwork. He realized now it was what she did when she was particularly bothered or upset. After the events of the afternoon, he guessed they'd have a fine meal tonight.

She turned a beef mixture into a casserole as her brows pulled together in a frown. She lifted a fragile square of pastry and laid it over the top of the beef, pricking it with a fork. But he heard the deep sigh that seemed to come from her very toes.

"Penny for your thoughts."

She spun, her hand flying to her chest in surprise. He smiled. At least he could still surprise her.

"Only a penny?" She tried to joke, but her attempt at a jaunty grin wobbled. It appeared she hadn't bounced back as well as she was trying to portray.

"Maggie, are you sure you're okay?" He dropped his arms and started into the room.

She took a deep breath and squared her shoulders. "Of course I am."

She slid the dish into the oven. Turned and faced him, pasting on a smile that he understood was clearly for his benefit. She wiped her hands on her apron.

"It's chinooking. Which means tomorrow you'll be slogging it out in the muck."

He pushed away the urge to simply cross the floor and kiss her. He'd been thinking of it ever since she'd lain in his arms. But she was too raw, he could see that. "Chinooking?"

Maggie took a dishcloth and began wiping down the counter. "It's a wind that comes over the mountains, and it'll melt all the snow that's left. Some days it seems to blow and blow, but when it's done, it'll feel like spring around here."

Great. Warmer weather meant walking, and walking in muck. He'd actually hoped the cool weather would prevail a little longer. He frowned. Wished Maggie had an ATV he could borrow. Only then she'd ask why, and where he was going…dammit. Things were growing more complicated by the second.

"You don't have a headache, do you?" She took a few steps forward. "A lot of people get them, especially if they're not used to the pressure change. If your head is bothering you, I have painkillers in the cabinet."

She was the fragile one here and she was worried about his headache? The only headache he had wasn't from the pressure change, but from finding ways to keep his reasons for being here private without telling bald-faced lies. How to remain focused on his job without thinking about her every waking minute.

He was starting to fall for her, he realized. His head really did start to ache.

"My head is fine."

"Oh."

The short, quiet word told him he'd been too harsh and he tried to soften his expression. He hadn't meant to snap at her. "But thanks for asking." He pushed his thoughts away and tried a smile. "How long until dinner?"

"About an hour."

Her reply was cool and he guessed she wasn't quite ready

to forgive him for his snappishness. "I guess I'll go read or something, then."

"Nate?"

He paused. Lord, but she was beautiful. She'd wiped away any trace of her earlier tears and her eyes shone the most perfect shade of blue, like his grandmother's china bowl on his mom's cabinet, the one he was never allowed to touch as a boy. Blue Willow, he remembered now. Timeless and beautiful, like Maggie. Her lips were slightly puffed and he wanted to kiss them until they both ran out of breath. His chest tightened, strangling. He wanted to carry her upstairs, undress her, run his fingers over her creamy skin. Make love to her on the homemade quilt until the shadows grew long and disappeared. He wanted to tell her the truth and be free of it. He couldn't do any of those things.

She was watching him as though she could read his mind and he shuddered.

"What, Maggie?" It came out almost a whisper and the line of tension crackled between them.

She broke eye contact first, and half turned, breaking the spell. "Let's go for a walk while dinner's cooking. I'll show you what a Chinook arch looks like."

Getting outside was probably a really, really good idea. Otherwise he'd do something foolish that he couldn't take back. Like kiss her again. Like tell her how he was feeling. Ridiculous.

They pulled on boots and jackets, leaving their hats behind and putting their hands in their pockets.

Once outside, Maggie led him down the driveway to the road. It was paved, but barely. Narrow with no lines printed on it. Just a country road leading to the only place she'd called home in almost twenty years. He was a city boy, born and bred. The wide-open space, the simplicity of it, was a revelation. He breathed deeply, the sharp wind buffeting his chest. Felt a little of the tension slip away.

"See that?" She lifted her finger and pointed to the white sweep of clouds in the west. "That's a Chinook arch. Like a horizontal rainbow of cloud front. I've seen it warm over ten degrees Celsius in less than an hour. I've seen snow melt so quickly that you'd swear by the sound of the drips that it was raining."

"You love it here." He shook off the feeling of guilt from prying again, torn between caring for her and wanting to see the whole picture. It was like she was trying to forget all about their earlier conversation, and pretend it had never happened.

She kept walking, and he listened as her footsteps squeaked on the melting snow of the shoulder of the road.

"I've never been anywhere else. This is home."

"It's very different from where I'm from."

"Florida?"

He laughed. He'd only been in Florida for the last few years, although he loved it there and considered it his home base. "I was brought up in Philadelphia. Where my parents are. But yes, Florida, too. Have you ever been?"

She shook her head. "I've been to Vancouver. Once."

They walked on, Maggie's hair blown back by the force of the westerly wind. "I always had Jen, and she had school. And during breaks, I always had guests. I've never had the chance to travel."

His chin flattened. "Until a few weeks ago, and you got saddled with me instead. I'm sorry about that."

He loved how she smiled back. It was free of agenda, unfettered by awkwardness and with a hint of growing trust at the corners. Had he inspired that?

"I'm starting to not regret that quite as much as I did at first." She tried tucking her hair behind her ears. "You've been everywhere, I suppose," she commented.

"I've been around. The Middle East, Europe with the marines. All over North America with the Marshal Service. But…"

Maggie turned her head to look up at him, a strand of hair

whipping around her face and catching in her mouth. She plucked it out with a finger. He reached out tucked it back, his finger lingering by her earlobe.

"But…"

He dropped his hand. He doubted she could really comprehend the places he'd been or the things he'd seen. "But there's no place like home. Other than my mom's place, here with you, at Mountain Haven, is as close as it gets."

"What about your place in Florida?" The moment suspended as the wind howled around them.

What about it? It was empty and functional and a place for him to sleep and eat. Had been for several months.

"My house there doesn't really feel like a home."

He could tell by the look in her eyes she wanted to ask more but didn't. Instead she placed a hand on his forearm, unaware of how the simple gesture touched him.

"Then I'm glad you're happy here."

That was it. He was surprised. Any woman he knew would have asked long ago if there was a wife or girlfriend in the wings. But not Maggie. He understood now that she'd learned long ago to simply accept. He almost wanted her to ask, just so he could tell her there was no one. No one with a claim on his heart.

Maggie turned to keep walking and he clasped her hand in his. She smiled softly, squeezing his fingers.

"Thank you, Nate, again. For being there today. It helped. More than you know."

Their hands swung gently between them as they ambled along rough pavement. It hit him as being a bit surreal, walking down a country road, holding hands with a beautiful woman. "Something's happening between us, Maggie, we both know it."

"I…I'm not prepared for that."

"I know."

His low words were almost lost in the power of the

Chinook, but she heard them. He looked over at her, saw her swallow, look down at her feet as their steps slowed.

"Maggie, don't run, okay? We've both been dancing around it until neither of us knows how to act or what to say. So I'm just going to get it out of the way. I'm attracted to you. More than I thought possible."

Her mouth opened and shut a few times before she could speak. "I know. And I've started to trust you, Nate, and it scares me to death. I don't have it in me to start anything. There are so many reasons not to."

His lip curled at the thought of trust. The one bugbear in all of this was that he knew she trusted him more with each passing day. And he knew she shouldn't. Knew that she'd be more hurt if she knew he'd been keeping secrets all this time. He wondered again whether it would be better to just tell her.

Then he remembered the look in her eyes today when she'd thought Jen was hurt, when she'd told him about all the loss she'd suffered. He couldn't tell her and walk out the door each day that was left, knowing how she'd worry. She didn't need that. She had enough to worry about. Not only that, if he told her, he'd lose any hope of finding out what it was he already suspected. That Maggie knew a hell of a lot more than she was saying.

He felt her eyes on him and he turned his head, his face softening slightly. "Sorry. I didn't mean to disappear." He took her other hand in his, stopping their progress in the middle of the road, running his fingers over her soft knuckles.

He leaned forward, just a little, and touched his lips to her forehead, catching a strand of her hair in his mouth as the wind whipped it around. He pulled it out with a finger.

Their time together was growing short. He wouldn't have to worry about seeing her every day, knowing he was keeping secrets from her. Another week was all that was left in his stay and they would probably never see each other again.

It was crazy how empty the thought of that made him feel.

Her hair whipped around and he reached out, threading his fingers through the long strands, pushing them back so her pale face was framed by the darker skin of his hands. It was wrong to feel this way and he knew it. But in the end the pull to her was too strong to fight.

"I'm sorry, Maggie. I have to."

He pulled gently with his hands, drawing her closer and up, dipping his head until he touched her lips with his.

She was sweet, so very sweet, and a little salty from her earlier tears. His eyes slammed shut and he focused on the feel of her, real and alive and responsive. Despite her earlier protests, despite all the reasons why she couldn't, her mouth opened beneath his and he squared his feet, planting his weight, taking it as deep and as dark as she'd let him.

The wind howled around them, warm and wild, swirling up dust. He lowered one hand, pressing it to the small of her back, pulling her closer so that their bodies were meshed as closely as their outerwear would allow. Her arms reached up, circled his neck as she adjusted the angle of her head to better fit his and his blood sang. He gripped her hair, tugging to tilt her head back and he ripped his mouth from hers, sliding his tongue up her neck.

She whimpered, and he felt the vibration on his lips.

He froze. God, here he was doing the very thing he'd promised himself he wouldn't, not today. This was what going for a walk had been meant to avoid. Breathing heavily, he gently released her and backed away.

"You're stopping." Her cheeks flamed red but she met his eyes bravely.

"You're too vulnerable, Maggie. We both know it."

"I think I'm old enough to know what I want." She lifted her chin.

He couldn't stop the surge at her words. She wanted him.

That was clear. Her response had told him plainly she wanted him as much as he wanted her.

Maggie held his gaze, trying to seem stronger than he knew she felt. She wasn't the kind to take something to a physical level and be cavalier about it. He took a step backward. "But I'm not sure you'd see it the same way tomorrow, and I don't want to take advantage. And the last thing I want to do is hurt you in any way." He tried slow, steadying breaths. "Besides, we're in the middle of the road."

Maggie looked left and right while the only sound was the Chinook and dripping water from melting snow. Then she snorted, a tiny, ladylike bubble of noise.

"Oh goodness, we are, aren't we?"

"Yeah."

Things seemed back to normal for a few minutes. They turned back in the direction they'd come and the wind was at their backs, buffeting them along. Maggie tried tucking her hair behind her ears, but it wouldn't stay. It blew wildly around her head.

It was good they'd stopped when they had.

When they reached the lane up to the house, she stopped suddenly. He looked at her, then at the house. It seemed to be waiting for them to go in.

"So what do we do now?"

Nate knew what he wanted to do, but it would cause more problems than it would solve. He sighed.

"Damned if I know, Maggie. Damned if I know."

Maggie hummed as she folded the clothes in her basket, laying them in two piles on her bed; one for her, one for Nate. He'd offered to do his own laundry if she'd let him use her facilities, but she didn't mind doing it for him. When she'd offered, there'd been a slightly tense moment as she'd worried he'd think she was just after billing the service.

Truth be told, it was nice to have someone to do for. Washing his clothing was nothing at all. She'd merely made the comment that she could throw it in with her own and the awkward moment had passed.

She smoothed her hand over a pair of his jeans, rubbing out the creases from the dryer. Her fingers lingered over the denim, picturing how the fabric molded to his frame. Not in many, many years had she felt such a need for a man, such desire. Not only that, but she'd never expected that she'd find those things that made him a cop—the haircut, the penchant for neatness, the physicality—so alluring.

When he was gone on his ramblings during the day, she couldn't believe how wantonly she'd behaved during their walk. In the middle of the road, of all things. But the moment his arms went around her and he kissed her, she forgot everything beyond the feel and taste of him. For those few moments, she forgot the fear. When she was in his embrace, she forgot all the reasons why he was wrong for her. He made her feel young and alive and the novelty was intoxicating.

They'd walked back to the house and she'd wondered how on earth they were going to coexist in the same house for the next several days. Wanting him to kiss her again, knowing it was inadvisable. Wanting much more from him, yet afraid to take that giant step into being intimate with a man. She didn't take those things lightly.

But she needn't have worried at all. Nate had reverted to his pleasant, normal self. Full stop. No more long looks, intimate smiles, toe-curling kisses. None.

And she missed him.

The laundry finished, she put her own clothes away and stacked his, along with the guest towels, back in the basket to take upstairs to his room. Maybe he'd put on the brakes because she'd never given him a reason to move forward. And yes, he was only here for a short time. But he understood her.

That much she knew. She'd trusted him with her past and that was a subject she rarely talked about. And he'd made the first move each time they'd kissed, touched.

What if he was waiting for her to make a move now?

Maggie swallowed as saliva pooled in her mouth. After seventeen years of celibacy, she was afraid. Afraid of looking silly. Afraid of the intensity. Afraid of another man seeing her body. She wasn't twenty anymore. She'd had a child. She'd aged. And his body was youthful and perfect.

"Maggie?"

Nate called as he came in the door and she couldn't stop the flood of welcome that rushed through her. When had she started truly looking forward to his return every day?

"I'm in here."

She let out a slow breath. This was silly. He was only a man. This was only a crazy reaction to having him so close; to being alone together.

She hefted the laundry basket, settling it on her hip. It wasn't in her to make the next move. No matter how much she wanted to.

She turned the corner into the kitchen, the basket sliding off her hip to the floor as she saw his face.

"Have you got bandages, Maggie?"

His voice was calm, reasonable, but all Maggie saw was blood streaming from a gash that ran down his forehead to just below his eyebrow.

"Maggie. Bandages."

She sprang into action, the sight of the cut always before her eyes as she ran to the bathroom for the first-aid kit.

When she came back, he'd pulled out a kitchen chair and sat in it. Maggie grabbed an ivory hand towel from the spilled basket and immediately pressed it to the cut, staunching the blood as it seeped darkly through the cotton. "Hold this for a minute."

She opened the kit and saw her fingers trembling. He was fine, it was just a cut, she reassured herself. But seeing the blood, the open gash, had sent pins and needles through her extremities. What if he had a concussion, or needed stitches?

She looked up, gauze and scissors in her hand, and watched as Nate's face paled and he weaved slightly.

She dropped the items to the floor and knelt before him, pressing one hand to the towel and the other to the back of his head, pushing him forward.

"Put your head between your knees," she commanded, hoping to God he didn't pass out or get sick. Either one might mean concussion.

He obeyed, saying nothing.

"Take slow, deep breaths, Nate."

She moved to the side a bit, still holding the towel to the wound and rubbing a hand over his shoulders. The movement gave her time to find her own bearings, and she realized something shocking.

In the instant she'd seen his blood, known he was injured, her only thoughts had been for him. Not of Tom. Not of Jen. Not of fear born from years of loss and anxiety. But for *him*.

It was more than lust, more than feeding a hunger. It was Nate, the man, and he inspired feelings Maggie had thought long extinct. For her, it had suddenly become much deeper and meaningful. And complicated.

"I'm okay now."

His voice came through, deep and rough and she blinked back tears at the mere sound of it.

"Sit up slowly, that's it." She helped guide him up until he was upright in the chair once more. Once he was stable, she put his hand on the towel and moved quickly to grab a chair so she could sit facing him.

"I'm going to pull the towel away now," she murmured,

gently pulling the cotton from his head. She swallowed at the amount of blood staining the ivory. With light fingers, she held his forehead and examined the cut. "You should have stitches."

"I'll be fine, just bandage it up."

"Nate, it's huge. Even with stitches, you'll likely have a scar. You can guarantee it if I patch you up. Not to mention it'll take longer for it to heal."

"There's steritape in my bag. I'll get it."

"Tell me where it is and I'll get it for you."

"No. I mean, I'm feeling much better."

"Don't be stupid. You asked for my help, let me give it."

"The bleeding's nearly stopped. I'll get the tape and let you do it, all right?"

She sat back at his sharp tone. She wasn't sure why she'd been so worried, if he were going to be this stubborn. Men. Why was it that admitting they needed help was so difficult?

He got up from his chair and made his way to the stairs.

She took the towel and threw it in the trash; there was no saving it. What on earth had happened to him, and how long had he walked before getting to the house?

"Maggie."

Her head snapped up. Nate's voice was weak and thready. She rushed toward the stairs. Why hadn't he let her go after the supplies rather than playing the tough guy?

"Oh my stars, Nate."

He was halfway down the stairs, clinging to the banister and holding a small kit in his hands.

She went up half a dozen steps and slid beneath his right arm, bolstering his weight. "You big ninny. Trying to do this yourself. From now on, you're doing exactly what I tell you."

"Yes, ma'am."

Carefully they made their way to the bottom of the stairs and she helped him back to the chair. He sat heavily, closed his eyes while she took the kit from his hands.

"This isn't my forte, just so you know. You really should see a doctor."

"No doctors. It's just a scratch."

"Don't be stupid."

A muscle in his jaw ticked. "I just don't like doctors, okay? I've had worse wounds, trust me. I've been patched up by medics, by colleagues and even by a tribal leader in Africa."

"You are so stubborn." Maggie held the first strip of tape. "Take a breath. Now let it out. Slowly."

As he exhaled, she pushed the edges of the wound together and applied the tape.

His eyes opened, the blue-green of the sun through a bottle. They focused on her face. "Thank you for doing this."

She caught the tip of her tongue in her teeth as she applied the next strip.

"I want it noted that I thought you should see a professional."

His gaze never wavered, and her stomach tumbled, both from the first-aid and from his intense focus.

"You can charge for services rendered. I'll speak up for you."

Her lips twitched. "So you're not *that* badly injured, if you're cracking jokes."

"It's a scratch," he repeated. "I've got scars much worse."

Her hand halted, another strip of tape stuck to her index finger. She wondered where he had scars; what they looked like. Her body heated as she imagined touching him, kissing all the places where they marked his skin.

And just as quickly, she cooled. She couldn't forget that the very presence of the scars were a real reminder of the life he led. And the danger he represented.

"What happened, anyway?"

He cleared his throat. "I was walking the creek. Don't know exactly what happened, but I must have slipped in some mud. Hit my head on a rock, I guess. And got my bell rung pretty good."

Maggie reached for a swab, cleaned the bottom of the cut and reached for the gauze. It made sense, she supposed. The creek bank could be slick this time of year, and a stripe of dried mud ran up his leg.

"And you walked all the way back here with your head bleeding."

He nodded slightly, wincing. "Yeah. Used a mitten to control the bleeding—it's a write-off by the way—and hit for home."

She sat back, packing the kit again. "You're patched up, for what it's worth. I still think you're probably concussed."

"Then you'll have to keep an eye on me, won't you?"

He smiled his most charming smile, and suddenly the life went out of her legs.

She sat heavily. She hated the sight of blood, but her immediate concern for his health had overridden it. Now that he was attended to, the aversion came back heavy and strong. The smell of blood was the smell of death. She would have taken him to the hospital out of sheer worry, but she didn't like hospitals any more than he apparently did. Hospitals were always a reminder of what she'd lost.

"You need tea, Maggie. Now you're pale."

She nodded. "I'll make some. I think we could both use it. I've got to keep my eye on you for the next while."

She would have moved to get up but he stayed her with a hand on her knee. "I don't know how to thank you. You've always gone above and beyond, but today…that's different. I owe you, Maggie."

She rose, his hand sliding off her leg. "It's fine. It's the smell of the blood, that's all."

She forced herself to smile. He couldn't know, and she didn't want him to. For all he was aware, Tom had been killed on the job. And he had been. But it hadn't been an accident. No indeed. Tom had been shot. And by the time she'd reached the hospital he was in a coma. He'd never regained consciousness. All she had for parting memories were the sights and smells of his blood.

Too late she realized she was trembling. Nate lifted his hand and cupped her jaw with his fingers, steadying her. It was the most natural thing in the world to put her arms around him, try to gain strength from his.

He pulled her close and she linked her hands behind his back. That's when she felt it beneath her fingers, hard and cold. She pushed out of his arms.

"You're carrying a gun."

CHAPTER NINE

MAGGIE stepped back, away from him. She could still feel the cold lump of the steel, the shape of it, tucked into the waistband of his jeans.

He was in her house, carrying a weapon. He had to have brought it with him, she realized. He'd had it all along. Her blood ran cold at the thought. In those moments all of Maggie's old feelings reared up, making her next words strangled and raw.

"You're carrying a gun."

The words echoed through the room. For long seconds Nate simply stared at her, as if determining what would be the best thing to say. She drew in a shaky breath. Tom had carried a handgun during his duties. To her recollection, he'd never fired it.

Not until the night he'd had to protect himself. Not until the night he'd come face-to-face with another weapon and he'd fired back. The end result was that he'd lived long enough to make it to hospital and the other man hadn't. And because the trespasser—a so-called activist—had also died, it didn't matter that Tom had died defending himself. His name had been sullied by the press, bandied about in the news like some political trick. One side placing the blame on him, the other side blaming the other man. Maggie had been caught in the middle, trying to grieve and defend him while being left alone with an infant daughter and a teenage cousin.

The very thought of Nate carrying a gun and being so calm about it made her sick to her stomach. She'd trusted him. He'd told her about his leave of absence and she'd believed him. Now she realized it was all a lie. The day it had hit her—he was on assignment—she'd known. And she'd let him divert her from the truth. But a man on a leave of absence, on vacation, didn't carry a gun.

Maggie folded her hands, keeping them from fidgeting and twisting by sheer willpower. He'd more than misrepresented himself to her. He'd insinuated a place for himself at Mountain Haven. With her.

She swallowed against the bile in her throat. He'd known all along and yet he'd let things grow between them. The sting of betrayal was made worse by her acute embarrassment at her actions. She'd kissed him. Wanted him. She'd started to care for him, deeply. Had considered taking it further, knowing he was leaving. Thank goodness she hadn't articulated her feelings. She clenched her fingers, turning the tips white. But she refused to turn away. Gathering all her strength, she squared her chin.

"Get out."

Nate froze. "You want me to leave?" He picked his words carefully, keeping his voice neutral.

"Do you or do you not have a gun tucked into the back of your jeans?"

She already knew the answer even as he sighed. At his brief silence, she raised an eyebrow.

"Yes, Maggie. I'm carrying a weapon."

She folded her arms, putting even more distance between them. "Why would that be, Nate? Am *I* some kind of threat to you?"

"I'm a marshal, Maggie. I don't go anywhere without a weapon. Ever."

Instead of reassuring her, her lips thinned. She'd accepted him at face value and it had been a terrible mistake on her part. She'd believed everything he'd said, had wanted to help him. Had wanted to nurture him. Knowing she'd been duped stung her pride, her self-judgment. She asked the question simply to clarify what she already knew.

"You mean you've had a gun on you the whole time you were here?"

"Yes, Maggie."

She swallowed. She had to know all of it. Know how blind she'd been to what was going on around her. There was no turning back now. "When we went to Olds?"

"Yes." His eyes settled on hers steadily. She wanted him to look guilty, but he didn't. She wrinkled her brow. If she didn't know better, she'd almost think he looked relieved.

"When you went snowshoeing?"

"Yes."

"And walking each day?"

She wished he'd show some emotion, rather than standing tall, unflinching before her. His eyes were honest but unreadable, a look she realized he probably used in his job every day.

"Yes."

Maggie paused, her eyes widened. "The day we went walking in the Chinook?"

She waited for his answer, her heart in her throat. That day she'd been vulnerable, and that day she'd made the choice to trust him with much of herself. He'd held her as she'd cried in his arms, listened as she'd told him about Tom. She couldn't have been so wrong, could she?

"Yeah. That day, too." His eyes searched hers, like he was asking her to understand. But she didn't understand anything. He hadn't really told her anything. How could he have held her and kissed her and been kind all the while having a handgun tucked in his jeans?

She turned away and he bent a little, trying to explain.

"Maggie, listen, what I said is true. I don't go *anywhere* without a gun." He stepped forward, holding out a hand but she backed away. If he was asking her to say it was all right, to understand why he'd done it, he could forget it. She'd been honest with him. He obviously didn't think he needed to reciprocate.

"It's a part of who I am," he continued. "You shouldn't take it personally."

"Not take it personally?" Maggie raised her voice, and she laughed a little at the end, the sound sharp and dry with disbelief. How could he possibly think she wouldn't take it personally? He'd come into her home. He'd brought guns into her home. And he hadn't told her. What else hadn't he told her? Was his whole story a fabrication?

She pointed to the door. "I want you to leave, Nate. You can get in your truck and drive into Olds and find a room at a motel. I'm sure your superiors will pay for it."

"I can't do that."

His reply was strong and definite, like he was giving an order, she thought. It would be much easier if he'd look away, or at least have the grace to look uncomfortable. But he kept her pinned with his eyes, begging her to understand. To accept. She'd done enough accepting. She'd accepted the death of her parents, leaving her orphaned. She'd accepted Tom's death, accepted the findings of the RCMP in their official report. She'd accepted Jen's troubles and had taken them on herself, done what she could to minimize the damage. She'd let Nate into her house and accepted his story about the girl as his reason for being here.

But she was done. She refused to turn away from him. He had to know she meant what she said. She leveled her gaze. "You're not welcome here. Not with your weapons."

"Maggie, you have to listen to me." He implored her with an outstretched hand, but she took another step backward. "I have to be here. *I have to.*"

"Why? Why here? And tell me the truth. I think I've earned it."

"Because I've been put here. I wish I could tell you more. But I can't. It's for your own protection."

She half turned, refusing his reply. It wasn't enough. Her heart pounded. All the little feelings she'd had but dismissed over the past few weeks bubbled up again. Tiny things that hadn't added up but that now made sense. "You're not on leave, are you?"

"No, I'm not."

Those three words took the starch out of her knees. She reached out and gripped the back of a chair. *His* chair, the one he sat at during meals and with his morning coffee.

She looked away, staring past him toward the kitchen window. Outside she could see her grass, working hard to grow and turn green, and the dark earth of the garden, yet to be planted. This was her world. The one that had been her mainstay for years. Her safe place. Right now she wished she could get it back, that sense of normalcy. Wished she could forget all the long forgotten things Nate had made her feel. That extraordinary world, with him, wasn't real. Knowing he'd deceived her made her long to return to normal more than anything.

At her drawn out silence, he added quietly, "If it's worth anything, I didn't like it. Didn't like having to pretend."

"It's not worth much. It was all a lie then," she affirmed. She walked over to the counter and braced her hands on the top. The first time she'd considered truly moving on, doing something adventurous, out of her normal pattern, and this is what came of it. She'd thought she was safe with him. How could her judgment have been so off? She felt like a complete fool.

"Not all of it." He finally moved, going to stand behind her, yet keeping a subtle distance. He was close enough she could just feel the warmth of his breath on her neck. It made her remember how he tasted, how his arms felt, strong and sure around her. She had to stop thinking about it. It had been nothing more than momentary weakness. A flaw she wouldn't repeat.

"I was put on leave. The story I told you was one hundred percent true. But I was called back to work before it was over."

"And you're here on assignment." Everything she thought she knew melted away, leaving a dry, empty space.

"I'm sorry, Maggie."

Nate wanted to go to her, pull her into his arms and beg her to understand, but he wouldn't do that to her. He'd already done enough. He could see that as she spun to face him, her eyes wide with shock at the turn of the afternoon. He shoved his hands into his pockets to keep from reaching out. This was exactly what he hadn't wanted to happen. But his earlier encounter changed everything.

"What sort of assignment brings you to the middle of nowhere, Alberta? I don't understand. How do you even have jurisdiction here?"

He wished he could tell her everything, but he couldn't, not yet. Not without clearing it first. "I can't tell you the specifics."

She snorted. "Of course not. I'm just supposed to accept what you've told me and be a good girl and not question, right? I'm sorry, I can't do that."

Nate's frustration bubbled over. "Don't you think I wanted to tell you? Every time I looked into your eyes? Every time I kissed you, or you told me a little more about yourself? I hated having to lie to you, Maggie! But there's bigger issues at stake here!"

The outburst cost him. His head pained sharply and he exhaled slowly, trying to will it away. Yelling at her wouldn't solve anything.

"How on earth could I know that?" Her shout echoed through the kitchen.

This was why he'd kept the plan from her. Knowing what he knew about Peter Harding had made it clearer than ever that he had to keep her from harm. The more people that knew, the more danger they would all be in. If Peter found out who he was and where he was staying they could lose their opportunity. Or worse. No, it was necessary they keep it on a need to know basis. He reminded himself of that, drawing on all his strength to try to make her see reason.

"I know. And that's part of why I didn't say anything. You'd naturally have questions. Worries. I wanted to tell you, I did. I have reasons why I didn't."

"I don't care about your reasons." She tried to slide past him but he caught her with a hand on her wrist.

"Maggie, don't. Let me give you what I can. Sit down and we'll talk."

Nate kept the pressure on her wrist. He looked down at his fingers circling the pale skin of her arm. Why did he care? His cover was blown. Maggie knew who he was. How long before she put the rest together? But that wasn't all. He'd known all along he wasn't being honest and he'd gotten close to her anyway. And more than trying to find out information. He'd started to get involved with her personally. He couldn't begin to count the mistakes he'd made.

He should let her walk away and get on with the job, get it finished and get out. But he couldn't. Couldn't let her think everything between them had been a lie. Because it hadn't been. It had been, perhaps, the most real thing he'd experienced in a long time.

He cared about her. And not just the physical attraction, although there was that. He cared about Maggie, her hurts, her fears. Wanted to protect her. Wanted…damn. He wanted to love her, if it came to that.

"It wasn't all a lie," he began. But stopped, looking away for a moment. What was he trying to do? Get her to butt out or make her understand how deep his feelings really went? Trying to argue semantics wasn't the right strategy.

Maggie was glaring at him like he was the villain, for God's sake. The horrible thing was, he *felt* like a villain. All because he hadn't been able to be honest with her all along. And because he still couldn't. Not about the case, not about his feelings for her. Grant had been specific in keeping Maggie out of the loop until they knew for sure; to protest he cared about her would only come across as a diversion.

"Don't try to justify it now, just because you're caught."

"I won't."

She'd asked earlier if she were a threat, and she'd been sarcastic. But the answer that had jumped into his brain at the time had been *more than you know.* It was true in more ways than one. In the back of his mind he remembered what Grant had told him that day at the coffee shop. His gut said he could trust her. But what if he was wrong? After what had happened before his leave he wasn't sure he trusted his instincts anymore. What if Grant's suspicions were true and Nate let personal feelings get in the way? It would ruin everything. There was no way he could put people in danger based on a feeling. It was too much of a risk.

Right now he had to decide exactly how much to tell her. Enough to ease her mind and not enough to compromise things. Smooth things over. Get her to let him stay long enough to finish the job. He couldn't let his growing feelings for her cloud the priority. He pushed away the need to pull her into his arms, kiss away the hurt marking her face right now. He wasn't foolish enough to think she was only angry at him. She was hurt, too, and she had every right to be. What a mess.

He released her wrist and forced himself to relax, one muscle at a time, to make his body and expression as normal as possible. As he did it, her response mirrored his, until they both were more at ease.

"I'm asking you, please. Give me a chance to explain."

She hesitated long enough that he could take the opportunity to press his case. "I owe you an explanation. Let me give it."

She nodded and led the way back to the kitchen table. His head was aching now that the adrenaline had burned off but he forced it to the back of his mind. He could take something for the pain later.

He sat heavily, turning the chair to the side so he was facing her. "You know that Grant and I met at a conference in Toronto a few years ago. When this case came up, it was a natural fit for me to work with him on it. It was all set up before I had a chance to think."

"So you're working with Grant." She crossed her right leg over her left.

"He's the local liaison, yes. And it's true, I was on a leave of absence and they brought me back. At the time it seemed the logical cover. It's a small town, Maggie. What would people say if they knew I was here? I had to keep under the radar. It was much easier to come under the ruse of a vacation. Only…only I met you and I hated lying to you from the beginning."

"He says conveniently."

She was going to be a hard sell, especially without the details she seemed so intent on getting. Right now she was sitting in her chair, legs crossed and arms folded close to her body. Defensive to cover the pain. Unwilling to listen. But he knew it was there. Her eyes evaded his as he attempted to make contact. She had every reason to be hurt. He'd let himself become personally involved with her under false pretenses. He knew better.

"I still don't understand how someone from the States gets to come up here. Isn't there a whole jurisdiction issue?"

This was the one part Nate knew he could explain easily. "There's a Memorandum of Understanding between the U.S. authorities and Canadian. I liaise with a local department or contact, and here I am."

"So when you met Grant, it wasn't about catching up."

"No. We were information sharing."

"And you'd deliberately come along that day. When I took Jen to the bus station." Her arms crossed tighter. Her blue eyes flashed, accusing. She deserved an honest answer. He wished he could give her one, prevent her from building a wall around herself. He didn't want her to shut him out. Even if what Grant thought was true, the more he could keep Maggie out of it now, the better. He could at least give her some kind of protection.

"I did. We met to discuss...details."

"Who could you possibly be looking for?"

Nate sat back in the chair. This was the one question he couldn't answer right now. How could he tell her? She was more wrapped up in it than she knew. It wasn't only the proximity that made her the perfect choice. And how on earth could he ask her what he needed to know? Grant had aired his suspicions and Nate admitted to himself that they weren't groundless. The problem was, he'd lost his objectivity. The evidence on paper didn't fit the person sitting before him now. There was more at stake than just the two of them. He had to be cautious.

"I can't tell you that."

"Again, convenient." She pushed her chair back but he put both hands on her thighs, keeping her seated.

"It's for your protection, Maggie, can't you see that?"

"Frankly, I can't."

The pounding in his head was increasing. It didn't matter that he'd been hit today. They had to move and move now. If he ruined this case there'd be no leave of absence. Two mistakes in a row wouldn't go over well. But it was more than that. Maggie was at the center of it, whether she knew it or not. Things would escalate from this moment forward. He had to take the time to explain things the best he could. For now. Then he'd deal with her innocence. He knew in his heart that whatever Maggie had done, it had been unwittingly. Had to have been.

They should have had more time to make their move against Harding. But Nate had been distracted, he'd gotten careless. He'd ventured in closer to the farm and was on his way back out again when Pete had driven up in his truck. Nate had stopped, intending to see what was in the back of the vehicle when he'd frightened a flock of geese. The resulting flapping of wings and honking had sent up the alarm and he saw the rifle. And it hadn't been pointed at the birds.

He'd made himself a moving target, but Pete was a good shot. A graze was lucky.

He couldn't blame her for being scared. And she was under the impression that he'd only taken a fall.

The silence drew out as they stared at each other.

It was like they were holding a conversation without saying any words. When she finally spoke, he understood exactly what she was asking.

"When?"

Nate stood, walked a few feet and hooked his thumbs in his belt loops. Maggie looked away. He understood why. And hated it. It would be unfair of him to ask her for more.

"Tomorrow morning, best guess."

"So soon." The words were strangled.

"We need to move fast, before he takes off again."

"He?"

The name sat on his tongue and he debated. What would she do if he told her? And had Harding found out where he was staying yet?

Lord, he'd gotten careless and had put her in danger anyway. They had to strike first before Harding had a chance to regroup. He looked into Maggie's ashen face. And ignored the evidence for once. She was as innocent in all this as Jen had been. He'd stake his life on it. "I promise I'll tell you. Tonight."

"Nate, you'll be in danger," she repeated.

"I know." He ignored the searing pain in his head and squared his shoulders. "But this is what I'm trained for, Maggie. It's what I do, and I do it well."

"And afterward?"

She had to know how this was all going to end. There could be no other way. "Afterward Grant and I transport him back to the U.S. to stand trial."

This would be his last night at Mountain Haven. They both knew it. What Nate wanted and what he knew was possible were two very different things. He wanted to be with her. To love her. To take away that beautiful memory. Instead he'd be planning an op. Working to keep her safe. The thought left him hollow.

"This person is wanted. A *fugitive,* Maggie. It's what I do. I bring in criminals who are running from the law. Do you think we go after the small-time shoplifters? Do you?"

To his relief she stayed put in her chair. Her face paled further and her eyes widened. He hadn't wanted to frighten her but perhaps now it was the only way. To make her see why he'd felt the need for keeping her in the dark.

"The people I bring in are armed robbers, murderers, rapists, child predators. What do you think could happen if someone like that knew I was here to find them, knew you were involved?"

"If you're trying to scare me, it's working."

"Good. Because that's how important this is. It's the reason—the *only* reason—I had to keep quiet."

She looked away. "It doesn't change that you…"

He swallowed. She was right. He'd put his feelings for her above his duty. It was the first time he'd ever done that and he knew it had been a mistake. It served no purpose save to hurt both of them.

"No, it doesn't. I let myself become personally involved with you and I had no right. If you'd been anyone else…"

"You'd what?"

His breath caught as she turned liquid blue eyes on him. It was a day of truths. All too soon he'd be gone and perhaps if she knew, she'd accept his partial silence a little easier.

"I'd never have started to fall for you."

Calmly she rose from her chair. "You deceived me, used me. There is no excuse for that. You blew it, Nate."

I sure did, he thought, watching her walk away.

"Maggie."

She stopped at the doorway, refusing to turn around and face him.

"Can I stay, Maggie?"

Her words came, brittle. "I honor my commitments. I accepted your reservation and your bill is paid."

On the contrary, he knew he'd be paying for this for a long time to come. A day wouldn't go by that he wouldn't think of her. The scent of vanilla and cinnamon, the sound of her laugh or howl of the westerly wind.

Maggie disappeared into her living quarters and Nate sighed. There was a lot to be done and a limited amount of time. He'd have to sort things out with her later. Right now he had a phone call to make.

They couldn't let Pete slip through their fingers again. He had to call Grant, assemble the team and prepare to go in. And add attempted murder to the list of charges.

Because he knew he'd gotten lucky. And he couldn't count on his luck to hold.

Maggie held it all in until she was in her living quarters. She shut the door with a firm click, then went and sat in the chair by the window, staring outside but seeing nothing.

Had he really fallen for her? Or was that his way of trying to smooth things over?

She didn't know what to believe anymore. She only knew

that for the first time since Tom's death, after all those long, lonely years, she'd finally let someone in. She'd finally started to care. It had gone beyond simple flirtation and the physical. She'd *fallen*. She'd fallen for the man she thought he was. Kind, caring, strong, trustworthy.

Now she felt like a complete fool.

In the isolation of her room she let the tears come. Tears for all she'd lost, tears of humiliation. She hated her weakness, for allowing herself to fancy he was truly interested in her. She'd spent the majority of her life seeing things exactly as they were.

And where they were right now was that she was a forty-two-year-old widow with a teenage daughter and a bed and breakfast. Full stop. After years of protecting her heart, she'd let down her guard and had become vulnerable, trusting. She'd cautioned herself not to let herself get hurt again but she'd done it anyway. She'd let herself be seduced by the magic and romance of the situation, conveniently forgetting that reality would come crashing through.

She'd been stupid to believe he'd wanted her. She'd been naive. He was staying now, but not for her. For the job.

She should have done *her* job and put a stop to any personal connections they'd made. She'd been foolish and fanciful and…weak. The tears were bitter and cold and she resented them nearly as much as she resented Nate right now. Damn him for making her feel this way…hopeless and vulnerable. She hadn't cried often since Tom's death, and not once had it been over a man. Until now.

She swiped her hands roughly over her cheeks, brushing away the moisture. She'd indulged enough. She went to the bathroom and washed her face, covered the redness with makeup and vowed she'd never cry over a man ever again.

He was gone from the kitchen when she entered it again. The remnants of her first-aid treatment had disappeared, too, except for a bottle of painkillers that remained on the counter beside an empty glass. She should have realized his head would be hurting after the bump he'd taken.

The house was deathly silent. If he were concussed, he shouldn't be sleeping. Or if he did, she should at least wake him frequently. Just because she was angry and hurt didn't mean she wanted anything to happen to him.

She went upstairs, her feet creaking on the old steps, sounding louder than normal in the awkward silence that seemed to envelop the house. She should have insisted he see a doctor.

His door was open a crack and she tapped gently, pushing it open a few inches.

"Come in, Maggie."

Her body trembled at the sound of his soft, sure voice. In her anger it had been easy to believe he'd felt nothing for her, had used her. But as she pushed the door open with a squeak, and faced his eyes as they looked at her, she knew there was something between them. Something tenuous and tender, and now tainted with mistruths.

He was different, even if it was only her own perception that made him so. He wasn't Nate Griffith, reevaluating, but Nate Griffith, U.S. Marshal, back on the job.

"You're awake. I was worried."

He was sitting in the straight-back chair, and the laptop was open in front of him. He spun so that he was facing the door, but he didn't get up. As much as she hated the lies, as much as she hated the guns…something about him made her feel safe. It had always been that way; hating what he did while still feeling proud and protected.

His flak jacket lay on the bed in plain sight. There was no point in hiding it from her now. She could say she didn't care about him all she wanted. The surge of relief she felt knowing he'd at least had a vest on told the truth.

"I didn't mean to worry you. Believe me, Maggie. I wanted to save you more worry. You've had your fair share."

"I saw the pills downstairs. Does it hurt much?"

Automatically his fingers found the bandage on his forehead and he winced. She fought back the urge to go to him and examine the wound.

"It's paining a bit yet. Nothing I can't handle."

"You shouldn't sleep for long periods of time. I'm pretty sure you probably have a concussion." Her fingers curled on the doorknob. Her first instinct was to care for him. But things were too tenuous between them. She didn't want him to think all was forgiven just because she was concerned about his medical well-being.

"Me, too. That's why I'm…" He paused, then unsmiling, treated her with the truth. "That's why I'm working."

Her muscles stiffened. "Working."

He nodded. "The investigation is moving forward quickly now. We need to speak about that."

Her head spun as all the possibilities ricocheted in her mind. She couldn't imagine an empty house again, without him to cook for, talk to, laugh with. How could that be, knowing what she knew now?

He'd be going away. But before that, she supposed he'd get what he'd come for. And that wasn't her, even as a tiny voice inside her wanted it to be. And after what he'd said…there would be risks.

She kept her hand on the knob of the door. Better she know now. Other than Jen and Mike, it had seemed like everyone she'd cared about in her life had met a tragic ending. And even Jen could have been in more trouble if Maggie hadn't worked hard to change things. It would be better all around if she kept her distance from Nate.

"What do I have to do with it?"

He glanced at the laptop and her eyes followed. It seemed to be some sort of mapping diagram. She knew without him saying that it was a plan.

"Grant Simms will be here within the hour. Two at most."

Maggie's lip curled. Grant Simms again. He'd been at the local detachment for probably five years and he had a way of looking at Maggie like he *knew* things. When she'd pleaded Jen's case, she hadn't liked the way he'd watched her. Assessing. Like he was trying to figure her out, when her only motive had been to minimize the damage to her daughter. Jen had made a mistake. Maggie didn't think it should follow her around indefinitely. She realized now that Grant had probably told Nate everything about last summer and he'd never mentioned it. More secrets.

"You trust Grant."

"Of course I do."

She pulled back a little. It felt too much like choosing sides and she needed to distance herself again. Being close to him made it too easy to forget the many ways he had wronged her.

She would rather they met somewhere else. But it was hardly fair to ask that of him when he was already popping pills for his headache. She'd do it, knowing that it would make things move faster, letting her get her life back in order sooner. Then she could put this all behind her, once and for all.

"I'll put some coffee on."

She left the room, but turned to pull the door closed behind her. Before it was latched, she saw Nate already facing the computer again, his hand on the mouse.

He was a cop, a fugitive hunter, focused on the job. There was no room in his life for her. It was just as well she knew now before something happened she'd truly regret.

CHAPTER TEN

IT WAS probably good Grant was coming. At this rate, the deep freeze would be full and she'd have to send a care package to Jen. Maggie stared at the pile of dirty dishes on the counter and the cooling racks full of baked goods on the table. She was more upset than she'd initially realized.

Baking meant she could avoid Nate. She could distract herself from thinking about how he'd lied to her, how he was putting himself in danger again, how in danger *she* felt when he kissed her and touched her, lighting her body on fire.

Only the distracting wasn't working so well this time.

She was sliding another batch of muffins out of the oven when the doorbell rang. She put the muffin tins on top of the oven and pulled off her oven mitt as she went to the door.

Grant Simms was on the other side, dressed in plainclothes but with his issue pistol in plain sight.

"Good evening, Maggie."

"Constable Simms."

She knew she sounded frosty and didn't care. She stepped back, holding the door open, the only invitation to come in that she offered. He stepped into the breach.

With Jen behind him.

"Jennifer!"

For a moment she wondered if Jen were in trouble again,

but dismissed it. She had no doubt that Jen had learned her lesson. Still, what was she doing here?

"Constable Simms sent for me this afternoon. He wanted me to answer some questions about Peter Harding."

Peter Harding?

"Hey, Grant."

Nate's voice came from the stairs and the three of them turned to look up.

He was fully dressed, in jeans and a dark long-sleeved T-shirt that accented the breadth of his chest and the curved muscles in his arms. "U.S. MARSHAL" was emblazoned down the sleeve. He'd shaved, changed the gauze and tape on the bandage. For the first time since arriving, he had on a holster and his handgun was in it. All pretenses were officially gone. Maggie blinked. Everything was upside down. What was now reality seemed surreal to her.

When Nate got to the bottom, he and Grant shook hands, the grip strong as their eyes met. And Maggie knew that despite her personal feelings, Nate and Grant were a team. They were cut from the same cloth, and she was oddly reassured.

"Hell of a thing, you getting trimmed."

Maggie's face blanched as the words seemed to bounce around. All the blood drained from her head, leaving her spinning as Jen's and Nate's faces blurred. Nate frowned at Grant. The bandage glared white on the corner of his head.

"You didn't tell her?" Grant's voice echoed in her head. She knew what trimmed meant. She knew it meant he hadn't fallen and hit his head on a rock. Trimmed meant he'd been grazed by a bullet.

She heard Nate's voice, it sounded far away. "No. I didn't want to worry her."

She closed her eyes, willing away the shock and numbing fear. Nate put his hands on her shoulders. She wanted to lean back against his strength but resisted. He'd lied to her over and over again. When would she learn?

"You were shot." She shook off his hands, knowing being touched by him made her vulnerable. She wanted to escape but didn't know how. He was blocking the door and Grant and Jen were watching it all. There was nowhere safe in the house. Yet how could she deal with this?

"Give us a minute, Grant. Jen, if you wouldn't mind waiting in your room, we'll call you when we're ready." Nate took charge, gripping her arm and leading her down the hall to the kitchen. Once there he squeezed her arms and bent his knees so he was looking in her eyes. "I was grazed, that's all."

"You were shot." She shook her head wildly, stopping when his grip tightened. "A man fired a gun at you with intent…the fact that he was slightly off the mark is irrelevant. And you wouldn't even go to the hospital!"

"I know a flesh wound when I see one, Maggie. And there wasn't time for a trip to the emergency room."

She'd had his blood on her hands.

"No time," she echoed. What did that mean? She pulled away but stopped by the kitchen table, standing next to the first chair. The one he'd sat in while insisting that she bandage the wound.

"I don't know what to say. I didn't want you to panic. And we can talk about this, but not now. There isn't time for it."

She nodded. This couldn't be happening. It was all becoming a big blur that she didn't understand. Things were moving too fast. She'd barely begun to assimilate that he was actually on the job. Now everything else came crashing around her. Grant was here. Jen was here, of all things. Maybe Nate cared, maybe he didn't. But the one thing that was clear was that he'd used her. Used her to get to this particular moment in time.

"Maggie, is there coffee?" Nate's voice was efficient but calm, and it grounded her. She turned her head, focused on his face. The truth had changed him. He was taller, somehow.

More commanding. There was a force about him that was magnetic. He was a man to be reckoned with; a man who would protect what was right. She should hate him for it but couldn't help but admire it.

"Yes, and fresh muffins."

"That would be great. We'd like it very much if you'd join us."

"What do you need me for?"

"It'll all make sense, Maggie."

Grant had only ever been coolly polite to her, and now they were asking, no demanding, that she accommodate their meeting.

Lord, she had so many mixed feelings over the matter she felt like making more muffins. Why couldn't they go back to the way it was before? It had seemed complicated, but it was simple compared to this. Before, it had been new and foreign. Now Nate was putting his life on the line and nothing she could say would make any difference.

Nate put his hand on hers as she retrieved a plate. The firm warmth of it heated her cold fingers.

"Thank you, Maggie. I know this isn't easy for you."

"No, it's not." She avoided his face, focusing instead on arranging the muffins on the plate.

"And I don't mean to make it any harder…so I'm going to ask you something in private."

Her hands stilled over the butter dish. There was more? How much more could she possibly take today?

"What could you possibly want to ask of me now?"

Surprise held her still when he took both her hands in his own. She risked a look up; his eyes held apology and understanding.

"You shared things with me these last weeks. Things about your life. And we…we developed an attachment. Yet…" He paused, looked at his toes, then looked up again.

"Just ask what you want to ask, Nate. We're too far along for niceties now."

"I find it hard to believe you haven't been involved with anyone since Tom."

Maggie's brows drew together. She couldn't read his face; he'd switched back into cop mode. What did her sex life, or lack of it, have to do with anything?

"What does it matter?"

The pressure on her fingers tightened. "Damn, I wanted to wait to ask you this at a better time. Maggie, have you been involved with anyone? Say, last summer?"

Last summer? She looked up into his face, her eyes widening with confusion. "You're asking me if I've had a boyfriend since Tom. Specifically about a year ago."

"That's what I'm asking."

"I don't see what business it is of yours, but no."

She pulled her hands away and resumed arranging the tray. What reason could he possibly have for delving into *her* past? It was dry as dust. There hadn't been anyone since Tom. Not even close, until…

Until Nate. It always came back to Nate.

"You weren't involved with Peter Harding?"

Peter Harding? This is what this was about? It was the second time she'd heard his name tonight and Maggie's stomach dropped. Why in the world would he think she was involved with Pete? How could anyone? She had very real reasons to hate the man, not have an affair with him. Her fingers tightened on the edges of the tray.

She looked up at Nate, surprised to find him serious. "I have no use for Peter Harding. None whatsoever. He's despicable."

The relief on his face was so profound that suddenly it all fit together. Pete was Nate's assignment. Pete, the man responsible for Jen's arrest, had shot Nate today. The thought made her knees go weak but she stood her ground. "He's who you're here for, isn't he?"

Had he thought she was involved all this time? She took a step back.

"Did you seriously think that I had an affair with a man like that?" And suspecting it, had he seduced her anyway? Or had he tried to get close to her so she'd betray Pete? The very idea turned her stomach.

"I believe you when you say you didn't," he conceded. "Once I got to know you, I knew it couldn't be true. But I had feelings that I recognized might be clouding my judgment." His voice grew stronger. "But Grant is going to ask you and I wanted to give you the heads-up. I thought it might be easier for you if it came from me first."

Grant, of course. She wondered if that was why he always looked at her with that cold, assessing glare. At least Nate had judged her correctly. She stared down the hall at the entrance to the den, her distrust growing. He'd let Jen go, but he hadn't been pleasant about it. Now he'd dragged her into this mess once again, when it would be best if it were all forgotten. She simply wanted to go on as if Peter Harding had never existed!

"What has Pete done?" She collected herself and put the plate of muffins in the center of the tray. "After all you've put me through, you can at least tell me that."

"Bring in the coffee, Maggie. We'll talk."

She put the carafe on the tray and Nate took it from her hands. This was all happening so quickly. Only this afternoon she'd been humming and folding Nate's laundry and now she had the RCMP sitting in her den, talking about bringing in fugitives over coffee and muffins.

Nate put the tray down on the coffee table and Maggie poured three mugs of the steaming brew. She sat on the couch, surprised when Nate sat down beside her instead of in the chair closest to Grant, almost as if he were choosing her side.

She stared at his thigh, lean and muscled even through the denim. She put down her spoon in time to see Nate meet Grant's gaze and give a small shake of his head. Grant shifted in his seat.

"Maggie," Grant began, "first of all I want to apologize for putting you in the middle of this. It was my idea completely. I certainly didn't mean to cause any upset."

She wasn't sure whether to believe him or not. Yet something in his tone rang genuine, something she hadn't heard before.

"You're after Pete Harding." She took a sip of the coffee, trying hard to appear calmer than she felt.

"Yes, we are." Nate broke in. "Your place was the natural fit. You're geographically close by, I could stay here legitimately and your known connection to him helped."

"My connection," she echoed, lost. "I already told Nate I wasn't involved with him."

"Through Jennifer," Grant said gently.

Maggie turned and looked at Nate. "You did know." Her heart sank. She'd been aware from the first what he did for a job and she'd wanted to spare him the details of Jen's arrest. But he'd known all along. Of course he had.

He nodded. "I did. But it didn't matter. Jen told me about it anyway before she left to go back to school. She felt very sorry about putting you through so much trouble."

Maggie's eyes stung. Pete Harding was a waste of space in her opinion. Bootlegging and selling pot, petty stuff to most but she knew how it could cause lasting damage. Jen had been quiet when the whole arrest happened, unwilling to share much information at all and it had scared Maggie to death. She'd wanted Pete pulled in but she'd been informed at the beginning that there wasn't enough to warrant his arrest, so she'd focused on what was best for Jen. For months she'd lived in the same community resenting his presence and his above-the-law attitude.

She was glad Jen seemed to be on the other side of her troubles now. And yet here was Pete again, front and center in Maggie's life. She huffed out a breath.

Grant spoke into the breach. "I'm glad to hear there was nothing going on with you."

Maggie turned her attention to Grant. "Why on earth would you have suspected such a thing? How could you? All I did was try to protect my daughter!"

Grant rested his elbows on his knees. "You're about the same age, you've been a widow for a lot of years. And you were very persistent in dropping the matter last summer when Jennifer was arrested. It looked like you were protecting him. We couldn't take chances. When we found out who he really was…we had to act."

Maggie put down her cup. "My only concern was minimizing the damage to Jennifer, and I was as much as told that there wasn't enough on Pete to charge him with anything. You haven't been here long, Grant, but if you'd talked to anyone in the community they would have told you point-blank that I'd never have anything to do with someone like Pete Harding."

"The only thing we had on file for you was Tom, and the questions brought up from his death…on paper it was very plausible."

Maggie looked at Nate. The eyebrow not hindered by gauze was wrinkled; like he was confused about something.

"Paper isn't enough." She turned her attention to her coffee cup.

"I know. Please accept my apologies, Maggie."

His words, his tone, his expression, were all earnest. Maggie looked at Nate again. He'd been thoughtful enough to ask her about it in private. Perhaps it made no sense in light of recent truths, but if Nate trusted Grant, it was good enough for her.

"Let's just move on, shall we?"

Nate angled himself on the sofa. "If you have anything you know about Pete that you'd like to share, that would be helpful."

Maggie couldn't think of a thing. "I only know he operates off his property. Booze and drugs. Wouldn't surprise me to find a grow operation on the property somewhere."

Nate grinned suddenly, the expression lighting up his face. "Oh, we found it. Thanks for the snowshoes, by the way. I don't think there's going to be much of a crop this year."

So he hadn't been going for walks, either. He'd been haunting the fields. "You were staking him out."

Nate nodded. "I took what I needed in my backpack and made do."

His backpack. Maggie now understood that he'd not only carried his lunch but very likely firearms and ammunition as well as surveillance gear. She fought against the sense of the surreal, tried to remain in the moment. It didn't seem possible that this was happening in her house.

Who was this man? The more she discovered, the more he seemed a mystery. How could he be the same man she'd kissed? The same man she'd told secrets to, the one who'd inspired feelings in her that no man had since she'd been married to Tom?

"You don't know anything more?"

She shook herself out of her thoughts in time to register the question.

"No, nothing."

"Then I think it's time to bring Jen in. If there's anything she can share that she didn't last fall, it could be helpful."

Grant went out and returned a moment later with Jen, who kept her eyes downcast and picked at a fingernail.

"Jen, honey, Constable Simms and…and Nate—" she still couldn't seem to bring herself to call him a marshal "—just want to ask you a few questions about Pete Harding. You're not in any trouble. Right?" She aimed the last at Nate, giving him a warning eyebrow.

Nate nodded. "That's right. You haven't done anything

wrong. Why don't you sit down, and we can see if you remember anything that might be important."

Jen sat on the sofa beside Grant and met her mother's gaze with red-rimmed eyes.

"I'm sorry, Mama," she said, swallowing.

Maggie's eyes misted. Jen hadn't called her Mama for several years and it took her back to those uncomplicated days of her childhood.

"You're forgiven."

Why it had taken nearly a year for them each to say those important words, Maggie didn't know, but as soon as they were spoken, everything changed. Her daughter was back. Really back. The relief hit her square in the chest.

"Jennifer," Grant began, "Last summer you didn't give us a lot of details and we think that you may have been afraid to say much of anything. I want you to forget that fear now. Nate is here, and I'm here, to take Peter Harding in for good. He can't hurt you, Jen. But you can help us so he doesn't hurt anyone else."

"What do you want to know?"

Jen's face was pale but somehow strong, and Maggie realized what a treasure she was. She met Jen's eyes and nodded.

"Did Pete ever threaten you?"

"He said that if I ever ratted him out I'd be sorry."

"Anything more specific? Did he use several girls to run his product?"

Jen shook her head. "Not that I know of. At first…at first he was kind of cool, you know? Then he got a little scary. I felt weird around him but by that time I was afraid to walk away. Then he…"

She stopped, turned away and Maggie's heart stopped.

"Then he what, Jen." She tried to keep the shake out of her voice but failed.

"He showed me a trapdoor in the barn. It was where he hid

his stuff. And he said if I did anything to cause trouble he'd hide me there, too."

Maggie's stomach tumbled clear to her toes as the ramifications covered her in waves.

Nate's mouth fell open and Grant's face turned red.

"Why in God's name didn't you tell me this last summer?" Grant's elbows came off his knees and his fingers flexed tightly as he raised his voice.

Jen sniffled. "I was too afraid! I figured if I kept on the low it would go away and it would be okay."

Maggie stood, crossed the room and pulled Jen into her arms. "Oh, baby," she whispered, holding her daughter close as she sobbed. "You should have told me. We could have stopped him months ago."

"You were so mad, I didn't want to upset you anymore. And then you sent me away and I thought that…"

The childlike plea in Jen's voice touched her. In all this time, she hadn't considered that Jen might have felt turned away. She'd only considered her daughter's well-being. The backs of her eyelids burned.

"You thought what? That I didn't want you anymore?" Maggie put her hands on either side of Jen's face and looked her dead in the eyes. "Oh, honey, I hated being without you. You're all I've got. But I wanted to keep you safe. To get you away from your troubles. I could never stop loving you! I certainly wouldn't ever punish you by sending you away!"

Jen's arms tightened around Maggie's neck and Maggie closed her eyes, feeling the tears trickle on her cheeks and not caring that Nate and Grant stood by watching. She'd sent Jen off to school somewhere else, tried to pretend none of it had happened and all the while her baby girl had felt the sting of rejection. Had thought she wasn't wanted, which couldn't be farther from the truth.

Grant's voice interrupted quietly. "Jen, if there's anything else you have to tell us, now's the time. I wish you'd said something last summer."

Jen's voice came out in a hoarse whisper. "He said if I told anyone he'd lock me in there. I didn't think the cops would take it seriously, they'd think he'd only said it to scare me. But I saw the look in his eyes. I believed him."

Nate ground out an earthy curse, then the den fell eerily silent.

Whatever Pete had done, it had been enough that the U.S. Government had seen fit to send Nate up to get him. And they didn't do that for simple bootleggers. Maggie's body felt like stone; she couldn't move. Implications of what might have happened to Jen fell on her, heavy and cold. And for the first time, she was glad that it was Nate with her. Glad he was on the job. Grateful and…proud. Her arm tightened on Jen's shoulder as they faced the men together.

"I'm sorry," she whispered. "I have to know. What is it he's done? What's he charged with?"

After a moment's silence, Nate answered. His tone was clear, strong and the words sent an icy chill up the backs of her legs.

"He's charged with three counts of kidnapping and sexual assault, and one count of murder."

A cry escaped her throat as she crumpled, sliding away from Jen. Nate's arm reached out, supporting her as shock rippled through her body.

Harding's threats didn't seem so harmless now. Delayed fear pulsed through her veins at what she could have lost. She'd lost everyone else. She couldn't have borne losing her baby girl, too. And she'd come closer than she'd thought possible.

Nate ignored Grant. Instead he put a finger under her chin and lifted it. When she looked up into his face, ashamed of what she'd done, frightened of what she'd just heard, what she saw in his eyes warmed her soul.

He would do whatever it took to make things right. He

would protect her. He would protect Jen. She knew it in her heart. How could she hate him now for hiding the truth? Now that she knew all of it, she understood.

"It will be over soon, Maggie, I promise. Peter Harding will be gone from your life forever. You won't have to be afraid. Jen won't have to be afraid."

She closed her eyes briefly. "Thank you."

He pressed his lips to her forehead and she let herself lean into it, just for a moment, gathering a little strength.

After a few minutes, she squared her shoulders. Nate had said that things were moving fast. That meant he and Grant had to be planning how to make the arrest. Her heart beat erratically, nerves bubbling over. Nate would be in danger. The best thing she could do now to help was make sure they had the time and space to plan, to prepare. To ensure there would be no mistakes.

"We'll leave you to talk now. You must have things to discuss."

"Maggie?" Grant's voice interrupted. "Jen isn't staying. I want her away from here, and safe. I have an officer ready to take her back to Edmonton as soon as we're finished here. I'm sorry."

"But…" Maggie looked up at Nate, then back to Grant. It would sound silly, insisting that she'd only just gotten Jen back. But now that she knew everything, she didn't want to let her go.

"Can't I stay here, with Mom?"

Nate's hand squeezed Maggie's and he looked down into her eyes. "It would be useless to ask *you* to leave, I know that. But we can keep Jen away from it. It would be one less thing for us to worry about."

Maggie knew that right now it was more important to keep Nate focused on his job. She looked up at Jen, raised an eyebrow. Jen looked stronger now, less frightened. Nate had a way of doing that and she loved him for it.

Jen wrapped her arms around herself. "It's okay, Mom. Once it's over I'll come home. I promise."

Maggie rose, her thigh tingling as Nate's free hand lingered over the fabric of her trousers. "I'll come and get you myself." She held out her hand and Jen took it. Maggie's knees trembled but she made herself take one step, then another, to the door. She avoided Grant's gaze as she left the room with Jen, closing the door behind her.

She leaned back against it. Yes, Peter Harding would be gone for good. But so would Nate.

And the thought of being without him made her very lonely indeed. She hated it almost as much as she hated the fact he'd be putting himself in danger.

A half hour later, after a quick cup of tea and a restorative, albeit brief conversation with her daughter, Maggie heard voices in the hall; heard Nate say "that's it then." Maggie put down her teacup and held Jen's hand as she went to see Grant—and her daughter—away. She'd been remiss in her manners earlier, but she saw things differently now.

Very differently. Knowing what Pete had done, knowing how much trouble Jennifer could have been in...Grant deserved her gratitude and respect, certainly not the curtness she'd treated him to on his arrival.

When she walked toward the front door, Grant's eyes seemed to smile at her. She was no longer intimidated by his size, his bearing. Instead she was oddly reassured that he'd do everything in his power to make sure things turned out the right way. The animosity she'd felt for him all these months evaporated.

"Thank you, Maggie, for the hospitality—and for the information."

"You're welcome," she said, meaning it. She caught Jen in a quick hug. "Love you. Call when you get in. And I'll see you soon."

Grant lifted a hand in farewell and jumped the two steps off the porch, Jen following behind.

"Constable Simms?"

He stopped. Maggie sensed Nate behind her and knew what she was about to say was as much for him as it was for Grant. "Be careful."

He smiled at her, a genuine, wide smile. She hadn't known his face could change that much. He looked ten years younger. "I'm always careful." His smile faded as he looked up at Nate, standing just behind her. "Nate...I'll see you at the staging area at five. Get some sleep, will ya?"

Nate nodded. "I'll be there with bells on."

He reached over and squeezed Maggie's hand. "I've got things to do. I'll see you later."

He left her on the cold porch, shivering in the frosty spring air and watching Grant and Jen drive away. More than ever, she had no idea what it was she wanted. She only knew she wanted it over.

By midnight she was sufficiently worried. She'd heard nothing out of Nate since Grant's departure, not a whisper of him moving around upstairs. The vision of his cut loomed before her eyes. He'd held it together during Grant's visit, but she'd seen the gray pallor beneath his usual healthy color. She'd kept hoping he'd stir, perhaps come down to the kitchen for a snack. She'd bathed and changed into a pair of sleep pants and a T-shirt, but nothing. Her conscience nagged at her, telling her to forget her hurt feelings and check on him. The few hours of frenetic activity had subsided. And she was left feeling raw and open. It brought back so many memories she'd tried to bury.

She hated to wake him. He had to be up early and needed his rest. Yet...she was pretty sure he'd suffered some sort of a concussion.

She crept upstairs, although she couldn't figure out why. She was going wake him anyway, so why was she worried about making noise? Perhaps it was simply that now they were forced to tiptoe around each other. Hold a fragile balance. She didn't feel prepared to tip the scales in favor of the anger or the hurt she felt. The betrayal at his lies and the fear of the danger he was putting himself in, all mixed together with gratitude that he was there in the first place. None of her emotions matched up and she was completely off balance.

She opened his door. It was dark inside and he was in bed, sprawled beneath the covers. One ankle curved outside the quilt, the skin of his foot pale in the muted moonlight pouring through his window. His lips were slightly open in sleep, the white bandage on his head a stark reminder of all that had transpired that afternoon.

She didn't want to touch him. Not now. It would do nothing but stir up memories and futile longings.

"Nate." She whispered it, willing him to wake. But he never moved, his chest barely rising and falling.

"Nate." She put a little more force behind it, to no avail.

Heart pounding, she sat tentatively on the edge of the bed. One of his arms was spread wide, his forearm sprinkled with dark hair visible under the edge of the blanket. She touched it lightly, the warm skin tingling on her fingertips. She'd never met a man like him. He was strong and deliberate, even in sleep.

"Nathaniel," she whispered, her throat tight.

His lashes fluttered up as he opened his eyes. The turquoise color glowed darkly in the shadows, focusing on her face.

"Maggie," he murmured, the soft sound an endearment.

Her body warmed. Lies or not, the undercurrent of desire hadn't abated. She'd had time to think since the events of the afternoon, and even knowing there was no future for them, she understood his reasoning for secrets. He'd done it to protect her, to protect everyone, and had put himself in danger in the process. She didn't like it but she understood it. He'd only done what he'd needed to do.

What she didn't understand was why he'd let things progress between *them*. Why he hadn't kept his distance. If he was here on business, why hadn't he kept it as business?

But was that what she really wanted? Then she would have missed out on the last few weeks, and despite the pain, both from dredging up the past and from learning about his deception, she couldn't bring herself to be sorry any of it had happened. She wasn't sorry that he'd made her feel more alive than she had in years. She'd never be sorry he'd kissed her and held her.

"I'll go," she murmured. "I wanted to make sure you were awake. You shouldn't sleep for long periods at once."

"Stay."

He hadn't moved. His foot curled around the blankets at the end of the bed, his arm stayed beneath the covers. But his eyes, and that one word, held her there.

"Don't," she whispered. She swallowed. Hadn't there been enough pretense today? He didn't need to act like there was still something between them. The truth was out, and it was bigger than both of them.

"Not everything about my being here was a lie, Maggie."

"How can you say that," she whispered furiously. "It was a cover from the moment you called and gave your reservation to Jen." She turned away from his gaze. "Your interest in me was a cover."

She didn't want him. But even knowing it, her heart begged him to dispute it.

The arm shifted. His fingers reached up until they touched the skin of her face and it was all she could do to not close her eyes at the tender touch. She couldn't seem to move off the side of the bed, anchored there by the gentle graze of his fingertips and the intensity burning in his eyes.

"I lied about the professional side, because I had to, and now you know why." The backs of his fingers caressed her jaw. "But everything…personal between us was the truth. It was not part of the plan. I wasn't anticipating *you*."

"Why should I believe you?" She jerked her head away from his hand. She couldn't think, couldn't remain objective when he touched her this way.

"Because if you don't it means you were wrong." He didn't let her get away. His fingers curled over her ear and beneath her hair as he raised up on the opposite elbow. "Wrong when you felt this *thing* building between us. Wrong when you touched me and I touched you. Wrong when you trusted me."

His lips curled ever so slightly into a smile. "You weren't wrong, Maggie. Those feelings—they're real."

She wanted desperately to believe him as his soft words wooed her. To believe that everything that had transpired… their confidences, the little touches, the way her heart soared when he kissed her…had been true. But she couldn't escape the memory of the cold steel tucked beneath his shirt today. Or the way she'd had his blood on her hands. She hated guns. Hated them with a passion. Even knowing he was a cop hadn't meant that much to her. He'd been on holiday, and for the brief time he was at Mountain Haven she'd chosen to ignore the fact when it suited her. He hadn't been on duty. He'd been someone else.

"I'm sorry about the gun," he whispered, as if he could read her mind. "You have to know I'd never hurt you. You have to know I'd do anything—*anything*—to protect you. Even lie."

"I feel used," she admitted, amazed that she still felt she could confide her feelings. How could she be so angry and yet feel so close to him? Yet they'd always seemed able to talk. She remembered how he'd held her in the den earlier when she realized the depth of the danger Pete Harding represented. He had told her the truth when he could.

Perhaps in an odd way, that was the one thing that had been truthful between them. The ability to talk when it was necessary. He had a way of bringing out her secrets. Most of them, anyway. She still held a few close to her heart. She didn't want to see pity on his face. And without telling him, he'd never understand why she had reacted as she had to discovering his gun, or knowing he could have been killed.

His eyes searched hers. "I know you do, and I'm so sorry. And I did want to tell you. I even mentioned it to Grant, but he thought it would be better if I didn't."

He tugged with his hand. She was sitting on one hip and lost her balance, falling slightly to lay over his chest.

"Nate, I…"

He stopped her words with his mouth. First lifting and seeking her lips, and once finding them, pushing up and twisting so that she fell beneath him.

It was different from the other times. This time it went beyond the sexual and hit her straight in her heart, and she didn't fight it. Maybe it was the freedom of the truth that changed it, maybe it was knowing it was all coming to an end, but despite everything he still had the power to do this; to make her feel like a desirable, loved woman. It was more than knowing he was younger, or the fitness of his firm body. It was in the way he touched her, like he couldn't help himself. Like she was something treasured.

But he was leaving tomorrow, and she wanted to absorb the feeling and keep it locked inside for safekeeping. To be able to look back and remember it when he was gone, to cherish it like she did the items she kept in her special box. For once, she stopped analyzing the pros and cons and let herself *feel*.

In the dark, on a rumpled bed, they were horizontal with his weight pressing her into the mattress. Her hands lifted, only to find the warm, bare skin of his shoulder, curved and dipped with hard muscle. Her fingers drifted lower, over his shoulders and back, stopping at a rough wrinkle. One of the scars he'd mentioned? She couldn't tell in the dark.

"This isn't a lie." His lips hovered over her ear before trailing down her neck. His weight pushed her deeper into the mattress. "What you do to me isn't a lie."

His mouth claimed hers again and she met it eagerly. She'd let fear stand in her way for too long. Now his time at Mountain Haven was drawing shorter with each fleeting moment. She'd been waiting for someone. Someone she could feel safe with. It shocked her to realize she still felt Nate was that man. Even after everything that had been revealed today.

He shifted slightly, his hand slipping over her T-shirt. He cupped her in his palm and her body surged from the contact, long-lost desire settling in her core. She arched, pressing herself more firmly into his hand, glorying in the feeling she'd nearly forgotten in her long abstinence.

He lowered his head until she felt his moist breath through the cotton.

A moan ripped from her throat and she gripped his hair with her hands.

And he stilled, his muffled cry of pain vibrating just below her heart. In the heat of the moment, she'd forgotten about his head and the gash that had unraveled everything.

"I'm sorry," she whispered. She was sorry she had hurt him. She was sorry they'd stopped, because being with him made her feel alive.

But it was madness and nothing good could come of it, no matter how much she craved him. He would still be leaving. He would still put himself in harm's way every day. She'd already been through it once. She couldn't deal with it again.

Nate didn't move. He simply dropped his head, resting it for a moment on the softness of her diaphragm. She closed her eyes and imprinted the feeling of him there on her soul.

"It's all right." His voice grated in the darkness. "We should stop. I promised myself I wouldn't do this."

Maggie suddenly felt very exposed, though she remained completely clothed. She put her hands on the bed, pushing herself upward a few inches. The fantasy was over, reality firmly back in its place. The need to protect herself overrode the longing to be with him one last time before he left.

Nate rolled to the side, propped up on an elbow. "I promised myself I wouldn't let this go too far. I can't make love to you, Maggie. No matter how much I want to."

His explanation fell flat. He didn't really want her and she'd been foolish to indulge in rolling around on the bed with him. Things were far too complicated. He probably thought she'd come up here with this very purpose in mind. Her cheeks burned at the thought.

"I don't recall asking you to."

Her icy words cooled the room considerably.

"No, you didn't."

She pulled away, stood beside the bed glaring down at him, angry at herself for falling under his spell yet again. He'd been the one to tug her down and kiss her first. To what purpose? Surely he didn't feel like he had to pretend anymore.

"What were you trying to do, anyway? Distract me from the fact that you've been pretending all this time? Or just smooth things over to soothe my hurt feelings? I assure you, I'm over it."

His nostrils flared but he didn't move from his position. "That's not it at all. I wanted to show you that despite every-thing, *this* much was real." His lip curled with the bite of sarcasm. "At least it was for *me*."

How dare he. He'd been the one to lie and pretend and she'd done nothing but be honest with him. Brutally honest, she remembered, her cheeks burning. Now he was accusing her of using him? Declaring his intentions to be pure while challenging that hers were anything but? And then pushing her away in the end anyway.

"When will you be wrapping this thing up?"

Nate pushed up off his elbow, sitting up in the bed. His brows pulled together in the middle.

"Tomorrow, then if it goes as planned, transport the day after. Why?"

Maggie smiled coldly. "Then I only have one more day of doubting every word that comes out of your mouth."

She instantly regretted her statement, but gathering every last shred of pride she had left, she swept from the room, shutting the door behind her.

CHAPTER ELEVEN

THE coffee was brewed, but Maggie stared out the kitchen window, seeing little in the predawn hours. She'd slept fitfully, waking every few minutes, worrying, thinking too much. Finally at four she'd risen, dressed and put on coffee. She'd sleep later. She'd have lots of time for sleep.

Nothing made sense. She'd been mad about the lies; she wasn't anymore. She was proud of who he was, but it scared her to death. She cared about him, more each day, but she wanted him gone. Wanted this over.

Wanted to come out of it unhurt, and the longer it went on, the more she was sure that was impossible.

Her head tilted as she heard sounds echoing through the upstairs. Nate was up. He was packing his things to walk away, leaving forever. She should be glad things hadn't gone further than they had. In her head she knew that was true. But all her heart felt was an aching loss at an opportunity missed; a return to a life that was lackluster and plain. Most of all she was sorry she'd lashed out at him last night. He had enough to worry about without her throwing around accusations. It didn't solve anything.

She couldn't stand the thought of sitting here, waiting for news throughout the day. Listening for his footsteps when he came back…or didn't. No, it would be better if they said their goodbyes now.

He'd be down soon. Maggie took out a frying pan and got eggs from the fridge. The last thing she could do for him was make him a decent breakfast. It had nothing to do with any service she was being paid for; nothing to do with him being a guest in her home. It was, simply, the last caring act she could give him.

The eggs were delicately done when his steps echoed on the stairs. Maggie turned off the burner and went to the cupboard to fetch a plate. When she spun back around, she froze.

He was magnificent.

There was no other word for it and it frightened her almost as much as it exhilarated her. There was no hiding who he was from her this morning. He stood in the breach between hallway and kitchen, dressed in his customary jeans. But everything else seemed different. A long-sleeved shirt hugged the muscles of his chest and arms, and for the first time she caught sight of his USMS badge. It hung from a silver chain around his neck, a plain star within a circle with the words "United States Marshal" engraved in the perimeter. In his hands he carried more gear—a vest with several pockets, and two holsters. They made him seem so very large, imposing. Only she couldn't help but notice the dark circles beneath his eyes and a stab of worry went through her. He needed to be alert this morning. Was it her fault he wasn't rested?

"I made you breakfast."

It was all she could think to say. Anything more would open a door she didn't want to walk through today. They both knew what he was going to do. They both knew that he was leaving. There was nothing more to say without bringing up recriminations and regrets.

He put his gear on an empty chair and sat down as she placed the plate at *his* place. "Are you joining me?"

Food was the last thing on her mind and she didn't think she could stomach it anyway. "I'll just have some coffee," she murmured.

Gone was the easy banter they'd shared over mealtimes. Gone was the subtle flirting, the friendly smiles and eye contact. The sound of his knife and fork were amplified through the kitchen and each clink was torture. She got up from the table and refilled his coffee cup.

"Maggie, I'm sorry about everything I've put you through. I've been incredibly unfair."

The emptiness crawled in again. His job came first and that was how it should be, she realized. And she didn't want anything permanent from him, so why did it hurt so much?

"Don't say anything. We both know it's what you do. We knew all along that this moment would come."

"This isn't easy for me, Maggie," he said quietly. "I wasn't counting on finding you."

Her fingers tightened on the back of a chair. He didn't understand how she felt the need to pull back. To save herself from more pain. Seeing him hurt was bad enough. Finding out he'd been shot was another story. A fresh bandage shone on his forehead, a bright reminder of the consequences of his job. It was too close, too fresh. Even after all these years. She couldn't handle the danger. She knew it as surely as she was breathing.

"Maggie, please. Talk to me."

She lifted her head, her vision blurred with angry tears. "And say what, Nate? You could have been killed! And don't shrug it off, because I know what it's like, okay? You're not the only one keeping secrets!"

His lips dropped open as her voice raised.

"I don't know what you mean. What secrets?"

She snorted, looking away for a moment. "What am I thinking. It was probably all in the background check you did."

"What on earth are you talking about?" He came forward, placing his hand on the countertop. "You're not making any sense!"

She put her hands on her hips. "Tell me you don't know, then. Tell me you don't have a clue that my husband died because he was shot on the job!"

The words came out so quickly she had no chance to hold them back. She'd never hidden the fact that Tom had died, but she'd also never let on he'd been shot.

His body stiffened. "He what? I swear to God, Maggie, I didn't know."

"How could you not know? Stop lying to me!"

The outburst rang through the silence. "Maggie, I'm telling you truthfully. I didn't know about your husband. I only knew you were a widow. I promise. Grant didn't tell me anything more." He came forward, reached out to touch her. "It explains so much. Why you held back. Why you were so upset about the gun and the shooting. What Grant said last night about the file. I never knew. How did it happen?"

Maggie remembered the look of confusion on Nate's face the previous evening when Grant had mentioned Tom's death. Perhaps he hadn't known after all.

But talking about it still hurt. It still brought back all the bitter memories of that night and she had to swallow the bile that had risen in her throat thinking about what she'd been put through.

"He was a security guard for one of the oil companies. An activist didn't look kindly on their policies. Tom paid the price for that. We paid the price, too, living with the inquiry, living without him."

"I'm so sorry, Maggie. Such a senseless way to lose a husband and a father."

She warned him off with a raised hand, blinking furiously. "Don't. Please, don't be kind. I can't handle any more."

The last thing she needed now was sympathy. Her eyes darted up to the clock, ticking along steadily as if they had all the time in the world. But they didn't. He had to go, and soon.

"You'd better finish your breakfast."

Her cold tone put an end to further conversation. Nate sat. Maggie didn't know how he could eat, her own stomach was tied in knots over the whole thing. She supposed this was an ordinary day for him. Perhaps it was routine for him. Get up, get dressed, eat and go to work. For her, this would never be normal.

Finally it was over. Nate rose from the table and brought his plate to the sink.

"Thank you, Maggie."

The words were deep and hushed in the quiet. Maggie closed her eyes, wanting to get goodbye over with and yet desperate to cling to every second she had with him.

"You're welcome."

Her throat thickened so that it was difficult to swallow. It was silly, she told herself, that she'd come to care so much about someone in a few short weeks. Someone who had misrepresented himself and lied to her. But she was smart enough to realize it wasn't that easy. Without intending to, Nate had broken through so many barriers she'd erected since Tom's death. She'd started to feel again—to want, to need. For a few glorious moments, it had been bliss.

But in the end it wasn't worth the thud and she knew it.

"Nate, I…"

She turned but he was gone.

She found him near the front door. He'd shrugged into his vest and she could do nothing but stare. Never in her life had she been so glad to see Kevlar and she prayed it would keep him safe. Each pocket contained some piece of equipment he would need. The marshals crest appeared again on a flap that lay over his heart. As she watched, he propped his foot on a stair step and fastened a holster over his thigh, his movements practiced and efficient.

From his pack he took a handgun, placed it in the holster and straightened. When he did he spied her watching him and their eyes clashed, held.

"You look so different," she whispered. He was a stranger yet not. He was the man she was attracted to, but so much more.

"This is who I am, Maggie."

"You're more than that, Nate. Don't think I don't know it." Her lower lip quivered, she bit down to stop it.

Five more minutes. That was all she had to get through.

"I want you to take it all, Nate. When you leave this morning that has to be it."

His gaze fell on something by the front closet and she turned her head. His duffel waited, already packed.

It was what she wanted. It was. That didn't mean seeing him walk away wasn't going to hurt.

She met his gaze. He waited, strong and steady. How she wished she were brave enough to take a step forward, to tell him what it had meant to her, knowing him. To feel his arms around her one more time, to breathe in his scent.

"I've got to go, Maggie."

"I know."

They were whispering now. He shouldered his pack and picked up his duffel. Put his hand on the doorknob. And paused.

Maggie's body trembled. How could this be it? How could he walk out with nothing more than a goodbye? Yet to say more would take more than she could give.

The bags slid to the floor and he reached out, pulling her close and pressing his mouth to hers.

Her heart leaped as she wrapped her arms around his neck, pressing as closely as she could though the thickness of his vest held them apart. The hard metal of the gun on his leg dug into her thigh; she didn't care. She just wanted to tell him at last how much he meant to her despite the complications.

"Oh God, did you sleep at all?" she wailed, pulling back and cradling his jaws in her hands, her thumbs touching the shadowed half-moons beneath his eyes.

"I couldn't. I could only think of you, Maggie." He crushed his mouth to hers again. When they finally came up for air, his voice was raw. "I wish you'd never left my room last night."

Her heart thundered. She'd started to wish it, too, even knowing it was wrong. How was it that she could be so afraid for him this way—wrapped in Kevlar and strapped with weapons—and yet be so fatally attracted?

"I'm sorry, Nate. I'm not mad anymore, I promise." She gulped in air, trying to control the urge to cry.

She couldn't go through this again. His lips touched her eyelids gently and his hands cupped her face. She knew this had to be goodbye. He needed to go, to get what he'd come for and finish it. There was no sense in going over again what couldn't be changed.

"I've got to go," he repeated. "I just couldn't leave without you knowing…" He lowered his forehead to hers. "Damn, Maggie. This wasn't just some assignment and we both know it. I'm sorry I hurt you. More sorry than you know."

"How can I be angry with you?" She tried to smile but it faltered. Soon his touch would be gone for good. "You did what you had to, Nate, I understand that."

"It wasn't just the job."

His breath warmed her cheek and she closed her eyes, swallowing. Oh Lord, this was turning into the farewell she'd craved and dreaded all at once.

"I wanted to protect you, you and Jen. I see every day what men like Pete can do. I'd die before I let him hurt either of you more than he already has."

Her blood chilled. The danger was real and imminent. Yet

she was proud. "Do you know how rare you are?" At the shake of his head, she persisted. "You are. You take responsibility for *right* when most of us shy away."

"But...you want me to walk away."

"And it's the only thing to do." His thumb grazed her cheek and she fought back tears. "Now go. Grant will be waiting."

He picked the bags up again and opened the door. And just as quickly dropped them again.

And faced her, looking as serious as she'd ever seen him.

"I love you, Maggie."

The words stopped her cold.

He loved her? Maggie stepped away. No, no. They'd said all that they needed to say. He didn't mean it. He was supposed to be going to meet Grant. They were supposed to have their goodbye and she'd put her life back together. It was all supposed to be temporary.

But in a moment he changed everything with those three little words. This was different. *Love* was different. Love hurt. She didn't have room for love.

She turned her back. "You're just reacting to today, that's all. What you need to do, what happens next. You can't love me...you've only known me a few weeks. You're just getting caught up in the moment."

"No, I don't think so."

Maggie faced him. This wasn't happening. He couldn't love her. It was supposed to be a beautiful goodbye, that was all.

"Nate, don't do this. I can't love you. You live thousands of miles away. And my life is here, with Jen."

"I know that." He took a step closer, unwilling to let her get away. "It's confusing, but it doesn't change how I feel. Or that I had to tell you."

Something inside her broke, a quiet snap that pierced the dam of denial. She'd told herself for so long that no one would ever love her again, but she'd been wrong. Nate loved her. It would never work, but simply knowing it filled her with a warmth she'd long forgotten.

She pushed it aside, that lovely joy and replaced it with the stark reality of what he did for a living.

"What is it you want, Nate?"

He came closer still until Maggie felt the cool wood of the banister pressing against her back.

"I want you. I want all of you, Maggie. I don't know how, but I can't let you go."

"You're talking about a future beyond today."

He was so compelling. His weight was balanced squarely over both feet, a pillar of strength and fortitude. He was everything a woman could ever want, so why was she determined to run in the opposite direction?

Because she knew what happened to people she loved, and Nate already faced enough risk every day. She wouldn't survive going through that again.

"Marry me, Maggie Taylor."

Her mouth dropped open for the briefest of seconds before she forced it shut again. Everything in her felt like weeping, only she couldn't. She couldn't fall apart now.

"Oh, Nate, you know I can't." She turned away.

"Why not?" He grabbed her wrist and turned her back around.

Maggie set her lips, looking from his fingers circling her wrist up into his oh-so-earnest eyes. "First of all, my business and home are here."

"Sell it and start a new one. I can sell my house and we'll buy a new place on the water."

She shook her head. "Jen goes to school here."

"Bring her along. She can transfer her credits. Or she can go to school here and fly to Florida on holidays. Most kids would kill for spring break in the Sunshine State."

He was tearing down her arguments one by one and panic threaded through her veins. Why had he ever come here?

She'd learned how to live her life her own way and he waltzed in changing everything. She couldn't handle that. Didn't know how to do it.

And the fact remained that she was a forty-plus widow with a grown daughter and he was nearly a decade younger, just embarking on that phase of his life. It wouldn't be fair to either of them.

"What about children?"

Nate paused and Maggie knew she'd hit a spot. She grabbed at it, persisted. "Don't you want children, Nate? I already have Jen. I'm forty-two years old. And look at you. You're in your prime. Thirty-three and ready to start a family. And I don't want any more babies, not at my age. I'm sure of that."

"You're playing the age card. And that's not fair. I don't give a damn that you're older than I am. I never have, and you know it."

But she shook her head, stopping him. "No, I'm thinking ahead. It wouldn't be fair to you."

She skirted past him and into the den. It was true. She didn't want to have kids in her forties. Didn't want to be sixty and going through the teenage years, or trying to pay for college as she was retiring. But she couldn't blame Nate for wanting a family. It was another in a long list of reasons why it would be better to walk away. Perhaps one he could actually relate to.

"I don't want kids."

He followed her into the den. Maggie reached out and picked up a knickknack, turning it over and over in her hands. "You say that now, but…"

"No, Maggie. I don't want kids." His voice was firm, definite. "I've seen too many who weren't loved. I have nieces and nephews and I love them, but I've never wanted any of my own. I'd rather put my energies into helping ones who need someone to care. I'd hate to do that and not have energy for my own at home. That wouldn't be fair. So I'm okay with not having children."

He closed the gap between them. "Do you have any other roadblocks you'd like to erect? Because none of it changes the fact that I love you."

She could throw out the fact that he was asking her to uproot her life while his remained unchanged, but she knew she could never ask him to change who he was. Perhaps he'd change jobs, but he'd always be in law enforcement. There was no point even bringing it up. Not when she knew the real issue was that she never wanted to love and lose like she already had too many times in her life. Today had shown her that losing Nate would hurt. How much more would that be magnified after months, or even years of marriage? How could she stand waiting at home every day, wondering if he was all right, wondering if this would be the day he wouldn't come home? How could she stand to have her heart broken a second time?

There was only one way. And in her heart she silently apologized for it before she opened her mouth, knowing that while it hurt him, having to tell it was tearing her apart.

"I will never love anyone the way I loved Tom. I'm sorry, Nate."

He stopped cold and her heart wept as the light went out of his eyes.

"That's it then. I can't compete with a ghost."

"What did you expect me to say?" she whispered. "You know me better than anyone has known me in a long time. You had to know I wouldn't pick up and leave my life behind. Not for…"

The pause said more than the words ever could have.

She couldn't love and lose so horribly. Not again.

"Please, Nate, don't make this harder than it already is." Everything in her longed to reach out and touch him but she couldn't afford the moment of weakness. "I can't love you the way you want me to."

"I can't argue with that." He ran a hand over his short hair, leaving little bits in spikes. "I can argue with logistics. I can't make you feel something you don't. I misread."

He shrugged his shoulders, inhaled. "That's it then. After we pick up Pete I'll be spending the night in town. In the morning I'll be leaving with Grant."

His eyes, dark with disappointment, caught hers one last time. "I know it's not nearly enough, but thank you, Maggie. For everything."

He turned and walked out the door, and she let him go, wishing he'd do it quickly now instead of prolonging the pain.

He stepped off the porch and toward the SUV that would take him away from her.

"Nate?" She couldn't help calling out to him as he lifted the tailgate and put his gear inside.

"Be safe."

He raised a hand in farewell and slid behind the wheel. Maggie closed the door and walked numbly back to the kitchen, putting his dirty dishes in the dishwasher for the last time.

She'd thought that once he was gone the tears would come, but they were locked deep inside, too deep for her to give them license. She sat at the empty kitchen table, closing her eyes.

After a time she rose and went to do the morning chores, anything to keep herself occupied. Returning to his room was another reminder of how close they'd come to making love last night and Maggie regretted how she'd acted. She wished now she had that beautiful memory to carry her through, but she hadn't been able to let down the wall she'd built around herself. When he'd stopped them, she'd convinced herself he was rejecting her.

But what she'd really been afraid of was herself. And now she'd hurt him without intending to.

But Nate had broken through her barriers anyway. She finished making his bed and turned, only to find the St.

Christopher medallion he always wore, twined around the base of the bedside lamp. She sat on the edge of the bed where she'd lain with him, holding the heavy pewter in her fingers. Fighting the feeling of superstition that he should be without his good luck charm today of all days.

And when she realized how long she'd been sitting there, she fastened it around her neck. Tomorrow she'd put it in the trinket box she kept of reminders from those she'd loved. For that's what he'd done to her.

For the first time in fifteen years, she was in love.

And he was in love with her.

And now he was gone. Even knowing he wasn't coming back, she wouldn't rest until it was over and she knew he was safe.

CHAPTER TWELVE

WHEN the car door slammed, she leaped up in anticipation.

But it wasn't Nate's SUV. Instead it was Grant's cruiser and he walked, alone, toward Maggie's front door.

"No," she breathed, a hand lifting to cover her mouth. Everything in her body went icily cold. She shook her head, backing away from the door. *Not again.*

Grant took off his cap and tucked it under his arm before ringing the doorbell.

She couldn't answer it. She pressed both her hands to her face, refusing to touch the doorknob. She couldn't listen to him say the words that she knew would come next. Oh God, she'd done that once before and it had blown her whole world apart. Tears seared the backs of her eyelids as she remembered the officer telling her Tom had been killed. And this morning…

The doorbell rang again. "Maggie?"

A single sob escaped. This morning Nate had told her he loved her and she'd told him that she wouldn't love anyone the way she'd loved Tom. She'd cast him off and sent him into a dangerous situation believing she didn't love him at all.

But she did. She loved him so much she refused to believe in a world where he didn't exist.

"Maggie, for God's sake, open the door!" Grant shouted now and for some reason the command jolted her to action and she turned the knob, pulling the door open. And saw the smear of blood on his shirt.

He took one look at her face and his own gentled. "You're pale. Come sit down."

She shook her head. "Just say it, Grant. Please, just say it and get it over with."

His eyes were kind, so kind and she hated him for it.

"He's not dead, if that's what you're thinking."

Her breath came out in a rush. "I think I'll sit down now." She made it to the first chair on the veranda and her knees gave out.

Grant knelt before her, chafing the sides of her thighs with his hands. The connection gave her something to focus on.

"Thanks to you, and to Jen, we found a stash of drugs, money and weapons beneath the barn. And we were right in bringing him in, and none too soon. We found the cell. There were restraints. We're checking it now for DNA evidence."

The thought that it could have been Jen in there momentarily made Maggie's heart stop.

"But that's not all, Maggie. I'm just going to tell it to you straight, okay?" He squeezed her hand and met her gaze squarely. "I came alone because Nate was shot and he's been taken to hospital."

"How bad is it?" She pulled away, twisting her pale fingers together, trying to hold it together and absorb everything Grant was telling her. Trying not to panic. Trying not to act like her whole world was crumbling around her.

"He's alive, but beyond that I really don't know."

Dread and fear froze her.

"I…" She halted; this was Grant whom she barely knew, yet she had to say it. "I turned him away this morning. I was wrong to do that, Grant." Her words came out childlike and contrite.

"I can take you to the hospital. Grab what you need and I'll wait."

Maggie nodded dumbly. Her only thought now was seeing Nate and telling him she loved him before it was too late. He couldn't leave her, not when the lie was there between them. Not before she had a chance to make it right. She got to her feet woodenly, stopping only to grab her purse and lock the door.

Grant opened the door to his cruiser and helped her inside. He got in the driver's side and called something in on his radio before reversing and pulling out of the lane.

He didn't spare speed and she was glad of it as they hit the main road. A call came back on the radio and Maggie tried to interpret it, but she couldn't seem to make sense of the words.

Grant answered back. Then turned to Maggie.

"Nate's stable for the moment, but they're airlifting him to Edmonton."

Maggie didn't move; it was simply another layer of shock. He was ill enough that he had to be transferred to a bigger hospital. He had to hold on until she got there, he simply had to. Flashes hit behind her eyes, of arriving at the hospital and finding Tom in a coma. All the things she wanted to say to him were meaningless. And then he'd been gone.

Nate had to hold on. He had to.

"I'm going to take you there, Maggie. Pete's in custody and not going anywhere. And odd as it seems…Nate's my partner. We'll go together."

Maggie sat back in the seat, surprised when Grant turned on his lights but not the siren, taking the highway north to the capital city. She didn't know what to say to him…her normal ability for small talk had evaporated.

But Grant suddenly seemed able to fill the gap.

"Maggie, I looked into what happened with Tom. It wasn't as simple as him just being shot. And a thing like that…I can see how it would change a person. I know you got to the hospital too late. And the investigation was no picnic…especially on top of all the grief you must have been feeling."

His clear eyes were unrelenting as he turned his head to look at her, like he could see her thoughts. The notion didn't unsettle her now, not like it used to.

"It's normal to be scared. And there are no guarantees. But…for what it's worth…I think it would be a crying shame to walk away from something, from *someone* who loves you as much as Nate does because you were afraid. You'd miss out on something wonderful, don't you think?"

Maggie tried to swallow around the lump in her throat. He made it sound so easy. Nothing about loving Nate Griffith was easy. When she'd said she couldn't love him like she had Tom, it hadn't been a complete truth. She did love him and it scared her to death. She loved him so much that she couldn't imagine losing him. That was what she'd meant and she'd deliberately let him draw his own conclusion as to her meaning.

"It can be damned lonely being a cop. Sometimes it's family that keeps us grounded. Wives put up with a lot, but…"

He kept his eyes on the road, smoothly passing a tractor-trailer and moving back into the right lane again. "Sometimes having that anchor keeps us going." He cleared his throat and looked back at her. "Think about it," Grant concluded.

There were so many questions. She had the bed and breakfast and a daughter and nearly crippling fears about being involved with such a man.

How badly had he been hurt?

And how could she let him do this alone?

At the hospital, Grant sidestepped a news crew, which had already arrived. An officer being shot was news and Maggie had no desire to be captured on camera. As Grant snuck them through, Maggie stared at the TV crew openmouthed, the lingering sense of déjà vu pervading again. A nurse directed them to the Intensive Care Unit and from there to a waiting room outside the closed, quiet doors.

When the time came, Grant went in first. Maggie tried to straighten her hair, make herself look presentable. But Grant was back within a few minutes, unsmiling.

"He's still unconscious."

"I want to see him."

Grant nodded. "The doctor says it's all right. I'll take you to him."

Once inside Nate's room, Maggie forgot all about Grant. Nate, her Nate, lay pale and prone on the bed. Tubes ran from his nose and more from his arm. His lashes were still on his gray cheeks, and as she watched, one finger twitched against the blanket.

But that was all.

"He lost a lot of blood," a nurse whispered, padding into the room softly and deftly adding a bag to his IV stand. "It's perfectly okay that he's not awake."

Maggie's shoulders slumped as she pulled up a chair to the bed, as quietly as she could. "Thank you. Is it all right if I wait?"

"We usually only let visitors in for a few minutes."

"I just want to sit with him. I don't want him to wake up alone."

The nurse looked at Maggie a long time, then at Grant, still in uniform, still with the stripe of dried blood.

"As long as you sit quietly."

Maggie nodded.

Grant stepped forward. "I'm going to get us some coffee."

She nodded dumbly; coffee was the last thing she wanted but didn't have it in her to argue.

And then the room was quiet, except for the soft beep of a monitor.

She looked at Nate's slumbering form. It was clear from the position and bandaging that the shot had hit his leg. A thousand questions flooded her brain…how bad was it, would he be permanently injured, did his head injury of yesterday

ffect his health now, did they get the bullet out, did it hit the
rtery…but all of them were subverted by a single thought:
lease don't leave me.

Grant brought coffee; stayed awhile, but in the end he had
o return home. There was paperwork to be done and arrange-
nents to be made now that Nate would not be transporting
arding himself. With a promise to come back as soon as he
:ould, Grant left and it was only the two of them. Maggie
:hafed Nate's hand between hers.

"Hold on, Nate. Please hold on."

The haze was white, then gray, and then blurry shapes came
nto focus.

Nate swallowed—his mouth was bone-dry—and realized
:hat the beeping sound he heard wasn't his alarm clock, but
a monitor that was attached to somewhere on his body.

He was in the hospital, and in that moment, he remembered
exactly what had happened. The sound of the shot and the explosion of pain, and he instinctively stiffened. Only tensing
brought the pain back and he forced himself to relax.

And when he did, he realized there was a mop of dark hair
on the bed beside his hip.

Maggie.

He turned his head a half inch and tried to whisper her
name, but nothing came out. He sighed and lay his head back
against the pillow, closing his eyes, marveling that she was
there, sleeping on his hospital bed.

He was a marshal, he knew that. He also knew that never
in his life had he felt as strong a connection as he did to
Maggie. He loved her, and it was different than anything he'd
experienced before. Nothing about Maggie was easy. Perhaps that was why she was so perfect for him.

Why in the world couldn't she see that?

He sighed, knowing he couldn't place one iota of blame

on her. Not after today. Before today he could have insisted that he wouldn't get hurt. He could have told her about all the cases he'd been on where he'd come out without a scratch.

But after today...there was no denying it. What he did had risks. And after the way her husband had died, hell, he couldn't blame her for not taking that on again.

He moved a hand until it could touch the soft silk of her hair and he rubbed a few strands between his fingers. She had said this morning that she couldn't love anyone as she'd loved her husband. But that wasn't what had made him walk away.

He had sensed her desperation and panic, and he knew he couldn't pressure her into taking the chance. It wasn't fair to ask that of her, not after all she'd been through already. She'd already risked and lost everything. She'd fought him so hard this morning that he had known he couldn't hurt her more than she'd already been hurt.

Yet here she was. Waiting for him in a hospital room. He couldn't imagine how difficult this must be for her. He licked his lips.

"Maggie," he managed this time, his voice a rough croak.

She lifted her head slowly, one cheek red from being pressed against the blanket, her hair untidy and she began to tuck it behind her ears by what he knew now was force of habit.

"Nate."

As soon as she said his name, her eyes welled with tears and a few slid past her lashes and down her cheeks. To Nate, she'd never looked more beautiful. Her voice was soft and musical like he remembered. He'd heard it enough times in his head. Played it over and over like a favorite song, only he never tired of it.

He raised his hand, cupped her cheek and closed his eyes. Home.

This was how it felt then. Everything he had known was missing came down to this very moment. Home wasn't his place in Florida or the Haven or a place at all. It was Maggie. Maggie was the home he'd been looking for.

He looked at her tear-stained face, drawn with worry and anxiety and he knew he'd been wrong to propose. Every argument she'd put up had been justified but easily disputed. Until the end. Maggie would never intentionally hurt anyone, so for her to say what she had, told him exactly how frightened she was. As much as he loved her, he knew that her feelings for him only caused her pain. The kindest thing he could do is accept her words and let her go.

"What are you doing here?"

Maggie linked her fingers with his. "Grant brought me. You're in Edmonton. You were shot."

His eyes widened. She'd said the last without flinching at all.

"I remember. Pete?"

"Is in custody. Grant was here…he brought me…but he left several hours ago to look after things. He's coming back in the morning."

Nate nodded. "I'm sorry I worried you. I'll be fine, though. You don't have to stay."

"Just try to get rid of me and see what happens."

Nate's mouth dropped open and for the first time, Maggie smiled.

It made him hope, even as pain shot from his leg into his gut. But hope was all he had, and he didn't want to squander a second of it. "I'll take you for as long as you'll let me."

"How does forever sound?"

Maggie laughed at the expression on his face. He hadn't been expecting that. But she'd had a good long time to think, and cry, and worry, and pray. And every single time she came up with the same answer: Any time with Nate was better than no time at all.

He winced and she stood up, glancing at the IV bags. "I'll call the nurse. You are nearly due for pain medication, I think."

He stopped her. "No, not yet. They'll put me to sleep. And right now I want to see you."

Her body warmed. All day she'd had images of what he was doing and they blended with the memories of the night Tom was killed. And then her fears had come true. And with them, truth—she loved him. But she hadn't known what to do with it.

Only hours spent at his bedside had shown her what was real, and right.

"Let me get you some water, at least," Maggie chided. "You need fluids. The doctor said so."

She wanted to kiss him but wasn't sure if it was the right thing or not. In the end she waited so long she just smiled and scooted from the room.

She was coming back from the ice machine when she spied Jen, curled up in a chair in the waiting room.

"Honey?"

Jen came awake instantly, standing up and tucking her hair in the same way her mother often did. "How's Nate? Is he all right?"

Maggie nodded, going into the room and sitting down next to Jen. "He just woke up. He's okay. In a lot of pain, but fine."

Jen's shoulders relaxed and Maggie's brows pinched together.

"I didn't expect to see you quite this soon. How long have you been here, waiting?"

"A few hours. Constable Simms called me at the dorm and told me what happened. Said maybe you'd like some company. But when I got here and peeked into Nate's room, you were asleep. So I came out here to wait." She reached over and took Maggie's hand in hers. "How are you holding up?"

"Me?"

Jen nodded. "Yeah. You. This couldn't have been easy for you, Mom. Not after Dad."

Maggie wiped her lashes; how many times was she going to cry today anyway? "When did you grow up so fast?"

"I dunno." Her old grin was back, impish. "Fast enough to see that you're in love with him."

Maggie's head snapped back to stare at her daughter. Jen's dark ponytail bobbed as she nodded her head. "You are. I knew when I came home there'd been something between you. You were different. And the way he held you last night…"

Maggie's heart thumped hard as she looked into Jen's eyes, ones so like her father's.

"How would you feel about that?" She posed the question carefully.

"Dang, Mom, you've been alone too long. And Nate's cool, you know? He's one of the good guys." Her cheeks pinked. "He took care of Pete, didn't he?"

"Yes, yes, he did," Maggie murmured.

"Well, then, I think you'd be a fool to let him get away."

Maggie couldn't help but laugh a little. "You do, do you?"

"I do. Now, do you think it'd be okay if I said hi to Nate and then went home? I have a nine-thirty class in the morning."

"I think that would be fine."

They went into the room together, Maggie holding the plastic cup of ice chips and Jen with her hands in her pockets. But when she saw Nate, she went over to the bed, leaned over and kissed his cheek. "Thank you," she said quietly. "Thank you for helping me. For helping us." She threw a quick glance at her mother.

"You're welcome," he whispered, his voice too hoarse for anything stronger. "And we owe you, too, Jen. I'm proud of you."

Jen squeezed his hand. "I'm going to leave you two alone, but I'll come back after class tomorrow. Do you want anything? The only thing worse than dorm food is hospital food. I can sneak it in."

Maggie swallowed thickly. It was so much like a family. Yet she'd turned Nate away just hours ago. Would he believe her now, when she was ready to tell the truth?

"Chocolate pudding," he murmured. "I love chocolate pudding."

Jen laughed. "Talk to you soon," she said in farewell, before closing the door behind her, leaving them alone in the dim light.

He patted the bed beside him. "Come here," he commanded, his voice still weak but warm.

She put the cup of chips on the table beside the bed and perched on the mattress gently, trying to disturb as little as possible.

He took her hand in his. The hospital band chafed at her a bit, but his other hand was connected to the IV.

"Let's go back. Why don't you tell me what you meant about the forever bit. Because this morning you were prepared to never see me again."

It had hurt her to hurt him. And during the long day, waiting for news, she'd looked around her. What did she have at Mountain Haven? Nothing more than a list of excuses. A house, a home. A garden and a roof that needed repairs. She'd considered it her safe place but now knew she'd only been hiding.

She had a daughter who was already moving away, embarking on a new stage in her life. And what had Maggie done? She'd let her fears dictate her actions, letting her grief have control. She'd been so afraid of what might happen that she'd pushed away the one true thing.

Only Grant had shown up and had told her Nate was hurt, and none of it mattered anymore. Saying goodbye had done nothing to quell her feelings, or her worry. She knew in that moment that she wanted to stand by him *through* it, not pretend it didn't exist.

"You left, and I waited. It was awful, not knowing. But not near as awful as seeing your blood on Grant's uniform. Or hearing him say you'd been shot."

"I'm sorry I put you through that. I realized this morning that I had asked too much of you. It's never easy being married to a cop, for anyone. And after what you've already been through...I should have realized."

Maggie's heart skipped. "Are you saying you don't want to marry me?"

His eyes met hers, the blue-green glittering darkly in the pale light. "That's not the issue. The truth is, I should have been more sensitive. I knew all along how you felt and I pressured you anyway."

"Maybe I needed it." She straightened her shoulders. After all she'd been through today, it wasn't as hard being brave as she thought it would be.

"I love you, Nate."

Saying the words, finally saying them, filled her with something so surprising she didn't know what to do with it. It was like everything in her expanded, awakened. There was power in it, beautiful power she hadn't expected.

She ignored the trembling in her hands and gripped his fingers. She longed to touch him, wished he weren't hooked up to monitors and medication. Instead she had to make do with their tenuous connection.

"It's true. I do love you, and I'm sorry I let my fear dictate how I acted. I think I need to explain," she murmured, her voice shaking a little. He'd opened his heart to her that morning, now it was her turn. And she wanted to do it. It didn't mean it was easy.

"Losing Tom was the hardest thing I ever did," she began. "Not only was he shot, but he killed a man in the process and he was made out to be both hero and villain. Like my parents, I'd loved him and counted on him and he was suddenly gone. I had Jen and Mike to look after and I had to do it alone. I swore from that point that I would never give myself over to that sort of hope again. It hurt too much to lose. That's what I meant. I couldn't love like that again, not because I didn't love you but because the need to protect myself was too strong to give in to it."

"I knew that."

"You did?"

"All the other arguments were logical and easily remedied. But that one…I could see how afraid you were. And I knew you were too precious to hurt that way again. So I walked away, knowing at least I wouldn't be the one to cause you that sort of pain."

Tears flooded her eyes. "You knew."

"Of course I knew. Did you think I didn't get it? We got to know each other over the last weeks. I fell in love with you."

"When Grant said you were hurt, I knew without a doubt. I had to tell you that I had been afraid to love you. Afraid of what it meant to change my life for you. Afraid to live."

"Oh, Maggie."

"I want to live, Nate. I didn't realize I wasn't…didn't realize I could…until you came along. You changed everything. None of it matters without you."

"But I'm still a marshal. Look at me. I was really hurt today. I still have a job to do. And I'm not sure I'd be happy doing anything else."

"I'd never ask you to."

"What about being afraid? You were so angry when you discovered who I was. When you thought Jen might be hurt and when you found out I'd been shot."

"And I'll still worry. But I'll worry whether we're together or not. Grant said something to me today. He said that sometimes family is the glue that holds you together. I want to be that for you. Don't you see, Nate?" Her lip quivered but she kept on. "You always put yourself in danger. I want to be your safe place. The way that you've become mine. I always thought I was safer in my little corner. But I was so wrong."

"I love you, Maggie. And I'd do anything to be able to hold you right now."

Six inches lay between his body and the edge of the bed,

but Maggie didn't care. She stretched out, aligning herself with his good side, her cheek resting against his shoulder. "Will this do?"

His voice rumbled, slow and sexy in her ear. "For now."

He was warm and strong and for the first time in nearly half her life she felt exactly where she belonged. Now, safe in his arms, the relief flooded her, and she finally let the tears come as she wept against his shoulder.

"Don't cry, Maggie. Please don't."

His voice, that smooth baritone with the hint of grit rumbled from his chest against her cheek. She shook her head against the cotton of his shirt. "I was sure of how I felt. But I also knew I might be too late. I was so afraid I'd be too late to tell you…"

"You're not."

He caught sight of the chain around her neck and the medal hanging from it. "You found my St. Christopher."

She nodded. "I was going to put it in my special box of memories. Only it's not a memory. I'm not ready to give up on the future yet."

He squeezed her. "Oh, Maggie. I'm so glad." He released her and she lifted her chin so she could gaze into his eyes. Those beautiful, turquoise eyes that had somehow seen her from the very beginning.

"Is this a good time to ask you again?"

Her heart tripped over itself.

"Will you marry me, Maggie? We can figure the rest out later. Just say yes."

"Yes." And she shifted a little, pushing herself up on the bed so she could kiss him properly.

When she pulled away, she stayed propped up on an elbow. "Is your house big enough for one more? Maybe two?"

"You mean in Florida? You'd move there to be with me?"

A tiny smile worked its way up her cheek. "I would. I can

sell Mountain Haven. And find a job there, or open a business. I think I might become very partial to palm trees."

"You would really give up your life here?"

"I would."

"What about Jen?"

"Didn't you already solve these arguments this morning?" She teased him. "Jen's finding her own way. In another few years she'll be on her own completely. She's becoming an adult and making her own decisions. I'll leave it up to her what she wants to do."

He closed his eyes and Maggie was shocked to see a tear gather at the corner of his eye. "Nate? What is it? Should I get the doctor?"

He shook his head. "No…it's just…" He opened his eyes again, struggling with emotion. "This morning when I was shot I thought I was going to die. And now here you are. It doesn't seem possible. I lied to you, Maggie, and led you on and did nothing but confuse your life. And here you are ready to give up everything for me. It doesn't seem right. It should be me making the sacrifices."

"No, Nate. You changed everything for me. Why should you give up your life? I'm not giving up anything, not really. Because I wasn't really living. I was only existing. You did that. Only you."

"You actually mean that?"

"I do. I want to be with you. I know a part of me will always be afraid you're not coming back. But I can't sacrifice all the good stuff. Living without you isn't living at all. It's just putting myself in a box and hoping I'll never get hurt. And it's not what I want anymore."

"I want to touch you, do all the right things," he whispered in the semidarkness. "I don't have a ring for your finger, but if you'll say yes I'll rectify that problem as soon as I get out of this bed."

"I don't need a ring to know what's true. All I need is you."

He traced a finger down her cheek with his free hand. "This sounds odd considering where I am. But there are things I can promise and things I can't. And you know that, Maggie. But I can promise you that when you're my wife I'll do my best to come home to you every night, to love you and protect you. Those things will never change."

"That's all the guarantee I need," she whispered, pressing her lips to his once more. "It's more than enough."

* * * * *

The Colton family is back!
Enjoy a sneak preview of
COLTON'S SECRET SERVICE by Marie Ferrarella,
part of THE COLTONS: FAMILY FIRST *miniseries.*

*Available from Silhouette Romantic Suspense
in September 2008.*

He cautioned himself to be leery. He was human and he'd been conned before. But never by anyone nearly so attractive. Never by anyone he'd felt so attracted to.

In her defense, Nick supposed that Georgie could actually be telling him the truth. That she was a victim in all this. He had his people back in California checking her out, to make sure she was who she said she was and had, as she claimed, not even been near a computer but on the road these last few months that the threats had been made.

In the meantime, he was doing his own checking out. Up close and exceedingly personal. So personal he could feel his blood stirring.

It had been a long time since he'd thought of himself as anything other than a law enforcement agent of one type or other. But Georgeann Grady made him remember that beneath the oaths he had taken and his devotion to duty, there beat the heart of a man.

A man who'd been far too long without the touch of a woman.

He watched as the light from the fireplace caressed the outline of Georgie's small, trim, jean-clad body as she moved about the rustic living room that could have easily come off the set of a Hollywood Western. Except that it was genuine.

As genuine as she claimed to be?

Something inside of him hoped so.

He wasn't supposed to be taking sides. His only interest in being here was to guarantee Senator Joe Colton's safety as the latter continued to make his bid for the presidency. Everything else was supposed to be secondary, but, Nick had to silently admit, that was just a wee bit hard to remember right now.

Earlier, before she'd put her precocious handful of a daughter to bed, Georgie had fed his appetite by whipping up some kind of a delicious concoction out of the vegetables she'd pulled from her garden. Vegetables that, by all rights, should have been withered and dried. She'd mentioned that a friend came by on occasion to weed and tend it. Still, it surprised him that somehow she'd managed to make something mouthwatering out of it.

Almost as mouthwatering as she looked to him right at this moment.

Again, he was reminded of the appetite that hadn't been fed, hadn't been satisfied.

And wasn't going to be, Nick sternly told himself. At least not now. Maybe later, when things took on a more definite shape and all the questions in his head were answered to his satisfaction, there would be time to explore this feeling. This woman. But not now.

Damn it.

"Sorry about the lack of light," Georgie said, breaking into his train of thought as she turned around to face him. If she noticed the way he was looking at her, she gave no indication. "But I don't see a point in paying for electricity if I'm not going to be here. Besides, Emmie really enjoys camping out. She likes roughing it."

"And you?" Nick asked, moving closer to her, so close that a whisper would have trouble fitting in. "What do you like?"

The very breath stopped in Georgie's throat as she looked up at him.

"I think you've got a fair shot of guessing that one," she told him softly.

* * * * *

Be sure to look for *COLTON'S SECRET SERVICE*
and the other following titles from
THE COLTONS: FAMILY FIRST *miniseries:*
RANCHER'S REDEMPTION by Beth Cornelison
THE SHERIFF'S AMNESIAC BRIDE by Linda Conrad
SOLDIER'S SECRET CHILD by Caridad Piñeiro
BABY'S WATCH by Justine Davis
A HERO OF HER OWN by Carla Cassidy

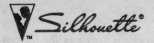
Romantic
SUSPENSE

**Sparked by Danger,
Fueled by Passion.**

This was wrong. This was fool's gold. This was also the only thing on earth she wanted right now. He tasted of warm, hungry man—clean, so good.

But she shouldn't...they mustn't...

Ethan was backing her relentlessly toward the door. She waited until he slipped the lock before lacing her fingers through his thick dark hair and making him her prisoner. "Shall we be captives here for long?"

"As long as it takes," he promised huskily.

Susan Stephens

THE RUTHLESS BILLIONAIRE'S VIRGIN

International Billionaires

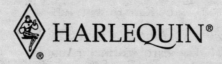

HARLEQUIN®

TORONTO • NEW YORK • LONDON
AMSTERDAM • PARIS • SYDNEY • HAMBURG
STOCKHOLM • ATHENS • TOKYO • MILAN • MADRID
PRAGUE • WARSAW • BUDAPEST • AUCKLAND

Recycling programs
for this product may
not exist in your area.

ISBN-13: 978-0-373-12822-8
ISBN-10:   0-373-12822-3

THE RUTHLESS BILLIONAIRE'S VIRGIN

First North American Publication 2009.

www.eHarlequin.com

Printed in U.S.A.

All about the author...
Susan Stephens

SUSAN STEPHENS was a professional singer before meeting her husband on the tiny Mediterranean island of Malta. In true Harlequin Presents style they met on Monday, became engaged on Friday and were married three months later. Almost thirty years and three children later they are still in love. (Susan does not advise her children to return home one day with a similar story as she may not take the news with the same fortitude as her own mother!)

Susan had written several nonfiction books when fate took a hand. At a charity costume ball there was an after-dinner auction. One of the lots, "Spend a Day with an Author," had been donated by Harlequin author Penny Jordan. Susan's husband bought this lot and Penny was to become not just a great friend, but a wonderful mentor who encouraged Susan to write romance.

Susan loves her family, her pets, her friends and her writing. She enjoys entertaining, travel and going to the theater. She reads, cooks and plays the piano to relax, and can occasionally be found throwing herself off mountains on a pair of skis or galloping through the countryside.

Visit Susan's Web site, www.susanstephens.net. She loves to hear from her readers all around the world!

CHAPTER ONE

SOME said confidence was the most potent aphrodisiac of all, but for the man the world of rugby called 'the Bear', confidence was only a starting point. Confidence took courage, something Ethan Alexander proved he had each time he faced the world with his disfiguring scars.

A change swept over the Stadio Flaminio in Rome when Ethan took his seat to watch Italy play England in the Six Nations rugby tournament. Men sat a little straighter, while women flicked their hair as they moistened their immaculately made-up lips.

Without the Bear, any match, even an international fixture like this one, lacked the frisson of danger Ethan carried with him. Tall, dark, and formidably scarred, Ethan was more than an avid rugby supporter, he was an unstoppable tycoon, a man who defied the standards by which other men were judged. His face might be damaged, but Ethan possessed a blistering glamour born of keen intelligence and a steely will. His grey eyes blazed with an internal fire women longed to feel scorch them, and men wished they could harness, but today that passion had ebbed into simmering frustration as he contemplated

human frailty. How could something as simple as a sore throat lead a world-famous diva like Madame de Silva to pull out of singing the national anthem for England at such an event as this?

The same way a damaged spine could end his own career as a professional rugby player, Ethan's inner voice informed him with brutal honesty.

He'd brought in a young singer as a replacement for Madame de Silva. Savannah Ross had recently been signed to the record company he ran as a hobby to reflect his deep love of music. He hadn't met Savannah, but Madame de Silva had recommended her, and his marketing people were touting the young singer as the next big thing.

Next big thing maybe, but Savannah Ross was late on pitch. He flashed a glance at the stadium clock that counted down the seconds. Hiring an inexperienced girl for an important occasion like this only reminded him why he never took risks. He'd thought it a good idea to give his new signing a break; now he wasn't so sure. Could Savannah Ross come up with the goods? She better had. She'd been flown here on his private jet and he'd been told she'd arrived. So where was she?

Ethan frowned as he shifted his powerful frame. The execution of last-minute formalities was timed to the second to accommodate a global television audience. No allowances could be made for inexperience, and *he* wouldn't allow for last-minute nerves. Savannah Ross had accepted this engagement, and now she must perform.

This wasn't like any theatre she'd ever played in before, or any concert-hall either. It was a bleak, tiled tunnel filled with the scent of sweaty feet and tension. She didn't even have a proper dressing-room to get changed in—not

that she minded, because it was such an honour to be here. Hard to believe she would soon be singing the national anthem on the pitch for the England rugby squad—or at least she would once she found someone to tell her where she was supposed to go and when.

Poking her head through the curtain of the 'dressing-room' she'd been allocated, Savannah called out. No one answered. Not surprising, in this shadowy tunnel leading to the pitch. The lady who had issued Savannah with a visitor's pass at the entrance had explained to her that what rooms there were would be needed for the teams and their support staff. Knowing Madame de Silva always travelled in style with an entourage, including Madame's hairdresser and the girl whose job it was to care for Madame's pet chihuahua, Savannah guessed the management of the stadium had been only too relieved to release the many rooms Madame would have taken up. And she was grateful for what she had: an adjunct to the tunnel—a hole in the wall, really—an alcove over which somebody had hastily draped a curtain.

And she had more important things on her mind than her comfort, like the clock ticking away the seconds before the match. She had definitely been forgotten, which was understandable. Taking Madame's place had been so last-minute, and her signing to the record label so recent, that no one knew her. How could anyone be expected to recognise or remember her? And though she had been guided to this alcove everyone had rushed off, leaving her with no idea what she was supposed to do. Sing? Yes, that was obvious, but when should she walk onto the pitch? And was she supposed to wait for someone to come back to escort her, or should she just march out there?

Hearing the chanting of the excited crowd, Savannah knew she must find help. She was about to do just that when she heard the rumble of conversation coming closer. A group of businessmen was striding down the tunnel and they must pass her curtained alcove. She would ask one of them what to do.

'Excuse me—' Savannah's enquiry was cut short as— whoosh, splat!—she was flattened against the wall like an invisible fly. The men were so busy talking they hadn't even noticed her as they'd thundered past, talking about the man they called the Bear, a man who had made his own way to his seat when all of them had been jostling to be the one to escort him.

The Bear...

Savannah shivered involuntarily. That was the nickname of the tycoon who had sent his jet to fetch her. Ethan Alexander, rugby fanatic and international billion-aire, was an unattached and unforgettable man, a shadowy figure who regularly featured in the type of magazines Savannah bought when she wanted to drool over unat-tainable men. No one yet had gained a clear insight into Ethan's life, though speculation was rife, and of course, the more he shunned publicity, the more intriguing the public found him.

She really must stop thinking about Ethan Alexander and concentrate on her predicament. To save time she would put on her gown and then go hunting for help.

But even the sight of her beautiful gown failed to divert Savannah's thoughts from Ethan. From what the men had said about him, having Ethan at the match was akin to having royalty turn up—or maybe even better, because he was an undisputed king amongst men. Taking into account the man-mountains in the England team, the Bear

was the best of all the men there, they said; he was the deadliest in the pack.

Savannah shivered at the thought of so much undiluted maleness. By the time she had wriggled her way into her gown she had worked herself into a state of debilitating nerves, though she reasoned it wasn't surprising she was intimidated, when this tunnel led onto the pitch where the atmosphere was humming with testosterone and almost palpable aggression.

The thought took her straight back to Ethan. The power he threw off, even from the printed page, made him physically irresistible. Perhaps it was the steely will in his eyes, or the fact he was such a powerfully built man. He might be a lot older than she was, and terribly scarred, but she wasn't the only woman who thought Ethan's injuries only made him more compelling. In magazine polls he was regularly voted the man most women wanted to go to bed with.

Not that someone as inexperienced as her should be dwelling on that. No, Savannah told herself firmly, she was gripped more by the aura of danger and tragedy surrounding Ethan. In her eyes his scars only made him seem more human and real.

Oh, really? Savannah's cynical-self interrupted. *So that would be why these 'innocent' thoughts of yours regularly trigger enough sensation to start a riot?*

Prudently, Savannah refused to answer that. She had no time for any of these distractions. She poked her head round the curtain again. There was still no one there, and she was fast running out of options. If she continued to yell she'd have no voice left for singing. If she put her jeans on again and went looking for help, she'd be late onto the pitch. But she couldn't let Madame de Silva

down, who had recommended her for this important occasion. She couldn't let down the squad, or Ethan Alexander, the man who had employed her. She'd put her dress on, then at least she'd be ready. Or her parents who had scrimped and saved to buy the dress for her, and she only wished they could be here with her now. Secretly she was happiest on the farm with them, up to her knees in mud in a pair of Wellington boots, but she would never trample on their dreams for her by telling them that.

As her mother's anxious face swam into her mind, Savannah realised it wasn't singing in front of a world-wide audience that terrified her, but the possibility that something might go wrong to embarrass her parents. She loved them dearly. Like many farmers they'd had it so hard when the deadly foot-and-mouth disease had wiped out their cattle. Her main ambition in life now was to make them smile again.

Savannah tensed, hearing her name mentioned on the tannoy system. And when the announcer described her in over-sugary terms, as the girl with the golden tonsils and hair to match, she grimaced, thinking it the best case she'd ever heard for dyeing her hair bright pink. The crowd disagreed and applauded wildly, which only convinced Savannah that when they saw her in person she could only disappoint. Far from being the dainty blonde the build-up had suggested, she was a fresh-faced country girl with serious self-confidence issues—and one who right now would rather be anywhere else on earth than here.

Pull yourself together! Savannah told herself impatiently. This gown had cost a fortune her parents could scarcely afford. Was she going to let them down? She started to struggle with the zip. The gown had been precision-made to fit her fuller figure, and was in her favour—

ite colour, pink. With the aid of careful draping it didn't even make her look fat. It was all in the cut and the boning, her mother had explained, which was why they always travelled up to the far north of England for Savannah's fittings, where there were dressmakers who knew about such things.

'You can't wear that!'

Savannah jumped back as her curtain was ripped aside. 'Do you mind?' she exclaimed, modestly covering her chest at the sight of a man whose physique perfectly matched his reedy voice. 'Why can't I wear it?' she protested, tightening her arms over her chest. It was a beautiful dress, but the man was looking at it as if it were a bin liner with holes cut in it for her head and arms.

'You just can't,' he said flatly.

Taking in the official England track-suit he was wearing, Savannah curbed her tongue, but she wasn't prepared to let the man continue with the peep show he seemed intent on having, and she held the curtain tightly around her. 'What's wrong with it?' she asked with all the politeness she could muster.

'It's not appropriate—and if I tell you that you can't wear it then you can't.'

What a bully, she thought, and her flesh crawled as the man continued to stare at her curvy form behind the flimsy curtain. Did he mean the neckline was too low? She always had trouble hiding her breasts, and as she'd got older she hated the way men stared at them. She would be the first to acknowledge her chest was currently displayed to best advantage in the low-cut gown, but it was a performance outfit. She could hardly hide her large breasts under her arms! 'Not appropriate *how*?' she said, standing her ground.

The man's disappointment that she didn't fold immediately was all too obvious. 'The Bear won't approve of it,' he said, as if that was the death knell of any hopes she had of wearing it.

'The Bear won't approve?' Savannah's heart fluttered a warning. To walk out onto the pitch and have Ethan Alexander stare at her... She had dreamed of it, but now it was going to happen she was losing confidence fast. That didn't mean she wouldn't defend her dress to kingdom come. 'I don't understand. Why wouldn't he approve of it?'

'It's pink,' the man said, his face twisting as if pink came with a bad smell.

Savannah's face crumpled. It was such a beautiful dress, and one her mother had been so thrilled to buy for her. They had discussed the fact that hours of dedicated work had gone into the hand-stitching alone, and now this man was dismissing the handiwork of craftswomen in a few unkind words.

'You'll have to take it off.'

'What?' Savannah felt the cold wall pressing against her back.

'I understand you're a last-minute replacement,' the man said in a kinder tone, which Savannah found almost creepier than his original hectoring manner. 'So you won't know that a major sponsor has supplied a designer gown for the occasion, which he expects to be worn. The dress has received more publicity than you have,' the man added unkindly.

'I'm not surprised,' Savannah muttered to herself. Well, it could hardly have received less, she thought wryly, seeing as she was a last-minute replacement. She kept a pleasant expression on her face, determined she wouldn't give this man the satisfaction of thinking he'd upset her.

'And the Bear expects all the sponsors, however small their donations, to get their fair share of publicity, so you'll have to wear it,' he finished crossly when she refused to capitulate.

Perhaps he would like her to cry so he could play the big man to her crushed little woman, Savannah reflected. If so, he was in for a disappointment. Because she was plump and rather short, people often mistook her for a sweet, plump, fluffy thing they could push around, when actually she could stick her arm up a cow and pull out a newborn calf during a difficult birth, something that had given her supreme joy on the few occasions she'd been called upon to do so. Her slender arms were kinder on a struggling mother, her father always said. She didn't come from the sort of background to be intimidated by a man who looked like he had a pole stuck up his backside.

'Well, if that's the dress I'm supposed to wear,' she said pragmatically, 'I'd better see it.' She hadn't come to Rome to cause ripples, but to do a job like anyone else, and the clock was ticking. Plus she was far too polite to say what she really wanted to say, which was *what the hell has it got to do with the Bear what I wear?*

Someone pretty important to your career, Savannah's sensible inner voice informed her as the man hurried off to get the dress; *someone who is both the main sponsor for the England squad and your boss.*

When he returned the man's manner had changed. Perhaps he believed he had worn her down, Savannah concluded.

'Madame Whatshername was pleased enough to wear it,' he said with a sniff as he handed the official gown over to Savannah.

Savannah paled as she held up Madame de Silva's

gown. She should have known it would be fitted to the great singer. Madame was half her size, and wore the type of couture dress favoured by French salon-society. The closest Savannah had ever come to a salon was the local hairdresser's, and her gowns were all geared towards comfort and big knickers. 'I don't think Madame's gown will fit me,' she muttered, losing all her confidence in a rush as she stared at the slim column of a dress with its fishtail train.

'Whether it fits you or not,' the man insisted, 'You have to wear it. I can't allow you onto the pitch wearing your dress when the sponsor is expecting to see his official gown worn. Putting his design in front of a worldwide television audience is the whole point of the exercise.'

With her in it? Savannah very much doubted that was what the designer had had in mind.

'You have to look the part,' the man insisted.

Of team jester? Savannah was starting to feel sick, and not just with pre-concert nerves. In farming lingo she would be classified as 'healthy breeding stock', whereas Madame de Silva was a slender greyhound, all sleek and toned. There was no chance the gown would fit her, or suit her freckled skin. 'I'll do my best,' she promised as her throat constricted.

'Good girl,' the man said approvingly.

Savannah's chin wobbled as she surveyed the garish gown. She was going to look like a fool, and beyond her little drama in the tunnel she could hear that the mood of the crowd had escalated to fever pitch in anticipation of the kick-off.

Where was she? Ethan frowned as he flashed another glance at his wristwatch. A hush of expectancy had swept the capacity crowd. It was almost time for the match to

start, and he was more on edge than he had ever been. He had promised the squad a replacement singer, and now it looked as if Savannah Ross was going to let him down. In minutes the England team would be lining up in the tunnel, and the brass band was already out on the pitch. The portly tenor who had been booked to sing the anthem for Italy was busily accepting the plaudits of an adoring crowd, but where the hell was Savannah Ross?

Anxious glances shot Ethan's way. If the Bear was unhappy, everyone was unhappy, and Ethan was unusually tense.

Madame's fabulous form-fitting gown had a sash in bleakest white and ink-blot blue, which like a royal order was supposed to be worn over one naked shoulder.

Fabulous for Madame's slender frame, maybe, Savannah thought anxiously as she struggled to put the sash to better use. If she could just bite out these stitches, maybe, just maybe, she could spread out the fabric to cover the impending boob explosion—though up until now she had to admit her frantic plucking and gnawing had achieved nothing; try as she might, the sash refused to conceal any part of her bosom.

And as for the zip at the back...

Contorting her arms into a position that would have given Houdini a run for his money, she still couldn't do it up. Poking her head out of the curtain, she tried calling out again, but even the creepy man had deserted her. She peered anxiously down the tunnel. The crowd had grown quiet, which was a very bad sign. It meant the announcements were over and the match was about to start—and before that could happen she had to sing the national anthem! 'Hello! Is anyone—?'

'Hello,' a girl interrupted brightly, seemingly coming out of nowhere. 'Can I help you?'

After jumping about three feet in the air with shock, Savannah felt like kissing the ground the girl was about to walk on. 'If you could just get me into this dress…' Savannah knew it was a lost cause, but she had to try.

'Don't panic,' the girl soothed.

Savannah's saviour turned out to be a physiotherapist and was using the tones Savannah guessed she must have used a thousand times before, and in far more serious situations to reassure the injured players. 'I'm trying not to panic,' she admitted. 'But I'm so late, and the fact remains you can't fit a quart into a pint pot.'

The girl laughed with her. 'Let's see, shall we?'

The physio certainly knew all there was to know about manipulation, Savannah acknowledged gratefully when she was finally secured inside the dress. 'Don't worry, I'll be fine now,' she said, wiping her nose. 'That's if I don't burst out of it—!'

'You'll have a fair sized audience if you do,' the girl reminded her with a smile.

Yes, the crowd was wound up like a drum, and Savannah knew she would be in for a rough ride if anything went wrong out on the pitch.

As the physio collected up her things and wished her good luck, Savannah stared down in dismay at the acres of blood-red taffeta. It was just a shame every single one of those acres was in the wrong place. Madame was a lot taller than she was, and how she longed for the fabric collecting around her feet to be redistributed over her fuller figure. But it was too late to worry about that now.

'You'd better get out there,' the girl said, echoing these thoughts, 'Before you miss your cue.'

Don't tempt me! Savannah thought, testing whether it was possible to breathe, let alone sing, now she was pinned in. Barely, she concluded. She was trapped in a vice of couture stitching from which there was only one escape, and she didn't fancy risking that in front of the worldwide television audience. She'd much rather be safely back at home dreaming about Ethan Alexander rather than here on the pitch where he would almost certainly look at her and laugh.

But…

She braced herself.

The fact that she could hardly move, let alone breathe, didn't mean she couldn't use her legs, Savannah told herself fiercely as she tottered determinedly down the tunnel in a gown secured with safety pins, made for someone half her size.

Here goes nothing!

CHAPTER TWO

SHE had forgotten how much her diaphragm expanded when she let herself go and really raised the rafters. How could she have forgotten something as rudimentary as that?

Maybe because the massive crowd was a blur and all she was aware of was the dark, menacing shape of the biggest man on the benches behind the England sin bin, the area England players sat in when they were sent off the pitch for misdemeanours.

Sin.

She had to shake that thought off too, Savannah realised as she lifted her ribcage in preparation for commencing the rousing chorus. But how was she supposed to do that when she could feel Ethan's gaze in every fibre of her being? The moment she had walked onto the pitch she had known exactly where he was sitting, and who he was looking at. By the time she'd got over that, and the ear-splitting cheer that had greeted her, even the fear of singing in front of such a vast audience had paled into insignificance. And now she was trapped in a laser gaze that wouldn't let her go.

She really must shake off this presentiment of disaster, Savannah warned herself. Nervously moistening her lips, she took a deep breath. A very deep breath…

The first of several safety pins pinged free, and as the dress fell away it became obvious that the physio's pins were designed to hold bandages in place rather than acres of pneumatic flesh.

His mood had undergone a radical change from impatient to entranced, and all in a matter of seconds. The ruthless billionaire, as people liked to think of him, became a fan of his new young singing-sensation after hearing just a few bars of her music. The crowd agreed with him, judging by the way Savannah Ross had it gripped. When she had first stumbled onto the pitch, she had been greeted by wolf whistles and rowdy applause. At first he had thought her ridiculous too, with her breasts pouting over the top of the ill-fitting gown, but then he remembered the famous dress had been made for someone else, and that he should have found some way to warn her. But it was too late to worry about that now, and her appearance hardly mattered, for Savannah Ross had him and everyone else in the palm of her hand. She was so richly blessed with music it was all he could do to remain in his seat.

She refused to let the supporters down. She carried on regardless as more pins followed the first. She was expected to reflect the hopes and dreams of a country, and that was precisely what she was going to do—never mind the wretched dress letting her down. But as she prepared to sing the last few notes the worst happened—the final pin gave way and one pert breast sprang free, the generous swell of it nicely topped off with a rose-pink nipple. Not one person in the crowd missed the moment, for it was recorded for all to see on the giant-sized screen. As she

started to shake with shame, the good-natured crowd went wild, applauding her, which helped her hold her nerve for the final top note.

Thrust from his seat by a rocket-fuelled impulse to shield and protect, Ethan was already shedding his jacket as he stormed onto the pitch. By the time he reached Savannah's side, the crowd had only just begun to take in what had happened. Not so his target. Tears of frustration were pouring down her face as she struggled to re-pin her dress. As he spoke to her and she looked at him there was a moment, a potent and disturbing moment, when she stared him straight in the eyes and he registered something he hadn't felt for a long time, or maybe ever. Without giving himself a chance to analyse the feeling, he threw his jacket around her shoulders and led her away, forcing the Italian tenor to launch into *Canto degli Italiani*—or 'Song of the Italians', as the Italian national anthem was known—somewhat sooner than expected.

There was so much creamy flesh concealed beneath his lightweight jacket it was throwing his brain synapses out of sync. Unlike all the women he'd encountered to date, this young Savannah Ross was having a profound effect on his state of mind. He strode across the pitch with his arm around her shoulders while she endeavoured to keep in step and remain close, whilst not quite touching him. As he took her past the stands the crowd went wild. *'Viva l'Orso!'* the Italians cried, loving every minute of it: 'hurrah for the Bear'. The England supporters cheered him just as loudly. He wondered if this compliment was to mark his chivalry or the fact that Ms Ross could hardly conceal her hugely impressive bosom beneath a dress that had burst its stitches. He hardly cared. His overrid-

ing thought was to get her out of the eyeline of every lustful male in the Stadio Flaminio, of whom there were far too many for his liking.

It crossed his mind that this incident would have to have happened in Italy, the land of romantic love and music, the home of passion and beauty. He had always possessed a dark sense of humour, and it amused him now to think that in his heart, the heart everyone was so mistakenly cheering for, there was only an arid desert and a single bitter note.

By the time Ethan had escorted Savannah into the shelter of the tunnel she was mortified. She felt ridiculously under-dressed in the company of a man noted for his *savoir faire*. Ethan Alexander was a ruthless, world-renowned tycoon, while she was an ordinary girl who didn't belong in the spotlight; a girl who wished, in a quite useless flash of longing, that Ethan could have met her on the farm where at least she knew what she was doing.

'Are you all right?' he asked her gruffly.

'Yes, thank you.'

He was holding on to her as if he thought she might fall over. Did he think her so pathetically weak? This was worse than her worst nightmare come true, and it was almost a relief when he turned away to make a call.

It couldn't be worse, Savannah concluded, taking in the wide, reassuring spread of Ethan's back. This was a very private man who had been thrust into the spotlight, thanks to her. No doubt he was calling for someone to come and take her away, nuisance that she was. She couldn't blame him. She had to be so much less in every way than he'd been expecting.

While he was so much more than she had expected…

Ethan Alexander in the flesh was a one-man power source of undiluted energy, a dynamo running on adrenalin and sex. At least that was what her vivid imagination was busy telling her, and she could hardly blame it for running riot. No television-screen or grainy newspaper-image had come close to conveying either Ethan's size or his compelling physical presence. And yet the most surprising shock of all was the way his lightest and most impersonal touch had scorched fireworks through every part of her. He'd only touched her elbow to help steer her, and had draped his jacket across her back, and yet that had been enough to hot-wire her arm and send sparks flying everywhere they shouldn't.

Her thoughts were interrupted by the young physio coming over to see if she could help. 'It wasn't your fault,' Savannah assured her, hoping Ethan could hear. She didn't want him blaming the young girl for Savannah's problems. 'It was my breathing,' she explained.

'What a problem we'd have had if you hadn't breathed!' The young physio shared a laugh with Savannah as she started pinning Savannah back into the dress. 'And I'm really glad you did breathe, because you were fantastic.'

Savannah had never been sure how to handle compliments. In her eyes she was just an ordinary girl with an extraordinary voice, and no manual had come with that voice to explain how to deal with the phenomenon that had followed. 'Thank you,' she said, spreading her hands wide in a modest gesture.

But the girl grabbed hold of them and shook them firmly. 'No,' she insisted, 'Don't you brush it off. You were fantastic. Everyone said so.'

Everyone? Savannah glanced at Ethan, who still had his back turned to her as he talked on the phone. She

pulled his jacket close for comfort; it was warm and smelled faintly of sandalwood and spice. Tracing lapels that hung almost to her knees, she realised that even though Ethan's jacket was ten sizes too big for her it did little to preserve her modesty, and she hurriedly crossed her arms across her chest as he turned around.

'Okay, I've finished,' the physio reported. 'Though I doubt the pins on Ms Ross's dress will hold for long.'

'Right, let's go,' Ethan snapped, having thanked the girl.

'Go where?' Savannah held back nervously as the physio gave her a sympathetic look.

'Ms Ross, I know you've had a shock, but there are paparazzi crawling all over the building. Don't worry about your bag now,' Ethan said briskly when Savannah gazed down the tunnel. 'Your things will be sent on to you.'

'Sent where?'

'Just come with me, please.'

'Come with you *where*?' The thought of going anywhere with Ethan Alexander terrified her. He was such an imposing man, and an impatient one, but with all the paparazzi in the building the thought of not going with him terrified her even more.

'After you,' he said, giving her no option as he stood in a way that barred her getting past him.

'Where did you say we were going?'

'I didn't say.'

Savannah's nerve deserted her completely. She wasn't going anywhere with a man she didn't know, even if that man was her boss. 'You go. I'll be fine. I'll get a cab.'

'I brought you to Rome, and like it or not while you're here you're my responsibility.'

He didn't like it at all, she gathered, which left one simple question: did she want this recording contract or not?

She couldn't take the chance of losing it, Savannah realised. She hadn't come to Rome to sabotage her career. She might not like Ethan's manner, but she was here on his time. Plus, she didn't know Rome. If her only interest was getting home as quickly as possible, wasn't he her best hope?

She had to run to keep up with him, and then he stopped so suddenly she almost bumped into him. Looking up, Savannah found herself staring into a face that was even more cruelly scarred than she had remembered. Instead of recoiling, she registered a great well of feeling opening up inside her heart. It was almost as if something strong and primal was urging her to heal him, to press cream into those wounds, and to…*love him*?

This situation was definitely getting out of hand, Savannah concluded, pulling herself together, to find Ethan giving her an assessing look as if to warn her that just looking at him too closely was a dangerous game well out of her league. 'It's important we leave now,' he prompted as if she were some weakling he had been forced to babysit.

'I'm ready.' She held his gaze steadily. This was not a time to be proud. She didn't want to do battle with the paparazzi on her own, and she would be safer with Ethan. There were times when having a strong man at your side was a distinct advantage. But she wouldn't have him think her a fool either.

'After you.' Opening the door for her, he stood aside.

He looked more like a swarthy buccaneer than a businessman, and exuded the sort of earthy maleness she had always been drawn to. Her fantasies were full of pirates and cowboys, roughnecks and marines, though none of them had possessed lips as firm and sensual as Ethan's, and his hand in the small of her back was an incendiary device propelling her forward.

'What's wrong now?' he said impatiently when she stopped outside to shade her eyes.

'I was just looking for a taxi rank.' By far the safest option, she had decided.

'A taxi rank?' Ethan's voice was scathing. 'Do you want to attract more publicity? Don't worry, Ms Ross, you'll be quite safe with me.'

But would she? That was Savannah's cue for stepping back inside the stadium building. 'I'm sure someone will find the number of a cab company for me.'

'Please yourself.'

She couldn't have been more shocked when Ethan stormed ahead, letting the door swing in her face. Defiantly, she pushed it open again. 'You're leaving me?'

'That's what you want, isn't it?' he called back as he marched away. 'And as you don't need my help...'

'Just a minute.'

'You changed your mind?'

Savannah's heart lurched as Ethan turned to look at her. 'No, but.'

'But what?' He kept on walking.

'I need directions to the nearest taxi rank, and I thought you might know where I should look.' She had to run to keep up with him, which wasn't easy in high-heeled shoes, not to mention yards of taffeta winding itself like a malevolent red snake around her feet.

'Find someone else to help you.'

'Ethan, please!' She would have to swallow her pride if it meant saving her parents more embarrassment. 'Can you really get us out of here without the paparazzi seeing?'

He stopped and slowly turned around. 'Can I get us out of here?'

The look of male confidence blazing from his eyes was

at its purest. When she should be considering a thousand other things—like how long before the paparazzi found them, for example—a bolt of lust chose that moment to race down her spine. His eyes were the most beautiful eyes she'd ever seen, deep grey, with just a hint of duck-egg blue, and they had very white whites, as well as the most ridiculously long black lashes.

'I'm done waiting for you, Ms Ross.'

He was off again, but this time he grabbed her arm and took her with him. Savannah yelped with surprise. 'Where are we going?'

'To something that travels a lot faster than a taxi,' he grated without slowing down.

What did he mean—a helicopter? Of course. She should have known. Like all the super-rich, Ethan would hardly call a cab when he could fly home. 'Can we slow down just a bit?'

'And talk this through?' he scoffed without breaking stride. 'We can take all the time in the world if you want the paparazzi to find you.'

'You know I don't want that!' *Okay, no reason to worry*, Savannah told herself. They would fly straight to the airport in Ethan's helicopter, from where she'd fly home. Traffic snarl-ups were reserved for mere mortals like herself. In no time Ethan would be back in his seat at the stadium ready for the second half, while she returned to England and her nice, safe fantasies. Perfect.

Or at least it was until a door burst open and the press-hounds barrelled out. It only took one of them to catch sight of Ethan and Savannah for the whole pack to give chase.

'This way,' Ethan commanded, swinging Savannah in front of him. Opening a door, he thrust her through it and, slamming it shut, he shot the bolt home.

If she hadn't left her sensible sneakers in the tunnel she might have been able to run faster, Savannah fretted as Ethan took the stairs two at a time, but now the straps on her stratospheric heels were threatening to snap.

'Leave them!' he ordered as she bent down to take them off. 'Or, better still, snap those heels off.'

'Are you joking?'

'Take them off!' he roared.

'I'm going to keep them,' Savannah insisted stubbornly.

'Do what you like with them,' he said, snatching hold of her arm, half-lifting her to safety down another flight of steps. 'And hitch up your skirt while you're at it, before you trip over it,' he said, checking outside the next door before rushing her out into the open air again. 'Your skirt—hitch it up!'

Hitch it up? The photographers would surely be on them in moments, and when that happened she didn't want to look like a...

'Do it!'

'I'm doing it!' she yelled, startled into action. But she wouldn't ruin the shoes her mother had bought her. Or Madame's dress. Slipping off her high-heeled sandals as quickly as she could, Savannah bundled up the gown, noting she barely reached Ethan's shoulder now. Also noting he barely seemed to notice her naked legs, which shouldn't bother her, but for some reason did.

'Come on,' he rapped impatiently, still averting his gaze. 'There's no time to lose.' Taking her arm, he urged her on.

Savannah was totally incapable of speech by the time they'd crossed the car park. Yet still Ethan was merciless. 'There's no time for that,' he assured her when she rested with her hands on her knees to catch her breath.

Straightening up, she stared at him. She didn't know

this man. She didn't know anything about him, other than the fact that his reputation was well deserved. The Bear was a dark and formidable man, whom she found incredibly intimidating. And she was going who knew where with him. 'You still haven't told me where we're going.'

'There's no time!'

'But you do have a helicopter waiting?'

'A helicopter?' Ethan glanced towards the roof where the helipad was situated.

He had a helicopter there, all right, she could see the logo of a bear on the tail. She could also see the scrum of photographers gathered round it.

'A useful distraction,' Ethan told her with satisfaction.

A red herring, Savannah realised, to put the paparazzi off the trail. 'So what now?'

'Now you can sit,' he promised, dangling a set of keys in front of her face.

Ah…She relaxed a little at the thought that life was about to take on a more regular beat. She should have known Ethan would have a car here. His driver would no doubt take them straight to the airport, where the helicopter would meet him and she would fly home. She was guilty of overreacting again. Ethan was entitled to his privacy. He'd taken her out of reach of the paparazzi and saved her and her parents any further humiliation. She should be grateful to him. But she still felt a little apprehensive.

CHAPTER THREE

EVEN with the knowledge that comfort was only a few footsteps away, Savannah reminded herself that this was not one of her fantasies and Ethan was no fairy-tale hero. He was a cold, hard man who inhabited a world far beyond the safety curtain of a theatre, and as such she should be treating him with a lot more reserve and more caution than the type of men she was used to mixing with.

'Put this on.'

She recoiled as he thrust something at her, and then she stared at it in bewilderment. 'What's this?'

'A helmet,' he said with that ironic tone again. 'Put it on.' When she didn't respond right away. he gave it a little shake for emphasis.

It was only then she noticed the big, black motorbike parked up behind him and laughed nervously. 'You're not serious, I hope?'

'Why shouldn't I be serious?' Ethan frowned. Dipping his head, he demanded, 'You're not frightened of riding a bike, are you?'

'Of course not,' Savannah protested, swallowing hard as she straightened up. Was she frightened of sitting on a big, black, vibrating machine pressed up close to Ethan?

'If you have any better suggestions, Ms Ross…?'

Watching Ethan settle a formidable-looking helmet on his thick, wavy hair, she mutely shook her head.

'Well?' he said, swinging one hard-muscled thigh over the bike. 'Would you care to join me, or shall I leave you here?'

She was still staring at the tightly packed jeans settled comfortably into the centre of the saddle, Savannah realised. 'No…no,' she repeated more firmly. 'I'm coming with you.' Remembering the door incident, she already knew he took no prisoners. Holding up her skirt, she hopped, struggled, and finally managed to yank her leg over the back of the bike—which wasn't easy without touching him.

'Helmet?'

As Ethan turned to look at her, Savannah thought his eyes were darker than ever through the open visor—a reflection of his black helmet, she told herself, trying not to notice the thick, glossy waves of bitter-chocolate hair that had escaped and fallen over the scars on his forehead. But those scars were still there, like the dark side of Ethan behind the superficial glamour of a fiercely good-looking man. Her stomach flipped as she wondered how many more layers there were to him, and what he was really thinking behind those gun-metal-grey eyes.

'Helmet,' he rapped impatiently.

Startled out of her dreams, she started fumbling frantically with it.

'Let me,' he offered.

This was the closest they'd been since the stadium, and as Ethan handled the catch he held her gaze. In the few seconds it took him to complete the task every part of her had been subjected to his energy, which left her thrum-

ming with awareness. And he hadn't even started the engine yet, Savannah reminded herself as a door banged open and a dozen or so photographers piled out. Snapping his own visor into position, Ethan swung away from her and stamped the powerful machine into life. 'Hang on.'

There was barely time to register that instruction before he released the brake, gunned the engine, and they roared off like a rocket.

Propelled by terror, Savannah flung her arms around Ethan, clinging to as much of him as she could. Forced to press her cheek against his crisp blue shirt, she kept her eyes shut, trusting him to get them out of this. But as the bike gained speed something remarkable happened. Maybe it was the persistent throb of the engine, or the feel of Ethan's muscular back against her face—or maybe it was simply the fact that she had a real-life hunk beneath her hands instead of one of her disappointing fantasies— but Savannah felt the tension ebb away and began to enjoy herself. She was enjoying travelling at what felt like the speed of sound, and not in a straight line either. Because this wasn't just the ride of her life, Savannah concluded, smiling a secret smile, but the closest to sex she'd ever come.

As Ethan raced the bike between the ranks of parked cars she was pleased to discover how soon she became used to leaning this way and that to help him balance. She could get used to this, Savannah decided, sucking in her first full and steady breath since climbing on board. She felt so safe with Ethan. He made her feel safe. His touch was sure, his judgement was sound, and his strength could only be an asset in any situation. There was something altogether reassuring about being with him, she concluded happily.

When she wasn't being terrified by him, her sober self chimed in.

Ignoring these internal reservations, she went with the excitement of the moment—not that she needed an excuse to press her face against Ethan's back. As she inhaled the intoxicating cocktail of sunshine, washing powder and warm, clean man, she decided that just for once she was going to keep her sensible self at bay and ride this baby like a biker chick.

Ethan was forced to slow the bike as he engaged with the heavy traffic approaching Rome, and Savannah took this opportunity to do some subtle finger-mapping. She reckoned she had only a few seconds before Ethan's attention would be back on the bike and his passenger, and she intended to make the most of them. He felt like warm steel beneath her fingertips, and she could detect the shift of muscle beneath his shirt. She smiled against his back, unseen and secure. She felt so tiny next to him, which made her wonder what such a powerful man could teach her, locking these erotic reveries away in record time when he gunned the engine and turned sharp right.

The bike banked dramatically as they approached the Risorgimento Bridge spanning the river Tiber, forcing Savannah to lean over at such an angle her knee was almost brushing the road. As she did so she realised it was the first time she had ever put her trust in someone outside her close-knit family. But with the Roman sun on her face, and the excitement of the day, clinging on to a red-hot man didn't seem like such a bad option, she told herself wryly. In fact, who would travel by helicopter, given an alternative like this?

She was feeling so confident by the time Ethan levelled

up the bike again, she even turned around to see if they were being followed.

'I thought I told you to sit still.'

Savannah nearly jumped off the bike with fright, hearing Ethan's voice barking at her through some sort of headphone in her helmet.

'Hold on,' he repeated harshly.

'I am holding on,' she shouted back.

As if she needed an excuse.

They took another right and headed back up the river the way they'd come, only on the opposite side of the Tiber. Ethan slowed the bike when they reached the Piazalle Maresciallo Giardino where there was another bridge and, moored under it, a powerboat...

No.

No!

Savannah shook her head, refusing to believe the evidence of her own eyes. This couldn't possibly be the next stage of their journey. Or was that one of the reasons Ethan had been making that call back at the stadium, to line everything up?

'Come on,' he rapped, shaking her out of her confusion the moment they parked up.

As she fumbled with the clasp Ethan lifted her visor and removed the helmet for her. As his fingers brushed her face she trembled. Staring into his eyes, she thought it another of those moments where fantasy collided with reality. But was Ethan really looking at her differently, as if she might be more than just a package he was delivering to the airport? The suspicion that he might be seeing her for the first time as a woman was a disturbing thought, and so she turned away to busy herself with the pretence of straightening out her ruined hair. She still had her

precious high-heels dangling from her wrist like a bracelet, which turned her thoughts to her mother and what she would make of this situation. Her mother was a stand-up woman and would make the most of it, Savannah concluded, as would she.

'Are you thinking of joining me any time today?'

She looked up to find Ethan already on board the boat, preparing to cast off. He leaned over the side to call to her, 'Get up here, or I'll come and get you!'

Would you? crossed her mind. Brushing the momentary weakness aside, she called back, 'Wait for me.'

'Not for long,' he assured her. 'You're not frightened of a little mud, are you?' he added, taunting her as she teetered down the embankment.

Frightened of a little mud? He clearly hadn't seen their farmyard recently. 'What sort of wet lettuce do you think I am?'

'You'd prefer me not to answer that.'

'I'm not all sequins and feathers, you know!' She kicked the hem of her gown away with one dirty foot for emphasis.

'You don't say.' Ethan's tone was scathing, and then she noticed their chins were sticking out at the same combative angle and quickly pulled hers in again.

'There is an element of urgency to this. Paparazzi?' Ethan reminded her in a voice that could have descaled a kettle.

And then car horns started up behind her. She was providing some unexpected entertainment for the male drivers of Rome, who were slowing their vehicles to whistle and shout comments at her. They must think she was still in evening dress after a wild night out with an even wilder man, Savannah realised self-consciously. A man who was threatening to make good on his promise to come and get her, she also realised, detecting move-

ment in her peripheral vision. 'Stay back,' she warned Ethan as he took a step towards her. 'I don't need your help.'

It was a relief to see him lift his hands up, palms flat in an attitude of surrender. She had enough to do picking her way across the splintery walkway without worrying about what Ethan might do.

It was just a shame she missed his ironic stare. The next thing she knew she was several feet off the ground travelling at speed towards the boat. 'Put me down!'

Ethan ignored her. 'I can't live life at your pace. young lady. If you stay around me much longer, you'll have to learn to tick a lot faster.'

She had no intention of 'staying around' him a moment longer than she had to, Savannah determined. But, pressed against Ethan's firm, warm body, a body that rippled with hard, toned muscle... 'Please put me down,' she murmured, hoping he wouldn't hear.

Ethan didn't react either way. He didn't slow his pace until they were onboard, when he lowered her onto the deck. Having done this, he surveyed her sternly. 'The race is still on,' he said, folding massive arms across his chest. 'And I have no intention of giving up, or of allowing anyone to hold me back. Is that clear?'

'Crystal.'

'Good.'

Savannah smoothed her palms down her arms where Ethan's hand prints were still branded.

'Well, Ms Ross, shall we take this powerboat on the river?'

'Whatever it takes,' she agreed, watching Ethan move to straddle the space between the shore and the boat.

'I'm going to free the mooring ropes,' he explained, springing onto the shore. 'Can you catch a rope?'

Could she catch a rope? He really did think she was completely useless, Savannah thought, huffing with frustration. Ethan had got her so wrong. 'I might have smaller hands than you, but I still have opposing thumbs.'

Was that a smile? Too late to tell, as Ethan had already turned away.

'In that case, catch this.'

He turned back to her so fast she almost dropped the rope. It was heavier than she had imagined and she stumbled drunkenly under the weight of it.

'All right?' Ethan demanded as he sprang back on board.

'Absolutely fine,' she lied. Summoning her last reserves of strength, she hoisted it up to brandish it at him.

'Now coil it up,' he instructed, pointing to where she should place it when she'd done so.

'Okay.' She could do this. Quite honestly, she enjoyed the feel of the rough rope beneath her fingers—and enjoyed the look of grudging admiration on Ethan's face even more. But she needed to even the playing field. Ethan was dressed appropriately for taking a powerboat down the river. She was dressed, but barely. 'Do you have a jumper, or something I could borrow?'

Ethan made a humming sound as he looked her over. 'I see your point.'

Savannah felt heat rise to her cheeks and depart southwards.

'I'll see what I can do for you,' Ethan offered, brushing past her on his way across the deck. 'I must have an old shirt stowed here somewhere...'

Her nipples responded with indecent eagerness to this

brief contact with him, just as a fresh flurry of car horns started up on shore. Who could blame the drivers? Savannah thought. The sight of a decidedly scruffy girl in an ill-fitting evening dress onboard a fabulous powerboat in the middle of the afternoon with a clearly influential man of some considerable means would naturally cause a sensation in Rome. But why couldn't Ethan notice her?

'What's wrong?' he said when he straightened up, and then his stare swept the line of traffic. One steely look from him was all it took for the cars to speed up again. 'Will this do?' he said, turning back to Savannah. He thrust a scrunched-up nondescript bundle at her.

The shirt was maybe twenty sizes too large, Savannah saw as she shook it out, but in the absence of anything else to wear she'd have to go with it. Plus it held the faint but unmistakeable scent of Ethan's cologne. 'It's absolutely perfect. Thank you.' Slipping it on, she realised it brushed her calves, but at least she was decent. She pulled the shirt close and, inhaling Ethan's scent deeply, gave a smile of true contentment, the first she'd unleashed that day.

He was stunned by the sight of Savannah wearing his shirt. She looked…adorable. She looked, in fact, as he imagined she might look if they had just been to bed together. Her hair was mostly hanging loose now, and the make-up she'd worn for her appearance on the pitch was smudged, which made her eyes seem huge in her heart-shaped face, and her lips appeared bruised as if he'd kissed them for hours. His shirt drowned her, of course, but knowing what was underneath didn't help his equilibrium any. Hard to believe he had looked at her properly, critically, for the first time just a few moments ago when she'd asked for the shirt. Nothing on earth would have

induced him to stare at her out on the pitch where she'd been at such a disadvantage. But now? Now he couldn't take his eyes off her fuller figure.

Savannah tensed guiltily as unexpectedly Ethan's gaze warmed. What was he thinking—that she was a fat mess? A nuisance? As sophisticated as a sheep? Before her imagination could take her any further, she took her seat. 'I'm on it,' she assured Ethan when he glanced at the harness.

She couldn't do the darn thing up. And now Ethan was giving her the type of superior male appraisal that got right up her nose.

'I don't seem to have the knack,' she admitted with frustration. Maybe because her hands were shaking with nerves at being in such close proximity to Ethan.

'Would you like me to fasten it for you?' Ethan offered with studied politeness.

As he leaned over to secure the catch for her, Savannah felt like she was playing with fire. Ethan's hair was so thick and glossy she longed to run her fingers through it. And he smelled so good. His touch was so sure, and so…disappointingly fast. She looked down. The clasp was securely fastened. 'Is that it?'

'Would you like there to be something more?'

As he asked the question Savannah thought Ethan's stare to be disturbingly direct. 'No, thank you,' she told him primly, turning away on the pretence of tossing her tangled hair out of her eyes. But even as she was doing that Ethan was lifting his overlarge shirt onto her shoulders from where it had slipped.

'Are you sure you're warm enough?' he asked gruffly. 'Only it can be cold out on the river.'

Or hot to sizzling. 'I'll be fine, thank you.' Each tiny hair on the back of her neck had stood to attention at his touch, and it was a real effort not to notice that Ethan had the sexiest mouth she had ever seen. She would have to make sure she stared unswervingly ahead for the rest of the boat ride.

'Now what are you doing?' Ethan demanded. He had just opened up the throttle, and as the boat surged forward it pitched and yawed; Savannah had chosen that very moment to shed her harness, which forced him to throttle back.

'I'm calling my parents.'

'Calling your—?' He was lost for words. 'Not now!' he roared back at her above the scream of the boat's engine.

'They'll be worried about me.'

This was a concept so alien to him it took him a moment to respond. 'Sit down, Savannah, and buckle up.' He spoke with far more restraint than he felt and, after congratulating himself on that restraint, he conceded in the loud voice needed to crest the engines, 'You can speak to them later.'

She reluctantly agreed, but he detected anxiety in her tone. He also detected the same desire to protect Savannah he'd felt out on the pitch, except now it had grown. His intention to remain distant and aloof, because she was young and innocent and he was not, was dead in the water. There was too much feminine warmth too close. 'I'll speak to them,' he said, wanting to reassure her.

Savannah was right, he conceded, her parents must be

worried about her, having seen everything unfold on television. 'You can speak to them after I do,' he said. 'But for now *sit down*.' And on this there could be no compromise.

Even Savannah couldn't defy that tone of voice, and he made sure she was securely fastened in before picking up speed again. It amused him to see she had pushed back the sleeves on his overly large shirt and pulled it tightly around her legs, as if she felt the need to hide every bit of naked flesh from him. He supposed he could see her point of view. They were diametrically opposed on the gender scale. He was all man and she was a distraction. Fixing his attention to the river, he thrust the throttles forward.

'This is wonderful!' she exclaimed excitedly as the powerboat picked up speed and the prow lifted from the water.

It pleased him to see her looking so relaxed, and he even allowed himself a small smile as he remembered her jibe about opposing thumbs. There was a lot more to Ms Ross than the circumstance of their first meeting might have led him to suppose.

What exactly that might be was for some other man to discover, though, because this was strictly a taxi service to get Savannah out of harm's way as fast as he could.

Oh, yes, it was, he argued with his unusually quarrelsome inner voice.

She was only here because she had no other option, Savannah reassured herself as the powerboat zoomed along the river. She was glad she'd been able to catch the rope and prove to Ethan she wasn't completely helpless—after the debacle at the stadium she certainly needed something to go right, but she still had some way to go. She cupped her ear as he said something to her. It was so hard to hear anything above the rhythmical pounding of the boat.

'You're not feeling seasick, are you?'

'On the river?' she yelled back. This riposte earned her a wry look from Ethan that made her cheeks flame. He might be stern and grim, but she still thought he had the most fantastic eyes she had ever seen, and there was some humour in there somewhere. It was up to her to dig it out. But for now... To escape further scrutiny, she dipped her head to secure the strap on her sandals.

'You can't put those on here.'

Savannah's head shot up. 'But my feet are filthy. Surely you don't want them soiling your pristine deck?'

'I don't want them anywhere near me,' Ethan assured her, which for some reason made Savannah picture her naked feet rubbing the length of Ethan's muscular thighs and writhing limbs entwined on cool, crisp sheets.

Swallowing hard, she quickly composed herself whilst tucking her feet safely away beneath the seat. Such a relief she had Ethan's shirt to wrap around her; Madame's gown was split to kingdom come, and what little modesty she had left she had every intention of hanging on to.

But as the river rushed past the side of the boat, and Savannah thought about the flicker of humour she'd seen in Ethan's eyes, modesty began to feel like a handicap. If only she knew how to flirt...

Flirt? Fortunately, she wouldn't be given a chance. Savannah's sensible inner self breathed a sigh of relief as at that moment Ethan looked behind them. He must think they were still being followed, Savannah reasoned. She did too. The paparazzi would hardly have given up the chase. But she felt safe with Ethan at the helm. With his sleeves rolled back, revealing hard-muscled and tanned forearms, he gave her confidence—and inner flutters too. In fact the sight of these powerful arms was apparently

connected to a cord that ran from her dry throat to a place it was safer not to think about.

Had she lost her grip on reality altogether?

With every mile they travelled she was moving further and further away from everything that was safe and familiar into a shadowy world inhabited by a man she hardly knew. As the boat spewed out a plume of glittering foam behind them, Savannah couldn't shake the feeling she was racing into danger, and at breakneck speed.

There were many things he could do without in life, and of all them this fluffy thing in the oversized shirt was top of his list—though Savannah could be feisty. She had a stinging retort, for example, should she wish to use it. Far from that being a negative, he found it very much in her favour. She was also a real family girl, and, given that her parents would have undoubtedly seen everything unfolding live on television in their front room she had kept a cool head and thought not of herself but of them. A quick glance revealed her checking her feet. No doubt her pedicure was ruined. She was the smoothest, most pampered and perfect person he'd ever met, and possessed the type of wholesomeness that could only be damaged by him.

Feeling his interest, she looked up. He should be glad they couldn't hold a conversation above the thundering of the hull on the water. He had no small talk for her; he'd lived alone too long. His passion for rugby, one of the roughest contact-sports known to man, defined him. The majority of his business dealings were conducted on construction sites, where he loved nothing more than getting his hands dirty.

He was well named the Bear, and the contrast between him and Savannah was so extreme it was almost laugh-

able; only the music they both loved so much provided a tenuous link between them. Forced to wrench the wheel to avoid some children fooling around in a dinghy, he was surprised at the way his body reacted when Savannah grabbed hold of him to steady herself.

'Sorry!' she exclaimed, snatching her hand away as if he'd burned her.

He was the one who'd been burned. Savannah was playing havoc with his slumbering libido and, instead of shouting at her to sit down, he found himself slowing the boat to check that she was all right.

'I am now,' she assured him, and then they both turned around to make sure the children were okay.

As their eyes briefly clashed he was conscious of the ingenuous quality of her gaze. It warmed him and he lusted after more of that feeling. He needed innocence around him. And yet he could only sully it, he reminded himself. But he hadn't meant to frighten her, and it didn't hurt to take a moment to reassure her now.

'You're not such a baddy, are you?' she said to his surprise.

In spite of his self-control his lips twitched as he shrugged. A *baddy*? He had to curb the urge to smile. He'd shut himself off from all that was soft and feminine for too long. Living life by his own very masculine rules and preferences, he hadn't been called upon to take anyone else's feelings into account for quite some time. And a woman like Savannah's? Never. 'A baddy,' he repeated. 'I've never been called that before.'

It was as if she saw him differently from everyone else on the planet. He smiled. He couldn't help himself. Paying close attention to the river, he didn't look at her, but he knew that she was smiling too.

No sooner had he begun to soften towards Savannah than he reverted to coldly examining the facts. Did he need this sort of distraction in his life? Savannah was very young and had a lot of growing up to do. Did he want the attention of the world centred on him, when he'd successfully avoided publicity for so long? He'd gone to the match with the sole intention of supporting his friends in the England squad, and it was them who should be getting the attention, not him. He felt a stab of something reprehensible, and recognised it as envy. The days when he'd hoped to play rugby for England weren't so far away, but the past could never be recaptured. He had learned to adapt and change direction since then; he'd moved on. But the facts remained: the injuries he'd sustained during a prolonged beating by a gang of thugs had meant the club doctors had been unable to sign the insurance documents he needed to play his part in the professional game. And so his career had come to an abrupt and unwanted end.

But none of this was Savannah's fault. He might be drawn to her, but he wouldn't taint her with his darkness. He would fight the attraction he felt for her. Some might say he needed a woman like Savannah to soften him, but he knew that the last thing Savannah needed in her life was a man like him.

'I'm sorry you've missed the match, Ethan.'

The river was quieter here and he cut the engines. 'Don't worry about it. I'll watch the replay on television later.'

'But you can't detect the scent of excitement on a screen,' she said with concern.

Or feel the ravages of failure, the blaze of triumph... Yes, he knew that, but he was surprised Savannah did. 'It's no big deal.'

'Yes it is,' she said, pulling a face that made him think

how pretty she was. 'You'd be there now if it wasn't for me.' Frowning with concern, she began plucking threads from his ancient shirt.

He didn't prolong the exchange. He didn't like people getting close to him. He was a bear licking his wounds in the shadows, full of unresolved conflict and bitterness, and chose not to inflict himself on anyone—least of all an innocent young girl like Savannah.

'Watching England play must be both a passion and a torment for you.'

Why wouldn't she let it rest?

'Perhaps,' he agreed, accepting she meant no harm by these comments and was only trying to make conversation. It was public knowledge that the damage to his spine had ended his career. Lifting he could do, running he could do, but to risk another knock, another blow…

'You could let me off here, if it's quicker for you.'

He followed her gaze to a nearby landing stage. 'I could let you swim to the far bank,' he offered dryly. 'That might save some time.'

Her expression lifted, which pleased him. He didn't want to intimidate her, though his appearance must have done that already. Mooring up and calling a cab to take her to the airport was what he should do. He should let her go.

But the decision was taken out of his hands by the sound of rotor blades. The paparazzi's helicopter was still some way off, but it was approaching fast. There was no time to do anything more than hit the throttle and tell Savannah to hold on.

'They've found us?' she shouted above the roar of the engines.

Oh, yes. The race was back on. And no way was he going to let them catch her. 'Yes, they've found us,' he confirmed grimly. 'Sit tight.'

The spray was in her hair, her eyes, and her knuckles had turned white with holding on. If she'd been nervous before, she was terrified now. It was one thing showing a brave face to the world when things were going well, but the black, menacing shadow of the paparazzi helicopter would soon beam a travesty of the true situation around the world. Adding fuel to the paparazzi's fire, she was forced to cling to Ethan as he pushed the powerboat to its limits, because he was the only stable element in a world that was tipping and yawing as the currents played bat and ball with their hull.

Nothing had gone right for Ethan since she'd turned up in Rome, Savannah thought guiltily, and though he hardly knew her he had insisted on fighting her corner in spite of the personal cost to him. He must be wondering what he'd done to deserve such aggravation!

CHAPTER FIVE

As A surge of water threw the delicately balanced boat off kilter, Ethan fastened his arm protectively around Savannah's shoulders. At first she tensed, but then slowly relaxed. Ethan had no idea how profoundly his protective instinct affected her. Coming from a man as cold as he was, his smallest touch bore the intensity of a kiss. She could get used to this physical closeness all too easily. But they would soon reach the airport, she would fly home, and she would be nothing more than a tiresome memory to him. But at least the helicopter was wheeling away. 'Fuel shortage?' she suggested hopefully.

'I think you're being a little over-optimistic,' Ethan said as he powered back the engines. 'My best guess is they got the photographs they came for and their work is done.'

'How can you be so calm about it? Don't you care?'

'I don't waste time regretting things that can't be changed.'

'But they breached your privacy. Won't you make some sort of protest?'

Her heart jolted to see Ethan's lips tug in a smile. 'I hope you're not suggesting I should try to curb the freedom of the press?'

'Of course not, but.'

'But?' he pressed.

'Well, I just can't roll over.'

'You don't have to,' he pointed out. 'It's happened and I'll deal with it.'

'Okay, well, my parents are going to be devastated. What if the press are there right now, hammering on their door? Ethan, I have to call them.'

He couldn't imagine anyone else on earth in this predicament thinking of placing an international call, but he was fast learning that Savannah's first thought was always for others, and he envied the loving relationship she obviously enjoyed with her parents and would never stand in the way of it. 'I'll speak to them first to reassure them, and then you can speak,' he suggested, warming to her.

'Would you really do that?'

Her relief made him think he should have done it sooner. 'Number?'

As she recited it he punched it in to his mobile phone, and it occurred to him that Savannah must have no idea how lucky she was to have a loving family.

'You didn't have to do that,' she said several minutes later when she had finished speaking to her mother.

'I wanted to,' he admitted. 'It was the right thing to do,' he added sternly when Savannah's face softened into a smile.

'It was very kind of you.'

'It was nothing,' he argued, turning his attention back to sailing the boat. 'All I did was point out that my legal team will handle any press intrusion, and reassure your parents that they mustn't worry because you were safe with me.'

'You gave them your private number.'

'How else are they supposed to call me?'

'Well, thank you,' she said sincerely.

'Your mother seemed reassured,' he said, unbending a little. His reward was to see Savannah's face softening into a smile.

Her mother had been reassured, Savannah reflected with relief. Her romantic mother had always been a sucker for a strong man, though she preferred them safely corralled on the cover of a book or on a screen at the cinema, and kept a well-trained beta hero at home. She wondered if her mother would be quite so reassured if she could see Ethan in the flesh.

'I have another call to make,' Ethan told her, turning away.

As Ethan stood in profile his scars were cruelly exposed, and it appalled her to think one person could do that to another. But surely it couldn't have been one person—it had to have been more—a gang, maybe? She'd felt a fraction of Ethan's strength today and he was bigger, stronger and fitter than most men. What kamikaze group of yobs would have dared to take him on?

Trained yobs—professional thugs, truly evil men— was the only conclusion she could possibly come to. No casual attack could result in such serious injuries. But who would pay such men to beat Ethan so severely he'd nearly lost his life and *had* lost his sporting career? Professional rugby might be a highly competitive sport, but it was hardly a killing ground.

As Ethan finished his call and stowed the phone, turning the wheel to negotiate a bend in the river, Savannah was wondering if the person behind Ethan's beating also accounted for the darkness in his eyes. If so Ethan carried far more scars than were visible to the

naked eye. 'Are we going to the airport?' she said, noticing he was steering the boat towards a tributary.

'To the airport first, and then to my place in Tuscany— just until the heat dies down.'

'To Tuscany?' She was feeling more out of her depth than ever.

'Unless you'd prefer me to leave you to the mercy of the press?'

Savannah's heart turned over as Ethan looked at her. How childish he must think her. Women would scratch each other's eyes out for the chance to be with Ethan like this, and yet she had sounded so apprehensive at the prospect of staying with him. 'I don't want to be left to that pack of hounds,' she confessed. 'But I've put you out so much already.'

'So a little more trouble won't hurt me,' Ethan reassured her dryly.

Maybe his lack of enthusiasm didn't match up with her fantasies, but what Ethan had suggested was a sensible solution. And his place in Tuscany sounded so romantic— such a pity it would be wasted on them. 'Are you sure it wouldn't be easier for you if I just fly home?'

'If you do that you won't be able to take advantage of the security I can provide. It would take me quite some time to get the same level of protection set up for you in England, which is why I've made some arrangements for your parents.'

'Arrangements? What arrangements?' Savannah interrupted anxiously.

'I decided a cruise would take them well out of the range of prying eyes.'

'A cruise?' She gasped. 'Are you serious?'

'Why wouldn't I be serious?'

'You mean you booked a holiday for them?'

'It's the best solution I could come up with,' he said, as if booking fabulously expensive trips was nothing unusual for him.

Savannah couldn't stop smiling. 'You have no idea what this will mean to them. I can't remember the last time they went away—or even if they ever have been away from the farm.'

'The farm?'

'I live on a farm.' She shook her head, full of excitement. 'You must have seen my address on file?'

'Lots of addresses have the word "farm" in them. It doesn't mean a thing.'

'Well, in this instance it means a great deal,' she assured him, turning serious. Savannah's voice had dropped and emotion hung like a curtain between them, a curtain Ethan swiftly brushed aside.

'Well, I'm pleased I've made the appropriate arrangements.'

'Oh, you have,' Savannah said softly, thinking of all the times she'd wished she could have sent her exhausted parents away for a break, but she had never had the money to do so. Their grief when they'd lost their herd of dairy cows to disease had exacted a terrible toll, and they'd only survived it thanks to the support of the wonderful people who worked alongside them. Those same people would stand in for them now, allowing them to take the holiday they deserved.

'You've no idea what you've done for them,' Savannah assured Ethan.

He brushed off her thanks, as Savannah had known he would. But because of his generosity she thought he deserved to be wholly in the picture, and so she told him

how her parents had stood by and watched their whole herd being slaughtered—animals they'd known by name.

'That must have cost you all dearly,' he observed, looking at her closely. 'And not just in financial terms.'

It was a rare moment between them, but Ethan scarcely gave her a chance to enjoy it before switching back to practicalities. He treated emotion like an enemy that must be fought off at every turn, Savannah thought as Ethan told her that her bags would probably arrive at the *palazzo* before she did.

'Just a minute,' she said, interrupting him. 'Did you say "the *palazzo*"?' Of all the day's surprises, this was the biggest. Ethan had just turned all her points of reference on their head. As far as Savannah was concerned, a *palazzo* was somewhere people who existed on another planet lived.

'There are a lot of *palazzos* in Tuscany,' Ethan explained, as if it were nothing, but as Savannah continued to stare incredulously at him he finally admitted, 'Okay, so I've got a very nice place in Tuscany.'

'You're a very lucky man,' she told him frankly.

In the light of what Savannah had just told him about her parents' hardships, he had no doubt that was true. At least they'd be able to put plenty of space between each other at the *palazzo*, he reminded himself thankfully.

'Tell me about your *palazzo*.'

Finding he was staring at her lips as she spoke, he turned away. 'Later,' he said, relieved to see his driver waiting exactly where he had asked him to, by the landing stage. He waved to the man as he cut the engines and allowed the powerboat to glide into shore. 'We'll disembark first, and then I'll tell you more about it when we're on my jet.'

But she was back on the ground and in the back of a second limousine before Ethan turned to answer her questions.

'The name of the *palazzo*?' he resumed, leaning over from the front seat where he sat next to the driver. 'The Palazzo dei Tramonti Dorati.'

'That's quite a name.' Savannah laughed as she tried to say it, stumbling over the unfamiliar Italian words, acutely conscious as she did so that Ethan was watching her lips move.

'Not bad,' he said, congratulating her on her accent.

'What does it mean?' Savannah found that she badly wanted to hold Ethan's attention.

'It means "the Palace of the Golden Sunset".'

He hadn't meant to enter into conversation with her, but how could he not when she glowed with pleasure at the smallest thing? It reminded him, of course, of how very young she was, but even so he couldn't subdue the urge to tell her about a home he loved above all his others.

'It sounds so romantic!' she exclaimed, her eyes turning dreamy.

'Yes, it's a very old and very beautiful building.' He knew he was being drawn in, but he would never forget his first sight of the *palazzo*, and he'd had no one to share it with before. 'The towers glow rose-pink at sunset,' he explained, though he left out the emotional angle, which had entailed a longing to own the ancient *palazzo* that had come from the depths of his soul.

'The *palazzo* is located in a glorious valley blessed with sunlight, and the medieval village surrounding it is inhabited by wonderful people who appreciate the simple things in life.' And who had taken him to their heart, he remembered with gratitude. As he tried to convey some-

thing of this passion to Savannah without becoming overly sentimental, she remained silent and alert, as if what he didn't say told her everything she needed to know.

She confirmed this, saying softly when he had finished, 'You're even luckier than I thought.'

'Yes, well…' He left the statement hanging, feeling he'd gone too far. He wasn't a man to brag about his possessions, or even mention them.

Ethan was full of surprises. His sensitivity was obvious once he started talking about the *palazzo*. He flew planes, he rode bikes, he drove powerboats, and he had a perfect command of the Italian language. The thought that he did everything well and was capable of such passion sent a frisson of arousal shimmering through her.

Which she would put a stop to right away! Savannah's sensible inner voice commanded. It was one thing to fantasise about sexual encounters with Ethan, but quite another to consider the reality of it when she was saving her virginity for some sensible, 'steady Eddie' type of bloke, and then only when they were married.

'Are you too warm?' Ethan asked, misreading the flush that rose to her cheeks as she moved restlessly on the seat. 'I can easily adjust the temperature for you.'

Savannah bit her lip to hide her smile.

'What's so funny?' he demanded suspiciously.

What was so funny? Ethan was the man most women had voted to go to bed with, and she was the woman most men had decided not to go to bed with—that was funny, wasn't it?

'I asked you a question, Savannah.'

The easy atmosphere that had so briefly existed between them had suddenly gained an edge.

'Is it my scars?' he pressed. 'Do they make you nervous?'

Ethan had read her all wrong, Savannah realised. He was so far off the mark, she shook her head in shock. 'Of course they don't.' It was no use, because Ethan wasn't listening.

'Is that why you're trying so hard not to laugh?' he demanded.

'I've told you, no!' She held his gaze. There must be no doubt over this. She would be the first to admit she was overawed by Ethan, and that he even frightened her a little, but those feelings were all tied up in his worldliness contrasted with her own inexperienced sexual-self, and had not the slightest connection with his scars. If he thought she was shallow enough to be intimidated by them… Savannah shook her head with disgust at the thought. As far as she was concerned, Ethan's terrible scars were just a reminder that even the strongest tree could be felled. 'I see the man, not the scars,' she told him bluntly.

In the confines of the limousine his short, disbelieving laugh sounded cruel and hard.

That had to come from some memory in his past, Savannah reassured herself, refusing to rise to the bait. Sometimes it was better to say nothing, she was learning, and to persuade Ethan she was more than the fluffy girl he thought her would take action, not words. She had been raised on a working farm and knew the value of hard work. She was used to getting her hands dirty and wasn't frightened of much.

Just as well, Savannah reflected as Ethan turned away with a face like thunder to continue his conversation with the driver, because there was nothing easy about Ethan Alexander. But whatever Ethan's opinion of her, she would stand up for herself. Perhaps he had learned that

much about her. If nothing else this journey was giving them both the opportunity to learn a little more about each other. What she'd learned might not be reassuring, but it hadn't put her off Ethan either—in fact, quite the reverse.

CHAPTER SIX

As THEY approached the end of the journey they sat in silence, and Ethan could sense Savannah's unease. For all her excitement at the thought of seeing his *palazzo*, she was wondering what she had got herself into. He had always been intuitive. His mother had told him he was keenly tuned, close to the earth and all its mystery. She'd told him that before the crystal sphere she'd kept next to her bed told her to marry for the fourth time, apparently. At seven years old he had begged her not to do it, believing it would be a disastrous move for his mother and for himself. She had ignored him and the marriage had been a disaster. So much for his mother's belief in his special powers. The beatings had begun the day his new 'daddy' had arrived back from their honeymoon. He'd gone away to school that September, and had been the only boy in his class relieved to be living away from home.

And why was he remembering that now? He moved so that Savannah was no longer in his eyeline in the mirror. Was it because for the first time since his rugby career had been ended he wished he could be unblemished inside and out? Was it because Savannah Ross was too innocent to know the ugliness inside him?

Realising he was only paying attention to half the things his driver was telling him, he made some token comment and started watching Savannah again. She looked so small and vulnerable, sitting all alone on a sea of cream leather. The Bentley was the right scale for a man his size, but she was dwarfed by it. And she was a distraction he couldn't afford, he warned himself, especially if he was going to remain aloof from her when they reached their destination.

Stately cypress groves provided a lush green counterpoint to the rolling fields of Tuscany, and with the sun burning low in a cobalt sky Savannah wondered if there might be enough beauty here to distract her from her main obsession—but her main obsession turned at that moment to speak to her.

'We'll be arriving at the *palazzo* at the perfect time.'

'Sunset,' Savannah guessed. A thrill of excitement overtook her fear that Ethan had not forgotten or forgiven her for the earlier misunderstanding. As the light faded his face was in shadow, so she couldn't see his expression to gauge his mood, but there was something here that had lifted it—his *palazzo*, she suspected. Following the direction in which he was looking she searched hungrily for her first sight of the building. The sky was a vibrant palette of tangerine and violet so dramatic, so stunningly beautiful, she had butterflies in her stomach at the thought of what might come next. She could sense Ethan was also buzzing with expectation, and try as he might to be stern all the time, an attractive crease had appeared in his face. He'd softened just a little. Now if he could only soften a little more and smile at her that would be a gift—the only gift she wanted.

'When we cross the river, you'll see the *palazzo* in this direction.'

As Ethan pointed towards the shadowy purple hills, she sat bolt upright, tense with expectation.

'I don't want you to miss the approach,' he said, seeing her interest. 'It's quite spectacular.'

'I won't,' she assured him as anticipation fluttered in her stomach. Something told her that this was one of those precious moments that would mean something all her life and must be cherished.

She was only half right, Savannah discovered. When it came into view the *palazzo* exceeded her expectations so far it took her breath away. Rising like something out of a legend from the mist was a winding road and an old stone bridge, and then the towering walls. A glittering snake of water travelled beneath the bridge, and as they crossed it she thought the restless eddies were like mirrored scales carrying the sun-fire to the sea.

'Now you understand why the palazzo got its name.'

Even Ethan couldn't quite keep the excitement from his voice.

'Understatement,' she breathed. The turreted spread of the Palazzo dei Tramonti Dorati appeared framed in fire, and even her fertile imagination hadn't come close to doing it justice. This wasn't the Gothic horror she'd feared Ethan might inhabit, but a palace of light, built from pink stone that might have been sugar-rock. Glowing warm beneath the red-streaked sky, it couldn't have appeared more welcoming.

'What do you think?' Ethan prompted.

Savannah was surprised her opinion mattered to him, and the thought touched her immensely—though she mustn't read too much into it, she reminded herself. 'I

think it's stunning,' she told him honestly. 'The colour of the stone is extraordinary.'

'Pink?'

The touch of irony in his voice made her smile. Were they connecting at last? Just a little, maybe? But she wasn't going to push it. 'You must admit, it's unusual,' she said, trying to sound grown up about it, though the prospect of staying in a pink palace, and one as beautiful as this, would have excited anyone.

'The stone is pink because millions of years ago this whole valley was a deep marine-gulf,' Ethan explained. 'The pink hue is due to the millions of tiny shells and fossils locked in the rocks.'

'What a magical explanation.' And romantic, Savannah mused as Ethan settled back to enjoy the last leg of the journey. He might fight as hard as he could to keep his distance from her, but he had brought her to one of the most romantic places on earth. Ethan might shun everything pink or soft or feminine, but he'd let his guard down by showing her his *palazzo*. 'The Palace of the Golden Sunset,' she murmured happily as the limousine made a smooth transition from slick tarmac to the winding cobbled streets.

'Can you see the fragments of the original walls?' Ethan said, turning towards her again.

His enthusiasm was framed in a scholarly tone, but he was clearly determined to share this with her, and he didn't need to tell her how much he loved his *palazzo* when she could feel his passion like a warm cloak embracing her. 'Yes, I see them,' she said, pressing her face to the window. In some places there was little more than raised ground to show where the original walls must have stood, but at others she could see what remained of them.

They looked like blackened silhouettes pointing crooked fingers towards the blazing sky.

'Much of the structure dates from medieval times,' Ethan continued.

Like the thinking of its master? Savannah wondered. What would it take to have Ethan see her as a grown woman rather than as a singing sensation recently signed to his record label? And was she sure she wanted him to think about her that way? Wasn't it safer to remain as she was—a ward under his protection?

It was beyond the scope of Savannah's imagination to conjure up the consequences of attracting the sexual attentions of a man like Ethan, and as the limousine slowed to pass beneath a narrow stone archway she told herself how lucky it was that this was only destined to be a short stay. Any longer and she'd definitely fall in love with him.

The paparazzi would soon find another story and she'd be able to return home. But if she was so confident about that, why was she wracked by shivers of anticipation at the prospect of staying with Ethan?

Because she was tired, Savannah told herself firmly. Who could blame her for feeling uncomfortable with what lay ahead when she was pinned into a dress that felt more like a medieval torture-device than a couture gown?

'This gateway is called the Porta Monteguzzo.'

She paid attention as Ethan distracted her, and was about to answer him when, embarrassingly, her stomach growled.

'Hungry?' he prompted.

'I'm starving,' Savannah admitted, wondering when she had last eaten. And did she dare to eat when another crumb of food on her hips meant she would definitely pop out of Madame's gown and she had no clothes of her own to wear yet? 'Porta Monteguzzo,' she repeated, both in an

attempt to distract herself from hunger pangs and to try
again to master the musical Italian language. 'Doesn't
"*guzzo*" mean "food", in Italian?'

'You're thinking of gusto, perhaps?'

She watched his mouth, thinking how well he spoke
the language…amongst other things.

'Which means taste,' Ethan explained.

Or tasty, perhaps, Savannah mused as she turned to
stare innocently out of the window while Ethan resumed
his conversation in fluent Italian with their driver. But as
they drove deeper into Ethan territory and the world he
dominated, and those tall, stone walls of his stole the
light, Savannah knew that, though the sight of Ethan's
fairy-tale castle had thrilled her beyond belief, it had sin-
gularly failed to reassure her.

Oh.

Savannah's heart sank as she stood in the hallway of
the *palazzo*. It was a struggle to marry up the exquisite
exterior with this dismal space. Wasn't it wired for electricity? She could hardly make out the faces of Ethan's
staff as he showed her round.

Okay, so maybe that was a slight exaggeration, but the
inside of the palace was like something out of a gothic
horror film—'dark and dismal' didn't even begin to cover
it. It might just as well have been lit by candlelight, it was
so shadowy and grim. To say she was disappointed after
the stunning run-up to the building was a major understatement. But she was more concerned about the fact that
Ethan chose to live like this.

As the housekeeper led the way up the marble staircase, Savannah's apprehension grew. Apart from the very
real risk of missing her footing on the dimly lit staircase,

the landing they were heading for appeared equally dingy. To go from fairy-tale *palazzo* to the haunted house was a huge disappointment. She only had to contrast Ethan's grand *palazzo* with her parents' simple farmhouse to know there was no contest: she'd prefer the sunny chaos of the farmhouse to this grand grimness any day.

Perhaps she should offer a few home-improvement tips, Savannah concluded as the housekeeper indicated they should follow her down a darkened corridor. 'Don't you worry about your staff tripping over the rugs?' She took the chance to whisper discreetly to Ethan.

'I can't say it's ever occurred to me,' he said with surprise.

'It would occur to me,' Savannah said worriedly as the housekeeper stopped outside a carved-oak door. 'What if someone was carrying a tray with hot drinks on it, or some glasses, and they tripped? They could really hurt themselves, Ethan. This is dangerous. There's hardly any light here at all.'

'No one's ever complained before.'

She knew she should hold her tongue, but it was about time someone did complain, Savannah thought, and Ethan's staff was hardly likely to.

The more she thought about it, the more Savannah became convinced that she must be one of Ethan's first guests at the *palazzo* in a long time. She wasn't sure exactly what she'd been expecting from a man known to be reclusive, but this was hardly the big, open house her family would have filled with light and laughter. She smiled as she thought of the cosy farmhouse back home with its rickety furniture and frayed old rugs, but it was a hundred times more welcoming than this.

The housekeeper was smiling at her expectantly, Savannah realised, quickly refocusing and smiling back.

Ethan was shifting restlessly, as if he couldn't understand the delay before the housekeeper got round to opening a door. But Savannah understood perfectly when the housekeeper finally revealed her surprise.

'*Signorina*, this is your room.'

Savannah didn't need to see the older woman's beaming smile to know that someone was keen to make her feel welcome. 'My room?' Savannah stood on the threshold, gazing in wonder. 'You did this for me?' The contrast between this well-lit space and the rest of the *palazzo* was incredible. No wonder the housekeeper had revealed her surprise with such a flourish.

'You're too generous.' But as Savannah looked at Ethan she realised he was as surprised as she was. He'd had nothing to do with it. His staff had done all this for her. They must have thrown open every window to air the room, and they had certainly lit every available light. There was a log fire blazing in the hearth, which illuminated all the beautiful old oil-paintings, and there were fresh flowers everywhere, beaming a rainbow welcome at her. 'Thank you; thank you so much!' she exclaimed, turning to grasp the housekeeper's hands.

'You bring us music, *signorina*, but all we can bring you in return is flowers.'

'What do you mean "all"?' Savannah exclaimed. 'This means everything to me.'

Tears stung her eyes as she remembered this was the sort of thing her family did for each other at home. The housekeeper had given her the one thing money couldn't buy, and that was a genuine welcome. Conscious of Ethan standing at her side, and knowing how difficult he found dealing with displays of emotion, she expressed her feelings more calmly to him. 'This is wonderful, isn't it?

You have great people working for you. I hope you appreciate them.'

He would think her presumptuous, Savannah realised, though she could read nothing on Ethan's face. But she had to say something, because his staff had carved an oasis of light and beauty for her from his cold, dark *palazzo*, and now she was eager to do the same for him.

He was shocked by his staff's initiative. All he'd done was call ahead to explain the situation to them and ask them to make a room ready for Savannah Ross. He should have known the Italians' great love of music meant they would already know everything about Savannah, and that it would have put wings on their heels when they learned he was bringing her to stay.

As his gaze embraced the room before him, he began noticing things he hadn't before, like the pink-veined, marble-topped console table where the telephone rested. He had bought it with the *palazzo*, and it was a beautiful example of a craftsman's art. Savannah was right; with the light shining on it, the furniture, like everything else in the room, was fully revealed in all its glory. No wonder she had been so relieved to see the efforts his staff had gone to for her. But the real difference here was Savannah, he thought, watching her shimmering golden hair bounce around her shoulders as she followed the housekeeper around the room. Savannah brought the light with her.

With emotions roused that he had thought were long buried, Ethan was suddenly keen to put some distance between them, so he found an excuse to leave Savannah in the care of his housekeeper. But she stubbornly refused to let him disappear so easily. 'I'm so excited,' she told him. 'I can't thank you enough for allowing me to stay here.'

'Then don't. This is nothing to do with me.' He dismissed the glowing room with a gesture.

'You're so wrong,' she assured him. 'This has everything to do with you.'

He shrugged. 'In this instance, Savannah, it is you who is wrong. This is a beautiful suite of rooms and nothing more. It has been aired and put back into use, and that is all.'

'And is that all you have to say about it?' she demanded, frowning.

'What else is there to say? I rarely come here, but it is beautiful, and I had forgotten.'

'But you never will forget again,' she insisted passionately. 'Not now the lights have been switched on.'

He gave her a look that stopped her in her tracks. It was a look intended to warn her not to go this far again. The contact between them was electric, and he let the moment hang for some reason. Anything might have happened as Savannah looked up at him had not his housekeeper coughed discreetly at that moment. It was only then that the rational side of him clicked into focus, and he took a proper look at Savannah and realised how exhausted she looked. She was still wearing his old shirt over the ill-fitting gown. She must have felt embarrassed, dressed that way when he'd introduced her to his staff, but not for a moment had she let it show. Her attention had been all on them, her only thought to make them feel special. 'Could you bring Ms Ross a robe, please?' he asked his housekeeper.

He wanted Savannah covered up. Her pale skin beneath the neck of his shirt was making him restless. She still had her precious sandals dangling from her wrist, like a child with a garish bangle, and she was scarcely taller than a

child. She couldn't have eaten since that morning, he remembered. 'Take a bath,' he said briskly, 'And then use that phone over there to call down for something to eat.'

'Won't you eat something too?' she asked with concern.

'Maybe.' He dismissed her with a gesture. He had no intention of prolonging this encounter. It occurred to him then that perhaps he didn't trust himself to prolong it.

'Where will you eat?' she pressed as he prepared to leave.

He hadn't given it a moment's thought. 'I'll take dinner in my room,' he said, remembering that that was what he usually did.

'In your room?' She pulled a face, and then immediately grew contrite. 'Sorry. It's none of my business where you eat.'

No, it isn't, he almost informed her, thinking of her other comments since they'd arrived, but the fact that she looked so pale held him back.

Fortunately his housekeeper returned at that moment with the robe, which put a halt to further conversation.

He took that as his cue. 'Goodnight, Savannah. Sleep well.'

'I'll see you in the morning?' Her eyes were wide, her expression frank.

'Perhaps.' With her innocent enthusiasm she made it hard for him to remain distant.

'For breakfast?' she pressed.

'Ah…' He paused with his hand on the door, as if to say he was a much older man with many better things to do than to entertain a young woman. 'We'll see.'

'Sleep well, Ethan. And thank you once again for allowing me to stay in your beautiful home.'

Who should be thanking who? he wondered, catching

sight of the luminous expression on his housekeeper's face. 'Goodnight, Savannah.' He didn't need a second dose of Savannah's radiant face before he walked out and closed the door to know his defences had been breached.

CHAPTER SEVEN

SAVANNAH waited for Ethan's footsteps to fade before asking the housekeeper shyly, 'Do you think it would be possible to put on some more lights?' The housekeeper had been so kind to her that Savannah felt her request might have some chance of success.

'More lights, *signorina*?'

'In the *palazzo*? I mean, it's very dark outside my room, and I just thought it might be safer for you—for all of us.'

The housekeeper studied Savannah's face before deciding. 'Come with me, *signorina*.'

As they left the room together the housekeeper called to a passing footman, who looked at Savannah with surprise when he heard her request via the housekeeper. As he hurried away, the housekeeper exchanged a look with Savannah. 'You are starting a revolution,' she confided.

'Oh dear.'

'No, it's good.'

'Is it?' If only she could feel confident that Ethan would agree.

Savannah approached the first light-switch.

It took all of her resolve just to switch it on. But when she did...

'*Bellissima!*' The housekeeper exclaimed, clasping her hands in front of her. 'This is what the *palazzo* has been waiting for.'

Her endorsement encouraged Savannah to ask if they could put a few more lights on.

The housekeeper drew in a breath and then, exhaling slowly, she turned to look at Savannah. Her eyes were sparkling. 'A very few,' she agreed. 'Let's do it!'

They hurried off in different directions, snapping on light switches like naughty children, and they didn't stop until the whole of the upper floor was flooded with light.

Down in the hallway Savannah could see more lights being turned on. It was like the curtain going up at the theatre, she concluded, feeling that same sense of wonder—but the only difference here was a glorious home was being revealed rather than a stage set.

The housekeeper rendezvoused with Savannah back at her room. 'It's amazing!' Savannah exclaimed softly, gazing at the transformation they'd created.

'*Si, signorina.* You have worked a miracle.'

'A very tiny miracle,' Savannah argued with a smile. 'I only turned on the lights.'

'Sometimes that's all it takes,' the older woman observed shrewdly.

They shared a smile before the housekeeper left Savannah, after asking her to promise she would call downstairs if she needed anything more.

Well, she would need all the friends she could find on the staff, if she stood a chance of leaving Ethan's home happier than she had found it, Savannah reflected. But with all his beautiful treasures bathed in light she had to believe he would share her enthusiasm for ancient

frescoes stepping out of the shadows, and carvings revealed in all their intricate detail after years of neglect.

But…would he be pleased, or would he be angry at her continued interference? She was only a guest, after all, and one that wasn't here for very long. She suspected she knew why Ethan avoided light, but her concern was for the main thoroughfares where safety was an issue. The more intimate areas like Ethan's rooms could remain discreetly lit. She could only hope he would agree it was a happy balance.

Deep inside, Savannah believed everyone needed light. And as for the *palazzo*, well, she'd already seen the results of the transformation Ethan's staff had brought about in her rooms, and their instincts were right. There should be light, love and music in such a beautiful home. There should be life at the *palazzo*.

Savannah took a long, soapy bath. Now the excitement was over, she realised how hungry she was, and until supper arrived a bath was the perfect distraction from hunger pangs as well as from the likely repercussions of her interference in Ethan's home.

Twiddling the taps with her toes, she sank a little lower in the fragrant bubbles. This story might not have a happy-ever-after ending, but she had fairy-tale accommodation for the night, and after the staff had gone to so much trouble it would have been churlish for her to refuse the setting they had prepared.

She had rifled through the full-sized luxury products on the glass shelves like a small child in a beauty salon, and now the scent rising from the steam had led her into a dream world of erotic images in which Ethan starred…

Wrapped up cosily in a warm robe some time later, she

stared into the mirror. It was so easy to imagine Ethan's dark face when she saw him in the shadows everywhere she went. It was torture, knowing he was somewhere close by, and almost impossible not to imagine him stripped and naked beneath an ice-cold shower. It would be cold water, because warm was too indulgent for him. And his bedroom would be spartan, she decided, because Ethan denied himself anything soft or superfluous— which didn't leave her with too much hope, Savannah concluded wistfully.

Rubbing her hair vigorously, she walked back into the bedroom. Kneeling in front of the fire to dry her long hair, she thought about Ethan's complex character. All he seemed to need was a clean bed and a floor to pace— perhaps with the addition of a giant television-screen in every room to catch up on any rugby matches he might have missed. Perhaps it was the legacy of those dreadful scars that made him so careless of his own comfort.

Thinking about them always made her so angry. Casting the towel aside, she began to pluck distractedly at the rug. Who would do that to him? Who could do that to a fellow human being?

Why don't you ask him? Savannah's inner voice prompted.

Because life isn't that simple?

But it could be, if she went to him, and spoke to him…

Rolling onto her back, Savannah stared up at the ornate plasterwork. All the *palazzo* could be like this, cared for and fully restored, and always welcoming. Or it could remain cold and full of shadows. How lonely it must be to live in the dark.

Sitting bolt upright, Savannah hugged her knees and, resting her chin, she stared into the fire. It didn't have to

be like this if someone changed it around—if she changed it around. An impossible task, perhaps, but not if she had the help of Ethan's staff. Even this gleaming fireguard, polished to a flawless sheen, was evidence of their care for him. They had to be as keen as she was to see the *palazzo* come back to life.

Impatient with inaction, she sprang up. She hardly knew where she was going, but as she crossed the room her spirits lifted. It was such a glorious ultra-feminine space it must have given Ethan a headache just to poke his head round the door. Everything that wasn't gilded or twinkling glass was covered in silk, satins or velvet, and all in the most exquisite pastel colours. Stretching out her arms, she turned full circle, thinking it the most appealing space she had ever inhabited. She was still smiling broadly when she reached the door and opened it. 'Ethan!'

'Savannah.'

She knew immediately from his voice that Ethan was furious. She felt instantly guilty, as well as silly and awkward, standing barefoot in front of him in her towelling robe. Her lips trembled and her smile died instantly.

'What have you done?' he snapped.

Her gaze slid away. 'I was taking a bath.'

'You know I don't mean that.'

Savannah drew her robe a little closer, conscious that Ethan's stare was boring into her, demanding an answer.

'I mean the lights,' he explained. 'I take it you're responsible?'

'Yes, I switched them on. Please don't be angry with your staff, Ethan.' She touched his arm. 'It was all my fault. I did it for them, for you.'

'For me? For them? What is this nonsense?'

Tears were threatening. She had been so looking

forward to sharing this moment with him, Savannah realised, and now it had all gone wrong. Far from wanting light, Ethan craved the darkness to hide his scars. She should have known and not been so insensitive. In trying to help him she had arrogantly assumed she was right, only seeing the world from her own perspective. And now he couldn't wait to turn those lights off, or for her to leave. 'I'm so sorry—'

'You'll have to leave,' he said, perfectly echoing her thoughts. 'I can't have this sort of interference. Please pack your bags.'

'Ethan—'

'There's nothing more to say, Savannah.'

'But it's nighttime. Where will I go?'

'A hotel, the airport, somewhere—I don't care.'

'You're throwing me out?'

'Save your melodrama for the stage.'

'Says you, living in the dark!' She couldn't believe she'd said that. But it was true. She was fighting for Ethan, and where that was concerned nothing she said was going too far. But as Ethan's stony stare raked her face, Savannah realised he didn't see it that way.

'Will you pack?' he said coldly, confirming her worst fears. 'Or must I call the housekeeper to do that for you?'

'Ethan, please.' It was no use. He'd closed off to her.

As he shook Savannah's hand from his arm, he saw her tears and his heart ignored the dictates of his head.

'Please don't be angry with your housekeeper,' she entreated, adding to the conflict boiling inside him. 'You must know this is all my fault.'

Every bit of it was Savannah's fault...or her blessing. He turned his back so he wouldn't have to look into her face, but still he felt her goodness washing over him. She

wouldn't stop until all the bitterness was cleaned away. She touched his arm, begging him. 'You've gone too far,' he growled, wanting even now to protect her from that black evil inside him.

She didn't argue, and instead she did something far worse: she confessed.

'You're right,' she said frankly. 'I interfered where I shouldn't have. This is your home, Ethan, not mine. I asked your staff to turn on some lights so it was safer for them, and for you. I can see I went too far with that plan when one or two lights would have been sufficient, and if you want me to leave I will. All I ask is your promise that you won't blame your staff for my thoughtless actions.'

He didn't need to see any more tears to know that Savannah was at her most vulnerable. Yet she fought on in the defence of others. He couldn't ignore that. Her appeal had touched him deeply in a way he hadn't felt, maybe, ever. He was still wondering how best to deal with this unusual situation when the housekeeper Savannah was at such pains to defend came unwittingly to their rescue.

'Something to eat, *signore, signorina*?' she said blithely when Savannah opened the door to her knock.

What perfect timing, Savannah thought, exhaling with relief as she smiled at her new friend. As her shoulders relaxed she quickly adapted her manner so as not to concern the older woman. 'Let me take that tray from you.'

'No, please, let me.' Ethan's innate good manners meant he had to step forward in front of Savannah to take the tray himself.

'Thank you, *signore*,' the housekeeper said politely, handing Ethan the tray without any sign that she had overheard their heated exchange. 'I've made enough for two.'

Hmm, Savannah thought, realising Ethan had no other option other than to carry the tray into her room. 'Let me clear a space for you,' she said, hurrying ahead of him.

To give her a moment to regroup, she rushed about, hunting for her slippers. Ethan placed the tray down on the low table between the two sofas and remained standing.

This was one consequence she could not avoid.

By the time she had found her slippers and slipped them on, she could hardly breathe, let alone speak as she came to a halt in front of Ethan.

When exactly had he become so hard and unfeeling? She had only turned the lights on, after all, which in the bright world Savannah inhabited was a very small transgression. As she ran her fingers through her still-damp hair, her face naked after her shower, he knew she was also naked under her robe. She looked nervous, apprehensive; fearful. She was certainly braced for a stinging rebuke. 'We shouldn't let the supper go to waste. That's if you don't mind…'

She looked surprised at his suggestion, as he had expected, but she quickly rallied, saying, 'Of course I don't mind. Please, sit down. You must be hungry too?'

'A little,' he admitted.

Savannah had to stop audibly sighing with relief as Ethan sat down. Maybe there was a chance, however slender, that she could change things for him before she left; it was all she wanted. But as always in the world of Savannah things never ran according to plan. She remembered that her underwear for the next day, having been rinsed out, was still hanging over the bath—large, comfy knickers included. What if he decided to go in there? 'D'you mind, if I…?' Flapping her hands, she glanced anxiously across the room.

'Not at all. Take your time,' Ethan invited.

She would have to, Savannah thought, resting back against the bathroom door. She wasn't leaving this room until her heartbeat steadied, which meant she could be in here quite some time. Ethan was full of surprises. She felt like he was giving her a second chance. But he was so complex, she had no idea what to expect next. But then she hardly knew him, Savannah reasoned. When she emerged from the bathroom, there was music playing.

'Do you like it?' Ethan asked as Savannah poked her head self-consciously round the door.

'Is it what I think it is?'

'If you think it's your first CD then, yes, it is.'

Savannah pulled back inside the bathroom, suffused with too many emotions to impose them on Ethan. She felt elated that her teachers' and parents' dreams for her had come true, and dread that Ethan only regarded her as a property belonging to his record label.

'Aren't you coming out to join me?' he called. 'Come and listen to your music.'

She could hardly refuse, since Ethan owned the record company. 'Do you like it?' she said anxiously when she returned.

'Like it? Your singing voice always makes me think of…'

Frogs croaking? Wheels grinding?

'Birds singing,' he said, settling back with a blissful expression on his face as Savannah's voice filled the room. 'Song birds,' he added dryly, without opening his eyes.

At least not crows squawking.

She should have more confidence, Savannah told herself, but in many ways she was as happy in the shadows as Ethan. In a different way, of course. But she

loved nothing more than the wide-open countryside back home, and the fact that she could walk for miles unnoticed as she soaked up all the glories of nature.

'I'm glad we signed you.'

Savannah refocused to find Ethan staring thoughtfully at her. 'Thank you.' She risked a small smile as her heart drummed wildly.

'You should eat something. It must be hours since you last ate.'

Probably. She had no idea. But she would have to lean past him to take something, and she was acutely aware that she was naked under her robe.

'Here,' he said, offering her the loaded plate. 'Take one of these delicious *ciabatta*.'

'Ethan, if I've offended you—'

'Eat something, Savannah, before you faint.'

'I didn't mean to,' she finished softly. 'Sometimes my enthusiasm carries me away.'

He hummed at this and angled his stubble-shaded chin towards the plate.

'Thank you.' Selecting a delicious-looking, well-filled roll, she bit into it with relish, expressing her pleasure in a series of appreciative sounds. Even now, beneath Ethan's unforgiving eye, she couldn't hide her feelings. 'You're very lucky to have such wonderful staff.'

'Yes, I am.' And when she thought that short statement was it, he added, 'You were right about the gloom making life difficult for them. And, yes, even dangerous. And, as for artworks, I hadn't even noticed.' He paused and then admitted, 'Who would think turning on the lights could make such a difference?'

She could.

CHAPTER EIGHT

ETHAN realised how much he had misjudged Susannah when his housekeeper, having returned with a fresh plate of food, took him to one side to inform him that she was glad to see how happy the *piccola signorina* was now the lights were on.

The way the older woman had held his gaze suggested more than the fact that Savannah was a guest with particular tastes to accommodate, or even that his housekeeper liked the young singer and wanted to make her stay as comfortable as possible. It was more the type of look the older generation gave the younger in Italy—and would sometimes be accompanied by tapping the side of the nose. Naturally, the older woman wouldn't dream of being so familiar with him, but she had got her message across. He'd brushed off her inquisitiveness with a rare smile.

Some time ago he had come to understand and even envy the Italian nation's fixation with love. And how could he be angry with Savannah, when all it took to make him smile was to watch her sucking her fingers with gusto before devouring another sandwich? Savannah had transformed the *palazzo* in the short time she'd been here, filling it with good things and raising the spirits of his

staff. It wouldn't last when she'd gone, of course, but she had unlocked one small portion of his heart, which was good news for his staff.

'It is a beautiful room, isn't it?'

As Savannah lifted her head with surprise, he realised he was seeing things through her eyes and how different things could be if he decided to make them so.

She'd go mad with grief if she heard that Ethan had returned to his old ways when she went home. And that wasn't overreaction, it was pure, hard fact, Savannah concluded, blushing when, having held the door for his housekeeper, Ethan remained leaning against the door frame with his powerful arms folded across his chest, watching her.

Her body reacted as if Ethan had just made the most indecent suggestion. His tight fitting T-shirt strained hard across his chest, and his jeans were secured with a heavy-duty belt. She had noticed all this in the space of a few seconds, and started nervously when Ethan moved.

'More sandwiches?' he suggested, strolling across the room towards her.

She was as tense as a doe at bay, Savannah realised, sitting straight. 'No, thank you.'

And then she decided she had better get up and clear some space on the table for all the new food, but being nervous and clumsy she moved erratically, and somehow a chair leg got in her way. Ethan called out, but it was too late, and as he reached out to grab her to stop her falling she ended up in his arms.

'Suddenly you've got more legs than a millipede, and each one of them travelling in a different direction,' he suggested.

'Pretty much,' she admitted, though the millipede analogy failed to grow on her. A better woman would have made the most of this opportunity, while all she could think was had she cleaned her teeth?

'Well, I'm still hungry,' he admitted, letting her go and heading back to the sofa.

She watched him stretch out his muscular legs, knowing she had never felt more awkward in her life. And yes—thank the dentist's warnings—she had cleaned her teeth, but Savannah Ross was about to play host to Ethan Alexander? It hardly seemed possible.

'Won't you help me?' He glanced her way as he reached for a sandwich. 'My housekeeper clearly thinks we both need feeding up.'

Or perhaps the older woman wanted to keep him here, Savannah thought, surprising herself with this reflection. They ate in silence until Savannah put down her napkin with a sigh of contentment. The hearty feed had reminded her of home.

'You were hungry,' Ethan commented, wiping his lips on a napkin.

As he continued to stare at her, Savannah's cheeks heated up. They were still talking about food, weren't they?

Of course they were, she reasoned, smoothing out her hair, or rather the tangles. What must Ethan think of her, bare faced and barely dressed? Having never entertained a man before whilst naked beneath a robe, she wasn't too sure of the protocol. And as Ethan still showed no sign of going anywhere, she suggested, 'Why don't I switch on the television?' Maybe they'd catch the news, she reasoned.

'The television?'

'I just thought maybe there would be a news report about the match…or us.' Her cheeks fired up as Ethan gave her a look. The word 'us' couldn't have carried more embarrassing weight had it tried.

'I try to escape the news when I'm here.' Ethan's tone was a chilling return to his former manner.

'But surely not items affecting your business—or world affairs—or sport?' She was running out of options, wishing she knew how to turn the clock back so she could remove all reference to 'us'.

'No,' he said bluntly. 'And, Savannah, I need to tell you something.'

By which time she'd switched on the set. Her timing was impeccable, Savannah realised, recoiling as she blenched. 'Why, that's ridiculous!' A news item had just flashed up on the screen. A news item featuring Ethan Alexander caught out, so the reporters said, with his latest squeeze, a young ingénue only recently signed to his record label.

'How could such a nice evening end so badly?' Ethan wondered, glancing at her.

Now she knew why he hadn't wanted her to turn it on. 'How can you take it so well?'

'Because I know what to expect. That's one of the reasons I came to find you. I wanted to tell you myself before you found out by some other means. But now…' Leaning across her, picking up the remote-control and pointing it at the set, he switched it off.

'Shouldn't we know everything before we do that?' Savannah exclaimed. Terrible lies were being told about them. 'Don't you care what they're saying about us?'

'Do I care about gossip?'

'Gossip? They're telling lies!'

Ethan responded calmly. 'What are they going to do? They'll soon tire of us, and in no time those pictures will be wrapped around somebody's fish and chips.'

'A famous tycoon saves the girl with the golden tonsils, blushes, in front of a worldwide television audience?' Savannah stuck a finger in her mouth to show what she thought of that. 'A story like that could run and run.'

'Gossip only hurts you if you allow it to,' Ethan told her evenly. 'And if you're going to let it get you down like this, Savannah, perhaps you should have another think about pursuing a career in the public eye.'

Were those her marching orders? She went cold immediately, thinking of all the people who had helped her along the way and who would be badly let down if she quit. 'But the press say we're sleeping together.' Surely that would get through to him?

Ethan's brow rose seductively. 'Is that so bad?'

He shouldn't tease her. Savannah's cheeks flushed crimson the moment he put the thought of them being sexually involved into her head. And why was he doing that when he had vowed not to think of Savannah as anything other than a young girl under his protection? Was it because sometimes a deeper feeling than common sense took the lead?

Before he had a chance to reason it through she begged him to switch on the set again so she could know the worst. She made him smile inwardly. Her voice was shaking with anger, not fear, and her hands were balled into fists as if she would like to punch out the screen. She was new to this, he remembered. 'You know what they're saying and so do I,' he soothed, 'So let them get on with it.'

'No,' she shot back fiercely. 'We have to issue a denial.'

'We have something to deny?' he queried, pouncing on her naivety before it had a chance to take root. Picking up the remote-control which she had cunningly re-claimed, he tossed it out of her reach.

Gradually she relaxed, hopefully seeing the sense behind his years of doing battle with the press. 'Thank goodness my parents are away,' she said, confirming this.

She looked so grateful it drove home the message that Savannah came from a strong and loving family. He couldn't shake a lingering sense of loss for something he'd never had. But her desire to go out and slay dragons soon distracted him. The expression on her face was so appealing.

It took Savannah a moment to realise Ethan was laughing. It was the first time she'd heard him laugh, without it being an ugly or mocking sound. 'What's so funny?'

He shook his head, unable to speak for a moment. 'The infamous hard man and his teenage songbird?' he managed at last. 'They make us sound like something out of a novel.'

'And I'm not a teenager,' Savannah pointed out. 'I was twenty last week.'

'Twenty?' Ethan's face stilled. 'As old as that?'

'Well, I'm not some teenage tweety-pie, if that's what you think—and I think we should sue them,' she said seriously, which only made him start laughing again.

'You can if you like,' Ethan suggested between bouts of laughter.

Using magic beans to pay the lawyers, presumably. But as she had a leading role in this mess she was deter-mined to do something about it.

'From my point of view.'

'Yes?' Savannah stared intently at Ethan, ready to jump

into armour and fight at his side at the first sign he was preparing to take on the press.

'I think you should ignore it, as I will. Unless—' he held up his hands when she was about to leap in '—they become a nuisance, in which case I shall act.'

That was just so disappointing. She didn't want to sit back and have rubbish thrown at her. She was about to challenge Ethan's decision when a knock came at the door and her bags from the stadium arrived.

'I haven't let you down yet, have I?' Ethan demanded as she checked them over. 'And I'm not about to start now. And where this newspaper rubbish is concerned you'll just have to try something new.'

'Such as?' Lifting her head, she stared at him.

'You could try trusting me.'

'But we're trapped here,' she pointed out.

'Yes, in this terrible place,' Ethan mocked gently. 'Poor us.'

He only had to say this for warning darts of fire to attack every part of her, and each tiny arrow carried a subtle message. She wanted him, but confronted by Ethan's worldliness, and by the thought of staying under his roof, she grabbed the edges of her robe and tugged it firmly shut. 'Haven't they've got anything better to do than speculate about us?'

'They're only doing their job,' Ethan pointed out. 'We're newsworthy. You. Me. Both of us together. Now that's a real story.'

'But this isn't a real story. They've twisted the truth and made innocent photographs seem so…'

'Suggestive?'

She hadn't wanted to say that, and when Ethan looked at her a certain way she wished she hadn't. Prior to this

she had been sure Ethan thought of her as a ward beneath his protection, and the thought that he was now looking at her as a woman was unsettling. It might be everything she had ever dreamed of, but as fantasy hurtled towards reality at breakneck pace she lost her nerve. Getting up, she assured him, 'Well, don't worry, if I do have to stay here for any length of time, I'll keep right out of your way.'

'How very thoughtful of you,' Ethan murmured. 'Tea?' he proposed. 'Hot and sweet, perhaps?' he added under his breath. 'It's good for shock.' He reached for the phone to call the kitchen.

Shock? He thought she was in shock? She probably *was* in shock after seeing the news bulletin, Savannah conceded. But tea? She didn't want tea. 'I think I need something stronger than that.'

Ethan held the phone away from his ear. 'Espresso?'

His face was poker straight, but his eyes were laughing at her. This humorous side of him—so unsuspected, so attractive—was unbelievably seductive. And terrifying. She had no idea how to handle a man—any man—let alone a man like Ethan. The situation was rapidly spiralling out of control. 'Gin and tonic, please,' she said firmly, thinking it might help. 'A large one.'

For a moment she thought Ethan might refuse, but then he crossed the room to the wet bar where he mixed a drink. At last he was treating her like someone over the age of consent.

'Here you are,' he said pleasantly, handing her the glass. 'I hope I got the balance right?'

She took a large swig in a pathetic attempt to maintain a confident image—and choked. Worse than choked she wheezed and choked, whilst waving her hands frantically in the air as fire consumed her gullet.

'So, you're a virgin,' he said with amusement.

She was aghast that he could tell. 'How did you know?'

Holding the crystal tumbler aloft, he stared into the clear liquid. 'You can't drink a decent measure of alcohol without…' His voice tailed away as he looked at her. 'Oh, I see. We're not talking about the same thing, are we? Well, are we, Savannah?' Ethan pressed, and, far from being humorous now, his expression was grim.

She couldn't answer. Her throat had seized up with embarrassment. In the silence that followed everything Ethan had ever thought about her seemed to grow in her mind to grotesque proportions. She was too young for him, too inexperienced, too naïve, and whatever hopes she'd ever had about them ever being together had just turned into dust. But that didn't stop her wanting him, it just pushed him further away, because Ethan was so principled he would never even think of making love to her, believing her innocence was under his charge.

A virgin? *A virgin!* Ethan recoiled inwardly. This made the situation so much worse. How much worse he could hardly quantify in thought, let alone words. Savannah was only here to enjoy his protection, yet until a minute ago he had arrogantly contemplated seducing her. She was still so young, and his first thought must always be to protect her. He had to hang onto that thought now if he was to save her from the greatest danger of all, which was him—the very man who was supposed to be taking care of her.

'Ethan, please don't be angry with me,' she begged him as he made for the door.

'Angry with you?' He was bemused she could think that. 'Goodnight, Savannah.'

'Ethan, please.'

He was halfway through the door when she ran towards him. 'Sleep well,' he said, closing the door firmly behind him with Savannah on the other side. He didn't trust himself to wait and listen to her reply.

She sat on the bed for a long time after Ethan left. With her arms pressed tightly on the top of her head, she knew she'd made such a hash of everything and that she didn't have a clue how to make it right. She had known for some time now that she loved Ethan. How could she care for anyone as deeply as she did for him and not love him? But he still frightened her. She had played a foolish game of make-believe. The first time Ethan had noticed she was a woman, she had taken fright, and now his principles meant they could never be together. *Well done, Savannah*, she congratulated herself; there'd be no encores here.

Climbing off the bed, she went to stare into the mirror. What did Ethan see when he stared in his? He lived his life in spite of his injuries. He had triumphed over them. Or had he? Was she only seeing Ethan's public face? Did those scars torment him when he was alone? Because she cared about him, she couldn't stop thinking about it. How could she leave Tuscany and Ethan with so many things unresolved? She would go to him and speak to him. She would reason with him in the hope that when she went away they could at least be friends.

The fact that she didn't have a clue what she was going to say was immaterial, Savannah thought, tugging on her jeans. This was just one of those moments when doing nothing wasn't an option. She refused to have Ethan think she was repulsed by his scars, or that she made a habit of accepting hospitality and then changing everything

around for her host. Caring about someone came with responsibility, which meant she couldn't turn her back on him. And as this might be her last chance to search beneath Ethan's public persona, and find the real man underneath, she had no intention of wasting it.

CHAPTER NINE

Maybe the fates had decided she deserved a bit of luck, Savannah concluded as she followed a group of servants carrying fresh towels and a tray with a pot of coffee on it. There couldn't be that many people staying at the *palazzo*, surely?

All she cared about was finding Ethan, and as she waited, concealed in the shadows while one of the servants knocked on a door, she thrilled at the sound of his voice. Finding him filled her with relief.

She waited for the staff to come out again, and when their footsteps had died away she came out of hiding and cautiously approached the door around which they'd been clustered. The handle yielded all too easily, and as she pressed the door open a crack she could hear the shower running.

Opening the door fully, Savannah slipped inside. She found herself in a mannish-looking sitting room where the scent of good leather and books was overwhelming. She looked around. Okay, so now what? There was hardly anywhere to hide. As she had suspected, Ethan's tastes were plain. The floors were polished wood, and the sofas were dark-brown leather. The walls were lined with books and not much else, other than some vibrant modern paintings.

Originals, Savannah noted with interest, signed with a letter B that had a diagonal line through it. She could imagine what a psychologist might make of that. And as for the content: frightened, wide-eyed children without faces or proper form. The paintings were brilliant—but, in the same way Edvard Munch's *The Scream* both fascinated and repelled, these paintings were deeply disturbing. And there were shadows in them…lots and lots of shadows.

Were the paintings an autobiographical account of Ethan's childhood?

She'd bet her life on it. And this window into his psyche was both more illuminating and far worse than anything she had imagined. That he had immense talent was in no doubt, and as another type of artist she found that bond between them reassuring—though everything else about the paintings troubled her and told her she was right to be concerned. Listening, she was reassured to hear the shower still running. What other secrets could she uncover in the time she had?

She wasn't here to pry, but to sense things, Savannah told herself, remaining motionless in the middle of the room. And then the water stopped running. And she was completely exposed. She braced herself. All the clever words and questions she'd been preparing for Ethan deserted her. But when he didn't emerge from the bathroom curiosity got the better of her. Tip-toeing to the door, she peeped through a crack. Sensation streamed through every inch of her at the sight of Ethan standing in front of a mirror with just a towel around him.

He was magnificent.

Although his scars were far, far worse than she had thought, she had never seen anyone half so virile or ap-

pealing. His legs were beautifully shaped and muscular, and his naked torso was everything she had dreamed of. The extent of his injuries, of his scarring, only proved it was a miracle he had made it through, and the thought of the pain he must have experienced cut her like a knife. He was twice the man she'd thought him. And more.

Savannah jumped back in alarm as Ethan thrust his fists down on a marble counter-top. For a moment she thought he'd seen her and that that must have prompted the angry action, but then she realised he was leaning over his braced arms with his shoulder-muscles knotted and his head bowed, as if the sight of his own body had disgusted him. She knew then that everything she had feared for him was true: Ethan's injuries had scarred more than his body, they had scarred the man.

'Savannah?'

She gasped out loud as he wheeled around.

'Savannah! I'm speaking to you!'

The ferocity in his tone made her back away.

'What do you think you're doing here?'

'Looking for you...' She backed away, hands outstretched in supplication. 'I knocked, but you didn't hear me.'

'You didn't hear the water running?'

'I heard it, but.'

'You didn't leave immediately?'

'No, I.'

'You what?' he flashed across her. 'Wanted to try out your amateur psychology on me?' As he spoke his glance swept the paintings which he knew she must have seen. 'I thought so,' he spat out with contempt when she didn't reply.

'Ethan, please.'

'I thought we'd agreed you'd stay away from me?'

'Did we?' Her voice was trembling. 'I don't remember that.'

Straightening up, Ethan dipped his head. His stare was menacing.

'Stop trying to intimidate me.' If only her voice would stop shaking.

'Then tell me why you're here.'

'Like I said, I was looking for you.'

'Because?' he prompted harshly.

'I wanted to speak to you.'

'And so you sneaked into my room?'

'No!'

'Go back to bed, Savannah.'

'No.' She shook her head. But how was she going to put all her thoughts and impressions into a few short sentences when Ethan would never give her the time? Shorthand was her only option. 'I care about you.'

'You care about me?' Ethan's laugh was cold and ugly. 'If you only knew how infantile that sounded.'

'Caring for someone is infantile?' Savannah threw up her hands. 'Then I'm guilty.' The feelings she had developed for Ethan were so deep and so complex, at this point she had nothing to lose. 'I'll admit, I'm not good with words.'

'No, you're not.' Grabbing his robe, Ethan threw it on, belting it to hide his mutilations from her gaze. 'Get out of here, Savannah.'

'I'm not going anywhere,' she informed him stubbornly.

'Must I throw you out?'

She wanted to run as far and as fast as she could from the expression on Ethan's face. He had turned so angry and dark, and so utterly contemptuous of her. 'You wouldn't—'

But her voice wobbled and Ethan pounced. 'Can you be sure of that?'

'I'm absolutely sure you would never hurt me.' Standing her ground, she stared him full in the face.

'Have you finished? Can I continue with my evening in peace now?'

'I've not nearly finished!' Like a cork in a bottle her frustrations had been tamped down long enough. 'You can't dismiss me. I'm not a child!'

'You certainly look like one to me.'

'Then you're not looking closely enough. I'm a woman, Ethan, a woman with feelings; a woman who won't let those feelings go just because you say I must.'

Ethan's answer was to curtly angle his chin towards the door. 'And now I'm asking you to leave.'

'I'm not going anywhere.'

He tried sweet reason. 'It's been a long day and you should be in bed.'

Savannah shook her head. 'I'm not a child you can order to bed. All I want to do is talk to you.'

'Well, I'm right out of conversation. Now, get out of here. Out!' He backed her towards the door. 'Try to get this through your head, Savannah...' Bringing his face so close she could see the amber flecks in his steel-grey eyes, Ethan ground out, 'I don't want your company. I don't want your conversation. And most of all I don't want you snooping around here, spying on me.'

'I'm not spying on you,' Savannah said, raising her voice too. 'And if it's these you're worried about—'

Sucking air between his teeth, Ethan knocked her hand away, but, ignoring him, she reached up anyway. Touching his face with her fingertips, she traced his cruel scars. 'I don't see them.'

'You don't see them?' Ethan mimicked scathingly. Rearing back, he turned his face away.

'No, I don't.' Savannah flinched as Ethan walked past her. And flinched again when, having poured a glass of water and drained it, he slammed the glass down so hard she couldn't believe it hadn't smashed. 'It's no use you trying to shut me out, because I'm not going anywhere, Ethan.'

He remained with his hostile back turned to her. Perhaps she had gone too far this time. Ethan's massive shoulders were hunched, and his fists were planted so aggressively on a chair back his knuckles gleamed white.

'Bad enough you're here,' he growled without looking at her, 'But you should have told me you were—'

'I'm sorry?' Savannah interrupted, reading his mind. 'Do you mean I should have told you I was a virgin?' She waited until Ethan turned to face her. 'Are you seriously suggesting I should have said, "how do you do, my name is Savannah, and I'm a virgin"?'

'No, of course not,' Ethan snapped, eyes smouldering with passion. 'But if you'd given me at least some intimation, I could have made arrangements for you to stay elsewhere.'

'In a nunnery, perhaps?' Savannah cut across him. 'In a safe place with a chaperon?'

'And this isn't safe, and I don't have a chaperon.'

'Correct.'

As they glared at each other it soon became apparent that neither one of them was prepared to break the stand-off.

'And if I tell you I feel quite safe here with you?'

'And if I tell you that the rest of the world will put a very different construction on your staying here with me?'

'But I thought you didn't care about gossip?' she countered.

'I care how it affects you.'

'From the point of view that I'm signed to your record

company as the next *young* singing sensation, which means I must appear to the world to be innocent?'

Ethan took her barbed comment with far better grace than she might have expected. It was almost as if they had got the measure of each other, and for once he was crediting her with some sense—though he drew out the waiting time until her nerves were flayed and tender. Relaxing onto one hip then, he thumbed his chin as the expression in his eyes slowly cooled from passion to wry reflection. 'That's a very cynical attitude for a young girl to have.'

'How many times—?'

'Must you tell me you're not the young girl I think you are?' he supplied in a low voice that strummed her senses.

'If I'm cynical,' Savannah countered, 'Surely you're the last person who should be surprised?'

'I'm going to say this as clearly as I can.' Ethan's voice held a crushing note of finality. 'I don't want you here. Please leave now.'

She waited a moment too, and then said, 'No.'

'No?'

'No,' Savannah repeated. 'You're asking me to believe I must do everything you say. Well, standing my ground where you're concerned might not be a big thing in your world, or easy in mine, but it has to be a whole lot better than agreeing to be your doormat.'

'Have you quite finished?' he demanded.

'I've barely started,' she assured him, but even she could see there was little point in pursuing this if she couldn't persuade Ethan to see her in a different light.

And she couldn't. He pointed to the door.

Lifting her head, she wrapped what little dignity she had left around her and walked towards it—but when

she reached it she just had to know: 'What's wrong with me, Ethan?'

'Wrong with you?' He frowned.

'Is it because I'm not pretty enough, not desirable enough, or is it the fact that I'm not experienced and savvy enough when it comes to handling situations like this?'

'Savannah, there is no situation—other than my increasing impatience with you, which means there may soon be a situation, and it will be one you won't like.'

Walking over to the door, Ethan opened it for her. 'Goodnight, Savannah.'

Ethan felt nothing for her and she had no answer to that. She was so lacking in female guile, she had no tricks up her sleeve, and it was too late to wish she'd learned them before she'd come here.

'What do you think you're doing?' Ethan demanded when she turned around and walked back in the room.

If he wanted her out, he was going to have to throw her out, and something told her he wouldn't do that. Now she just had to hope she was right.

He shook his head. 'Savannah, you are the most difficult, the most stubborn—'

'Individual in the world aside from you?' She held Ethan's gaze along with her breath, and sent a plea into the ether. If there was anyone listening out there, anyone at all…

'I was about to say, the most annoying guest I've ever had. You will have noted my use of the past tense, I hope?'

'You can't just dismiss me.'

'Watch me. Out,' he rapped, employing the full force of his laser stare.

'Why are you so angry all the time?'

'Why are you so slow to take a hint?'

'Well, clearly my experience of men is somewhat limited, but if you'd just allow me to—'

'To do what?' he cut across her, eyes narrowed in suspicion.

'Spend time with you?' Savannah trembled as she clutched on to this last all-too-brittle straw.

Ethan's laugh was scathing. 'You must think I make a habit of courting trouble. Out.' He pointed to the door.

'Can't we even have one last drink together?'

'Gin and tonic?' he mocked.

'If you like.'

'I don't like. Now, go to bed.'

He closed the door with relief. Leaning back against it, he let out a groan of relief. Mentally, physically, he was in agony. He shouldn't even be thinking this way about Savannah. And now he knew she was a virgin he had even less excuse—though how to stop erotic images of her flooding his mind was something he had no answer for. He wanted her. Wanted her? He ached for her. The urge to lose himself in her was overwhelming him, but he couldn't feed on perfection, or drain her innocence to somehow dilute the ugliness inside him.

That was a wound of such long standing he doubted he'd ever be rid of it. It had taken seed in him the day he'd realised his mother had chosen his stepfather over her seven-year-old son, and had germinated on the day she'd seen his bruises in the bath. Instead of questioning them, she had told him she'd take his bike away if he wasn't more careful. Had she really believed the buckle marks on his back had come from a fall? That bitterness was in full flower by the time he'd been ready to make his own way in the world, and those dark secrets had stayed with

him. Would he share a legacy like that with Savannah? Not a chance. She was like a ray of light with her whole life in front of her, and he would do anything to protect her. He would do nothing to stop that little candle throwing its beam around the world.

Pulling away from the door, he thrust his hands through his hair with frustration. He wanted Savannah. He wanted to make love to her. The most important thing to him was that Savannah remembered the first time she made love for the right reasons.

He tensed, hearing her footsteps returning. That sound was shortly followed by a tap on the door. 'Yes?'

'Ethan, it's me.'

'What do you want?' He tried to sound gruff. Had she forgotten something? He glanced round the room, already knowing it was a vain hope. He opened the door. She looked like a pale wraith beneath the lights she had insisted on, and they were blazing full in his face. He hardly cared or noticed these days when people turned away from him, but he noticed tonight that Savannah didn't flinch. 'What do you want?' he said wearily.

'You…'

Her voice was so small he couldn't be sure he'd heard her correctly.

'I want you,' she repeated. 'I want you, Ethan.' She held his gaze as she paused, as if she needed to prepare herself for the next step, and then she whispered, 'Will you make love to me?'

He was already closing the door. 'Don't be so silly.'

'I'm not being silly.'

The door was stuck. And then he realised she put her foot in the way. He wanted to laugh at the sight of

Savannah's tiny foot in his door, but, seeing the expression on her face, he knew this was no time for laughter.

'Please, can I come in?' she begged him.

As she looked anxiously up and down the corridor, he knew the answer to that had to be yes. He wouldn't let her make a fool of herself in front of the servants. 'All right,' he agreed, opening the door wide enough for her to slip through. He would soon sort this out. He would tell her it must never happen again and then send her on her way.

But as he closed the door she rounded on him. 'Ethan, what do I have to do to make you see that I'm a woman?'

Noticing Savannah's hands were balled with frustration, he reached out. She reached out too. Whether he intended to hold her off or pull her close, he wasn't sure, he only knew they tangled and collided, and when she closed her eyes he dragged her close and kissed her.

She was trembling like a leaf by the time Ethan pulled away to cup her face and stare into her eyes. This was everything she had ever dreamed of and more. Ethan was everything she had ever dreamed of and more, and his kiss sealed the meeting of two lovers who had to have known each other for longer than one lifetime, and who needed the immediate reassurance of pressing every fragment of their flesh against each other. As she gazed up at Ethan, with all the love she felt for him shining in her eyes, she could have sworn he asked her, 'Are you sure?'

'Yes, I'm sure,' she whispered back.

CHAPTER TEN

HE TASTED heaven when he kissed her. Dipping his head, he kissed her again, deepening the kiss, always acutely conscious that she was so much smaller than he was, and vulnerable—the very thing that held him back.

'Why did you wait so long?' she murmured when he released her.

Because keeping her safe had been paramount. Because he had feared the dark forces inside him might express themselves in contemptuous energy. He should have known Savannah's joyful innocence would defeat them. And now he felt nothing but the desire to cherish her, and to have one night; a night in which he would bring her the ultimate pleasure.

'Ethan?' she prompted, sensing his abstraction.

'I haven't forgotten you,' he murmured, sweeping her into his arms.

Her clothes slipped away in sighs and smothered laughter, and Ethan's kisses drove her remaining fears away as she clung to him, hidden from the world by the spread of his shoulders and the width of his chest. She wasn't even sure how she'd come to be naked, only that she was. And she wasn't embarrassed by that, because

Ethan was there to take care of her, and everything he did or said made her strong. He hadn't even touched her intimately, and yet every part of her was singing with awareness, and she only knew how it felt to soften and melt against him. She clung to him, asking—for what, she hardly knew. She had so much to discover. She had everything to learn.

Ethan carried her across the room to the bed and laid her down on it, where she rested with one arm above her head on a stack of pillows in an attitude of innocent seduction. The linen felt cool and crisp against her raging skin, and she was lost in an erotic haze when she noticed Ethan moving away. 'You're not leaving me?' She sat up.

'This is wrong.'

'What do you mean, "wrong"?' She was blissfully unaware of how nakedly provocative she was to him. 'What's wrong about it?' Now her cheeks were on fire. 'Do you still think I'm too young for you?'

'Correct.' Ethan sounded relieved that she had given him an out. 'Get dressed, Savannah.'

Grabbing his arm, she pushed her face in front of his. 'I won't let you do this.'

'You have no choice.'

'No choice but to be humiliated?' Her voice broke, but Ethan still shook himself free. As he stood looking down at her she thought he had never seemed more magnificent. Or more distant. 'Why?' She opened her arms. 'Why?' she repeated softly. 'Why are you doing this to me, Ethan? Why bring me here at all?'

Because he had thought mistakenly that for one short night he could forget. But the seeds of doubt had been planted deep inside him when his stepfather had assured

him in hospital that no one would ever want to look at him again. That message had been driven home when his mother had recoiled from her own child. Was he going to inflict that same horror on Savannah when she saw his others scars? Knowing they were the answer to finishing this, he turned his back so she could see them. The scars on his face were bad enough, but those on his back were truly horrific.

'What are you doing?' she demanded. 'If you expect me to exclaim in horror, you'll be disappointed. These scars make no difference to the way I feel about you.'

'No difference?'

'They don't change what I feel about you in here.'

Savannah's hand rested over her heart. He tried dismissing that with a shrug, but she called him back.

'The damage might be all that others see—but I see you, Ethan.'

'Me?' he mocked unkindly.

'Your scars don't change a thing for me, except that—'

'Yes?' he cut across her, certain now that he must have destroyed her argument.

'They keep us apart,' she finished softly.

Just when Ethan needed her to be strong, she was crying for him, and for what he had lost.

'Dry your face and leave me, Savannah,' he said harshly.

'I'm not going anywhere. Your scars don't frighten me.'

'Then you haven't looked at them properly,' he assured her.

'Oh, but I have,' she argued, seeing inside him more clearly than she ever had before.

'Look at me again,' he suggested in a voice that broke her heart.

There was only one way past this. Kneeling up on the

bed, she reached out while Ethan stood tensely, like a hostile stranger. But little by little the conviction in her eyes drew him to look at her, and she traced his scars with her fingertips, traced the tramlines that criss-crossed his back and which looked as if they had been carved by a serrated knife. She traced each one of them with her eyes and with her fingertips, until she reached his beloved face.

'I revolt you,' he said confidently. 'You don't need to pretend.'

'I don't need to be here at all,' she pointed out. 'Oh, Ethan, you couldn't possibly revolt me. You amaze me.' Ethan's scars would always be a hideous reminder of the cruelty one human being could inflict on another, but they didn't make one jot of difference to the way she felt about him.

'How can I make love to you?' Ethan demanded. 'How?' he repeated with the same passion Savannah had shown him, and when she didn't reply he cupped her chin to make her look at him.

'The usual way?' she suggested softly, and because she loved him so much she risked the ghost of a smile. 'Just don't look to me for any pointers.'

Ethan thought her so cosseted and protected she couldn't tolerate anything that wasn't perfect, when nothing could be further from the truth, Savannah realised as he stripped off his clothes. 'You think my world is all concerts and evening dresses, lace and perfume?' She reached for his hand and laid her cheek against it. 'I was brought up on a farm with straw in my hair, wearing dungarees, and that's where I've always been happiest. I can take reality, Ethan, in rather large doses.'

'So reality like this doesn't trouble you?' Ethan wiped one hand roughly down the scars on his chest.

'Please don't insult me.' As she turned her face up she was aching with the need to wrench the demons out of him. Placing her palms against his chest, she kissed her way slowly across it.

'Don't,' Ethan said, tensing, but she wouldn't stop, and finally he dragged her to him.

Those scars, terrible though they were, didn't even begin to scratch the edges of his power. Ethan was like a gladiator in some ancient etching, wounded but triumphant, and she was hard pressed to think of anything with more sex appeal than that. But inside his heart there was nothing, Savannah's tender inner-self warned her. Yes, she answered back, Ethan's heart was cold, but she had to hope that in time her love would warm him. 'I want you,' she murmured, staring up at him.

'I want you too…more than you know.' And that was true, Ethan realised as he teased Savannah with almost-kisses. She was tender and precious, young and vulnerable, and he would never hurt her. And maybe her innocence was the last hope he had to heal those scars he couldn't reach.

'So, are you coming to bed?' she whispered. Holding his hand, she sank back on the pillows and threw back the covers. 'Don't be shy.'

He laughed. She was so funny and sweet. She had stripped herself bare for him in every way, proving she trusted him, and he would never betray that trust.

As Savannah snuggled lower in the bed, waiting for Ethan, knowing he might change his mind again at any moment, she started having fears on a more practical level. His size alone filled her with apprehension. He

must have sensed it, for as he stretched out on the bed at her side he said, 'I think you're nervous.'

'A little,' she admitted, in a shaking voice that betrayed her true feelings.

'There's no need.' He stroked her arm into quivering anticipation, and as she looked into his eyes he promised, 'I would never hurt you, Savannah.'

How could he not? Ethan was so much bigger than the average man—bigger than most men—plus he possessed the power and the stamina of a natural athlete. She'd been around a farm long enough to know that nature allowed for this sort of unlikely coupling, but she wondered now if in some extreme instances such things weren't possible. This was without doubt an extreme instance. She might be plumper than she wanted to be, but she was small and soft compared to Ethan. There was nothing soft about him. He was huge and hard.

Expecting to be soothed and reassured, she was surprised when Ethan moved so quickly to pin her beneath him. And now he was straddling her with his powerful thighs, and she was completely at his mercy while he murmured erotic, outrageous suggestions in her ear that made her squirm with excitement.

'Better?' His lips were curving with amusement as he stared into her eyes.

There was passion in his eyes as well as humour, and she was reassured to a point beyond fear. 'Much better,' she admitted. With Ethan's thighs pressed close against her sides, there was nowhere else on earth she'd rather be. But still she asked for one last reassurance. 'You won't hurt me, will you?'

His answer was to kiss her tenderly until she relaxed, and then he deepened the kiss, which made her want to

do anything but relax. Lacing her fingers through Ethan's hair, she tried telling him by her eagerness alone that her nerve endings were screaming for his attention.

'There's a lot more to you than meets the eye, Ms Ross,' Ethan murmured, smiling against her lips.

Savannah stared boldly at Ethan's mouth, shivering with sensation as his kisses migrated down her neck. 'What are you doing?' she asked, writhing with pleasure when he reached the most sensitive hollow above her shoulders.

'Exploring,' Ethan murmured.

The feeling when he teased her nipples was beyond description, and while he suckled and teased the sensation travelled through to the core of her being, until it was impossible to remain still. Ethan could have done whatever he wanted with her, and yet he never once made her feel vulnerable, other than to put her at risk of overdosing on pleasure. Bucking against him, seeking contact, she moved restlessly on the pillows as she assured him, 'I can't take any more of this.'

'So, shall I stop?'

'Just you dare,' she warned him, seeing the laughter in his eyes.

'What's your hurry?' he demanded when she pressed against him.

'You,' Savannah complained fiercely. 'You're my hurry.'

'Then it's time for you to learn a little patience.'

'I don't want to learn patience.' She shivered with delight as he ran his hands down her naked body. 'But, if I do,' she proposed, 'can we do this again?'

'If you're good.'

'I'll be very good,' she assured him. And as he pulled away to look at her she pulled him back. She didn't have sufficient strength to compel Ethan to do anything, but for

now the pleasure machine was at her command. 'No more teasing,' she warned him.

'What, then?' His lips were tugging with amusement.

'Make love to me…' And she was deadly serious.

CHAPTER ELEVEN

HE PROTECTED them both, and then touched her in a way he knew she would like. As she moaned beneath him, inviting more of these touches, he feathered kisses down her neck.

He hadn't guessed he could be quite so gentle, or Savannah half so passionate. She brought out the best in him, more than he'd ever known he had, and as she clung to him, crying out his name, moving against him and driving him half-crazy with desire, he held back, knowing he had found someone who could reach him at a level no one else could.

That it should be a young girl like Savannah both surprised him and stirred his conscience. This was the start of a new chapter in Savannah's life as a woman, but when tonight was over he would have to end their relationship. But for now…

Listening to her beating time with her voice to the music of their pleasure, he knew he had never known such extremes of sensation. Gathering her into his arms to stare into her eyes, he brought her to the brink and tipped her over, staying with her through the ecstasy as she enjoyed the release she had been searching for. When she quietened and snuggled in to him, he felt sure as he gazed

into her drowsy face that time was playing tricks on them and that they had known each other much longer than one night. It was a short step from there to knowing Savannah should be with someone who could give her the kind of life she deserved.

'Ethan, where are you?' she murmured, reaching up to touch his face.

'I'm still with you,' he murmured.

'No, you're not,' she argued softly, with barely the strength to open her eyes.

She was right. He was in a dark place he wouldn't take her. Dipping his head, he kissed her deeply, and before she had a chance to question him further he made love to her again.

Savannah lay awake for the rest of the night, pretending to be asleep in the early hours when Ethan left her. She didn't know him well enough to call him back. That struck her as funny and a little embarrassing, because she might not know him but she loved him. And loving him meant she understood his need for space. What had happened between them, what they'd shared, had been so much more than either of them could have expected. Of course, Ethan would need space to consider the changes this must make to his world. The changes to her world were immeasurable. Ethan was her man and her mate, and she had welcomed him inside her body with triumph and excitement. Ethan knew everything about bringing her pleasure, and they had been as one until pleasure had consumed them.

Only one worrying incident had tarnished the night. Ethan had drifted off to sleep after they'd made love, but after a few minutes he had thrown up his hands, as if to

ward off a blow. It was some buried memory he couldn't bring himself to share, she guessed, and it hurt her to think of him locked in a nightmare where she couldn't reach him. She had to believe there was a key to breaking that destructive cycle, and that she held that key.

Turning her face into the pillows, Savannah inhaled Ethan's scent. Exhaling softly in the darkness, she turned on her back as contentment consumed her. Her whole being was drenched in a warm, happy glow. She had expected to feel different when she gave herself to a man, but she hadn't expected to feel quite so complete. She couldn't wait to see the same look of happiness in Ethan's eyes, and, as the lilac light of dawn was stealing through the heavy curtains, there was no reason why she shouldn't go and find him.

Stretching her arms, Savannah welcomed the new day with a heart full of joy. It was a new and better world with Ethan in it. She had never believed in love at first sight, but now she did. She'd heard that opposites attracted, and she'd proved that to be right. She was deeply in love, of that there was no doubt, and after last night it couldn't be long before Ethan told her that he loved her too.

He had left Savannah sleeping, and now he was avoiding her at breakfast, choosing instead to start the day with a dawn jog around the extensive grounds surrounding the *palazzo*. But even after that he craved more exercise to clear his mind. He moved on to the gym and after taking an icy shower he swam. As he powered down the Olympic-sized swimming pool there was one thing on his mind: Savannah. He could not get her out of his head.

Did he love her?

The thought was too fantastic to contemplate. He wasn't entitled to love anyone. His stepfather had drummed that into him from the start, and over the years he had come to see that it was the one thing the man had said to him that made sense.

CHAPTER TWELVE

He dressed in the changing rooms just off the swimming pool rather than return to his private suite of rooms where Savannah would still be sleeping. Snapping his watch into position, he prepared to face the day. Heading out of the leisure facility, he made straight for his office. This wasn't a relaxing room where he could watch sport in comfort, but a cold, flickering world where he kept a handle on his business empire. He had this same facility in all his houses. No one was welcome to join him, because this was his techno-version of an ivory tower. He sat in the swivel chair absorbing a blizzard of information, and realised immediately he'd been away too long. He had to go to Savannah now and update her on the current situation. Of course he'd take legal measures to protect her from the braying paparazzi, but the sooner she could leave Italy the sooner she could break free of his shadow and get on with her life.

Savannah ran down the magnificent staircase, consumed by excitement at the thought of seeing Ethan. She could see his servants bustling about in the hallway, and knew that one of them would be able to tell her

where he was. She didn't even try to hide her beaming smile, and was half-afraid everyone would guess she was in love with their *gran signore*, and half-afraid they wouldn't. She approached the first young man who smiled back at her to ask him where she could find *Signore* Alexander.

Signore Alexander was in his office as usual, the young man told her, adding that if she would like to wait out on the terrace he would make sure breakfast was served there, and that *Signore* Alexander would be told she was asking for him.

'Thank you!' Savannah exclaimed happily. She must look such a sight, she realised as the young man smiled back at her, but she hadn't wanted to waste a single moment on make-up or drying her hair. After her shower she had quickly thrown on her jeans and a casual top, and left her hair hanging loose and damp down her back. This was a whole new world to her. Catching sight of the house-keeper, she waved, and when the older woman came over to see if Savannah needed anything she took the chance to ask a few discreet questions about the paintings on Ethan's walls. As she expected, the housekeeper told her that Ethan had indeed painted them, but they had never been exhibited as far as the housekeeper could remember.

She'd expected that too, and asked if it would be possible to open more windows. 'And I'd like to pick some flowers, if that's all right. I'd love to fill the *palazzo* with flowers—if I'm allowed to.'

'*Signorina*, we have a hothouse full of flowers—and that's before you even start on the garden—but no one ever picks them.'

'Oh, perhaps I shouldn't.' It wasn't her house, after all, and she'd made enough changes.

'Perhaps you should,' the housekeeper encouraged. 'Why don't I show you where the vases are kept?'

'Are you sure Signore Alexander won't mind?'

'I'm sure the *palazzo* can only benefit from your attentions, *signorina*.'

With her fresh flowers newly arranged in the centre of the table, Savannah settled herself at the breakfast table on the terrace to wait for Ethan. Last night was still framed in a rosy glow. Her world had been turned upside down over the past twenty-four hours, and it was a very beautiful world indeed, Savannah thought as she gazed across the emerald parkland. There was a lake at the *palazzo*, as well as formal gardens, and with wooden shutters framing the sparkling windows and vivid bougainvillea tumbling down the walls, the ancient palace was like something out of her most romantic fantasy.

Savannah's gaze returned to the floral arrangement on the table. She had picked the flowers herself and had placed them in a vase. It wasn't much of a gift, on the scale of the things Ethan owned, but it was a love token given with sincerity.

'It's good to see you've made yourself at home.'

'Ethan!' In her euphoric state it seemed to Savannah she only had to think of Ethan for him to appear. 'You startled me,' she admitted, still clutching her chest. She sank down in her chair again, not wanting him to think her too excitable—or, worst-case scenario, too much in love with him. If he thought that it might prompt the unwanted opinion that she was too young to know what she wanted yet.

'I didn't mean to startle you. Perhaps you were daydreaming?'

'Perhaps I was,' she admitted shyly.

'No reason why you shouldn't. I want you to enjoy your short stay here.'

Savannah paled at Ethan's mention of a short stay. So last night had meant nothing to him. Of course it hadn't meant anything to him, Savannah realised, breaking up inside. Ethan was a sophisticated man, and she was...

What? A fool?

She was a farm girl from the depths of the country. And perhaps that was where she should have stayed.

She had jumped to so many conclusions, and all of them wrong. This man was not the tender lover from last night, but a stern and formidable stranger who was currently staring back at her as if she were a visitor he barely knew, and whom he was kindly putting up for the night.

'Do you have everything you need?' he said.

Not nearly, Savannah thought, following Ethan's gaze to her empty plate. 'I was waiting for you.'

'There's no need.' He appeared restless, as if he didn't even want to sit down.

'Is something wrong?' she asked him.

'I need to speak to you.' His voice, his manner, was a return to their former, professional relationship.

'It's not my parents, is it?' That at least would make a horrible sort of sense.

'No. They're both well,' he reassured her. He reached out a hand that didn't quite make it to her shoulder. 'Do you mind if I sit down, Savannah?'

Did she mind? It was the wrong question from the right mouth. 'Of course I don't mind.' Her heart squeezed tight. She was tense all over. 'Would you like some tea? Can I pour it for you?'

'I don't want anything, thank you.'

Normal, everyday things should make a crisis manageable, shouldn't they? It didn't work for her. Ethan hadn't even glanced at the flowers she'd picked for him. and now she braced herself, certain there was worse to come.

'The paparazzi are at the gates, Savannah.'

How right she was! 'Here at the *palazzo*?' She couldn't believe it. The stab of distress she felt at the thought that Ethan's privacy had been breached, and that it was all her fault, was terrible.

'You mustn't be alarmed,' he said, misreading her expression.

'Alarmed? I'm concerned for you.'

Ethan wasn't listening. 'If you stay in the grounds and let me handle them, you'll be safe. Savannah,' he said, staring at her intently, 'Trust me. I won't let them near you.'

All the ground she'd gained had been lost. Ethan thought she couldn't handle it. He was going to mop up the mess she'd created without her help. No wonder he'd cooled towards her. He'd had time to think, and had concluded she was a liability. A man who guarded his privacy as Ethan did must be eager to be rid of her. 'I can't tell you how sorry I am.'

'Sorry?' he cut across her. 'Please don't be. You have nothing to apologise for, Savannah. You've done nothing wrong.'

Other than to fall in love with him. Ethan was all concern for her—not because he loved her, but because she was under his protection—and he would do anything it took to keep her safe. Savannah knew she shouldn't want more than that, but she did. 'What can I do to help?'

'Stay out of the way?' Ethan suggested.

So she was to be compliant, invisible and ineffectual? She had never longed for the farm more. At least there she

could have shown Ethan another side of her. It seemed now that was a side of her he would never see.

'The only problem, as I see it,' he observed, thoughtfully thumbing his stubble, 'Is that you'll have to stay here a little longer.'

He couldn't have made it clearer. There never had been any long-term plans where Ethan was concerned. That was the price she must pay for playing the game of love without the necessary credentials. 'But I can't just sit here. I have to do something.'

'The best thing you can do,' he said, 'is stay out of my way.'

Ethan was right; what did she know? Life on a working farm was great, but it wasn't the best apprenticeship for this world of celebrity. Whatever Ethan did now would be swift and decisive. He'd deal with the press and then he'd come back for her, by which time she must be ready to leave.

He returned to his office where he immediately contacted his legal team. He wanted them to draft an injunction to keep Savannah safe and free from harassment by the press when she left him, which must be soon now. She preoccupied his thoughts, and he missed her already. He'd noticed the softening touches she'd made—the dust sheets had all been removed and the *palazzo* had been thoroughly aired. There were flower arrangements in many of the rooms, punctuating the ancient artefacts and imbuing the *palazzo* with fresh life, he reflected, tapping his pen on the table top as he waited for his call to connect.

He had to stop this! He was relieved when his call connected, and he heard the cool, impersonal voice of his lawyer on the other end. Savannah was a real danger to the status quo in his life. She had made him look at things

that had never mattered to him before—frescoes, carvings, and all the incredible paintings he'd inherited when he'd bought the *palazzo*. She was a Salome of the arts, he concluded, whilst firing instructions at his lawyer. Savannah had beguiled him with her voice, and then enchanted him with her innocence and naivety, tempting him beyond the logical and factual to appreciate the beauty and emotional wealth locked in the treasures he owned. Raking his hair into a worse state of disorder than before, he signed off, determined that Savannah's qualities would never be compromised. Thank goodness he'd recognised in time the imperative of putting a stop to this fantasy of loving her, and had brought cool legal minds to bear on the problem instead.

A few short words and his lawyer had got the picture. In fact, his lawyer had seen all the pictures. As he stowed the phone, he relaxed. Back in a familiar world without emotion, he could focus on the facts. Savannah's welfare meant everything to him. His feelings towards her might have muddied the water for a short time, but that was over now.

Over…

He still had her music. Picking up the remote-control, he turned on her CD. As Savannah's voice floated around him he found it impossible to remain tense—impossible to forget how very special she was, and how at all costs he must protect her.

At *all* costs, he reminded himself, as he left the room to make sure that Savannah had the chance to live her dream.

She wasn't good with make-up. In fact, she was useless, Savannah concluded as she peered into the mirror. She was back in her room and, having packed, she supposed

putting on make-up before she left was all about pride. She was going to leave the *palazzo* with her head held high, and not looking like some washed-out waif. But a good technique with make-up took more skill than she had. Professional make-up artists had worked on her for the photo shoot for her album, though when she appeared on stage she could pile on the slap with the best of them; no subtlety required. But she hardly ever wore make-up off-duty. It would frighten the animals, she concluded wryly.

Well, she would just have to do, Savannah decided, having pulled her face this way and that. With no outfits to choose from, she was wearing jeans and flip-flops. But at least she had combed her hair, and she was wearing the pretty, lacy cardigan she always packed to wear over her evening gown to keep her warm in the wings while she was waiting to sing.

Moistening her lips, she attempted a pout and quickly gave up. You could put the glitz into the farm girl, but you could never take the farm girl out of Savannah Ross.

And thank goodness for it. She'd need every bit of grit she had to part from Ethan and act as if it didn't hurt like hell.

After instructing his lawyers, Ethan went outside and issued a statement to the press. He went back to the office, and had barely walked through the door when he saw Savannah's face staring out of one of the monitors. It was so unexpected, he stood transfixed, and then realised one of the reporters had somehow managed to elude his security staff and had accosted Savannah as she was coming out of the bedroom on her way across the court-yard. She was going to say goodbye to his staff in a typical act of kindness, he realised. His eyes narrowed as he took

in the scene. Far from running scared, Savannah had the news hound by the elbow and was showing him the door. From the tilt of her chin he gathered she was about to send the man off with a flea in his ear. But were more opportunists hanging around? He was already through the door, this time with a look of murder in his eyes.

One reporter she could handle, but a jostling crowd…

CHAPTER THIRTEEN

HE WAS mobbed the moment he stepped outside the door by the paparazzi. Now that they'd seen Savannah leaving his private rooms, he would struggle to deny that anything was going on between them. Whatever Savannah had told them must have been good, he concluded as the reporters formed an arc around him. He gave them a look and they went scattering back. They had agreed to leave, and had been caught out. The photographers remained a safe distance away from him, hovering like slavering hyenas as they bumped each other shamelessly in an attempt to capture both him and Savannah in the same frame. He hadn't looked at her directly yet, but he was deeply conscious of her standing close by him. He made no attempt to close the gap. He had no intention of compromising her, and would keep his distance until he'd had his say.

'Is it true you and Ms Ross are an item?' one of them asked. 'I thought you told us that Ms Ross's welfare was your only concern.'

So, what had she told them? He had no way of knowing. His only concern was to protect Savannah and prevent scandal blighting her career. They had spent the whole day avoiding just this situation—but when she

gave him a look that said her brave act of ejecting the reporter from the palace grounds had gone badly wrong, and she was sure she had just shot her reputation to hell and back, he moved swiftly into damage-limitation mode. He had two options: he could deny a relationship, and make Savannah look like a fool if she had said something different, or confirm one and bring her firmly under his protection. There was really no decision to be made. As he strolled over to her an air of expectancy swept the reporters, and as they fell back he put his arm around Savannah's shoulders.

For a moment Savannah couldn't get her head round the fact that Ethan was standing next to her. And not just standing at her side, but supporting her. The shock of feeling his arm around her shoulders must have gummed up her brain, she concluded as he gave her a reassuring squeeze. She knew this must just be an act for the benefit of the press, but it was a pretty seductive fantasy.

'I never saw you as a security-guard before, Ms Ross,' Ethan murmured. 'But you handle yourself pretty well.'

Savannah felt a rush of pride and relief as she identified the reporter she'd firmly ushered out of the grounds standing in line with the others. They were quite a team, she thought wryly as Ethan dealt effortlessly with the hail of questions—much good it would do her as far as her non-existent romance with Ethan was concerned!

'One question at a time, ladies and gentlemen, please.' Ethan raised his free hand to bring everyone to order, and she noticed how his relaxed tone of voice set everyone at ease.

'I'll answer all your questions. At least—' Ethan tempered with a glint in his eyes '—those I am prepared to.'

This made the reporters laugh, and as Ethan turned to glance at Savannah she felt her body respond. 'Of course, I can't speak for Ms Ross,' he added, with another of those dangerously addictive, reassuring squeezes.

As the noise of conversation fell Savannah realised how tense she had become. Pressed up hard against Ethan, she had grown as stiff as a board. Ethan, of course, had no such inhibitions, and was perfectly relaxed in the spotlight. He felt great—fantastic, in fact—warm, strong and in control. The first surprise he launched was to announce that she had his full authority to say anything she wanted to say about their relationship.

Their relationship?

'Not that Ms Ross needs my authority to do so,' he added with an engaging shrug. 'She's got plenty to say for herself.' Ethan's eyes were darkly amused as he turned to her for confirmation. He went on to agree to answer three questions. After which he was sure they'd all want to get away. 'So choose wisely,' he added, which brought another chuckle from the crowd.

He'd got them in the palm of his hand, Savannah realised. The female reporters were practically panting to be first to ask him questions. They might as well have called out, 'Choose me! Choose me!' she thought tensely as a forest of red-gloss-tipped hands shot up. How were they supposed to resist Ethan's wicked smile when it was sending seismic signals through her own system? And something told her this was just the tip of the iceberg where Ethan's charm offensive was concerned.

So, was she jealous? And since when? Since she realised she couldn't have him. She might not be able to have him, but did she want other women going there?

Now she was supposed to convince him she knew this was only an act for the press. Well, she'd give it her best shot.

The first question came from a young woman, who moistened her lips and arranged them in a pout before asking him, 'So, do you deny there is a relationship between yourself and your protégée, Ethan?'

'Not at all,' he said. 'Why should I?'

'But Ms Ross said—'

He didn't even blink, though he couldn't have had a clue what she had said. 'Miss Ross was trying to protect me...' As Ethan turned to look at her and his voice softened, his eyes held everything she could have hoped for.

Except sincerity, Savannah registered, meeting Ethan's gaze and holding it so that he was in no doubt that she knew this was all pretence. He got the message loud and clear. There was more humour in his gaze than anything else— humour and warmth—which was a devastating combination in such a dark, forbidding man, and all the warning she needed to keep her feelings for Ethan in check.

'So you and Ms Ross *are* an item?' the same girl pressed.

'Take care.' Ethan cut in like this was a game. 'That's your second question. Don't you think you should give someone else a chance?'

Reluctantly, the girl stepped back.

'*Are* you and Ms Ross an item?' A well-known wily reporter from a national television-station asked the same question, with more relaxed laughter.

'Ms Ross has already given you her answer—and, before you ask me to confirm what she's said, please think about your stories and how you're going to flesh them out. The tycoon leaving the stadium with his star performer can only be old news now, right?'

Ethan's audacity made Savannah gasp. Was he going

to write the press release for the reporters? From hunted to hunter in the space of a few seconds was not bad going, she reflected, even as the wily reporter pressed his lips down in acknowledgement of a worthy foe. 'But you must admit it's a great headline?' he said, launching his own fishing expedition.

'Is that question two or three?' Ethan's eyes were glinting with challenge, and Savannah knew he was enjoying this. Everything was a game to Ethan, a game he was determined to win.

'Will Ms Ross be staying at the *palazzo* with you for long?' The reporter waited patiently for Ethan to reply while the rest held a collective breath.

'As long as she likes,' Ethan said, turning to look at Savannah when she started to protest.

Okay, so she was only trying to defend Ethan's dignity—forget her honour; he clearly had. Pulling her tight, Ethan kissed away her protest, leaving her trembling like a leaf and everyone else gasping. 'Which means Miss Ross might be here quite some time,' he announced.

By the time Ethan released her she was fit for nothing, and even the reporters were still reeling with surprise that the famous recluse had come out. Ethan, of course, was completely unmoved, and continued his verbal jousting as if nothing unusual had happened.

So, what was he was up to? Disarming the press with more truth than they could handle? Even she wasn't naïve enough to believe that. His behaviour towards her had to be an act. She should have known better than to try and fight Ethan's battles in his own back yard. He was hardly the type to let her take over.

As cameras swivelled to take a better shot of her, Savannah's arms flew up instinctively to shield her face,

and in that same moment Ethan stepped in front of her. 'We have a deal,' he told everyone firmly. 'And I expect you to honour that agreement, as I shall. I answer your questions, and in return you respect our privacy.'

Ethan's back cut off Savannah's view of the proceedings, but her pulse pounded a reminder that Ethan was a warrior who wouldn't allow her to stand alone. That didn't mean he felt the same about her as she felt about him, just that he was a natural born protector. She longed to tell the press that, whatever the future held for them, she adored Ethan Alexander and always would.

'And your third and last question?' Ethan prompted, reclaiming Savannah's attention as he drew her close.

'How long do you expect this *liaison* to last, Ethan?' the reporter asked him, making the word liaison sound sordid.

Savannah felt Ethan's grip change and soften, instead of growing angry, and she realised that she could have walked away from him at that point, had she wanted to.

'Don't you think it would be more chivalrous if you addressed that question to Ms Ross?' Ethan's tone was neutral, almost as if he was condoning the reporter's scathing tone. But as the reporter turned to her Savannah felt very strongly that Ethan had played some clever move.

'Well, Ms Ross?' the reporter demanded.

Before she could answer, Ethan held up his hand. 'You've had your three questions,' he pointed out wryly.

As a clamour of protest threatened to break out, Ethan smiled at her. 'Why don't we pose for an official photograph?' he suggested.

'Are you serious?' Savannah said incredulously, still reeling from Ethan's killer move.

'Never more so.'

As Ethan's mouth quirked with familiar humour,

Savannah realised she trusted him. It was that simple and that complicated, she thought, taking her place standing at Ethan's side.

That was the signal for the photographers to rush to grab the best positions. They called for them to look this way and that, and fortunately smiling came easily to her. It wasn't that hard to pretend she felt good pressed up close to Ethan, and when the photographers asked them to change position, and he brought her in front of him with his arms loosely slung around her waist, she could have happily stayed there for ever. How hard could it be to rest her head against the chest of the man she loved with all her heart?

'There's just one more thing, ladies and gentlemen of the press,' Ethan announced when everyone had had their fill of them. 'And my lawyers have mailed this information to your editors,' he added. 'My legal team has drafted an injunction protecting Ms Ross. It was placed in front of a judge this morning. Everything that falls outside what I have told you will be jumped on. And, of course, this order will protect Ms Ross when she leaves here and picks up her career. She will not be harassed or there will be legal consequences. She will be left alone.'

He didn't need to say more, Savannah realised, taking in everyone's expression. There wasn't one reporter there who was prepared to risk an expensive libel case that might put their job in jeopardy. Ethan had acted swiftly and effectively to protect her.

'But you've told us very little,' the wily older reporter complained. 'Other than the fact that what we have on you and Ms Ross is old news.'

As they looked at each other both men knew this was the end game. There was nothing left for the reporters to do but to pack up and leave. They did so without further

comment, but as they reached their vehicles the older reporter turned and tipped his head in Ethan's direction, as if acknowledging another man at the top of his game.

'With the lives we both lead, it's almost inevitable that our paths will cross again,' Ethan explained as they watched the reporter walk away.

'And you don't mind that?'

'Challenge always gives me a buzz.'

So Ethan's life would go flat now. And she hadn't been much of a challenge for him, had she? Savannah reflected, remembering she'd practically begged Ethan to make love to her.

His phone rang and he had to turn away to take the call. 'Will you excuse me?' he said politely.

Savannah waited.

'The England manager,' Ethan revealed, sounding pleased. 'The boys won their match and would like to come over for a celebration.'

'Oh, that's great news!'

He looked at her sternly. 'I was about to say, but—'

'But what?' Savannah cut in again.

'But, in case you hadn't noticed, I don't do entertaining.' Having slipped the phone into the pocket of his shirt, Ethan started walking back towards the *palazzo*.

'But I do,' Savannah called after him recklessly.

'You do what?'

Ethan stopped so abruptly, she almost ran into him again. 'I do entertaining,' Savannah explained, staying a safe distance away. 'In fact, I love entertaining.' The prospect of humiliation was very real, seeing as she was supposed to be leaving the *palazzo*, not arranging a party for Ethan. But what did she have to lose? 'So, if you need a hostess, you've got one.'

'No.' Ethan quickened his step.

'No?' Prompted into action, Savannah ran after him. 'Why not?'

'For the obvious reasons.'

'What obvious reasons? Ethan, please, just wait and listen to me.'

'I said no, Savannah. Thank you for the offer, but there isn't going to be a party here. Half the *palazzo* is shut up. It hasn't seen the light of day since I bought it.'

'Well, what a good excuse to open it up. It can be done, Ethan, just like my room.'

Shaking his head, he strode away from her. 'I've got business appointments.'

'I could handle everything for you.'

'You?' He didn't break stride as he headed back towards the *palazzo*.

'Yes, me,' Savannah said patiently, scurrying along at his side.

'The boys can come over for a quiet kitchen-supper.' She felt like punching the air.

'But I don't do celebrations.'

'There's always a first time.'

'That's a popular misconception put about by an optimist,' Ethan informed her, speeding up again.

'You wouldn't even have to be there,' Savannah added hastily, forced to run to keep up as they crossed the court-yard. 'Unless you wanted to be there, of course,' she added, seeing Ethan's expression darken.

'If I agree to anything at all, it will be a quiet meal or-ganised by my staff. And an early night for everyone,' he told her sternly, reaching for the door.

'Oh…I'm sure the squad will enjoy that.' Savannah pulled a face Ethan couldn't see as he lifted the latch on

the big wooden door that led through to the utility rooms at the back of the *palazzo*.

'So, what are you saying?' He swung round to confront her. 'You want to stay another night?'

It would have been nice if he'd wanted her to. She swallowed her pride. 'If it would help you, yes; I'm prepared to do that.'

Ethan's hum told her nothing, his expression even less, but she wasn't done yet. This was one straw she wasn't going to lose her grip on. 'You helped me. I'd like to help you.' She gave a nonchalant shrug. 'It's the least I can do.'

The very least.

CHAPTER FOURTEEN

'MY STAFF won't need your help with a kitchen-supper,' Ethan pointed out.

'I'd like to do a little more than that for the squad.' And when Ethan threw her a hard stare she added, 'Don't look so suspicious, Ethan. I'm not going to turn it into a bacchanalian romp.'

'I should hope not.' He held the door into the hallway for her.

'Just some good food and hospitality.'

'A kitchen-supper,' Ethan confirmed, which wasn't what Savannah had in mind at all. There was that cobwebby old dining-room to be brought out of wraps, just for starters.

'Either way,' she said, curbing her enthusiasm as more ideas came to her, 'we should consult with your staff first, as this is very short notice for them.'

'At the start of this discussion, tonight wasn't going to be an event my staff would need notice for,' he pointed out.

True, but she had learned when to speak and when to say nothing—and what was it people said about actions speaking louder than words?

* * *

She wasn't going to build any bridges with marshmallow and fluff, Savannah reflected, rolling up her sleeves to help Ethan's staff prepare the neglected dining-room. Beneath the dust sheets the furniture was still beautiful, and the upholstery, in a variety of jewel-coloured silks, was as good as new. Ethan had carved his own narrow path through the glories of the *palazzo*, looking neither left nor right, she guessed, until he'd reached the suite of rooms he had chosen to occupy.

Later that day as Savannah straightened up to survey the finished dining-room she joined Ethan's staff in exclaiming with delight. The transformation from spooky and dark to glittery and bright was incredible. But would Ethan share their pleasure, or would he be furious? Having given his tacit consent to a quiet evening in, he would hardly have expected her to expand that brief quite so radically. But the old *palazzo* deserved an airing and the England squad certainly deserved this.

Savannah thanked each member of the household by name before they left the dining-room, knowing she couldn't have done any of this without them. She had been accepted by the people who worked for Ethan, and their smiles were so warm and friendly that she felt quite at home. Which was a joke, because this was not her home. In twenty-four hours she would fly back to England and never see it again. That was her deadline for convincing Ethan that this scene of warmth, comfort and welcome didn't have to end when she left, and that it was better for everyone who lived in the *Palazzo dei Tramonti Dorati* than cobwebs, shadows and dust.

Taking one last look around before she left the glowing

room, Savannah thought of this as her one chance to give Ethan an evening to remember, as well as to restore the heart of his *palazzo* before she returned home.

Ethan's chef excelled himself, working non-stop in the kitchen, and when the housekeeper had finished lighting all the candles Savannah thought she had never seen a lovelier room. With its soaring ceiling and deep, mullioned windows, the flicker of candlelight, the long, oval dining-table dressed with fine linen, sparkling crystal glasses, and Ethan's best silver cutlery brought out of storage for the occasion, it looked quite magnificent. Ethan had sent a message to say he had been detained on business and to start without him. What he would think of her opening up the dining-room when he was expecting to hunker down in the kitchen, she could only guess. It wouldn't be good news for her, Savannah thought, but what mattered more was that Ethan saw the possibilities here. There was a palpable air of excitement amongst his staff, and at their urging she had even gone mad and donned her neglected pink gown for the evening.

Feeling a flutter of excitement at the thought that all that was missing now were the guests, Savannah slowly turned full circle one last time to take everything in.

He was annoyed at being late, but it couldn't be helped. The meeting had run on longer than he'd thought. The England squad was already here. He'd seen their coach in the courtyard. He could hear the sound of male laughter as he strode across the hall. He ran up to his room to shower and change, eager to get back down and support Savannah. There was too much testosterone floating around

for his liking. It was only on his way downstairs again that he realised the sounds he could hear were not coming from the kitchen, but from the dining-room. He frowned as he retraced his steps across the hall. The room had been shut up for years…

A manservant opened the double doors for him with a flourish, and as he stood on the threshold he was momentarily stunned. The scene laid out in front of him showed the oak-panelled dining-room fully restored to its former glory. It was a haven of colour and warmth, and the sound of fun and laughter drew him in.

If Savannah had chosen to be a theatrical designer rather than a singer, she couldn't have conjured up a more glamorous set. But in the centre of that set was the centre of his attention: Savannah, looking more dazzling than he'd ever seen her.

Looking…There were no words to describe how Savannah looked. With her soft, golden curls hanging loose in a shimmering curtain down her back, she looked ethereal, and yet glamorous and womanly. She was playing hostess to the squad in a stunning pale-pink gown that fitted her voluptuous figure perfectly. This was no child, or some wanton sex-kitten displaying her wares in front of a roomful of men. This was a real woman, a woman with class, with heart and light in her eyes, a woman he now remembered was accustomed to working alongside men on her parents' farm, which explained her ease of manner. That was what made it so easy for his friends on the squad to relate to her, he realised.

'Ethan…'

Seeing him, her face lit up, and as she came towards him he realised he had expected to be shunned after the

churlish way he'd treated her, but instead she was holding out her hands to invite him in. She was more than beautiful, he realised in that moment; Savannah was one of those rare people: a force for good.

'Come,' she said softly. 'Come and meet your guests, Ethan.'

His attention was centred on her after that moment, and though he was quickly immersed in the camaraderie of the team he was acutely aware of her every second.

The boys in the squad laughed goodnaturedly, and made him admit that what Savannah had organised for them was a whole lot better than a quiet kitchen-supper. He agreed, and eventually even he was laughing. What Savannah had done for the team had made them feel special. She made him feel special.

It thrilled Savannah to see what an inspiration Ethan was to the younger players. Everyone showed him the utmost respect. At Ethan's insistence she was sitting next to him. She couldn't bear to think this was the last occasion when she would do that.

'Here's to England winning the Six Nations,' he said, standing up to deliver the toast. 'And here's to the only one amongst us without a broken nose.'

It took Savannah a moment to realise Ethan was raising his glass to her, and as everyone laughed and cheered he added, 'To our gracious hostess for the evening, the lovely Savannah Ross.'

'Savannah Ross!' the squad chorused, raising their glasses to her.

Savannah's cheeks were crimson, but Ethan hadn't finished with her yet. 'Would you sing for us?' he murmured discreetly. As his warm breath brushed her cheeks her

heart beat even faster. She was touched by the request, but terrified at the thought of singing in front of a room full of people, all of whose faces she could see quite clearly. There was no nice, safe barrier of blinding footlights to hide behind here.

'I'm sure you don't want to hear my rendition of Rusalka's *Song to the Moon*!' She laughed, as if the aria's romantic title would be enough to put him off.

But Ethan wasn't so easily dissuaded. 'That sounds lovely.' He looked round the table for confirmation, and everyone agreed.

As the room went still, Savannah wondered could she do this? Could she sing the song of the water-sprite telling the moon of her love for one man? And could she do that with Ethan staring at her?

Help him in dreams to think of me…

'No pressure,' Ethan said dryly.

Pressing her fingertips on the table, she slowly got up.

Silvery moon in the great, dark sky…

Savannah hardly remembered what happened after the opening line, because she was lost in the music and the meaning of the words. She didn't come to until she heard everyone cheering and banging the table. And then she found Ethan at her side. 'Did I—?'

'Sing beautifully?' he said, staring deep into her eyes. 'Yes, you did.'

She relaxed and, laughing as she shook her head in exaggerated complaint, raised her eyes to the ceiling for the benefit of the squad. 'What can you do with him?'

'What can *you* do with him?' Ethan murmured, but when her quick glance brushed his face she saw his expression hadn't changed. It was always so hard to know what Ethan was thinking.

'Our only difficulty with Ethan,' one of the players told her, 'is that he refuses to consider anything that has his name, a team, a ball, and a rugby pitch in the same sentence.'

'Leave it,' Ethan warned goodnaturedly when he over-heard this comment.

Savannah kept her thoughts to herself. But didn't everyone know Ethan's injuries had prevented him from further involvement in the game? He just couldn't risk one of the man-mountains landing on top of him. Tactfully, she changed the subject. Tapping her water glass with a spoon, she offered to sing an encore if the boys would help her with the chorus. And as she'd hoped that soon took the spotlight off Ethan.

After murdering every song they could think of, the players retired to bed, while Savannah insisted on changing and staying behind to help the staff clear up. 'It's late,' she told Ethan, 'and everyone's tired. We've had a wonderful evening, thanks to your staff working so late, so I'm going to stay and help them.'

'Then so will I,' he said, giving his staff the night off.

'I never thought I'd have the courage to sing in front of such a small group of people,' Savannah admitted as they worked side by side, putting the room to rights.

'You could certainly see the whites of their eyes,' he agreed wryly.

But none of them had eyes as beautiful as Ethan's, Savannah mused, keeping this thought in a warm little pocket close to her heart. 'You gave me the courage to do it,' she admitted.

'Then I'm pleased if your short stay here has helped your confidence.'

Savannah didn't hear any more. The warm little pocket shrivelled to nothing. She'd been trying to tell Ethan they

were a great team, but it had fallen on deaf ears. And if that was all he thought this incredible time had meant to her she really was on a hiding to nothing. But at least she could stop worrying whether she had given away too much, singing her impassioned song to the moon, Savannah reflected sadly, for just as Ethan's talent for inspiring people and for his art was wasted so was her love for him.

'You were great tonight,' he said, reclaiming her attention as he toed open the door to carry a tray to the kitchen. But just as her heart began to lift, he added, 'I'm really glad we signed you, Savannah Ross.'

She was still flat when Ethan returned with the empty tray. 'Well, have we finished?' he said.

'Looks like it,' Savannah agreed, checking round. 'What?' she prompted when Ethan continued to look at her.

She would ignore that look of his. Memories of their love-making sent an electric current shooting through her body; she'd ignore that too. What she must do was leave the room. 'Excuse me, please.' She avoided Ethan's gaze as she tried to move past him.

'I thought you might want a nightcap.' One step was all it took to block her way.

That was the cue for her willpower to strike. She wanted Ethan to make love to her one last time, though in her heart she knew sex would never be enough; she wanted more; she wanted all of him.

But, if sex was all they had, what then?

CHAPTER FIFTEEN

'IT DOESN'T usually take you so long to decide, Savannah.'

True, Savannah accepted wryly. The way Ethan had pitched his voice, so low and sexy, was sending her desire for him into overdrive. 'Water's fine.'

What was she doing? So much for her intention to retire to bed and think chaste thoughts! She'd sold out for a glass of water, and now Ethan showed no signs of moving out of her way.

He wanted her. He loved her. Savannah had impressed him tonight in every way, but what he felt for her was so much more than pride in her achievements. She had filled his home with light and laughter, and he could never thank her enough for that. She'd worked as hard as any member of his staff to make his friends feel welcome. She'd mixed well with the men and had known where the boundaries lay and how to impose a few of her own without causing embarrassment. She'd told him more about the farm and her life there, and he only wished he'd had the chance to see it before their lives diverged. But at least she was leaving on a high note. He would never forget the way that men with battered faces had treated

her like a favourite sister, and how much trouble she had gone to for them. And how she had looked so beautiful, and yet not once had flaunted her appeal. In fact, quite the opposite; she seemed totally unaware of it.

'It was a great night, Ethan; let's not spoil it now.'

'Spoil it?' he queried.

'You know I have to go tomorrow.'

So let's not draw this out, she was telling him. And, yes, he should let her go. 'It was a very good night,' he agreed, fighting back passion. But there were forces inside him that overruled his modern take on the situation. She was his. He wanted her. He loved this woman. The desire to possess Savannah overwhelmed him, and as she sensed the change in him and her eyes darkened he dragged her into his arms.

This was wrong. This was fool's gold. This was also the only thing on earth she wanted right now. She put up a token resistance, pressing her hands against Ethan's chest, but as she stared into his eyes and he murmured something decidedly erotic she gave in. Ethan understood the needs of her body and how to turn her on in every way there was. He knew how to extend her pleasure until she was mad with it, mad for him, and now all expectations of sleeping alone and dreaming chaste thoughts were gone. She groaned softly as he teased her with his lips, and with his tongue and teeth, reminding her of what came next. He felt so hard, toned and warm as his hands found her breasts. And he tasted of warm, hungry man—clean, so good, and so very familiar. And she'd missed him in the few hours they'd been apart.

But she shouldn't... They mustn't...

Her hips were already tilting, thrusting, inviting, while

Ethan was backing her relentlessly towards the door. She waited until he slipped the lock before lacing her fingers through his thick dark hair and making him her prisoner. 'Shall we be captives here for long?'

'As long as it takes,' he promised huskily.

And as he brushed her lips with his mouth, and she sighed and melted, she murmured, 'Kiss me.'

'Since when do I have to be prompted?'

Since never. Savannah purred with desire, and then gasped as Ethan swept her into his arms and carried her across the room. 'What do you think you're doing?' she murmured as he laid her down on the rug.

'A nice, soft rug is so much kinder than a table, don't you think?'

Savannah's cheeks blazed red as she understood Ethan's intentions were to take her any place, any time, anywhere, much as her fantasies had dictated. 'Why didn't I think of the rug?' she murmured, arcing towards him.

'Because you've still got a lot to learn?'

'Everything,' she corrected him happily.

'So, I'll teach you. Where would you like me to start?'

'Right here…' She placed his hand over her breast, and uttered a happy cry when he turned her beneath him.

Holding her wrists loosely above her head, Ethan dealt with the fastening on her clothes. She loved it when his big, warm hands cupped her buttocks, subjecting her to delicious stroking moves as he prepared her. She loved to feel those hands caressing and supporting her as he positioned her. She loved everything about him—the wide spread of his shoulders, the power in his chest, and the biceps flexing on his arms when he braced himself above her. She felt protected and loved. She wanted this, needed him—needed Ethan deep inside her so she could forget

she had to leave him in the morning. Wrapped up in passion, she wound her legs around him and lost herself again.

His intention had been to take Savannah to bed and make love to her all night, but here, in front of a crackling fire in the candlelit room she had made beautiful, there were all the romantic elements she could wish for, and he wanted to give her the full fairy-tale romance. All that had ever stood in the way of that was his cold, unfeeling heart, but for tonight he had the chance to hold Savannah in his arms while she slept, and he wanted to remember how she felt in his arms, and how she looked when he held her safe. He wanted to keep her safe always. *Safe from him.*

He knew what he must do, Ethan accepted grimly. Easing his arm out from under her, he kissed Savannah awake like some prince in a distorted fairy-tale. There could be no happy ending here. She smiled at him groggily. Reaching for his hand, she brought it to her lips. As she gazed at him her lips moved, and the dread that she was going to say 'I love you' made him kiss her again, but this time not to wake her, but to silence her. He wouldn't lure her into his cold, dark world, but the moment he released her she asked the one question he had been dreading most. 'Ethan, tell me about your scars.'

He turned his face away for a moment, cursing his arrogant assumption that Savannah could ever be distracted from her purpose. She touched his face to bring him back to her, but he pulled away. 'What do you want to know?' he said coldly.

'Everything.'

Everything? The word echoed in his head. If he would

save her from him, he was blindingly certain he would save her from *everything*.

'Ethan, why is it so wrong for me to want to be close to you when we just made love? I want to know who did this to you and why. Surely you can trust me enough to tell me that?'

She had no idea. How could she? He removed himself a little more, both physically and mentally. 'I can understand your fascination.' He spoke in a murmur as he reasoned it through, his mind set on other occasions when he'd suspected the questioner had obtained some sort of foul, vicarious thrill out of the violence.

'Fascination?' Savannah's voice called him back. 'Ethan, you don't know me at all. How can you think me so shallow?'

'Aren't all women shallow?' The bitterness burst out of him before he could stop it.

'I don't know what kind of women you've met in the past,' Savannah countered hotly. 'And I don't want to. But I can assure you I'm *not* shallow.' Her voice was raised, her body tense, and her gaze held his intently—but after a moment she froze, and a change came over her. 'Is your mother behind this?'

Every part of him railed against this intrusion into the deepest part of his psyche. 'How could you know that?'

'Because I can't think of anything more terrible than betrayal by a mother, and whatever wounded you to this extent has to be that bad.'

'You know all about me in five minutes?' he demanded scornfully.

'I knew you from the moment I met you.' She said this with blinding honesty 'From that second on, Ethan, I knew you.'

For the longest moment neither of them spoke, and then he told her some of it.

'One man did this to you, Ethan?' Savannah's face contorted with disbelief, and her eyes betrayed her bitter disappointment that Ethan didn't trust her more than that.

'I don't believe you. I can't believe this was some random attack. There isn't a man alive who could do this to you.' Her eyes narrowed in thought. 'Unless you were unconscious at the time—were you unconscious? Did someone drug you to do this?'

'It would be a cold day in hell before that happened.'

He must have been attacked by a gang, Savannah reasoned. The way Ethan had described his stepfather, the man had been a cowardly weed who wouldn't have had the strength to hold Ethan down and inflict such terrible injuries.

'Can we drop the subject?' he snapped, jolting her out of her calculations.

'No, we can't,' she said bluntly. 'I want the truth, Ethan—all of it. We just did some very adult things, and it's time you stopped treating me like a child.'

CHAPTER SIXTEEN

ETHAN'S naked torso looked as though a pitchfork with serrated edges had been dragged back and forth across it several times. 'A gang of men must have done this to you,' Savannah insisted, sure she was right now.

'You tell me,' Ethan snarled, 'Since you seem to know so much about it.'

The tension in him frightened her. Wound up so tight, he surely had to snap. But she wouldn't let it go. She couldn't let it go. If she couldn't reach out now and touch him, she never would. She went for his machismo with all guns blazing. 'If a gang of thugs attacked you it's nothing to be ashamed of.'

'Ashamed?' Ethan roared, exactly as she'd hoped. 'You think I'm ashamed?'

His fury filled the room, but as the window of opportunity opened she climbed through it. 'What am I supposed to think if you won't tell me?'

'May I suggest you don't think about it at all, since it's no concern of yours?'

Savannah's heart was hammering in her chest at the thought of what she'd started, but if Ethan held back now there was no hope for him—for them. 'If we mean

anything to each other.' She could see the black void in Ethan, but stubbornly she kept right on blundering towards it. 'If you can't trust me.'

He was already reaching for his shirt. 'Get dressed,' he said, tossing her clothes onto the bed. He couldn't wait to leave her. She'd gone too far.

Savannah dressed quickly, determined to finish what she'd started, and with everything half-fastened and hanging off her shoulders she raced to the door. Pressing her back against it, she barred his way. 'Tell me—tell me everything, Ethan. I won't move until you do.'

He looked down at her from his great height as if she were an annoying flea he might choose to flick out of his way. She braced herself against the look in his eyes, and against the knowledge that Ethan could always use the simple expedient of lifting her out of his way. His expression assured her he had considered that, but to her immense relief he eased back. Several seconds passed while they measured each other and then he started speaking.

'A gang of men attacked me with baseball bats. When I was unconscious they cut me.' He said this with all the expression of a man reading out a shopping list. 'Are you satisfied, Savannah?'

'Not nearly.' She felt so sick she could hardly stand. 'Why did they do that?' she demanded.

'Don't push it.'

'Why?'

'I don't talk about this—not to you, not to anyone.'

He held her gaze, unblinking, until she was forced to look away.

'You were lucky to survive—'

'I said I don't talk about it.' His expression had turned to stone.

'You were lucky to retain your mobility. There must be many who have not been so fortunate.'

'Savannah,' he growled in warning.

'Or who have lived to tell the tale.'

'Comprehend this,' he snarled, bringing his face menacingly close. 'I don't want your understanding, and I sure as hell don't want your pity.' Pulling back abruptly, he unlocked the door and left the room.

She had prepared for this, but, even so, Savannah was stunned for a moment. The energy from Ethan's fury still rang in her ears, disorientating her, but she rallied quickly. Chasing after him, straightening her clothes as she ran, she followed him up the stairs. The lights had been dimmed as the staff had gone to bed, and tall, black shadows crossed with Ethan's, joining them by a tenuous thread. Driving herself to the limit, Savannah took the stairs two by two.

Catching hold of her as she came up to him on the landing, Ethan swung her round. 'Do you and I speak the same language?' he demanded, trapping her against the wall.

She fought him, warned him to get off her and railed at him, but Ethan stole each impassioned word from her lips with a kiss.

'Hiding the evidence of your arousal?' Ethan taunted, as when he released her she stood with the back of her hand across her mouth.

'I love you. Of course I respond to you. I have nothing to hide.' She pulled her hand away, revealing her love-swollen lips. 'Why do you hide your pain from me, Ethan?'

'My pain?' Ethan laughed. 'Spare me the psychobabble.'

'Is it too close to home?'

He greeted this with a contemptuous sound.

'So now you return to your ivory tower,' Savannah observed. 'And I go home?'

'It's safer for you there.'

'Safer,' Savannah repeated, shaking her head. 'There's no compromise with you, is there?'

'No,' Ethan confirmed.

'Then by those same rules you have to accept I won't give up on you.'

As the light played on Ethan's hard, set face, he folded his arms and leaned back against the door.

Ethan continued to stare at her with his dark eyes slumberous and knowing Savannah wanted him to seduce her all over again. He held a dangerous power over her, she realised, and that power was addictive. The pleasure Ethan could deliver was unimaginable, and she would never get enough of him. But with his warm, hard body possessing her, the realities of life would always be shut out. 'I won't leave until you tell me how you got those,' she said, refocusing determinedly.

He laughed. 'You're refusing to leave my house?'

'What's the worst that can happen, Ethan—you tear up my contract?' His eyes narrowed with surprise, as if that had never occurred to him. 'Your life is far more important to me than a recording contract.' The moment this was out in the open, Savannah felt naked and vulnerable. She would give up everything for Ethan, she realised, and now he knew that too. If he laughed at her now, everything was over.

Ethan remained where he was, with his arms folded, quietly watching her.

She pressed him again about his scars. 'Please,' she entreated, holding out her hands to him.

'Believe me, you don't want to know,' Ethan said, shifting position.

It was a start; it was a chink of light at the end of the tunnel and she groped towards it. 'Perhaps you think I'm too young to share this with you, though not to take to bed?' she suggested.

Ethan shrugged, and in the same monotone he'd used before he told her about the beatings that had started when he was little, and had gone on until he was too big for them, when his stepfather had employed a gang of thugs to finish the job. His stepfather's timing had been impeccable, she learned. He had chosen the week Ethan had heard he'd won a coveted place on the England rugby squad to finish the job.

'So I would never play again. And, as a bonus, he had me scarred.'

Ethan's early life had been so very different from her own, Savannah could hardly take it in. But it made everything clear, she realised as he went on. 'Before his arrest my stepfather and mother came to visit me in hospital. He must have wanted to be certain the job had been completed to his satisfaction before handing over his money, I imagine.'

Savannah's stomach churned at the thought of so much evil. 'Go on,' she prompted softly.

'His main purpose was to ensure no one would ever look at me again without revulsion, and who better to test this on than my mother?'

'I can't believe your own mother would turn from you. Surely that was the very moment when she would draw you to her heart?'

'Your experience of childhood was very different to mine. Let's just say my stepfather got his money's worth.'

'No, let's not,' Savannah argued fiercely. 'He failed. If anyone notices your scars, you make them forget. You

have a bigger heart and a bigger presence than your stepfather could possible imagine.'

'And there's a grisly fascination about me that makes me irresistible to the ladies?' Ethan interrupted dryly. 'Yes, I know that too.'

'Don't you dare suggest that's how I feel, because it's just not true. You're more of a man than anyone I know. And, as for your stepfather…' Savannah's rage was all the more vivid for being contained. 'The little worm!' she managed finally.

As Ethan's eyes flickered she poured her love into him. There was just a single step dividing them and she took it. Winding her arms around his neck, she stared into his eyes. 'I can't leave you like this.'

Gently untangling her arms, Ethan pulled away. 'Give up on this, Savannah.'

'Never!' But she could feel him withdrawing into himself, and she didn't know how to pull him back.

'Goodnight, Savannah.'

She heard the note of finality in his voice, and as Ethan turned away she wondered if she would ever be able to forget this moment and what might have been, or close her heart to the possibility of love.

Savannah's eyes were still drugged with sleep when her searching hands acknowledged an empty bed. Of course her bed was empty. Ethan wasn't here. Ethan never had been here in the way she'd wanted him to be, and last night he had made it clear he never would be. Fumbling for the light switch, she grimaced when she saw the time. He must have been up for hours saying goodbye to his friends, and hopefully, she wasn't too late to do the same.

When she entered the dining-room everyone cheered.

'What?' Savannah said, smiling as she stared around. Ethan's stare was boring into her, but she couldn't ignore those happy faces round the table.

Ethan's voice curled round her, underscoring her sense of loss. 'Your CD just debuted at number one on the classical charts.'

Number one? She should feel something. This was what she and the team behind her had been working towards for years. Her career was important to Ethan's record company, Savannah registered numbly, so she was pleased for him.

She had everything to be grateful for, she told herself firmly, prompting her reluctant facial muscles into a smile.

'We'll want your autograph before we leave,' one of the players teased, understandably oblivious to Savannah's troubled state of mind.

'And could you sign this for my sister?' asked another. 'My sister dreams of being a singer like you one day.'

Savannah jolted round immediately. 'I'll do better than that,' she offered. 'Piece of paper, anyone?' Ethan tore a sheet from a pad and handed it to her. Resting it on a magazine, she scribbled something and handed it to the player. 'Give this to your sister. It's my telephone number. Tell her to ring me. I'll give her any help I can.' Who knew more about dreams than she did?

Playing a role helped her get through the rest of the morning, and then the happy hostess standing at the leading man's side waved off the team.

Ethan waited until the coach was out of sight before asking Savannah to accompany him to his study.

'What's this?' Savannah said as he handed her an envelope. She gazed in dread at it, as if it contained the ashes of her future.

'It's your first-class ticket home.' His stare was un-swerving, and the fact that he'd put acres of desk between them wasn't lost on her. Closing her fingers around the envelope, she wanted to say something, anything, but the words just wouldn't come.

'I didn't think you'd want to travel back with the team.' Ethan had put her welfare first again, Savannah registered dully, as if he were her business manager rather than her lover. 'And I thought you should travel home in style.' He said this as if that style was the panacea for all ills.

'Travel home in style?' Savannah repeated.

'My chauffeur will take you to the airport, and from there you'll—'

'Ethan,' she cut across him. 'I don't need a chauffeur to take me to the airport, and I don't need to travel home in style.'

'There's around an hour until you leave.' He might not have heard her. 'It shouldn't take you long to pack, should it?'

Some toiletries and two evening gowns? 'No, it shouldn't take long.'

'Good. That's settled, then. And I don't want you worrying about the paparazzi.'

Ethan was nothing if not efficient, Savannah thought, already anticipating his next reassurances concerning security, guards and alarms.

'So you'll be fine,' he finished.

If that was all it took, Savannah thought wistfully, ex-pressing her thanks. Learning what she had about him, she could understand why Ethan's heart had grown so cold, but not why he refused to embrace the chance of love.

'Okay?' he said with one of those brief, forced smiles people used to bring an encounter to an end.

'Okay,' she agreed with the same false gusto.

Ethan had his fists planted on the desk and was leaning towards her, as if keen to underline his concern. Savannah thought she knew why. She was the valuable property of Ethan's record company, and it made sense to protect her. This was no personal relationship, other than in her self-deluded head. She stuck the envelope in the back pocket of her jeans, and when Ethan looked as if he was waiting for her to say something more she managed, 'First class? Exciting.'

'My apologies. I couldn't free up the jet for you, because I need to use it.'

'No problem,' she assured him. If Ethan wasn't with her who cared where she sat? But…more leg-room with the heart ache? She'd take it. 'I'll get ready, then.'

What more was there to say? Should she beg Ethan to let her stay on? And, if he agreed, could she ever soften him?

The reality of a man who had proved to be absolutely untouchable chilled her to the core. It was better to leave now before she said or did something she'd regret, Savannah concluded. She loved Ethan with all her heart, but in his eyes she could see not even a flicker of encouragement. Having thanked him again for the arrangements he'd so kindly made for her, she did the only thing possible and left.

CHAPTER SEVENTEEN

HE LISTENED to the limousine crunch across the gravel as it carried Savannah to the airport, waiting for the rush of relief that never came. She had sought him out immediately before leaving to thank him for his *hospitality*. His hospitality? When she'd left him to go and pack, he'd sat brooding in his study, supposedly finalising a bid for a country home in Surrey, but his thoughts were all of Savannah. He wouldn't inflict himself on her, which was the only reason he let her go. She was young and idealistic, and in time she'd come to see he was right. He was glad she had gone, he brooded, gazing out of the window at a view that was no longer perfect without Savannah in it. Perhaps if he repeated that mantra long enough he would come to believe it.

He pictured her face and remembered her parting words: 'You have a beautiful home, Ethan; take care of it. And start painting again.' She had smiled hopefully at him as she'd said this, adding, 'You have a real talent.'

For the macabre?

'Yours is the talent,' he'd told her.

'Paint some happy scenes, Ethan, and don't hide them away—put them on display.'

It was shorthand they both understood for 'keep the lights on'.

Savannah had done more than bring the *palazzo* to life, she had held up a mirror to his life, giving him a tantalising glimpse of how it could be. Which was all the more reason to set that pure heart free. He wouldn't weigh Savannah down with his dark legacy. Savannah deserved better than that, better than him, and with her career going from strength to strength there was no reason why she couldn't have it.

It was like the bottom falling out of your world twice, Savannah concluded as she closed the front door on the bailiffs. She was still reeling from her parting from Ethan, and had barely been back at the farmhouse in England five minutes when the two men had knocked at the door.

It was like a black-comedy sketch, she decided, crossing the room to put the kettle on the Aga; a very black comedy-sketch.

'Your parents have taken on too much credit, love,' the bailiffs had told her when she had assured them with matching determination that they must have got the wrong address. Unfortunately, the two men had had the right address and there was no mistake. They had shown her the legal documents they'd brought with them, and she had checked out the court order line by hateful line. The only reason they'd cut her a bit of slack was because they had wanted her autograph.

Understanding they were only doing their job, she had given them that before going to the bank to take out enough cash to send them away happy.

As she nursed her mug of tea, Savannah could only be thankful she hadn't got round to spending a penny of the

money from her first royalty-cheque before she'd left for Rome. At least she had been able to put that money to good use now. But how could this have happened? She had asked herself this same question over and over again. How could her parents' world fall apart like this in the space of a few days?

But it wasn't a few days, Savannah reflected, walking to the window and staring out bleakly at the well-kept yard. It was years of paying for the best teachers, the best gowns, and even the lovingly polished second-hand grand piano in the dining-room. It was years of sacrifice for her. And she hadn't seen it before. She had grown up taking such things for granted—the golf club, the tennis club, all the right places and all the right clothes—and all these things cost more money than her parents had, or could make from the farm.

'We've seen it all before,' one of the bailiffs had assured her as he'd taken an inventory of her parents' possessions. 'And not just in the leafy lanes where the people with money live, but more and more frequently on working farms just like this one.' He'd paused then and looked at her as if even he, collecting money from hard-stretched individuals for a living, had never quite got over the calamity that had hit the farming community.

Foot-and-mouth, Savannah reflected bleakly. The disease had devastated the countryside and the people that lived there, killing their cattle, killing their dreams. So many farmers had been forced to adapt or go under. Blinking away her melancholy, she forced her mind round to practical issues.

The court order still stood, and it was up to her to get this mess sorted out before her parents returned from their cruise. Returning to the kitchen table, she sat down

to make a list. But as she stared at the page of jottings in front of her she realised she could only raise half the money needed. And if she didn't come up with a solution by the end of the month the bank would foreclose and there'd be no farm. Heartache reminded her of Ethan. Briefly she considered asking him for a loan, but quickly discounted it because he would never let her pay him back. He might have the riches of Croesus, but that money wasn't hers to dip into. No. She would find her own solution.

An unexpected phone call provided Savannah with an equally unexpected opportunity, but not one she could take up. 'I'm the last person on earth who has any influence over Ethan Alexander,' she explained to the senior official from the Rugby Football Union. But the man from the governing body of English rugby was persistent, and as he went on talking Savannah thought she saw an opportunity that might just turn out to be the saving of them all.

'And I said no!' Frowning, Ethan sprang up from his swivel chair and began to pace the long-suffering floor of his study. 'My rugby days are over. You know that,' he snapped at the official from the RFU. 'Yes, what I'm saying is your suggestion is out of bounds. I can't possibly make it fly for you—and no is my final answer.

'*What?*' Ethan ground his jaw as the man kept on talking. 'No, I didn't know that—when did this happen?' His expression turned grim as he listened to the official's account of a recent news item he'd missed due to a business trip. He might say no to a lot of things, but he would never turn his back on Savannah.

'No' could no longer be his final answer.

* * *

Almost exactly a month later Savannah stood on a newly levelled field at her parents' farm, waiting for Ethan's helicopter to arrive. She had anticipated this moment, spending many sleepless nights planning for it—planning that had included closing off part of her heart that would never be brought into service again.

Everyone had rejoiced on the day Ethan had agreed to be patron of the rugby academy set on her parents' farm. Savannah had quietly celebrated, knowing it marked his return to the world. From the moment Ethan had given his agreement, things had moved quickly. Savannah had persuaded her parents to enter into a long-term lease with the RFU for the use of some land, and that money had saved the farm. She couldn't have felt more passionate about this opening today for all sorts of reasons, and the only anxiety she had was seeing Ethan again. As Ethan's helicopter cast a shadow over the field, she told herself she could handle it, and what better time than this? Everything was in place, and even the local mayor had accepted her invitation to cut the ribbon outside the new clubhouse. But seeing his face at the controls undid all her good intentions. Ethan helped so many people, and yet the one person Ethan seemed incapable of helping was himself. This would be their first face-to-face meeting since they parted in Tuscany, and she loved him as much as ever. But this was no time to be nursing a broken heart. The project was far too important for that. And now she must greet the guest of honour.

He saw her immediately. Even amongst the crowd of excited children and local dignitaries, she stood out. Savannah had real presence, and the place she still held in his heart drew him to her.

Though she should be in Salzburg giving a recital today, he remembered, not standing on a rugby pitch dressed in a track-suit and trainers with her hair drawn back in a simple ponytail but never looking more beautiful. Right now she was running on the spot, surrounded by a group of youngsters, as if sport was her only passion now.

He was hugely disappointed, but the love he felt for Savannah would never change. He had come because he would do anything on earth to help Savannah and her family, and this scheme she'd dreamed up benefited everybody. Which was so like her. Savannah Ross might be the most irritating woman he had ever met, but Savannah always put others before herself.

The next few hours were going to be tough training for a life without Savannah, but where that was concerned he hadn't changed his mind. He was still scarred and she was still beautiful—inside and out. Some things never changed.

As he ducked his head to clear the rotor blades he caught a glimpse of her pale face angled towards him at the edge of the field. Was she smiling? He hoped not. He hoped she would only remember the distance he had put between them before she'd left Tuscany. He didn't want to see a look of love in her eyes. He wanted to know she had moved on.

They would never have worked as a couple, he told himself firmly as he strode towards her. How could he live with someone with no sense of responsibility? Though the fact that Savannah had broken her contractual obligations had surprised him. This youth project was vital, but she didn't need to be here. She had sacrificed a great career move, and in doing so had put herself at risk of having her contract terminated.

Now he was within touching distance, he registered

explosions of sensation. He didn't trust himself to shake her hand, and was glad when the current manager of the England squad intervened. He moved on with relief, spearheading the group responsible for making this day a reality, conscious that Savannah was behind him. *As beautiful as ever, with her skin as flawless as porcelain, and her eyes...*

He breathed a sigh of relief as he approached the line of local dignitaries, but as he fell into easy conversation he was conscious of Savannah's wildflower scent coupled with her breathy laugh. But she'd let his team down, he reminded himself grimly, and anyone who did that let him down. As she'd shunned her engagement to sing in Salzburg to be here, Ethan was under pressure from his team to end her contract.

His heart lifted when he met the first youngster on the scheme, and he recognised the same determination to succeed he'd had blazing from the boy's eyes. It was more than possible that one of these boys would play for England some day, and he knew then that that even without Savannah's involvement this was the type of project he would gladly give his last penny to.

'But this time your money isn't enough,' one of the officials told Ethan goodnaturedly, glancing at Savannah, who had joined their little group for confirmation of this.

He didn't need his attention being drawn to Savannah when he was conscious of her every second. His attention might appear to be focused on the RFU official, but he was communing with her on some other level. His feelings towards her were as turbulent as ever, but he could understand now why she was so reluctant to leave the countryside for the anonymous bustle of the opera

world. However prestigious that world might be, it lacked the honest goodness of the soil, and the unspoiled beauty of these rolling fields and ancient trees. The delicate tracery of lush, green hedges and dry stone-walls surrounding her parents' farm created a quintessentially English scene, and one which he was even buying into with his purchase of the adjoining land. But even as a result of everything he could see here Savannah shouldn't have broken her agreement and let people down.

He was snapped out of these thoughts by officials ushering him into the recently erected club-house for tea. As he turned he found Savannah at his side. He steeled himself. What he had to say to her wouldn't be easy, and so he greeted her formally before glancing towards the private office where they wouldn't be overheard. 'Could I have a moment of your time?'

'Hello, Ethan,' she said softly, reminding him of another occasion when his fast-ticking clock had ruled out the space for proper introductions. He felt a pang of remorse for then, for now, for everything that could never be. And what was he thinking? Was he going to take her aside and tell her she'd lost her contract on this wonderful occasion for which she was largely responsible? Was that his way now? The look in Savannah's eyes contained a disturbing degree of understanding. She knew him too well. She knew that once his mind was made up there could be no turning back, but as she turned to walk ahead of him he did wonder at the flicker of steel in her gaze.

He launched in without preamble, listing all the reasons why breaking her contract to attend the opening of a training facility that had nothing to do with her career was unacceptable. She stared at him throughout with little reaction other than a paling of her lips. He always gave

right of reply in these circumstances, and when she didn't speak up immediately he prompted her.

He was shocked by the way Savannah's face contorted with fury, and then she croaked something unintelligible at him. 'If you'd just calm down,' he said with dignity, 'Perhaps I'd be able to understand what it is you're trying to say.'

She made a gesture, like a cutting motion across her throat.

'That's a bit over-dramatic, isn't it?' he commented with a humourless laugh.

'I've lost my voice,' she half-huffed, half-squeaked at him.

Every swear-word in the book flew through his head then. He'd been so wound up like a spring at the thought of seeing her again, he hadn't even paused to consider all the facts. So a sore throat accounted for her no-show in Salzburg.

'Please forgive me,' he said stiffly. He couldn't blame her for the way she was looking at him. He never made mistakes, and therefore lacked the technique to account for them. Or maybe he did make mistakes—maybe he had—and maybe the biggest mistake of all was his under-estimating Savannah. She was an integral part of this training project. He'd learned from the officials at the RFU that this training facility was all Savannah's idea, and that she had come up with the plan of leasing part of her parents' land to the club so they could have a proper training-facility for the youth squad, as well as all the other local youngsters who wanted to come along and taste the sport. There were scholarships and training programmes and grading examinations the various groups could work towards—funded by him, but all of it dreamed up by Savannah.

More silent swear-words accompanied this thought, with the addition of a grimace and a self-condemning shake of the head. 'Savannah, please accept my apologies, I didn't realise…'

If he had expected benediction and forgiveness, he was out of luck. Spearing him a look, she spun on her heels and left him flat.

CHAPTER EIGHTEEN

HE FOUND her in the cosy farmhouse kitchen where she was standing by the Aga, drinking a steaming glass full of something aromatic. She barely looked up when he walked in, and, other than stirring her brew thoughtfully with a stumpy cinnamon-stick, she didn't move. 'Savannah.'

Her eyes were wounded and her mouth was both trembling and determined when she did turn to look at him. She gestured for him to stay away from her, but since when had he ever taken orders? He stopped short halfway across the kitchen when he saw the tears in her eyes, and his guts twisted at the thought of what he'd done. 'Savannah, please.'

She shook her head and gestured that he should stay away from her.

'I had no idea. I just got back—I came straight here.'

She shrugged her shoulders, and made a sound that showed more clearly than words that she couldn't give a fig what he did, and her blue eyes had turned to stone.

'I should have double checked my facts before wading in, but I just wanted to…'

Her finely etched brows rose in ironic question.

'All right, then,' he admitted, raking his hair with stiff, angry fingers. 'I just wanted to see you. There, I've said it.'

She huffed.

'Savannah, please.'

Lifting her tiny hand, she used it to push him away.

He wasn't as easy as that to get rid of.

How was she supposed to have a go at him when she couldn't even speak? Gestures and angry looks only got you so far—and that wasn't nearly far enough where Ethan was concerned. 'You can't just walk in here and act like nothing happened.' She wasn't sure how much of that Ethan got, seeing as she could barely force a sound that wasn't a squeak out of her infected throat.

'You should be out there, enjoying your success,' he said, confirming her impression that he hadn't understood a word of what she'd said. She pulled a face. What was the point going outside without Ethan? The scheme needed him—and not just to give it a popular face. She needed him to take on a fuller role than that, but right now her angry look was telling him: *you're a selfish, egocentric brute, Ethan Alexander, and I never want to see you again.*

But Ethan remained undeterred. 'So, just as a matter of interest, who is taking your place in Salzburg?'

'Madame de Silva,' she managed to husk.

He smiled, remembering Savannah had looked sensational in Madame de Silva's slinky gown, which was another reason he'd been only too eager to drag her off the pitch. But while he was reminiscing the wounded look returned to Savannah's eyes. 'But Madame couldn't look half as beautiful as you do right now in your tracksuit,' he assured her gently.

And before he could stop himself he dipped his head

and kissed her very gently on the lips. He thought for a horrible moment she was going to push him away. She was certainly crying again; he could feel her tears wetting his face, and he could taste them.

'You'll catch it,' she warned, her eyes wide with concern when he released her.

'Your sore throat, do you mean? I certainly hope so,' he said, kissing her again.

She wasn't nearly finished with saying hello to Ethan yet, as he released her when the door opened and everyone piled in. In typical English spring fashion the rain had chosen that moment to pour down, and there wasn't enough space in the club house or even the large marquee her parents had erected to accommodate everyone who had turned up for the opening ceremony.

Ethan quickly went about introducing himself to her parents, and then Savannah watched him mingling easily with everyone else. They had a marvellous team of workers on the farm, some of whose families had lived on the land adjoining theirs for generations. It was thanks to these lifelong friends that Savannah's parents had been in a position to accept Ethan's offer of a cruise, and she was glad he had the opportunity to meet them and thank them personally. Maybe Ethan could never be part of her life, but perhaps he understood now how special her life on the farm was, and how family and friends were a precious and integral part of that life.

As Savannah watched Ethan ease his powerful frame through the crowd of noisy visitors in the cosy farmhouse kitchen, it wasn't possible to think of him as the same man she'd first met. When he came out to socialise he radiated friendliness. Perhaps that should be her next project. If she could bring youngsters with similar injuries to

Ethan's into contact with him, he could give them the confidence to live their lives to the fullest.

Was she only dreaming, or would that really be possible? The first step would be persuading Ethan to take a full part in the scheme...

She would just have to try a little harder, Savannah concluded, passing round the savouries she'd baked. 'Ethan.' She caught up with him by the window, where he was holding a conversation with the local mayor. It was so hard to make him hear her with a scratchy voice. 'Excuse me,' she squeaked politely. 'Do you think I could borrow you for a moment?'

'Would you excuse me?' Ethan asked the mayor politely.

As soon as they found a space, she launched right in, 'Ethan, we need you.'

'You're speaking again?' His facial expression ran the gamut from relief to wry to mock-weary in the space of a breath.

'Happily, my voice is coming back,' Savannah agreed, ignoring Ethan's groan. She couldn't sing the praises of hot water, honey and lemon stirred with a cinnamon stick highly enough.

'Sorry?' Ethan dipped his head very low until his ear was level with her mouth. 'You'll have to speak up; you're still croaking,' he teased, turning Savannah's ailment to his advantage.

'If you think you're going to distract me with that wicked look...' He probably would, she realised.

'Go on,' Ethan prompted.

'We need you, Ethan,' she said, not messing about. 'And not just for a flying visit every now and then.'

'Ah...' He looked down at her sternly, but he was smiling inwardly as he remembered the house he'd bought close

by. He'd see Savannah, though what she was proposing for the scheme was a step too far for him. He couldn't let the youngsters see his scars and put them off their game. 'You've touched on the one subject I'm not prepared to discuss,' he said flatly, and when she squeaked at him he put up his hand. 'Are you quite sure your throat is getting better? Only I can't tell you how peaceful it's been since you lost your voice.'

'Well, I found it,' Savannah assured him firmly. 'And it's getting better all the time.'

'No,' Ethan said flatly when Savannah put her proposition to him outside the club house by the fence. 'How many times do I have to say no to this idea of yours?'

'As many times as you're asked—until you say yes,' she told him steadily.

'Savannah, I should warn you, I don't succumb to pressure.'

'There has been the odd occasion,' she reminded him brazenly, using tactics she should be thoroughly ashamed of but wasn't.

'Don't you know you're playing with fire?' he warned, seeing her eyes darken.

'Am I?' she asked. She was all innocence as she angled her face towards him. 'Perhaps that's because I'll stop at nothing to get you properly into this scheme.'

'Well, I never thought you'd sink this low,' Ethan murmured with his lips very close to her mouth.

'Then you have a great deal to learn about me.'

Dragging her close, he kissed her again.

'Though I have to admit,' she admitted breathlessly when Ethan released her, 'That I usually try to make sure that when you and fire are concerned there's no one else around.'

Breaking off to say hello to some of the England squad—who, dressed in kit, were leading a group of youngsters out onto the pitch—he couldn't have agreed more. The moment he turned back to her, she said, 'I won't give up, you know.'

'I think I guessed that much,' he told her, drawing her after him.

'Where are you taking me?'

'Somewhere we can talk privately and your enthusiasm can be harnessed.'

'Sounds lovely,' she murmured as he helped her over a stile.

'It will be.' Vaulting over the same stile, he took her by the hand and led her waist-deep through a field of long grass.

'Well, I think we can talk here,' she agreed when he finally stopped in the middle of it.

'You can talk if you want to.'

'Ethan...'

Love, contentment and unimaginable happiness...as well as a nice, dewy meadow freshly watered by the rain. 'Thank goodness, you're underneath me,' Savannah murmured groggily to Ethan some time later.

'I didn't want you getting grass stains on your nice, new track-suit,' Ethan mocked softly as they recovered.

'Why worry? The sun is shining now and I'll soon dry out.' As she outlined Ethan's sensual mouth with her fingertip until he threatened to bite it off, Savannah wondered whether this was the right time to broach the subject at the forefront of her mind or not.

'Well?' Ethan pressed, knowing she had something on her mind.

'Well, what?' she said, pulling on her innocent face. 'Why must you always be so suspicious of me?'

'I might only have known you a short time, but I know there's usually something brewing when you have that look.'

She hesitated and then said bluntly, 'When you sprang over that stile…'

'Yes?' He wasn't going to help her.

'Well, I just thought, with your back and—'

'Oh, I see.' Moving his head, he dislodged her teasing finger. 'You want to know how I can do something like that when I can't play rugby. Or, more importantly—at least as far as your scheme is concerned—why I won't help out with the coaching.'

'Yes,' Savannah admitted, wriggling away from him and sitting up. Truthfully, she had a lot more in mind for Ethan than the occasional coaching session. She wanted him to take a much fuller role in the scheme for which he had already proved to be an inspirational figurehead.

'It's only weights landing on my back I have to be careful about,' he explained. 'My legs are fine.'

'Then…' Hugging her knees, she rested her chin on them, staring up at him.

'Then?'

'Stop pretending you don't know what I mean. And stop growling at me,' she added when Ethan made a mock-threatening sound. She fixed a stare on him. 'If there's nothing wrong with your legs, there can't be any reason why you can't take part in the training programme—just part-time, of course,' she added before Ethan could get a word in. 'Plus, the occasional guest appearance would make all the difference.'

Having buckled his belt, Ethan sat up beside her and

swung Savannah onto his knee. 'Is that what all this has been leading up to?'

'Not all of it,' she admitted truthfully.

'Well, at least you've got the decency to blush,' he observed dryly, drawing her into his shoulder.

'You still haven't given me your answer, Ethan.'

'Well, why don't I do that now?'

It was some time later when Ethan drew Savannah to her feet. As he helped to brush grass and twigs from her clothes, she sensed something had changed.

'My answer is no,' he told her quietly, confirming her worst fears. 'How can I let those kids see my scars? They'll see nothing else—they won't concentrate on the game, on my coaching—I'd hold them back.'

'No, you wouldn't.'

'For the last time, Savannah, no coaching sessions.'

Seizing his hands, she stared into his eyes. 'What if we brought other youngsters here—youngsters with disfigurements like yours—would you do it then? Would you bring everyone together so that no one was an outsider?'

She had silenced him and touched him as only Savannah could. 'I'll think about it,' he promised, silencing her in the most effective way he could. 'Now, will you be quiet?' he demanded when he released her.

'Of course I will,' Savannah agreed, tipping her chin to stare lovingly at him. 'The moment you agree.'

CHAPTER NINETEEN

THE REST of the day passed in whirl of activity, with Savannah and Ethan falling naturally into the role of host and hostess. They were a good team, Savannah thought, smiling across the crowded club-house at Ethan. No, she'd got that wrong—they were an excellent team—but she must stop looking at him as if she had to convince herself he was really there. She was feeling more confident he would agree to a little coaching. Hadn't he said as much when they were making love in the meadow? Or was it coaching her he'd had in mind? Time to pin him down, she decided as people started to drift off home.

When Ethan came to her he raised both her hands to his lips. Had the tender lover returned to her? She had to believe that was so. Conscious of her mother and father watching them from the other side of the room, she sighed with pleasure as Ethan brushed her cheeks with his lips.

'It's been a wonderful day, Savannah,' he told her gently. 'Thank you so much…'

'It's nothing,' she murmured. She was still staring up at him, feeling like she could fly.

'I want to thank you on behalf of everyone,' he added,

still holding her hands in his firm grip. 'And I promise to give serious thought to your suggestion.'

But? She could hear a 'but'. 'Thank you, Ethan.' Savannah's smile faded. There was something wrong. She could see no answering warmth in Ethan's eyes, just a rather detached interest. 'You're not going to take an active part, are you?'

'I'm the patron, and I've already donated a large amount of money.'

'I'm not talking about money, Ethan, the scheme needs you—hands-on you.' There was something else, Savannah suspected—something Ethan hadn't told her.

He released her hands. 'Anything else at all, you only have to ask.'

'I am asking. If everyone else can find time, why can't you?'

'You know why,' Ethan said grimly.

No, she didn't—and now he was being drawn away. She'd monopolised him too long, and all the people who had been waiting to say goodbye to him were jostling for his attention. She waited on tenterhooks until he was free again and then pounced. 'Ethan, look at me.' But there were more interruptions. How hard was it to do this in public when you were trying to capture the attention of the most important man in the room?

Ethan freed himself this next time. He'd seen her concern and he crossed the room to her side. 'Tell me,' he said.

'Everyone needs your magic,' she said. 'Just look around you...' There was a group of youngsters clustered round the team captain. They might be with one hero, but they were all looking at Ethan, the most formidable man in the room, with awe-struck stares. 'They need you. Just a few hours of your time, Ethan. They rate you so highly.'

'You know my position.'

'No, I don't!' Savannah exclaimed. 'Your scars? They know about your scars—they don't even notice them. What else is holding you back?'

Ethan's eyes narrowed. 'What makes you think there's anything else?'

'I know you, Ethan.'

'Enough,' he said sharply, leaning close. Putting his arm out, Ethan rested his clenched fist against the wall so that Savannah's face and his were shielded from the crowd. 'I'll do anything I can for these young people.'

'Then give them your time. Or can't you bear the thought of being on the same pitch as a bunch of enthusiastic amateurs? Aren't they good enough for you, Ethan?'

He knew she was goading him, reaching deep, and that she didn't believe it for one moment. 'Savannah,' he warned, his mouth almost brushing her lips now.

'No, I won't be quiet,' she replied, confirming his thoughts. 'You're due a wake-up call.'

'And who better to give it to me than you?' He didn't wait for her answer. Freeing the latch on the door behind her, he backed her through it holding on to her while he closed the door behind them, and then frogmarched her across the yard.

And still she peppered him with accusations. 'You paint wonderful pictures and hide them away—that's one precious gift wasted. You're an inspiration, a positive role-model for young people and a force for good—a second—'

Savannah gasped as Ethan thrust her through the entrance of the hay barn. Slamming the door shut, he shot the bolt. 'This time I talk and you listen,' he said. Bringing her in front of him, he held her firmly in place.

'I live my life causing the least inconvenience I can to everyone around me.'

'You mean you're stuck in the past and won't even glance into the future?'

'I'm sure my business analysts might have something to say about that,' he said with all the confidence of a hugely successful tycoon.

'Your business analysts? And I bet they keep you warm at night.'

'You don't know me, so just leave this—'

'I know enough about you to care.'

As her voice echoed in the lofty barn they both went still. Ethan's eyes were so dark and reflected a truth so terrible Savannah almost wished she hadn't brought him to this point. 'What is it, Ethan?' she said, reaching out to touch his face. 'Who did this terrible thing to you?' They both knew she wasn't talking about his scars.

Ethan moved his head away.

'And this time tell me,' Savannah insisted gently. 'Don't insult me with some pallid version of the truth because you've decided I can't take the facts. I can take anything for you—share everything with you—good and bad.'

Everything hung on this moment, Savannah realised, and yet all she could do now was wait.

After the longest moment, Ethan shrugged. 'My step-father beat me.'

She knew that.

'When I grew too big for him to beat me, he paid others to do it for him.'

She knew that too. 'Go on,' she prompted softly.

'There is no more to tell.'

No more Ethan wanted to tell, perhaps. 'I don't believe

you.' Her voice barely made it above a whisper, but he'd heard her.

Ethan stared over her head as the seconds ticked past, and then he revealed his innermost demon. 'When I had recovered from the accident I visited my mother to try to heal things between us. Whatever had happened in the past, she was still my mother, and I had to believe she didn't really understand what had been going on.'

As Ethan stopped speaking Savannah felt the pain of his disappointment so keenly she didn't even need to hear the rest, but she knew she had to let him say it.

'She had known,' he said in a voice pitched low. 'My mother had known all along. She knew all of it.'

What hurt Savannah the most was that she could still hear the surprise in Ethan's voice. For a moment she found it impossible to speak or even breathe, and could only communicate the compassion she felt for him with her eyes.

'She told me I got in the way… She said I was always in the way, and that she wished I had never been born. She said she never wanted to see me again, which I could understand, really.'

'No!' As Ethan made a dismissive gesture, Savannah caught hold of his hand and held it firmly. 'No, Ethan, no; that's not right. You must never think that. You did nothing wrong—not then, not as a child, not ever.' She understood now why Ethan kept so much hidden. Having been betrayed by his own mother, how could he ever reveal his feelings to anyone again? He had to know she was here for him on any terms, Savannah determined, and that part of the bargain said she would be strong—even strong enough to let him go, if that was what Ethan really wanted.

But as he shifted position, and she saw his wounded

face set in that distant mask, she knew she had to give their chance to be together one more try.

'What better scheme than ours to bury those demons in your past once and for all? What greater triumph could you have, Ethan?'

Ethan remained silent for the longest moment, and then he murmured with a flicker of the old humour, '*Our* scheme?'

'Why not *our* scheme?'

'Because you seem to be doing pretty well on your own.'

'But we can do so much more together.' She waited for his answer, tense in every fibre of her being.

'Is that right?' he said dryly, flicking a glance her way.

At least they'd made contact, Savannah thought with relief. 'I'm sure of it,' she said fiercely.

'So you've found a way out of the darkness?'

The glint was back in Ethan's eyes—and that was more than a relief, it was a reminder of their first night together at the *palazzo*. He had come back to her. Seizing his hands, she brought them to her lips. 'We'll get through this,' she promised him.

'I already have.'

'Then you have no excuse.'

'Not to shine a light?' As Savannah smiled, he wondered how he could ever have been foolish enough to imagine life without her.

'I need you, Ethan,' she told him passionately. 'We all need you.'

'Well, I don't know about everyone,' he admitted gruffly. 'But you've got me, Ms Ross—and for keeps.'

'What are you saying, Ethan?'

'I'm saying that I love you, and that I want to be with you always.'

Savannah swallowed deep as Ethan looked at her. 'I take it you'll be staying on, then?'

'Even a rugby match couldn't keep me away from you,' Ethan assured her. 'Unless England was playing, of course…'

EPILOGUE

THE SUN blazed down from a clear, blue Tuscan sky, and there were no shadows on the day that Savannah married Ethan. The world's press had gathered in the exquisite ancient city of Florence for what everyone was calling the celebrity marriage of the year.

For the farm girl, and the tycoon better known to the world as the Bear, this was quite an occasion, Savannah thought. As the bells rang out and the crowd cheered, it was a struggle to wrap her mind around the fact that she really was married to the man she adored. Standing on time worn steps next to Ethan outside the Basilica de Santa Maria di Fiore, a cathedral church only exceeded in size by St Peter's in Rome, she only had to see the guard of honour formed by the youngsters Ethan now made time to coach on a regular basis to know that miracles did happen—and that, yes, dreams did come true.

'All right?' Ethan murmured, squeezing her arm.

Better than all right. She adored him. He was without question the most wonderful man in the world. And apart from making her so happy he had extended the reach of the training scheme—which had meant leasing more space from her parents in order to house the office of the newly

expanded training business, saving the farm, as well as giving them the little luxuries they'd lived so long without.

And her recording career? Well, she'd just signed a contract to complete a new album, and after that studio work and the occasional personal appearance at the world-famous opera house Glynebourne in Lewes, Sussex, just down the road from Ethan's new home that adjoined her parents' farm. He'd told Savannah she was to have her cake and—for the sake of the large family they planned to have—to eat it as well. Their mission, the newly married couple had decided, was to fill all of Ethan's homes with love, laughter and lots of light—and if possible with a rugby team of their own.

'You look so beautiful,' Ethan said, standing a little behind Savannah so the crowd had a good view of her.

'And you are the most beautiful man on earth.' To her he was and always would be. Now Ethan's inners scars were healed, he had no blemishes. 'And I love you,' she said.

'More than life itself,' Ethan agreed, smiling into Savannah's eyes. 'Now, let them have a good look at your dress.'

Oh, yes, her dress… Her very special dress in ivory silk, lavishly embroidered with seed pearls and thousands of twinkles that sparkled in the sun. It had been lovingly made for Savannah by her regular team of seamstresses in the far north of England, who knew a thing or two about showing off the fuller figure to best advantage. Who else would she have chosen to make her wedding gown, to ensure there wasn't the slightest chance she would suffer a wardrobe malfunction similar to the one that had brought the crowd at the Stadio Flaminio to its feet in Rome? In this dress her assets were displayed to full advantage, a fact that had not gone overlooked by her adoring Bear.

'Cover yourself, woman,' Ethan growled as Savannah's silk-chiffon veil billowed back and away from her naked shoulders.

'If I don't, will you carry me off and keep me safe as you did on the day we first met?' Savannah asked him.

She managed a solemn face for as long as it took her to ask Ethan that question, and as his mouth tugged at one corner he allowed, 'With one small change.'

'Which is?'

'I wouldn't waste so much time before taking you to bed.'

'Is that a promise, husband?'

'You can count on it, wife,' he murmured as they posed for pictures.

'Then I may just have to stage-manage a wardrobe malfunction.'

'And I might just have to put you over my knee, and—'

Ethan paused, seeing the official photographer was hopping from foot to foot.

'Smile, please,' the man begged, indicating that a formal pose, rather than a lover's confab was called for.

He barely had to ask.

THE MARRIAGE BARGAIN

Bid for, bargained for, bound forever!

A merciless Spaniard, a British billionaire,
an arrogant businessman and a ruthless tycoon:
these men have one thing in common—they're all
in the bidding for a bride!

There's only one answer to their proposals they'll
accept—and they will do whatever it takes to
claim a willing wife....

**Look for all the exciting stories,
available in June:**

The Millionaire's Chosen Bride #57
by SUSANNE JAMES

His Bid for a Bride #58
by CAROLE MORTIMER

The Spaniard's Marriage Bargain #59
by ABBY GREEN

Ruthless Husband, Convenient Wife #60
by MADELEINE KER

www.eHarlequin.com   HPE0609

HARLEQUIN *Presents*

NIGHTS *of* PASSION

One night is never enough!

*These guys know what they want
and how they're going to get it!*

PLEASURED BY
THE SECRET MILLIONAIRE
by Natalie Anderson

Rhys Maitland has gone incognito—he's sick of
women wanting him only for his looks and money!
He wants more than one night with passionate
Sienna, but she has her own secrets….

Book #2834

Available June 2009

Catch all these hot stories where sparky romance
and sizzling passion are guaranteed!

THE ITALIAN COUNT'S DEFIANT BRIDE
by **Catherine George**

Alicia Cross's estranged husband has
reappeared—and is demanding his wedding
night! Francesco da Luca wants his feisty
runaway bride back, especially when
he discovers she's still a virgin....

Book #2830

Available June 2009

Eight volumes in all to collect!

*Sicilian by name...scandalous,
scorching and seductive by nature!*

THE SICILIAN'S
BABY BARGAIN
by **Penny Jordan**

Falcon Leopardi will claim his late half brother's
child from vulnerable Annie—but duty means he
must also protect her. The women of his sultry island
will mourn: Falcon is taking a wife!

Book #2827

Available June 2009

Look out for more fabulous stories
from Penny Jordan, coming soon
in Harlequin Presents!

REQUEST YOUR FREE BOOKS!

2 FREE NOVELS PLUS 2 FREE GIFTS!

PASSION GUARANTEED SEDUCTION

YES! Please send me 2 FREE Harlequin Presents® novels and my 2 FREE gifts (gifts are worth about $10). After receiving them, if I don't wish to receive any more books, I can return the shipping statement marked "cancel". If I don't cancel, I will receive 6 brand-new novels every month and be billed just $4.05 per book in the U.S. or $4.74 per book in Canada, plus 25¢ shipping and handling per book and applicable taxes, if any*. That's a savings of close to 15% off the cover price! I understand that accepting the 2 free books and gifts places me under no obligation to buy anything. I can always return a shipment and cancel at any time. Even if I never buy another book, the two free books and gifts are mine to keep forever.

106 HDN ERRW 306 HDN ERRL

Name _____ (PLEASE PRINT)

Address _____ Apt. #

City _____ State/Prov. _____ Zip/Postal Code

Signature (if under 18, a parent or guardian must sign)

Mail to the **Harlequin Reader Service:**
IN U.S.A.: P.O. Box 1867, Buffalo, NY 14240-1867
IN CANADA: P.O. Box 609, Fort Erie, Ontario L2A 5X3

Not valid to current subscribers of Harlequin Presents books.

Want to try two free books from another line?
Call 1-800-873-8635 or visit www.morefreebooks.com.

* Terms and prices subject to change without notice. N.Y. residents add applicable sales tax. Canadian residents will be charged applicable provincial taxes and GST. Offer not valid in Quebec. This offer is limited to one order per household. All orders subject to approval. Credit or debit balances in a customer's account(s) may be offset by any other outstanding balance owed by or to the customer. Please allow 4 to 6 weeks for delivery. Offer available while quantities last.

Your Privacy: Harlequin Books is committed to protecting your privacy. Our Privacy Policy is available online at www.eHarlequin.com or upon request from the Reader Service. From time to time we make our lists of customers available to reputable third parties who may have a product or service of interest to you. If you would prefer we not share your name and address, please check here. ☐

HP08R

HARLEQUIN *Romance.*

Coming Next Month

Fall in love this autumn with the Harlequin Romance man of your dreams... Texas ranger, society bridegroom, Outback baron, jet-set millionaire, playboy prince, Mediterranean boss—you can have them all!

#4045 WEDDING AT WANGAREE VALLEY Margaret Way
In the first of Margaret's *Barons of the Outback* duet, it's a real case of opposites attract. Wealthy and charming Guy wants a wife, and a queue of society beauties are at his door! Alana is from the wrong side of town—but she's shaken up his life, and he likes it.

#4046 ABBY AND THE PLAYBOY PRINCE Raye Morgan
In the second of the fantastic *Royals of Montenevada* series, Prince Mychale has come to his mountain château to get away from the world. Instead he finds runaway Abby and her adorable baby! She's hardly suitable, but this playboy prince is intrigued....

#4047 THE BRIDEGROOM'S SECRET Melissa James
The stunning conclusion to *The Wedding Planners* series. Sometimes you just know when someone's got a secret. With a millionaire's ring on her finger, Julie should be the happiest girl in town. But before she says "I do," she wants to know what it is that gorgeous Matt's not telling her.

#4048 TEXAS RANGER TAKES A BRIDE Patricia Thayer
Loving someone sometimes means letting them go—at least, that's what Mallory tells herself whenever her little boy asks about his daddy. Chase always put helping those in need first. He left town, not realizing Mallory and her unborn child needed him the most. Now he's back....

#4049 CRAZY ABOUT HER SPANISH BOSS Rebecca Winters
Isn't it funny how life can change in an instant? One minute Jillian's driving along a Spanish highway, the next she's working on Count Remi's olive estate. She knows he only hired her out of guilt: he'd rather be left alone. But there's no turning back when she awakens her brooding boss's heart!

#4050 THE MILLIONAIRE'S PROPOSAL Trish Wylie
Brides for all Seasons
Kerry is swept off her feet by a fall proposal in Paris as jet-setting playboy Ronan whisks her around Europe. But he has a secret that's casting a shadow over his life, and only Kerry can light up his world again....

HRCNM0808

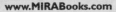